FOR THE PUSCH GIRLS

ALSO BY KATE CHRISTENSEN

IN THE DRINK

JEREMY THRANE

KATE CHRISTENSEN

BROADWAY BOOKS | NEW YORK

Broadway Books titles may be purchased for business or promotional use or for special sales. For information, please write to: Special Markets Department, Random House, Inc., 1540 Broadway, New York, NY 10036.

BROADWAY BOOKS and its logo, a letter B bisected on the diagonal, are trademarks of Broadway Books, a division of Random House, Inc.

Visit our website at www.broadwaybooks.com.

Library of Congress Cataloging-in-Publication Data

Christensen, Kate, 1962–
Jeremy Thrane: a novel / by Kate Christensen.—1st ed.
p. cm.
1. New York (N.Y.)—Fiction. 2. Fiction—Authorship—Fiction. 3. Socialites—Fiction. 4. Novelists—Fiction. 5. Gay men—Fiction. I. Title.
PS3553.H716 J4 2001
813'.54—dc21
2001025547

Permission credits for Jeremy Thrane appear on page 311.

FIRST EDITION

Designed by Gretchen Achilles

ISBN 0-7679-0801-5

1   3   5   7   9   10   8   6   4   2

PART ONE

I stood alone at the front of the boat. The deck sloped away from me, running with dew. The ferry's prow split the water into two clean lines of white froth as it plowed its way across New York Harbor, that grand old decaying basin rucked up with centuries of tides and traffic. As the wind, smelling of brine and diesel, lifted my hair from my forehead, I felt like the klieg-lit male lead in an old MGM musical, about to burst forth in a full-throttle tenor. Straight ahead, the Twin Towers' tops vanished into grizzled clouds. Off to the left was the Statue of Liberty, green as a garden gnome, and beyond, the improbably beautiful industrial banks of New Jersey: O brave old world, that had such smokestacks in it.

It was seven thirty-eight according to the radioactive little numbers on my wrist. I'd left Frankie splayed naked in the sheets, lying on his stomach with his shoulder blades folded together and his arms above his head, sucking a bit of pillowcase into his open mouth as he inhaled, wafting it back out again on the exhale. He hadn't been so beautiful awake, he'd been a wiry, unprofessional, foul-mouthed waiter. He was a complete stranger to me, and I to him. He'd waited on my friend Max and me the night before in a little Italian place on Carmine Street. It had been a nice job cracking him in two and showing him what was what. He'd put up a gratifying struggle. He was a bantamweight, but he was slippery and fast. Toward dawn I'd pinned him, then let him go to sleep and lay there watching him, listening to the mice in the walls, squinting in the glare of the bulb of his closet. He'd brought me to his house, entangled his body with mine. Now he slept peacefully, having allowed me to ravish him. Was it my low-key manner? The fact that

I'd put on a condom without being asked? But for all he knew, I was a mild-mannered, condom-wearing serial murderer. I wanted to shake him awake and warn him: Next time he might not be so lucky.

Instead, I got up and dressed, let myself out into the heavy, fresh morning air. The sidewalks were broad and cracked; the trees hung low overhead. I walked through a moist, spooky tunnel smelling of moss and water with a greenish light, like a dream, then hiked all the way down a long, sloping strip-mall-covered avenue to Bay Street. I must have unconsciously charted the landmarks and directions of our stumbling journey last night to Frankie's lair; retracing it, alone and in reverse, I found the vast gray empty ferry terminal and boarded the boat waiting there.

On a bench just inside the ferry's cavernous cabin slept a fat but frail old woman with her head wrapped in a dirty white bandage or turban, her belongings in bags under the bench. Her face was as purely beautiful in sleep as Frankie's had been, leathery and weary, but free of the disfigurements of dementia, mood, hunger, calculation. I could smell her. She reeked from stewing in her own animal juices day after day, eating garbage, drinking rotgut. I was sure if she awoke and caught me looking at her, she'd fix me in a hostile glare, but for now she was a sleeping beauty, sad but serene.

The towers of the financial district grew slowly until they loomed ahead, a forest of silent giants bigger than redwoods, denser than cliffs. A crowd gathered at the closed gates on the deck, waiting to be let onto solid ground. I felt them all around me, mild and still half asleep, heard their soft morning breathing, gentle as cows waiting for the farmer to open the pasture gates. I'd always felt an impersonal, brusque fondness for the fellow travelers I brushed up against on my way somewhere, strangers who neither got in my way nor let me get in theirs, all of us suspended together between past and future in a temporal tunnel of watery-green privacy like this morning's sidewalks. The ship docked with a thud and a grinding of underwater gears, a creak of the gangplank.

I walked out of the huge, echoing South Ferry terminal and headed up Whitehall Street. I caught pleasurable whiffs every now and then, the funky residue of Frankie wafting on gusts of warm air from inside my clothes. After several blocks, Whitehall became Broadway. The statue of a huge bull pawed at an island in the middle of the street. I crossed over to inspect it, and without thinking, reached down to cup its testicles. Giving them a gentle squeeze, schoolboy hilarity bubbled up in my chest. As I looked uptown with the bull's balls in my hand, the voice in my head sang "New York, New York, it's a wonderful town; the Bronx is up and the Battery's down—" After all these years, I could still be amazed by the cityscape on a fall morning, bronze testicles, skyscrapers, and blowing trash. The autumn air, whether cloudy or clear, had a quality that was present at no other time of year; in the fall, other New Yorks, past and future, real and imaginary, seemed to quiver just beyond the brink of the visible one. Other people's memories haunted me on every corner, as palpable as my own skin as I passed through them. A yellow cab slid by; its funhouse-like reflection smeared the green glass skin of one building, swelling then compressing to a vanishing blip.

O brave old world. Craning my neck like a tourist, I looked up the side of a skyscraper, straight up its ramrod-sheer belly. I'd never worked in an office. Most of my knowledge of offices came from sitcoms or movies. I thought of them as places where cadres of men with gym-cut muscles under Oxford shirts engaged in homoerotic banter; I imagined corporate men's rooms as the settings for rushed, silent, half-brutal encounters, a sullen mailroom boy collared in the hallway by an Armani-clad V.P., ordered to step into the gleaming empty room and stand against the wall with his hands splayed against the tiles. The image of the boy's tight khakis pulled down just far enough to cup his buttocks made me dizzy.

I found with my fingertips in my pants pocket a restaurant mint from last night, a small, pillowy square I fished out and sucked on. It crumbled chalkily on my tongue. I'd heard these mints were soaked in uric acid from patrons who didn't wash their hands after peeing, then scrabbled their fingers around the mint bowl. But urine was sterile, and anyway I'd always been clinically objective or, rather, cavalierly unconcerned about such things. You could go through life wiping every doorknob with a handkerchief and get picked off by a commonplace flu at fifty, or you could let all microbes take their best shots, thereby strengthening your resistance to them. I opted for the latter strategy, and as a backup maintained a steady level of alcohol molecules to confuse any invading bugs, in hopes that they would wander through my body's corridors like locked-out hotel guests, too blotto to find my cells.

It dawned on me then that I was ravenous and caffeine depleted. No wonder I was dizzy. Directly ahead lay an open deli, a bright little trading post on the canyon floor. I ducked in and loitered through the aisles for a moment until a small knot of people in suits at the counter concluded their business and cleared off. I breathed in the smells of Pine Sol, stewing coffee, and hot grease, glanced idly at boxes of prunes and instant chicken noodle soup. When I stepped up to the counter and ordered my breakfast, the counterman immediately handed me a cup of coffee. One of the things I deeply treasured about this city was the fact that people behind counters moved at least three times faster here than anywhere else in the country. The farther outside of Manhattan you got, the longer you had to wait in line; someone somewhere had probably figured out an algorithmic equation to express the exact ratios.

While my breakfast sizzled on the grill, I took the lid off my sweet, milky coffee and blew on it to make one static wavelet on its creamy brown surface that subsided the instant I stopped blowing. As I replaced the lid, my eye was caught by the cover of the top copy of the *National Enquirer* in the rack: "Sizzling Stars Heat Up the Sunset Strip." There were Ted and Giselle, looking smugly into each other's eyes. Her blond hair blew against his sculpted cheek. A flash of that irrational fondness I always felt when I unexpectedly saw anything familiar in a strange place was subsumed immediately by irritated envy. I was still half asleep; it wasn't fair of them to intrude on my solitary pleasures before I'd even had my coffee.

Giselle's husband, Ted Masterson, had been my boyfriend for the past ten years. Or, rather, Giselle had married my boyfriend, Ted, seven years earlier, having no idea that Ted had another life tucked away in New York. For his first several years in Hollywood, his star had seemed perpetually about to rise, but, until he'd married Giselle, it had stubbornly remained a red dwarf suspended about halfway between horizon and zenith. In the seven years since their splashy media-orgy of a wedding, his roles and asking price had steadily improved. He needed her; I had grudgingly accepted his marriage as a sound career move, but I didn't like it. And the few times I'd met Giselle, I hadn't liked her either; all the things I loved about Ted—his genuine acting talent, his sense of humor, his ironic cast of mind, and most notably his homosexuality—were quashed by her influence. She was a scrappy little white-trash kid who'd clawed her way up the glass mountain to land on the roof of the world. Her pre-stardom name had been Cathy Benitez, a castoff she'd abandoned along with her former self, a chubby, slitty-eyed, Valley-bred mall rat—I'd seen pictures—in favor of Giselle Fleece, white-blond movie star with upper arms as thin as stalks of celery and a practiced half-smile. They'd both married up, in a way. Her alliance with Ted, an old-money Ivy-League Connecticut WASP, gave Giselle a vicarious aura of aristocracy without eclipsing her. And as for Ted, there was no doubt about the career advantages he'd gained in exchange for his bargain with some internal devil, but I pitied him for it. His vanity was his greatest weakness. He'd given up more for its gratification than I could ever imagine sacrificing for anything, except maybe, come to think of it, Ted himself. But I hadn't made any bargains with any devil that I could think of. I just kept my mouth shut and did as I pleased while he was out of town.

In recent years, our once incendiary, inventive sex life had buckled under the combined weight of his double life and our mutual silence, mine tactful, Ted's withholding, on all the topics he and I had ceased over time to talk about. I had no high hopes for this weekend's visit. Half of me was tempted to get out of town for the duration, but the other, stronger half wanted to see Ted as often as possible, even if it meant pretending to be nothing more than his old friend the whole time. But I hoped that he would find a way for us to be alone together, if only for an hour or two.

I pulled the residual aura of my night with Frankie around me like a protective cloak and looked away from the newspaper rack, but the happy mindlessness of my hung-over reverie was shattered. Was there no escape for me from those two, nowhere I could go that I wouldn't find some reminder of their strategic public alliance? Their show went on every waking moment. Wherever they went, it seemed, the Fleece-Masterson family contrived to be caught in ostensibly casual but alarmingly flattering poses, and not only "heating up the Sunset Strip"—there seemed to be cameras awaiting them at the zoo, the gourmet grocery store, the video rental place, the fro-yo stand, Pink's, the Four Seasons. In recent published photos taken by enterprising photographers through long-range lenses in Tuscany and Venice, they glowed from a gondola, a balcony, a vineyard, a yacht, a cap of red curls nestled between them like a lapdog. This was their daughter, on whom they'd bestowed the unlikely name of Bretagne, Bret for short, when they'd adopted her five years ago. Giselle was too busy shooting back-to-back blockbusters to take time out for pregnancy, or so their publicists maintained. I'd never met Bret, but I'd seen plenty of pictures, and in all of them she looked like a terrifyingly precocious Hollywood kid, the type of enfant terrible who'd be pregnant, or worse, by the age of twelve.

The premiere for Giselle's new movie, to which I had been invited formally, by mail, was Monday night at eight at the Ziegfeld. Their private plane was scheduled to touch down early this evening at LaGuardia. Ted and Giselle would arrive in their limo with their entourage shortly thereafter at Ted's Gramercy Park house, where I lived; I'd hoped not to have to see them until much later, when the photographers had gone away and Bretagne was asleep and the house was quiet.

I paid for my breakfast and left the deli, heading into a thick breeze moving without undue haste past me and on into the depths of the financial district I'd just left behind. As I walked, I wolfed from its waxed paper bed the luscious fusion of salty thin-sliced ham, hot soft scrambled egg, and chewy poppy seed roll, then balled up the paper and tossed it into an overflowing trash can without missing a step or beat of my stride. The morning was cool and hazy, the city's edges softened and blurred by clouds boiling up from manholes, steam blowing from square aluminum-bright deli vents, the coal-black whiffets left hanging after buses pulled away. Every lungful of air I inhaled held this vaporous urban discharge from vents, grates, and engines, seething with the electric waves from millions of skulls, currents of mental activity to which my own were added along with my outward breath.

Walking through these early-morning streets, the idea of Ted's fame, no matter how minor compared to Giselle's, seemed almost ridiculous. How could a person project himself into such proportions all out of keeping with his common, limited, private consciousness? I recalled then a look Ted's face took on sometimes, a maddening expression of blue-blooded entitlement, his eyes glazed over like a sated overlord's, his mouth slack and his voice underlain with a flat, nasal Connecticut imperiousness that brooked neither interruption nor dissent. How could I love and hate someone so intensely, both at once? My loathing for parts of Ted felt like a noxious fuel, choking me while it propelled me through the summits and valleys of love, but keeping me to a narrow, strenuous track.

The sidewalk fell rhythmically away beneath my feet. Its surface was dotted with hard, black little tumors. This time of year, the chewing-gum mounds were interspersed with leaf-shaped black tattoos, ghostly negative silhouettes inked by rain and gravity pressing fallen leaves into the concrete. Bolts of cheap, glittering cloth were displayed in dusty old shopwindows along lower Broadway like ancient treasures in Aladdin caves. In SoHo, the women suddenly became huge-breasted and almost otherworldly in their aggressive chicness, and the air was charged with attitude as dizzying as perfume, even though it was the first thing in the morning.

"Jeremy," someone called.

I hated running into people on the street as much as I hated picking up the phone and having it be someone I didn't want to talk to. My first impulse was always to hang up or pretend I hadn't heard my name. But I overcame it now, and stopped and looked around.

"Jeremy," I heard again, and there was Sebastian Philpott, seventeen years older than he'd been the last time I'd seen him, minus a tonsure-sized skullcap's worth of hair. He sidled up to me and stood about a foot closer to me than I would have liked, his bulbous eyes peering intently into mine as he breathed quietly through his mouth.

"Hello," I said flatly.

A fleeting memory arose in my mind: Sebastian, trailing me one day after English class, sweating gently with the effort it took to catch up to me. He'd called my name exactly as he had a second ago. When I'd turned to see what he wanted, the naked admiration in his popout eyes might have struck me as poignant if I hadn't been an adolescent with my own popularity problems. I had just read my latest short story aloud in English class and wanted to flee the scene.

"What is it?" I'd asked impatiently.

"Could I—would you mind if I copied your story for myself?" he asked. "I'd like to see the way it looks on the page. I feel I missed so much of the subtlety and nuance, hearing it read aloud."

"You can have the fucking thing," I said, and thrust at him the wretched, toiled-over notebook pages covered with my crabbed hand-writing, multiple cross-outs, and splotches of whatever food I'd been eating as I wrote. The next day he tried to discuss my themes and imagery with me, and I'd said, "Oh, come on, Sebastian," and fled from him again.

"This is an amazing coincidence," he was saying now. "I was just thinking about you last week, wondering whatever happened to you. How have you been?"

We'd been the only two queers in our high school, or, rather, the only two I had known about at the time. Neither of us had kept our ho-mosexuality a secret, but neither had we broadcast it. We hadn't been friends and had never slept together; the mere idea of touching his white, frail, puffy body made me shudder. It wasn't his fault that he was white, frail, and puffy; he was asthmatic, hypersensitive to sunlight, and took thyroid medication that made him bloat, but nonetheless his personality did little to compensate for his physical shortcomings.

"Oh, I've been fine," I said.

"What have you been doing?"

"Not much," I said truthfully with synthetic breeziness.

"Are you still writing?"

"I'm working on a novel," I said, and would have left it at that, but pride compelled me to add, "and I recently finished a screenplay and got a movie agent."

"A screenplay!" he said, for some reason delighted by this news. "I'd love to read it."

"It's no masterpiece," I said, "to put it mildly."

"I don't believe you," he said with that same undaunted, eager ex-pression. "I would love to read it. Would you have your agent send me a copy? Here's my card." He thrust a small white rectangle of cardboard into my hand. "Because, well, to tell you the truth, I'm in the market for a good script, because I'm looking to produce a movie." He paused, then added with an embarrassment I would have suspected was feigned if it had been anyone but Sebastian, "My accountant recommended it, actually, I never would have thought of it on my own. He thinks up all sorts of ways of avoiding undue taxation. A number of years ago I started my own magazine, and it seems to be very popular with advertisers. Money keeps streaming in."

"Congratulations," I said.

"It's called *Boytoy*. It's pornography, primarily, but there are also celebrity profiles, health and lifestyle articles, that sort of thing." He paused as another bright idea bubbled up in his neocortex. "We are in desperate need of a new columnist, or, rather, I am, the editorial we; it's only me, I run the whole thing. I know it would be a comedown for a writer like you, but we try to keep the quality of the writing as high as possible. Jeremy, do you think you could write porn?"

"I'm not sure," I said, dismayed.

"We pay extremely well, which is to say, I do. Come and have lunch someday soon, and we'll discuss the terms and guidelines."

"Maybe," I said, and shook his hand, which was horribly soft, and so warm, it made me want to gag.

"Do call, Jeremy," he said over his shoulder as he proceeded on his way. "Don't lose my card. Well, if you do, it doesn't matter, I'm in the book."

Under Philpott or *Boytoy*? I was tempted to ask, but didn't care, although I did experience a mild and passing astonishment at the way he so casually broadcasted his telephone number's availability. This more than anything showed how unbridgeable the gap was between us. My own name hadn't been in the book in over ten years, and I had no desire ever to have it there again, because if people I didn't want to talk to had access to my number, then they might call me. Who these people were I didn't know, and I didn't want to know; anyone who was so casual about such things was clearly not my soul mate and never would be.

A while later, looking up, I found myself on my own street; I'd walked the last twenty blocks in a blur. In Gramercy Park, a gust of air lifted and tossed the trees' heavy, almost-bare branches with a barely audible creak, quick as a sigh. The paths were dim, deserted; the wrought-iron benches sat clenched and empty except for one purblind old man in corduroy pants, leaning on his cane, drooling quietly, harming no one.

Coming toward me on the sidewalk I heard the Dog Walker, talking as usual to his leashed charges. "Rosa, come on, don't do this to me, I need one good dog, at least. Jesus fucking Christ, George, don't fucking even think about it. Farkus! Farkus! Don't do that! Christ, I've told you twenty times in the last hour alone! You never fucking listen to me! You never listen! What's wrong with you guys today?"

He was a slight, grungy fellow with scraggly facial hair. His voice rose to a screech, subsided into resignation. The way he talked to his dogs reminded me of the way I had harangued my stuffed animals as a kid, fervently, without a shred of humor; part of me had suspected they were plotting to overthrow me and had to be kept in their place. The dogs, the center of all this emotional outpouring, walked calmly along on their leashes.

"Hi," their tormentor said clearly as he passed me, meeting my eyes with a steady, sane expression. He was cute. I felt a sudden stirring of attraction. Then he said, "Don't treat me like a fucking jackass. You think I'm in a bad mood now. I swear to God, don't start this shit with me so early in the morning." He was talking to the dogs, I thought, but I wasn't entirely sure. He rounded the corner, toward whatever imaginary dog-related dramas awaited him there.

The front stairs of Ted's house rose from the sidewalk to a heavy oaken door, into whose lock I fitted my key. He had bought this nineteenth-century town house fifteen years before. Its previous owners had rendered it unspeakably tasteless with shag rugs, lowered ceilings, and paneling. At huge expense, Ted had had it restored to a credibly somber replica of a nineteenth-century family house. Inside the foyer, light wavered palely through the glass fanlight above the door, casting smoky shadows over the umbrella stand, the coat tree, the parquet floor. A gold-leaf-etched mirror hung above a heavy mahogany table, on which stood a Chinese vase filled with dried sunflowers. The air smelled of pierogis, cabbage, meat-laden steam; through the French doors leading into the living room, I caught a glimpse of Yoshi's sinisterly angular form gliding into the kitchen, where, I knew by the smells permeating the house, Basia was preparing Polish delicacies for the master's homecoming.

Yoshi had heard me open the front door; I knew it by the casual flip of his slippers as he slid noiselessly into the kitchen. My coming in so early in the morning could mean only one thing, that I'd been tom-catting around the night before Ted was due back. In Yoshi's mind, I was almost certain, I was a freeloading layabout who'd scored the large, airy, sunny attic rooms, who sponged off Ted's largesse, coming and going as I pleased. In my mind, Yoshi was a complete phony who'd conned Ted into supporting him, so I supposed we were even.

I had a strong feeling that Yoshi was only pretending to be Japanese. He had a fortuitous Asiatic appearance, but I suspected that he was ac-tually of Finnish or Dutch extraction, I didn't know or particularly care which. He had long, straight black hair that he wore in a braid down his back, a short-legged, long-torsoed physique, and eyelids with a thick enough fold to render him plausibly Japanese. He had been Ted's personal trainer for his most recently released film, shot on location in the Australian outback. He had tutored Ted in kung-fu karate-chop jujitsu movements to give credibility to his portrayal of Brock Martel, action-Jackson with a cause, who in the name of saving the earth leapt from speedboats, scrambled over electric fences, ran through rocky deserts in the blistering sun. I only half believed Ted when he boasted about the challenges of playing such he-men; in addition to Yoshi, he was also furnished with stunt doubles, a masseur and yoga instructor, a gaggle of lackeys who flocked to him between takes with spring water, handheld fans, whatever else he required. One night nearly a year ago at their Alice Springs hotel bar over tisanes, Yoshi had confided to Ted that his secret dream was to be an indoor gardener in a private house, and once the film was wrapped, Ted had given him his wish.

Soon afterward, Yoshi had arrived at Gramercy Park with one solitary duffel bag containing, among other things, the tatami mat he did his yoga stretches on and the various pairs of enameled chopsticks he wielded ostentatiously at our occasional household dinners. He had taken possession of the basement suite, next door to the weight room and sauna, and seemed to be in no hurry to leave. I didn't blame him. I knew how well he was paid for fussing over the orange trees and orchids because I wrote his paychecks every month.

Since he'd moved in, an instinctive and mutual animadversion had hummed between Yoshi and me like a low-level magnetic repulsion. Sometimes it happened that he needed to water or prune plants in a room in which I happened to be lounging, the library, for example, where a cluster of persnickety potted orange trees lived. They required more attention than the average lapdog and went into a snit and dropped all their leaves whenever they got a draft or a teaspoonful too much water or just didn't like the way things were going. Sometimes when I sat reading peacefully in one of the leather chairs by the fireplace, the hair on my arms suddenly stood straight up. That was how I knew Yoshi was standing in the doorway and wished to come in as soon as possible to check on those damn trees. In the next half hour or so, I contrived to go elsewhere in a manner that showed him clearly that it was my own choice to leave the room, having nothing to do with anything he might have indicated to me. Once I'd left the room, he waited just long enough before he went in to prove that he hadn't been waiting for me to leave because he paid no attention to me either. The intensity of our non-contact was like an anti-obsession, the exact reverse of a crush.

Now I followed Yoshi into the kitchen to keep him from insinuating anything to Basia about my whereabouts last night. I always did my utmost not to offend Basia, primarily because I liked her, but also because I was a little afraid of her. She was a five-foot-tall fireplug, a former Soviet gymnast whose sedentary retirement had caused her to grow almost as big around as she was tall. She had snapping black eyes, a commanding voice, and wore her jet-black hair in a large braided bun. She owned a number of identical black dresses, long-sleeved and ankle-length, over which she tied capacious white aprons. Over the course of a typical culinary day, these became smeared with strange-colored substances whose sources I preferred not to speculate about. She ruled the kitchen, a despotic, beetle-browed suzerain, and although her food was invariably colorless, lardy, and salty beyond belief, I was careful not to bite the hand that fed me, lest it bite me back.

Ted had first become aware of Basia when he was eight and she was thirteen, and his grandmother had taken him to see her perform in New Haven. Her lithe little swaybacked form was his ideal; he'd worshiped gymnasts as a boy, he'd told me, because they were so bendable, beautiful, and strong. "A prepubescent girl has the most upper-body strength proportional to her mass of any human stage of development, male or female," he'd said as he handed me a few worn-out photos of little Basia, with her broad shoulders and wee hips, arching backward, flying over a bar. Her small, sharp, dark face was utterly expressionless, as if her mind had gone blank under the pressure. Ted had sent her a fan letter; she'd written back in a rudimentary English, which improved through the years as their pen-pal friendship continued. When she was ready to emigrate, he'd offered her a lifelong position as his cook and sponsored her green card application.

Ted had intended Basia's job to be purely nominal, but she'd taken it as intensely seriously as she'd once taken gymnastics. Her attitude toward cooking seemed to have been gleaned from her old coach's philosophy: Work made you strong, and then you died, and dough, lard, salt, and cabbage were all you needed in the meantime. Her citizenship classes hadn't impressed upon her the peculiarly American concept of the pursuit of human happiness. Pleasure was not in her lexicon.

Basia and Yoshi and I were all three, in one way or another, Ted's fully grown dependents, the wards he'd stowed here in his New York house like a trio of problematic relatives he preferred to keep stashed at a safe distance but had to support because no one else would. We all benefited from his generosity, especially, I had to admit, me. Ted had given me unlimited access to his New York bank account, from which I paid salaries, household bills, and any other domestic overhead. I was very well kept; my cage had always been as comfortable and well appointed as I wanted it to be.

"Good morning," I said, giving Basia a kiss on her dumpling-like cheek.

She scowled up at me. "You want breakfast?" she said.

"I just went out and got something," I said, "but thanks." I didn't look at Yoshi as I said this, but I could feel him listening as he lounged snootily on a stool at the center island, under a raft of hanging copper vats and soup pots big enough to boil a sheep in.

Basia didn't know that Ted and I were lovers. She didn't know that Ted was gay, and I doubted that she'd figured out that I was, or Yoshi, no matter how languidly he swanned around the house, post-workout, with a white towel around his neck and his muscles all agleam. All Basia knew was that she lived in a house owned by Ted, whom she adored, along with two single, passably good-looking younger men. She had never complained about this, as far as I knew.

"No breakfast," Basia repeated darkly.

"No, but thank you," I told her, suddenly eager to get upstairs; I had just remembered that Nina, the housekeeper, an old friend of Basia's, was coming at nine o'clock to vacuum, dust, air the bedding, whatever else housemaids did to prepare for the return of the master and his entourage. I wanted to stay well out of her way, because she despised her job and took it out on the floors she vacuumed, the shelves she dusted. She was a hostile, snarling dervish when she cleaned; once a week, crashes resounded through the house, followed by yowls in Polish I suspected were curses. I never let her anywhere near my own rooms.

"Yoshi," said Basia, turning her benign glare on him. "You want eggs, some fried potatoes? I have."

Without waiting to hear Yoshi's answer to Basia's offer of skin-tough eggs and slimy hash browns, which I hoped would be in the reluctant affirmative as he apprehensively drew today's chopsticks from the sleeve of his robe, I left the kitchen, threaded my way through the dining and living rooms, and started up the stairs. On the second-floor landing hung a dark oil painting in a gilt frame, the portrait of some long-dead English Masterson who bore a fleeting resemblance to Ted, with a jutting beak of a nose and ice-blue eyes turned inward, as if his nose conducted his public life while behind his eyes hid a complex soul. It was an interesting face, chilly and regal, but oddly vulnerable, if only because he had so far to fall. I called him Lord Muckety to myself, and as I passed his portrait, I winked at him.

On the fourth floor I unlocked my apartment door, stepped into my hideaway and closed the door behind me, kicked off my shoes and shed my jacket, and left them all in a heap by the door. My rooms had been furnished and decorated according to my own tastes. The enormous front room had a peaked ceiling and two large leaded-pane windows overlooking the park. I'd had three walls painted a warm, glowing tangerine with ivory trim on the moldings, and on the fourth I'd had a man come and build a floor-to-ceiling oak bookshelf, which was filled with books. In a corner cupboard were the stereo system, television, and VCR. My bed was firm, king-sized, its surface an expanse of charcoal-gray coverlet, with plenty of pillows and a good reading lamp on either side. A fully stocked liquor cabinet stood next to a small sofa and low coffee table; on the old hardwood floor was a dark gray wool rug. A cage in one corner, suspended from the ceiling, housed the other resident life-form, Juanita, a small green bird of average intelligence who liked to hop on my shoulder and nibble at my hair while I hand-fed her sunflower seeds and told her all my woes, which weren't many, given the particulars of my life.

Because my fear of Nina prevented me from taking advantage of her services and I seemed to be incapable of housekeeping for myself, my lovely, clean, airy rooms had transmogrified gradually into an archaeo-logical museum of my own recent past. I'd moved in with the sincere hope that living in this nice place would magically induce me to caper around at regular intervals with rag and feather duster, setting things to rights and polishing already gleaming surfaces, but the way things had turned out, I was three months past my thirty-fifth birthday and I lived in a pigsty. Banana peels so old they resembled small mummified ani-mals occasionally came to light from the couch pillows or between the dust-brittle curtains and the chalky windowsills. Encrusted plates lay under the couch, calcified with blood-brown lasagna residue, spattered with desiccated crusts of bread from some months-gone sandwich. My bed disgorged the occasional filthy sock or wadded-up Kleenex crusty with God knew what bodily discharge. The bookshelves were festooned with dust-laden spiderwebs. Bird shit had spattered here and there like hardened toothpaste; actually, some of it may have indeed been hardened toothpaste, since I'd never learned to brush my teeth without drooling, and tended to wander around my apartment while I did so.

Piles of books lay everywhere: My reading habits were scattershot and panicky. The better a book, the more frantically I dog-eared it, the more food I spilled on it. I almost couldn't tolerate too much verbal bril-liance flowing past my eyes; I was driven very nearly mad by my in-ability to physically ingest every word. I was currently halfway through *The Horse's Mouth*, and I'd had to create a minor disaster-area shrine of broken pencils and wadded-up paper and dirty dishes around the book itself, whose binding was actually coming unglued from my maddened efforts to dismantle and possess it. I would have to buy another copy if I ever hoped to finish the thing.

The smaller middle room, my office, held a desk and computer, a fil-ing cabinet, a telephone and fax machine: Ted had installed me in his house with the pretense of hiring me to be his archivist. In truth, of course, I was no more an archivist than Yoshi was a gardener or Basia a cook, and Ted's real-life archivist, a paragon of organization named Roy who lived in L.A., had things perfectly well in hand. I used the computer for my own work, a novel called *Angus in Efes*, whose eponymous pro-tagonist was based on the real-life Angus Thrane, my father. For fictional purposes, I'd changed his last name to Heyerdahl, since he'd once told me that Thranes were descended from Vikings and therefore never got seasick, and *Kon-Tiki* had been one of my favorite childhood books.

Back in the Bay Area in the sixties, when I was a little kid, my father had been a hotheaded Marxist lawyer who'd specialized in pro bono work for the Black Panthers, activists, demonstrators, and conscientious objectors during the Vietnam War. He was a hero to a lot of people, but those of us who lived with him saw another side of his personality entirely. When my mother asked him to help her with the housework a little too pleadingly for his tastes, my younger sister Amanda and I watched helplessly from the breakfast table while he ranted at her until finally, overcome by his helplessness to give himself over to what she wanted, he seized her, punched her in the breasts, and pulled her hair. She pulled it out in clumps as she sat, weeping, in a kitchen chair after he'd stomped out to one of his meetings or trials or protests. But for some reason, my father, not my mother, struck me as the weakling: He was enslaved by his own uncontrollable rage, whereas my mother was merely its shocked, involuntary target. I never, to put it mildly, identified with him all that much.

But he could be charming: In calmer moods, he took us camping in Mendocino, to baseball games at Candlestick Park, to Charlie Chaplin films and People's Park, where we watched naked grown-ups cavort around in tribal rituals called "happenings." A favorite Thrane family outing was going en masse to peace marches in San Francisco, where Amanda and I rode high above the crowd on our parents' shoulders. As the boy and the firstborn, I always got to ride Angus; I felt like a rajah on a prize elephant, kicking my heels happily against his chest to make him go faster, looking down on the sign-carrying rabble below.

Just after Lola was born in 1970, our mother finally left Angus with all three of us kids in tow. He turned his ramshackle Victorian house into a commune for fellow activists and politicos who reeked of BO and patchouli. Except for the occasional uncomfortable weekend (when our father called, always at the last minute, to insist that we visit him for a couple of days, not because he wanted us around, I later understood, but to irritate his ex-wife, who'd had the temerity to leave him), we didn't see much of him during those years. According to friends of both my parents, he'd had some kind of crisis or breakdown in 1974, left the Berkeley house to his comrades and chucked his San Francisco law practice. He then, according to legend, ran off to Turkey as crew on a freighter and disappeared into clouds of brazier smoke and dust. We didn't know why he'd vanished or how he'd managed to live, since he'd never had any money and it was unlikely he would have tried to start a law practice in Istanbul. I had long ago accepted that he was most likely dead, and whatever story he'd lived since his disappearance had died with him. *Angus in Efes* was my effort to imagine for myself what had happened, a way of laying him to rest.

In the rear of my apartment was a small but luxurious bathroom with a skylight and a huge claw-footed tub, thick towels, and a cupboard filled with bath salts and oils. The one cleaning task I performed faithfully was scrubbing the bathtub weekly with cleanser and clearing the drain of hair balls and gook. I routinely took epic baths, sometimes spending four hours in there at a stretch, working my way through most of a bottle of wine, listening to a flotilla of CDs, well-worn stack of boysie mags at hand (among them, now that I thought about it, a couple of moldy and bespattered issues of *Boytoy*) and a book or two. I'd dropped *Middlemarch* into the water at least three times already, having felt the immediate necessity of an osmotic soaking-in of Eliot's wizardry. To me the most palpable evidence of her mind-boggling genius lay in her character Rosamond, who was blond and gorgeous, while Eliot herself, not even her most devoted fans could deny, had been butt ugly. She must have resented her own creation and wished her ill, on some subterranean level anyway, but instead of making Rosamond a twittering caricature on whom to wreak all her ugly-girl revenge fantasies, Eliot had allowed her the dignity of an independent soul, making her accountable for her own choices and actions, however reprehensible they may have been. How had she created that living, rosy, awful girl out of words? I felt my own imagination on its knees before a mind as vast and inscrutable as the Sphinx. It gave me an excruciating pleasure I sought whenever I could bear it.

I filled the tub with hot water, took off my clothes, plunged in, scrubbed myself fast, and got out. I was tempted to lie there all day, staring up through the skylight at the shifting clouds and listening to the steady drip, drip from the faucet to the surface of the water, but I had work to do.

Next to the bathroom was the ship's-galley-sized kitchenette, which I'd had installed to allow me a third culinary option besides choking down Basia's food or eating in restaurants. This shipshape mini-kitchen was conducive to the kind of diet Amanda, Lola, and I had eaten as kids, sleeping three to a pup tent in southwestern campgrounds and on beaches in Baja California while our mother ran through much of her trust fund living the footloose life of the post-adolescent sixties flower child. We'd lived on peanut butter sandwiches, canned peas, granola bars, Life cereal out of the box, Fig Newtons, and Tang. Later on, during our commune period, our mother and the other grown-ups were all too busy "finding themselves" and "communing with nature" (in other words, dropping acid and lying around naked) to force us kids to eat their soybean stew and tofu-prune casserole, so we kids came and went all day, pillaging the larder as we ran through. These had been strange, lonely, formless, anxious years, but they hadn't been all bad by any means. Our mother had seemed to flourish under the dictates of free love as she'd never done in her fraught, violent marriage. We'd never seen her happy and youthful before, and since we looked to her for clues about how to feel about everything, some of her relief and pleasure was refracted onto us the way sunlight on a wall diffuses the gloom of an adjacent shaded alleyway.

I heated a can of chicken noodle soup while I slapped together a baloney sandwich with lots of mayo on honey-wheatberry bread. As I ate my second breakfast, sitting on the window seat tucked under an eave in my study, I spied on my neighbor, Dina Sandusky, in hers; my window looked directly down into her skylight, under which she sat at her desk, oblivious to me. She was playing solitaire. I watched her turn over a card, put it back, and turn over a different one. Then she changed her mind and went back to the first one. Dina was a freelance journalist who specialized in stories about rape victims, abortion rights, and similar "serious" topics for women's magazines. I also knew the following about her from living next door to her for four years: She donated regularly to Amnesty International, Doctors Without Borders, and Greenpeace, washed her dishes and hair in biodegradable gook, and took her own shopping bag to neighborhood mom'n'pops and local farmers' markets instead of cheaper, better-stocked, more conveniently located chain stores. This integrity extended to her research and interviewing tactics as well but not, apparently, to certain other activities, among them playing solitaire.

She was pretty in an interesting, bookish way; her chestnut-brown hair was cut in a semi-chic bob, she had a heart-shaped, asymmetrical face with strong, almost masculine features. She had a tense, quivering, greyhound-like quality, quite possibly because she was tormented by all the obsessive moral imperatives she was occasionally tempted to betray, but only in ways she hoped wouldn't count.

A few days before, I'd run into her on the street. When I saw the copy of *Middlemarch* she carried, I blurted out, "Oh, that's my favorite novel of all time."

"Mine too," she said.

"I love Rosamond."

"Do you?" she said, wrinkling her nose. "Why? She's so selfish and awful."

"She is selfish and awful, but that's the point. The book comes to life whenever she's around. Dorothea is such a sanctimonious prude. And that disgusting old man she marries—"

"Mr. Casaubon," she said immediately. "I agree, he's so awful. I think Dorothea is meant to represent—"

"See," I said, "that's the trouble, she represents something, she's some kind of paragon. She's the only character who reveals Eliot's didactic upbringing. No thank you."

Her eyes widened. "But to me she seems totally believable. She gives herself over to what she believes is the right thing. She marries Casaubon, and she's happy with him, he gives her the sense of being needed, at least at first. But when erotic love comes to her, she can't resist it. Erotic love is stronger than altruism or duty, Eliot knew that."

Then she looked at me with shining eyes, as if she were drinking me in, even though she had her own husband, Cory, a perfectly nice but stultifyingly boring senior vice president sort of fellow about twelve years her senior. She was literary, a daydreamer; I suspected that I reminded her of a dashing character out of a nineteenth-century novel. I could feel my wild, free-form hair lying romantically against the back collar of my black coat, my pale skin faintly flushed from the brisk walk I'd just had around town, checking out the Chelsea boys in their new fall outfits. "That's interesting," I said, making my voice go all rumbly; I felt a sudden powerful, uncharacteristically altruistic urge to confirm her fantasy of me. "I hadn't thought of it that way."

She gazed at me; I gazed back. I sensed that this moment was electric for her. I tried to sustain my end of it, but my eyes flickered sheepishly away from hers. We said good-bye and disappeared into our side-by-side houses.

Now I watched her wolf down half a bag of nonpareils, cramming them into her mouth. After this debauch, she stared into space with her hands hovering above her keyboard, her features distorted with wretchedness. I sat not twenty feet away from her, looking straight down at her through two windows and a well of air while she cried. "Poor Dina," I said, although of course she couldn't hear me. After a while she blew her nose and swept the cards to the side of her desk. A moment later she was typing away.

My phone rang as I was brushing the crumbs from my lap to join the other crumbs down there on the floor. I went into my bedroom, flopped down on my bed, and picked it up. "Hello?"

"So he didn't eat you alive," said Max with a chuckle I didn't much care for.

"Other way around, if anything."

"Did you have fun?"

I ignored this question. He would have to beg if he wanted sordid details. "He lives on Staten Island."

"Really," he said in a hushed voice, as if Frankie had taken me to a village up the Amazon. "What's it like there?"

"Primitive and mysterious," I said. "I just got home a little while ago, actually."

Max had insisted after we'd ordered our food that Frankie was definitely hitting on me, and when I went to the bathroom, he'd told

Frankie that I couldn't keep my eyes off his butt. Although Frankie and I hadn't initially noticed each other, Max's remarks had made us suddenly mutually irresistible. Max paid the check, leaving a huge tip, and then we went around the corner to a bar. When he was finished with his shift, Frankie showed up; Max had told him I'd be waiting for him. After a minimum of chitchat, Max said good night and got into a cab, leaving Frankie and me to share a nightcap and get to know each other a little. Frankie told me that he worked in his uncle's restaurant and lived in the basement of his parents' house on Staten Island, where he'd grown up. He was tired of sneaking around like a teenager: He was twenty-five years old, and he wanted to live his own life, and to hell with his parents. I put on my jacket and said, "Let's go," and off we went to Staten Island, where I'd done my best to fulfill his need for rebellion.

"I love to see young people pairing off together," said Max happily. "It warms my heart."

"You gave him to me only because you didn't want him," I said. "You know what I liked about him?"

"Let me guess."

"He's trying to get up the nerve to come out to his parents."

"And for what? So they can imagine him doing upsetting things they don't understand? Come on, don't start this whole thing up again."

"I'm only making a comment about Frankie," I said mildly.

"So," he said in the concerned voice he used to turn the tables on me whenever I tried to confront him about anything. "You ready for the homecoming tonight?"

"I don't know," I said. "I doubt I'll see much of Ted this weekend. Giselle's coming too, you know. And their kid."

"No wonder you liked Frankie," he said with a laugh. "Listen, I have a client coming in ten minutes and I haven't looked over his file yet. Good luck tonight, sweetie. Call if you need me tomorrow, I'll be around all day."

We hung up, I to turn on my computer, Max to counsel his nine o'clock client. I had never been in therapy, but I gathered that a therapist was, at least initially, a blank screen onto which his patient projected omniscience, wisdom, maturity, and stability. Max specialized in counseling recently out-of-the-closet gays and their families, which meant that homosexuals of all ages, along with their parents, children, spouses, or even the occasional sibling, trooped into Dr. Goldenberg's office, sat on couches and chairs, and talked or didn't talk for forty-five minutes, then emerged again and dispersed into the city for another week. During Max's off hours, he was an avid clubgoer, and at thirty-nine still a frequent user of poppers, X, coke, K, and even the occasional snort of heroin. He insisted that this steady nighttime debauchery didn't affect his ability to be an effective therapist, but I didn't buy it. It seemed to me to be a clear-cut case of "Shrink, heal thyself," or, rather, a continuation of unexamined adolescent acting-out, which in my opinion Max would have done well to face up to and resolve, for his health if nothing else. He was the only child of Orthodox Jewish parents. He'd been expected to become a businessman like his father and to marry a nice Jewish girl like his mother, and to provide little Rachels and Jacobs for his parents to shower with kisses and pinches on the cheek at Pesach and Yom Kippur.

Max and I had been friends for fourteen years, and during all this time I'd never met his parents, Fischl and Rivka Goldenberg, who called Max at least once a week, both of them together on separate extensions, to exhort him to come home soon for Shabbat dinner with Naomi Silverberg or Sarah Stein or Beth Berkowitz. For reasons I couldn't entirely understand, off he'd go once a month or so like a good little boy to Great Neck. He'd return well after dark on Saturday night, raring to go out and stay out until dawn. I didn't care much for clubs or drugs, but I went along to keep him company and make sure he didn't get lost, hold his head while he barfed into gutters or toilets; the next day I often brought him porn videos and chicken soup when he was too hung over to get out of bed. Since three years before, when Max had discovered his HIV-positive status, I'd known that my role of his nursemaid wasn't over by a long shot, depending on how long his regimen of pills kept symptoms at bay. I also knew that I'd be around when he needed me, because my own HIV status was negative, by some minor miracle, and I intended to keep it that way.

I'd also, as it happened, never spoken to or met Ted's parents, Chet and Betsy Masterson. Photographs of them showed a look-alike pair of tall, craggy-faced, well-groomed, fiercely smiling Connecticut Yankees, sheltered, correct, and set in their ways. Ted called them Martyr and Farter behind their backs, but to their faces he was a model son, courteous and solicitous to a degree that nonplused me, when I happened to overhear his side of their telephone conversations, as much as Max's hangdog filial obedience did.

I seemed to be slated to spend my life with closeted men—I, who'd announced that I was a homosexual one night at the dinner table at the age of twelve. At that time, we lived in a normal suburban house like a normal family for the first time ever, because my mother had finally burned out on her Bobby McGee vagabondage and utopian bliss. She'd married an architect and installed her brood in his split-level Phoenix ranch-style cinderblock house, complete with yard, dog, and TV set, our first.

I said out of nowhere, through a mouthful of potato, "I have an announcement to make, which is that I'm gay."

Amanda rolled her eyes; it was all over the playground at our school. Lola, who was eight, ignored me, her usual policy when confronted with something she didn't understand. My stepfather, Lou, shook my hand and said, "Congratulations, Jeremy, good for you."

To my puzzled irritation, my mother burst out laughing. "Oh, baby," she said. "Have you slept with a boy yet?"

"Mom! I'm only twelve."

"That is pretty young," she said, smiling.

"I'm gay, Mom," I said levelly.

Then I saw a flicker of something in her eyes, as if a wave of the New England Puritanism she'd spent her entire adult life striving to eradicate had risen up against the internal dam she'd built against it. But evidently her convictions held, because she eased back into her chair again.

"Well," she said. "Good for you for telling us, Jeremy, that took a lot of courage. And I hope you won't ever hesitate to ask for help or advice, and if there's any way I can give it to you, I will." She took a bite of pot roast, and that was that; the subject was changed, and dinner went on as usual.

But I remained edgy and tense throughout the meal, a feeling that had returned frequently since then. I had seen what I was up against.

3 | DOWNTOWN

I sat at my desk while Juanita unraveled the sleeve of my sweater, hopped along the back of my chair, perched on my shoulder, and nuzzled her hard little beak into my scalp. I always listened to NPR when I wrote; it provided such a soothing backdrop. My private motto for NPR was "Story time for grown-ups." The announcers' calm, correct pronunciation of every word, no matter how formidable, foreign, or vowelless, no matter what faraway or nearby calamities they were describing, allowed me to bask in the happy illusion that the world was safe and orderly and this latest catastrophe only an aberration.

Angus in Efes was my own small way of making sense of the rest of his life after my father vanished, and laying him to rest. When I'd begun the novel, it was with the idea that I'd bash out a first draft, revise it quickly, publish it, and move on, but after ten years I was still adding episodes, deepening scenes, polishing passages I'd already polished twelve times. And I hadn't been able to write the ending yet, possibly because in the years I'd been writing about him, I'd become almost as attached to the fictional Angus as if he had been an actual parent. During the solitude of Ted's lengthy absences, it was Angus who provided my days with meaningful structure, who gave me a reason to get up every morning. Instead of pining like Tennyson's pathetic, sighing, lovesick Mariana in her moated grange ("He will not come," she said./ She wept, "I am aweary, aweary/Oh God, that I were dead"), I conjured a verbal facsimile of my vanished father out of thin air and a computer screen, and made him say and do whatever I wanted him to. I couldn't keep Ted with me for long, but Angus was my captive. I was beginning to think I would write and rewrite this book for the rest of my life.

But no matter. My work was an internal sandbag to shield me from slings and arrows, not a target for them. I frequently tested whatever section or scene I was currently working on against the stark realities and blurred complexities I found in the world, and these checks shored me up, gave me a wholly private satisfaction, a pleasure having nothing to do with success or recognition. This in no way precluded fantasies of fame and glory, but it did forestall the rejection and criticism I'd have to undergo in order to attain them. I didn't mind being a crackpot attic-dwelling hermit far removed from such things as advances, reviews, promotion, because the idea of being misunderstood by reviewers, or even skewered and eviscerated for failing to uphold whatever subjective standards they espoused, horrified the bejeezus out of me. Like Bartleby, given the choice, I preferred not to.

Well, with one rather daunting exception. As I had just confessed to Sebastian, I had recently tossed off, just for fun, a screenplay I'd called with ironic pomposity *The Way of All Flesh*. I'd written it because I needed to take a break, write something disposable and mindless and over-the-top to temporarily dispel the earnest, analytical tone of my novel, replace Angus Thrane with a very different kind of father, Marxism with another obsession entirely. I had never for a moment expected this trifle to end up anywhere but the garbage. It was the most puerile thing I had ever written.

The screenplay's protagonist, an undertaker, was also a necrophiliac and a pedophile, although he tried to keep these under wraps. In act one, his own twelve-year-old son was killed by a speeding flower-delivery truck and wound up on his table. During a long night of sweaty moral wrestling, our hero paced back and forth by the laidout body of his son while a number of opinionated, diverse advisers—Plato, Lucrezia Borgia, Michael Jackson, Mr. Spock from *Star Trek*, Henry the Eighth, and Lizzie Borden—materialized and advised the bereft but aroused father on their own philosophies of life, death, familial bonds, fatherly duties, and man-boy love as they applied to his own particular dilemma. In a mockingly tender scene, the father finally made his decision and acted upon it. On the sound track, the Vienna Boys' Choir sang "Ruht Wohl," the heartrending lullaby-chorale from Bach's *Passion According to St. John*, as the camera rose above the man and dead child, circled them, then closed in until they were just flesh.

Nothing would ever have happened to this thing if it hadn't been for Max, the same Max who'd sent me home with Frankie last night and who, throughout the long tenure of our friendship, had caused me to do a significant number of other things I wouldn't otherwise have done. One night when he was over for dinner, I had laughingly explained its basic premise to him; over a couple of cognacs he'd managed to convince me to give him a copy. Without checking with me first, he'd mailed it to a friend of a friend who had just launched a small start-up agency and was desperately in search of "properties." I got a call two weeks later from some out-of-breath guy on a cell phone in what sounded like freeway traffic, saying that he'd loved the script and wanted to "shop it around." I was momentarily at a loss. "It's 'Kissed' meets 'Happiness,' " he said; I pictured highlighted hair slicked back with top-shelf gel, manicured hands, and a snarky frat-boy grin, and wrote him off as a perverted wing nut.

"I won't hold my breath," I said, "ha-ha," and hung up, ashen with embarrassment. I wasn't shocked that I hadn't received a single call from him in the three months since our conversation.

Today I was working on a scene in which Angus, lunching at a shady café table, watched as several village kids played with a feral dog, teasing and provoking him until the enraged animal bit one of them savagely. Rather than dashing to the rescue of the bleeding child, Angus leaned back in his chair, gazed at the sky, and mused to himself at some length about the superiority of socialism to the lamentably savage and seemingly ineluctable Darwinian struggle of natural law. This scene was proving tricky to write. It was hard to keep my narrative voice neutral, putting aside my scorn for my protagonist and imagining what had made my father tick. This was the crux of the whole book, but on some days I was more up to the task than others.

At eleven, the sun came out for a moment, then faded again behind the clouds. My ears pricked up when I heard a correspondent asking a Guatemalan woman about an annual festival in her village. A faint, melancholy bawk-bawk-bawk came in right on cue; I'd expected this, because I'd noticed that there was frequently a chicken clucking in the background when a native Spanish speaker was being interviewed on NPR. Maybe they had a tape of a chicken in their studio and dubbed it in, or maybe they arranged to have a chicken present for their Latin American interviews. I didn't know the reason, and I didn't want to know; it was one of the small but essential mainstays of my daily life like the Dog Walker's tantrums or Dina Sandusky's solitaire cheats.

Overcome all at once with fatigue, I went into the big room and stretched out on my bed on top of the quilt, and almost immediately I was plunged into a feverish, hazy, half-panicky dream in which Ted was walking away from me into a flickering light, into some sort of forest that darkened gradually and became a cavern into which he vanished. Standing at the entrance, I called his name, but he was gone. I awoke suffused with sadness. It was nearly one in the afternoon, but I felt as if I'd been sleeping for only five minutes. Disoriented and groggy, I splashed cold water on my face and put on my jacket.

"Did you invite your little boyfriend to the premiere?" I asked Felicia Boudreaux about half an hour later. We were facing each other in a booth at Benito's, our favorite Italian restaurant.

She stared at me. "What little boyfriend?"

"You have to ask?" I said. "How many do you have? I meant Wayne."

She flopped a hand at me. "Oh, get out of here."

"You get out of here. Every time I call you, he answers the phone, even if it's midnight or breakfast time. Where does he sleep, if not with you?"

"He's my assistant," she said. "We keep weird hours. Not everyone is as much of a slut as you are, Jeremy."

"Well, it's not easy sleeping around for two," I said without rancor; I loved it when she called me a slut, because she said it fondly, as if she vicariously admired me. "When are you going to do your share?"

She reached over and lightly scratched the tip of my nose with one red fingernail. "You know Dr. Wong told me I have to be celibate during my treatment. My system can't take the shock of transferring so much energy to someone else."

I wanted very badly to say, "Maybe if you quit shooting up—" but

I didn't want to piss her off. She brooked no challenge to her habits, any of them.

"Anyway," she said, "I don't blame you. It sucks that Ted is so unavailable, but you know. If he didn't live this way, he'd be stuck playing the heroine's loyal best friend or quirky hairdresser until he got old enough to play her weird bachelor uncle. I mean, think about it. What would you do if you were him?"

Felicia was one of Ted's oldest friends, and by now, one of mine. She had been his quote-unquote girlfriend at Yale. The day they met, he'd asked her to see a movie with him. A week or two later, at the point at which their nascent affair had to be either consummated or nipped in the bud, she had confessed to him, just as he was beginning to panic, that she loathed sex. They worked out a mutually satisfying arrangement: After a date together, he took her home to sleep by herself, and then he cruised New Haven gay bars and picked up townies.

"If I were him," I said, "I wouldn't have married Giselle."

"I wouldn't take their marriage so personally if I were you."

"Then how should I take it?"

She leaned her chin on one hand, her pointy elbow resting on the thick white tablecloth. Both cheekbone and hand were grotesquely, glamorously bony. The first two fingers on the hand that supported her chin held a long white mentholated cigarette whose smoke floated across her face like a film of nostalgia, as if this had all happened long ago. Her silk dress was the same bloodred shade as the booth. Her pale gold hair was piled on her head and stuck through with two chopsticks like a bowl of rice. She had rimmed her far-apart green eyes with black kohl and applied several layers of bloodred lipstick to her full, childlike mouth. Her face was serene and faintly, intelligently malicious, like a calm sea with a dark form skulking just beneath the surface.

"Ted's just like me," she said. "Selfish, and pragmatic. Sold to the highest bidder. You can't expect any more of him than that."

"That's not true of either one of you," I said hotly.

"Please," she laughed. "I can't believe you're still romantic about him after all these years. Maybe that's what's kept you together. You choose to see him as someone better than he is, and it flatters him because he respects you."

"Maybe I've seen parts of him that you haven't," I said stubbornly. "And maybe we truly love each other."

"It's possible," she said. "I wouldn't know. He's never shown me anything but his worst and truest self, the way I show him mine. He doesn't bother trying to impress me."

"What's that supposed to mean?"

"I'm starving," she said suddenly. This was a lie; she just wanted to change the subject before it turned into an argument. She was never hungry. She lived on menthols, vodka martinis, heroin, and weekly herbal injections from an old charlatan six flights up in a Chinatown tenement, Dr. Wong. He'd taken one feel of her pulse at her initial consultation and said, "Foggy brain. Very foggy brain." This was preposterous; Felicia had honed herself to a flesh-and-bone razor's edge of lucidity. The old quack was rooking her. But her romantic idea of herself was that she was poisonous and doomed, so she happily paid him to tell her this.

Apparently she was entertaining parallel thoughts about my own delusions, because she added then, "You shouldn't be threatened by Giselle, Jeremy. You have completely separate roles in Ted's life."

"Well, things haven't been so great between Ted and me lately," I said emphatically. I looked around for the spaghetti I'd ordered and beheld with an appetite-suppressing convulsion the rounded back of Phil Martensen two tables away, sitting across from Gary O'Nan. Phil was a photographer, Gary a gossip columnist. They both worked for *Downtown*, the weekly tabloid-style magazine whose offices, now that I thought about it, were right around the corner. Felicia and I had been talking rather loudly just then. "Oh my God," I said under my breath without moving my lips.

Felicia glanced over at Phil, then continued to skate her gaze around the room.

"Who are they?"

"*Downtown* magazine."

"They couldn't hear us," she murmured positively.

"We were almost shouting."

"No, we weren't," she said, and gestured for the waiter. As the reedy young man in the bow tie made his way over, I made a show of noticing them for the first time.

"Hello!" I called. "Phil, how are you? Oh, hi, Gary."

The lugubrious mask of a sad clown appeared in profile just above the pointy hump of Phil's back. Gary's glance was like the flick of a scorpion's tail. I gave a brief, hearty wave and looked up at the hovering waiter, my heart trying to rise through my esophagus to flee my body.

"I could use another one of these," said Felicia, tipping her near-empty martini glass into the ashtray. Two oily-wet olives rolled into the ashes and came to rest against a squashed butt. The waiter picked up the ashtray and replaced it with a clean one from his apron pocket. After he'd disappeared, I squeezed my eyes shut and groaned, "Aaaagh."

"I'm thinking of a number between eight and twenty-nine," said Felicia briskly.

I opened my eyes, narrowed my focus, and occluded my peripheral vision so that I could see only Felicia. We stared into each other's eyes.

"Between eight and twenty-nine," I repeated.

This was a trick we'd developed at parties, to look as though we were engaged in an intimate, emotional conversation whenever there was someone in the vicinity who needed to be prevented from approaching and causing either of us boredom or injury. It also worked as a distraction when one of us was upset about something. I could no longer see Phil or Gary; I was shielded by our taut, exclusive gaze. "Twenty-seven," I said fiercely.

"No," she said, but not without sympathy. "Let me narrow it down for you a little: It's an odd number, it's a prime number, and it's the age I was when Ted and I drove to New Orleans for spring break and stayed at that hotel on Prytania Street with that witchy proprietress who spooked us so much we had to leave."

"Nineteen," I said.

"That is it exactly," she said. "Do you feel better now? They didn't hear you."

"You mean *us*," I said. "You've got a big mouth too, you know, it wasn't just me." I took one of her cigarettes from her mint-green pack and lit it with a rasp of her thin gold lighter. The mentholated smoke numbed my lungs as if it were ice cold, and the head rush made me want to lie down. I took a second, deeper drag and stubbed it out in the fresh ashtray. My plate of spaghetti arrived, looking as obscenely horrific as the worms-and-clotted-blood jokes of my childhood. On the table in front of Felicia, oily brown liquid roiled in a vast white plate, the soup du jour. She was looking past it, at the table where Gary and Phil were sitting.

"Report," I muttered. "What are they doing?"

"They're paying," she said out of the side of her mouth. She appeared to be enjoying this. "The older guy is heading for the men's room. That other guy is picking up the tab. He's at the cash register now. Who is he?"

"I can't believe this is happening," I said.

"He looks so familiar," she said. "It's because he has a sadass. All the boys down south have 'em. Big baggy old rear ends. Comes from sitting around bossing the darkies all day."

"Darkies," I repeated in disbelief.

"Oh, yes, Jeremy. My grandmother once told my father when he was a little boy, 'We don't say "niggers," darling, we say "darkies." ' "

I stared at her.

"And you wonder why I left?" she added, shaking her head.

"No," I said, but I didn't say anything more. I'd always taken Felicia's references to her childhood in the Deep South with a big grain of salt, because I'd noticed that she and I had a peculiar effect on each other, something that happened all too often in these gay-man-straight-single-woman alliances, as if the ghost of Tennessee Williams hung over our conversations: I found myself playing up my homosexual mannerisms around her, just as I had the feeling I provoked her into acting more affectedly southern than she normally would have. "Okay, I'm going in. Watch my back."

"You're covered," she said in a cloak-and-dagger undertone.

I entered the men's room with a bright smile. "How are you, Phil," I said, trying to sound jovial. I assumed the stance right next to him at the bank of urinals. I hoped I'd be able to pee under these circumstances.

"How's everything, Jeremy," said Phil in a blandly friendly tone that left me just as uncertain as I'd been a minute ago.

"Okay." My gaze flicked uncontrollably over to Phil's penis, which turned out to be as thick, yellowish, and unprepossessing as the rest of him. If Phil was aware that I'd peeked, he didn't show it. I'd run into Phil for years at various parties and bars; we had several friends in common, but I knew next to nothing about him. He was a master of the smoke screen, betraying evidence of neither a personal life nor emotions. This colossally impenetrable sangfroid was one reason why people rarely noticed him until his flashbulb had gone off in their faces.

"The food wasn't too great today," I was saying now. "Felicia barely touched her soup."

Phil said without affect, "She's such a beautiful girl."

Then I heard myself saying something that made my ears blanch, something that went against everything I professed to believe. "She's Ted's ex-girlfriend," I said in a voice so palpably flat, the words didn't even bounce off the tiles, they fell to the bottom of the urinal and stayed there. "They dated for a while at Yale."

Phil gave his turnip-colored stub a waggle and put it away. "Well, maybe they'll get a new cook," he said as he scrubbed his hands at the sink.

"Let's hope so," I said as he headed for the door. I ran scalding water over my hands until I was certain that Phil and Gary were now standing the requisite two feet apart in the elevator on their way back up to *Downtown*'s offices. Then I walked briskly back to the table, where Felicia sat tapping a cigarette against the tabletop, looking at her watch.

"What happened to you?" she asked unhappily; I knew this mood all too well and was used to treating her like a soap bubble when it came over her. "I was afraid you'd hanged yourself with your belt from the light fixture."

"Why would I hang myself?" I asked as I handed the waiter the platinum Amex Ted had given me. "I never wear a belt."

She rolled the cigarette against her bottom lip, looking sideways.

"What happened?" I said, my gorge rising.

She sighed, then leaned her head back and gently dandled the spoon in her soup, which no one had bothered to remove yet.

"Tell me," I snapped.

She looked at me then. In her eyes was the infinite, fathomless sorrow of old idle hand-me-down money weary with the strain of reacclimatizing to each successive generation of antebellum decline. "Phil's friend came up to me and asked was I from South Carolina and I said yes, I am. He changed his name, that's how come I never realized who he was.

He used to be *Carstairs* O'Nan until his old granddad Carstairs the First cut him out of his will. I'm so sorry, I couldn't help it, his granddaddy and mine are actually old—"

"All right," I said witheringly. "What did he say?"

"He said he was looking forward to the premiere," she said. "And then he asked if you were talking about Ted just now, and I said no, of course not." Cradled in the hollow of her neck was an emerald on a short gold chain, a louche, cold, deadly green stone that jumped slightly with each beat of her pulse.

"Fuck," I spat at her. The armpits of my shirt were drenched.

Felicia slid into the booth next to me and put a fluttery hand on my arm. "I don't feel well at all," she said. She looked ghastly. Her black eye makeup was smearing into the tiny creases around her eyes, and she had a fleck of lipstick on her front tooth. Her knot of hair had slipped to one side of her head; the chopsticks looked silly and untethered. It was amazing how she could disintegrate in a moment like this.

"You're such a drama queen," I said as I took the pen the waiter handed me and made a squiggle on the signature line of the credit card slip.

"The tip," she reminded me, her head almost on my shoulder. Her breath smelled like sour milk heavily underlain with rubbing alcohol. "It's not enough. Two more is twenty percent."

"But the service sucked."

"We come here all the time. You want it to get worse?"

I added two dollars.

"I'm never too ill to remember the little people," she murmured, for an instant almost herself again. Then her face crumpled into a monkey vizard of agony.

I led her out onto the street and tucked her into a taxi. I was about to shut the door when her arm snaked out and twined around me. I tumbled in beside her, and the cab nosed itself into the traffic and set off downtown while Felicia sniffled and wiped her nose repeatedly on the back of her hand. A constant high keening noise came from way back in her throat. I handed her my handkerchief, then looked out the window and considered what had just happened.

"It's all your fault," Felicia said into my shoulder. "If you hadn't kept me waiting for so long—" I put my arm around her and she put her head down on my forearm.

"You pull out all the stops, don't you," I said.

"You're so mean," she murmured with a sickly smile. The cab stopped at a red light. Felicia sat up, dragged her knees up to her chest, and clasped her arms around them.

"We're crossing Canal. Almost there." I looked at my watch: just after three. "Turn left here," I said, and eased my wallet out of my back pocket. In the elevator of Felicia's building, I wedged my hands under her arms. Her skin was clammy and had turned gray. Her eyes were glassy and inward. I half carried, half dragged her across the blond-wood expanse of her loft to the bedroom, where I slung her up onto the billowing feather-quilted bed. In the bathroom, I opened drawers and cabinets until I found her syringes and little Chinese porcelain box of glassine packets. I lit the jasmine-scented candle she kept by the side of the sink, shook a packet of powder into a spoon, added a thimbleful of water, cooked the stuff until it bubbled, then set a cotton ball into the spoon bowl and sucked it up into the syringe. I tapped out the air bubbles on the way back into the bedroom, where Felicia looked up at me with fluttering eyes from the bed and turned over. I took in with horror her Barbie-doll thighs, skinny flanks bruised greenish blue from the endless hypos, the eye-searing shock of her pantiless bush, white-blond and pornographically trimmed.

I gasped as if I'd just been stuck with a pin and averted my gaze. "I'm not going to do this for you, Felicia," I said.

"Please," she answered breathlessly.

"No," I said, handing her the syringe. "I can't even watch."

I went out into the living room and sat on the couch for a while. I leaned against the deep leather cushions and looked out through the old factory window at the dense blue-white, boiling sky. All around me, facing me, were paintings of people arranged around restaurant tables or dance floors or bars. Their faces, lit by jukebox lights, votive candles, or matches held to cigarettes, were as sharply intelligent and unaccountably tragic as lemurs. They all looked deeply lonely, although they were in rooms filled with crowds and smoke and music; their expressions were a trompe-l'oeil blend of public arch amusement and inner clutching sadness. The colors were drenched and bilious, the skin tones as flat as the walls. Felicia was a great painter, I'd always thought, but no gallery owner had ever shown the remotest interest in her slides.

Felicia came out of her bedroom a few minutes later and sat next to me. She had put on fresh makeup and redone her hair, and wore a red silk robe tied at the waist. She was beautiful again and back in business.

"Sorry about that," she said breezily.

"I've got to go," I said.

"Jeremy. Accept my apology."

"This whole thing is bullshit. You started doing it because you liked the idea of yourself doing it. Now look at you."

She laughed loopily. "I don't have to answer to anyone."

"That's hardly the point, Felicia. Think about it."

"Oh, fiddle," she said, and cupped my face in her hands, which were as cool as a nurse's. "I want to be a drug-addicted neurotic semi-recluse. You want to be what you are; it's the same thing, Jeremy."

"What am I, Felicia?"

"You're a slut," she said, but this time it sounded like an insult.

"Okay," I said, aware that I was about to say something I couldn't retract, but I wanted to say it and I wanted her to hear it, because it would be like lancing a long-festering boil, "but it's not the same thing at all. Your choice is willfully self-destructive and mine isn't and that's a real difference, no matter how you want to justify it. I take care of myself." I hadn't known that I was this angry with her. The words themselves seemed to be drawing forth a poison from deep within me. "I'd never ask you to stick me in the ass with a syringe, for example."

"You didn't have to," she said, yawning, unperturbed. I knew I ought to rush back uptown and say something to Gary to convince him he'd misunderstood everything, and my mother was giving a poetry reading later on today, which I'd promised her I'd attend, but it wasn't easy to extricate myself from this couch. Felicia's head had dropped slightly; her forehead rested just an inch above my shoulder. Her face had softened and her eyelids were partially closed. The leather cushions we sat on seemed to draw us down together into a squishy, decadent vortex. Nothing seemed to matter here at Felicia's except staying here. I could see why she almost never went out.

"What kind of intervention was that, Jeremy?" she asked. "Was that the best you could do?" She laughed then, silently, but so hard she coughed, and I had to thump her on the back. "I'm sorry," she said finally, gasping, "but that was the most pathetic little confrontation I ever heard."

"I've got to go," I said, and stood up and went over to the door. I didn't look back at her because I was sure she was lolling her head back against the couch cushions, still convulsed with silent laughter, and I had no interest in seeing her like that.

"Jeremy, come back here and get your sense of humor," she called. "I think it's under the couch or somewhere."

I opened the door.

"Don't go," she said, and this time there was a note of pleading in her voice. "Don't leave all mad at me like that. I won't be able to get any painting done today, I'll be too upset."

Felicia had always frankly cared more about herself and her own needs and desires than just about anything else. But because I always knew exactly how she felt and what she wanted, I felt no need to cover up my own desires and moods. I found it oddly refreshing that her gestures of generosity were always offered on her own terms, which seemed much more genuine than the tactful equivocating or selfless white lies of "nice" people. Her self-centeredness infuriated me, but I didn't mind being infuriated when I didn't have to pretend I wasn't. For this reason, I always forgave her.

"I have to go," I said, softening. "I'll call you later."

"Give Ted my love," she called plaintively as I slammed the door behind me.

4 | SWEETNESS AND LIGHT

The Quill and Palette Club was a brownstone on West Tenth Street, a stately, high-ceilinged, former-single-family house very similar to the one in which I lived. I climbed the front steps and stepped into the bright, narrow front hallway, much less ostentatious than Ted's foyer and much more suited to my own tastes. In the big, crowded salon, I took a chair near the back, beyond the open French doors that divided the room in half. The old man next to me cupped his knees with his palms; the skin on the backs of his hands was an eerie, creamy white. The sight of these cool, gentle, pillowlike hands gave me a deep desire to go to sleep with my cheek resting on one of them. I closed my eyes for a moment, found myself nearly in tears, snapped them open again. The tears had come welling from somewhere deep inside me along with an immense fatigue. I had the sense of everything in the room around me, intolerably apart from me, a strange feeling of not fully existing, of having a skewed, incomplete perception of the world. My dream about Ted disappearing into the forest came back to me as if I were still in it: His plane was landing right about now.

People arrived, took seats, talked in small groups, laughed, and rustled their jackets off. I watched them, vaguely apprehensive that one of them would turn out to be an old family friend, and I'd have to get up and go through the tedious process of pretending to be delighted to see him or her, but luckily, I didn't see anyone I knew. Then my sister Amanda materialized all at once in the chair I'd saved for her.

Was Amanda losing weight again? I glanced briefly at her catlike little face with its small, straight nose and clear brown-gold eyes. Her cheeks were drawn and her skin too pale, I thought; she was beginning to look like our dead grandmother, who'd been a sticklike little bird with a dowager's hump. She was overdressed, as usual, so it was hard to tell; she wore an all-black, many-layered outfit that culminated, at its lowest point, in ugly, fragile shoes with enormous soles so ludicrously misshapen, they looked like Dr. Seuss buildings. I assumed they were Japanese.

"Hey, Jer," she said, giving me a dry peck on the cheek, which I immediately wiped off in case she'd deposited any maroon lipstick. She smelled of musk and cigarette smoke. She peeled off a sort of velvet capelet affair and sniffed. Amanda sniffed frequently, habitually, which I found, like so many things about her, wildly irritating: She didn't have a cold or allergies, and as far as I knew, she didn't use cocaine.

Amanda and I had always been semi-telepathically connected, so it wasn't necessary for us to tell each other what we thought of each other. From the air around her head I absorbed the opinion that I should get a life, try to publish my work, and stop hiding in Ted's attic. I thought, and knew she knew I thought, that she should dump her no-good live-in boyfriend and get over herself. She was incredibly self-serious about all aspects of her life, from the pretentious, overwrought music her band played to the way she sat there, her eyes narrowed, her neck very still, as if waiting for all eyes to fall upon her and widen in bewitchment.

"Ted get back yet?"

"He's coming in tonight," I said.

"With Giselle Fleece, right? I'd love to meet her. What's her schedule like while she's here?"

"I'm not her personal secretary," I said.

She sniffed. "There's Mom," she said.

"I see her," I said back.

Our mother, full name Emma Pepper Thrane Jackson Margolis, was striding to a chair near the podium, her posture ramrod straight as always, silver-black hair piled high on her head like a gypsy's.

A large elderly woman got up and tapped the mike.

"I'm very pleased to welcome you to the fall readings at the Quill and Palette Club," she said in a high, quavering voice like Julia Child's. "We have a wonderful treat for our opening reading today: Emma Pepper just won this year's Atlantic Poetry Award and also recently completed her fourth residency at the MacDowell Colony. Her work, which has been widely published, acclaimed, and anthologized, is known for its passion, lyricism, and metaphysical insight. We're very pleased indeed that she's agreed to read for us today. Please join me in welcoming Ms. Pepper."

My slender, somewhat fey mother might have appeared fragile to those who didn't know her, but these characteristics were in fact the source of her strength: Whenever she felt dissatisfied with the life she found herself in, she had always had the ability to generate a new persona for herself that seemed to have neither scars nor regrets but which contained the familiar hallmarks of her personality, and then to transplant this fresh self into more fertile ground. Where more rigid souls might have broken or soberer ones imploded, she changed her skin and slipped away like an inmate walking unnoticed through a prison gate in borrowed street clothes.

She had begun writing poetry shortly after she'd married Lou Jackson, the stepfather who'd shaken my hand and congratulated me when I'd made my big announcement. The oppressive heat, air-conditioned silence, and dead boredom of our Phoenix neighborhood had caused her mind to go into creative hyperdrive. She'd turned from free spirit into mad housewife almost overnight. Finding herself home alone all day, she exploded into fierce monomaniacal activity. Often we came home from school to find her at the dining room table surrounded by scribbled-on papers, a wineglass and half-empty bottle of white wine, cigarette burning in an ashtray. As we burst en masse through the door, yapping about our days at school, she waved us frantically away, commanded us to go help ourselves to cookies, candy, whatever the hell we wanted, just please leave her alone for ten more minutes.

She went off to writers' workshops during the summers, began submitting her work to literary magazines. She gave readings, won a small prize or two, kept writing. When I was in college, she left Lou and moved to New York, where she eventually met and married Leonard Margolis, her current husband, a physicist. She sold a poetry collection to Milkweed Press for a tiny poetry-sized advance, then sold a poem to *The New Yorker*, then another to *Harper's*. She'd hit the big time, poetrywise. She was asked to teach at Breadloaf and the New School, went to both Yaddo and MacDowell, and gave frequent readings wherever she could.

She was at the forefront of a group of middle-aged poetesses whose intensely melodious free verse had as its common theme the subject of femaleness and its attendant joys and tribulations: coming of age, sex, marriage, giving birth, divorce, aging, loss, hysterectomies, their rage at their mothers, passion for their children, fond bemusement for their husbands and yearning for their lovers, past, present, and imaginary. My mother was beautiful, well spoken, dramatic, and husky-voiced. She was shamelessly crowd-pleasing, hotly exhibitionistic.

She began today's reading with a poem made up of disparate images: a raccoon who'd wandered into the garden of her house in Saugerties, memories of playing in her grandmother's closet as a child, the sound of her husband's voice calling her name in his sleep. I listened straight-faced, breathing rapidly and shallowly, as if in the grip of mild nausea that threatened to worsen with any sudden movement. I sensed, but didn't turn to see, Amanda's rapt expression. She had stopped sniffing.

Just then I caught sight of my mother's old friend Irene Rheingold sitting a few rows up with her husband, Richard, and their daughter, Beatrice, a big, strapping, shy girl of twenty-seven I was almost certain was gay, even though she herself may not have realized it yet. In my initial reconnaissance of the room, I'd somehow missed the Rheingolds, or maybe they'd arrived late. Irene Rheingold was the one of my mother's friends I'd most dreaded having to pretend to be delighted to encounter. What was she wearing? A purple velvet medieval-maiden dress with leg-of-mutton sleeves and an Empire waist, a chunky wood-bead and squash-blossom necklace. As her body had expanded in girth, her clothes, retaining their girlish, hippie-dippy whimsy, had simply grown along with her.

Irene sporadically reviewed novels and poetry, and although she wasn't professionally affiliated with any particular magazine or publication, her reviews tended to cluster in *The Village Voice* and *The New York Review of Books* and *The New York Times Book Review*, an impressive ré-sumé that might have suggested her opinion was valuable and worth cultivating, an implication belied by her unqualified championing of purple-prosy memoirish semiliterate "novels" by minority, lesbian, or otherwise disadvantaged women, and her ecstatic spasms of devotion for "feminist" poets like my mother, whom she had recently dubbed, without a trace of irony, "Walt Whitman with a womb" in *The Voice*.

My mother, to her own discredit, had seen nothing to question in this praise, not a whiff of hyperbole or fatuity. The day it came out, I had been at her apartment, and had cringed through her side of the ensuing telephone conversation with Irene. "Such high praise," she'd said breathily, "coming from such a brilliant critic. I'm actually weeping, Irene!" Her friendship with Irene itself betrayed this same lack of discrimination, a selective gullibility and glibness I had always found deplorable in her; she was so easily taken in by some things and some people, including herself. My mother could be incredibly naive and daft in ways I didn't understand, given her perceptiveness and probity in other matters. If she had inculcated in herself a more rigorous, skeptical, demanding cast of mind, I couldn't help thinking with a twinge at my involuntary perfidy, she might have been led to expect more both from her friends and her own work, which might have made her a better poet, and would certainly have engendered more respect in her son. But then, adult children always imagined they were vastly more sophisticated than their parents; that was part of the illusion of human evolution.

Because I was preoccupied with these thoughts about my mother, I didn't notice until well into the reading that she wasn't projecting her usual élan. Hearing an uncharacteristic tremor in her voice, I noticed then that she looked pale and tense, which was odd: Was she having an attack of nerves or stage fright? If so, this would be the first time ever, so I had to doubt it. Now that I thought about it, there had also been a tremor in her voice when she'd called yesterday to make sure I was coming to her reading, and to tell me she needed to talk about something important afterward. Was she leaving Leonard? If so, I wouldn't blame her a bit; Leonard was an odd duck, to say the very least, a beetle-browed, silent fellow who drifted off into brown studies during dinner parties and couldn't be interrupted, although he was given to outbursts whenever something wasn't exactly right in his immediate environment. "Emma!" he might yell out of nowhere during dinner after passing most of the meal in dense silence, "you know I like the blue plates! Why are you using these?" Maybe Emma had finally become fed up with him. If she had, I wouldn't blame her.

She lost her place at one point, and near the end of one poem about Leonard her voice cracked, and she had to clear her throat several times before she could proceed. That was it, I thought. She was getting another divorce. She had her work, her friends; she'd be all right on her own. I'd been subjected at ages six and fifteen to her lengthy, self-imposed trials in which she played both defendant and prosecutor, with me representing judge, jury, and bailiff. Both times, after reviewing far more evidence than I'd ever wanted to be made aware of, I'd pronounced her innocent of any blame or fault. I could do it again, no problem.

"Jeremy, where are you? Oh, I see you, there you are," said my mother suddenly. A chill finger of dread snaked its way down my spine as she fixed an unwavering gaze on my face, and several members of the audience turned and smiled at me. "This next poem," she said in a voice rich with love, "is entitled 'To My Firstborn Child.' "

The poem was very long, and described without mincing words the nearly twenty-four hours of labor she'd endured before I'd finally deigned to poke my head out and greet the world, her uterine spasms, shaved pubic region, distended belly, my head cresting bloody and wet from gaping vaginal lips, ripping her open. I cringed, feeling like an overgrown mama's boy, trying to assemble my features into an adult expression instead of scratching myself frantically all over the way I very much wanted to do. I was no prude, to be sure, but I didn't enjoy this public graphic portrayal of my natal self. The whole ordeal hadn't been a picnic for me either, but that was beside the point.

To distract myself, I kicked around my head and teased silently with my tongue two words that had recently lodged in my brain, demanding a certain percentage of my running semiconscious attention: "Squanto" and "bughouse." Was Squanto, I wondered now with all my heart as several more people turned to gaze moistly at me, the Thanksgiving Indian who had brought the Pilgrims a leather pouch in which were wrapped a few withered corn kernels, a plug of tobacco, and a squash? Did "bughouse" mean crazy, or did it mean loony bin? It didn't matter; I'd gotten stuck on the whole question of what was in that leather pouch.

The audience, meanwhile, seemed completely rapt right up to the final lines: "And then at last I held you in my arms, my bloody scrap of flesh, my spark of life." There was a hush, then an explosion of applause. Then my mother shut her book, said "Thank you all very much for coming," and moved away from the podium as regally and sternly as an airline stewardess gliding behind her drinks cart.

As we all clapped with a fervor that seemed somehow unrelated to the quality of this particular reading and indicative more of a blanket admiration, I felt obscurely guilty in spite of myself, seeing how well regarded she was. I was her firstborn child and only son, and as such I'd been given the distinct impression, although of course she'd never actually said this out loud, that I was expected to become some sort of successful something. I'd always suspected (maybe this was just paranoia) that she'd hoped I would become a lawyer like my father, discarding the rough spots in his personality, of course, but embodying his idealism and political fervor; unfortunately, I had inherited neither. After I graduated from college, I announced that I was going to be a writer. To this my mother (herself a writer) had said something earnest and concerned but carefully nonjudgmental, to the effect that kids who had no idea what to do next called themselves writers and flailed around for a decade or so, working at bad jobs and getting depressed and feeling alienated, and she hoped this wouldn't be the case with me. Ever since, she'd maintained a tactful silence on the subject of what the hell I did with all my free time. I mentioned my novel every so often, but whether or not she took this seriously, I was never entirely sure because she never said. She'd always made it a point not to tell her children what to do, a policy that while admirable in principle made me extremely uneasy in practice; not knowing what she thought, I was free to imagine the worst.

I stood and inched my way toward the door, aimed a cursory "Hello" at Irene and the other Rheingolds, then turned to Amanda, who was right behind me, to whisper that I'd see her and Emma outside. Richard Rheingold meanwhile had lumbered his way over to my mother and was clasping both her hands in his like a hungry, friendly bear. In spite of myself, I found myself embroiled suddenly in some sort of conversation with Irene.

"Jeremy," she was saying in her girlish, affected voice, "I want to hear all about this new agent. That's just wonderful news; your mother must be terribly proud of you. Who *is* he? What *agency* is he with?"

I narrowed my eyes at Amanda, who seemed to be deeply interested in something Beatrice was telling her about her preschool teaching career. The news that I had somehow managed to convince an agent to represent me must have zipped over the phone lines from Amanda's Williamsburg apartment to the Upper West Side; I could almost hear them, their amused surprise, "He has an *agent*? Finally! You must be so relieved, Emma! Have you read the screenplay?"

I mumbled the man's name and agency. "But he's not necessarily going to do a thing for me," I added.

"Oh, yes, what a heartbreaking industry," Irene said with sympathetic woe, fixing me with her small, flickering eyes. As she talked, she pursed her lips, fluttered her hands, grimaced in an oddly parodic actressy way, as if she were unflatteringly mimicking herself. "But someone took you on! That means you've made tremendous progress with your work. Well, you must have in all these years since you last showed me anything. That was back when you were just out of college, wasn't it? That funny little play you were writing, I remember it reminded me a bit of early Ionesco. It was absurdist and dark in the most charmingly post-collegiate way, as if you weren't quite sure yet what you wanted to write about."

This sort of mewing insult was all too typical of her, but I couldn't be truly offended by anything she said, because even her most cutting remarks seemed devoid of any edge or intent; they always sounded as if they had quotation marks around them. I attributed this to the fact that Irene had never had to struggle or work for a living or worry about money, so her cattiness was more a nervous habit than an indication of any genuine cast of mind. Richard was a famous and well-loved concert pianist and could have had any number of other women, I was sure—I had never understood what kept him with Irene, but no one knew better than I did how impossible it was to tell anything about couples' private lives from watching them together in public.

Three middle-aged women, I saw out of the corner of my eye, had converged on my mother with a flurry of compliments and comments, edging Richard out. He stood by the radiator, listening politely to them.

They all looked as if they lived on Central Park West, held season tickets to the Philharmonic, pursued "culture" the way their small-town heartland-dwelling counterparts did jigsaw puzzles and needlepoint, and never missed an issue of *The Atlantic Monthly*. They were all, I realized, near clones of Irene; they wore the same pseudo-ethnic clothing and had identical girlishly long gray hair.

"You have such a wonderfully metaphorical but at the same time grounded way of expressing the most private and profound female experiences," the one with the longest hair said.

This was my cue. "I've simply got to run now," I said in my homo voice, an affected drawl I reserved for social occasions such as this one and for people like Irene. "Ciao, Irene, lovely to see you."

Irene waggled her fingers at me before turning, probably with relief, to Amanda and her daughter, Beatrice. I escaped at last to the front stoop, where I sat down and leaned back against the top step and muttered "Squanto was bughouse to squander his bounty" over and over again to myself. Just where did I get off, being so catty about my mother's best friend and her ilk, when I myself was kept in lavish splendor by a famous man who supported me and my own so-called writing career? Just then, into my line of vision strolled a superb example of sapiens, genus homo—young, moist-lipped, tight-buttocked, such stuff as dreams were made on. I tracked him through narrowed eyes, a low growl bubbling deep in my throat.

Ted was probably getting home right about now. I was extremely relieved to have an excuse to miss the homecoming. I imagined it as a scene out of a Gothic novel, the seasonal return of the Lord of the Manor bounding up the front stairs, followed by his wife and child, the nanny, his valet, Giselle's lady-in-waiting or whatever the fuck she was called, and the limo driver with the bags. As the secret mad wife in the attic, I wasn't due onstage until around midnight, carrying a burning candelabrum and wearing a soiled white nightgown. After supper with my mother and sister, I planned to cool my heels in a movie or bar while the household went through its paces, while the valet and lady-in-waiting unpacked the haute-couture finery and hung it in the walk-in closet in the master bedroom in readiness for Monday night's premiere and party, and the nanny installed little Bret in the nursery, Ted and Giselle admired Yoshi's obscene-looking orchids in their second-floor glassed-in balcony hothouse. At eight o'clock would come Basia's summons to the dining room table for body-temperature borscht, fleshy dumplings that resisted the teeth, and her specialty, pork cutlets as chewy as slabs of latex. After dinner, bath time and bedtime for the Kewpie-faced angel, the grunt work done by the nanny, the adoring parents standing by . . . and then? Then Ted might start to wonder where the hell I was, and I didn't want to be too easily located when his attention, as it must, turned to me. I had my pride.

"There you are," said my mother.

I looked up at her through a thick fog. She looked fragile and upset.

"Where's Amanda?" I asked.

"She'll be out in a minute," said my mother.

"What's wrong?"

She sat next to me on the stoop and leaned against me. "I'll tell you at dinner, when Amanda can hear too."

"That was a good reading, Mom."

"I was so distracted. But that's very nice of you to say." She squeezed my arm and gave me a kiss on the cheek.

"And you look beautiful, as always."

"Oh, Jeremy, if only everyone were exactly like you."

There were a few things I could say to this, but I chose to say none of them. A few minutes later, all the members of our dinner party, with one unwelcome addition, had assembled on the sidewalk, freed of extraneous conversational entanglements, ready to roll. Irene, it developed, had been invited along, whether by my sister or my mother I hadn't been able to ascertain, so my blame had no object and remained stuck in my craw. "The reservations were for three," I said weakly but mulishly.

"Well, they can pull up an extra chair," said my mother, equally mulishly but much more assertively. She had never understood my aversion to Irene; it was one of the few things she refused to indulge in me.

We were going, at my own suggestion, to a little bistro I frequented whenever possible. The three women strolled, yapping, while I surged ahead, eager to get this over with and also a bit peckish. Since that awful scene at Benito's this afternoon, I'd been looking forward to the sheer comfort of a St. Émilion I particularly liked to drink with an order of garlicky snails, chèvre-beet-mesclun salad, moules frites, and finally a cognac with mousse au chocolat and café au lait. The evening had just begun; it was absurdly early to eat dinner, but my mother ate this early almost every night, yet another of her eccentricities in a city where some people might have considered even an eight o'clock dinner invitation much too early.

When we arrived, it appeared that reservations had not been necessary; the staff were all still lounging at the bar with pre-shift cigarettes and demitasses, and seemed mildly put out by our arrival. No one else was there except a couple of old fruits sipping wine at the bar. I felt their eyes rake over me; I didn't return their glances, but it perked me up to be viewed as a morsel, my rose having long ago given up the ghost of its first bloom. Actually, now that I thought about it, "first" implied a second.

We faced off in a booth, Amanda and me against Emma and Irene. Amanda lit a cigarette while I scanned the wine menu to see whether they'd added anything that sounded better than the old standby.

"I wish you'd quit smoking, Amanda," said Emma. Lucy, her mother, had died two years before of lung cancer and emphysema.

"I'll stop in two years," said Amanda. "You were thirty-five when you quit."

"Isn't it ironic," my mother said to Irene, "how our children emulate us only in the things we most dislike about ourselves?"

"Beatrice has just decided to cut off all her hair," said Irene, peering through her reading glasses at the wine menu. "My own greatest mistake at her age."

"At least don't smoke in front of Mom," I said to Amanda. "Her mother died of lung cancer, for God's sake."

Amanda didn't look at me or acknowledge what I'd said except to send a wave of dislike my way, from which I gathered that I had been sent to a penalty box in her head, but I was tired of her disdainful silences, and now made it a policy to ignore them. If she had something to say to me, she could say it aloud.

"Where is Leonard tonight?" I asked my mother, although the thought of spending an hour or two or, God forbid, three with my brooding, intimidating stepfather, with his lashing out and unpredictable querulousness, was not a pleasant one; I wanted to change the subject before Amanda and I started bashing each other over the head with our plates. It was appalling the way we turned into overgrown kids whenever we were with our mother.

"Leonard," she said. "That's what I—"

"We'll have the Beaujolais," Irene was saying to the waiter with a shuddering little moue. He nodded and disappeared before I could protest. I noticed cruelly that her jowls had softened and drooped even more since the last time I'd seen her, sometime last spring. Mentally, I liposuctioned her neck and lifted her face, stapling the flaps to her ears, causing her to grimace in a permanent deranged smile.

The wine arrived, was pronounced drinkable by Irene, who had no idea what she was talking about, and was poured all around.

"To Emma," said Irene. "A wonderful, wonderful reading."

Our glasses met over the breadbasket and clinked gently. We drank.

I sighed and set down my glass. "What were you going to say about Leonard?" I asked Emma.

My mother looked bleakly at me.

She and Leonard lived up on West Eighty-seventh near Riverside, a world away from Gramercy Park. I'd been sitting at their kitchen table recently, doing the crossword puzzle and drinking coffee, when Leonard came in, rifled through the cupboard as if he were looking for something, and then slammed the door shut and banged the counter with his fist.

"What's going on out here?" my mother said, coming into the kitchen.

"Where is the cheese?" said Leonard. "Why didn't you buy some more or at least put cheese on the shopping list! I just went out and came back and there is no cheese for my lunch!"

She stared at him. "Leonard," she said, "it's only eleven o'clock. There's plenty of cheese. What's wrong with you?"

"With me? Me? I have to go out to the store again, Emma!"

"I just bought a cheddar and a Muenster yesterday."

"At least put them where I can find them!"

Emma opened the door of the refrigerator, reached into the cheese compartment, and took out two blocks of unopened cheese. "Here you are," she said briskly, setting them on the counter.

They looked at each other; I might as well not have been there. Leonard was flushed. His wool cap was still on, slightly askew. He had a wild-eyed look, as if he'd been drinking or doing something illicit.

Now I rehearsed in my head the words "It's going to be all right, Mom. He'll be okay without you. You'll be fine on your own."

"So, Mom," Amanda asked, "what is it?"

"I thought he was just acting like a bastard, but it isn't that." She laughed and blew her nose in her napkin, which she replaced in her lap and smoothed over her thighs. "The irony is that I was about ready to give up on him. Then he went for a routine checkup, and the doctor suspected he might have something going on with his brain and ran some tests. And well, he's apparently in the early stages of Alzheimer's."

We all stared at her.

"Poor man, all he cares about are waves and particles! He'll forget everything he knows." Her tears fell onto the piece of buttered bread she'd abandoned on a small white plate.

"Is there anything they can do?" I asked stupidly.

"They're going to run more tests; we're getting a second opinion."

"Are we ready here?" said the waiter. Then he caught sight of my mother's face, put both hands up briefly in apology, and withdrew. He had a lovely dimple in his cheek.

"Emma, this is so very, very shocking and painful," Irene was saying. "I can't imagine what it would be to lose Richard, little by little, his mind only. And Leonard has such an extraordinary brain . . . really one of the best I've ever encountered, so original and interesting—oh," she said with a small cry of shared pain, "God, it's just so sad, so infuriating, Alzheimer's, so cruel and unfair."

"Do you need me to come and stay with you guys for a while?" said Amanda, rubbing my mother's hand.

"No," said Emma. "Thank you. No, I just wanted to tell you all, just so you know. There's really nothing anyone can do at this point." Emma drew herself up, took her hands back, and dabbed at her eyes. She caught the waiter's eye and nodded. He returned and we all ordered, and then when he'd gone she said, "Oh, poor Leonard," and burst once more into tears. Amanda and Irene immediately leapt into comforting action, Amanda patting her hand, Irene proffering a napkin and making concerned lowing noises. The air suddenly felt violet with estrogen, the small space of the booth crowded with soft, heaving breasts. I'd grown up with women, I was used to this sort of atmosphere, but it never failed to make me feel somewhat detached. I was suddenly extra aware of my cod all snug in its lair, my bifurcated testosterone-charged brain and flat, unencumbered chest, my bristly chin and cheeks.

Just then, my snails were set down before me, green and glistening in their hot dish, redolent, half repellent. I speared one with the tiny fork provided for this purpose and put it into my mouth. Its rubbery muscular texture was slightly nauseating in a way I liked a lot. As Irene watched me with a delicate sneer of revulsion she probably was not aware of, a three-piece jazz combo, stand-up bass, piano, and saxophone, finished setting up right near us and began to play "St. Louis Blues." They always had good live music here; it made this place feel like a Parisian basement bistro. "I hate to see the evening sun go down," my internal voice sang along with the melody. I wished I were in Paris with Ted right now in a place like this, that we were drinking a bottle of St. Émilion and playing footsie under the table, even though Ted and I had never played footsie in public and probably never would.

"Oh, goodness," said Irene, scowling theatrically at the musicians. "I just hate it when there's music in restaurants. It gets so *loud*."

"They're not even amplified," I said.

She pursed her lips and raised her eyebrows at me. "Yes, but people will come in and start shouting at each other, it always happens whenever there's music."

I looked blankly at her, then ate another snail.

Our salads arrived. My plate was piled with mesclun, glistening with herb-flecked oil, and stained deep red from scattered cubes of peppered beet. Chunks of goat cheese soaked up some of the red stain. My mouth watered. "Fresh pepper?" asked the waiter, who looked faintly piratical all of a sudden; a piece of his dark hair had fallen over one eye. He proffered a large, phallic pepper mill; I wanted to make a tiger claw with my hand and go "Grrrr." Instead, I nodded and took a sip of wine while he went to work over my plate. I loved Frenchmen, their earnest yet devil-may-care philosophizing, the way they said "toopty puh" to mean tiny bit, the way they ate with ferocious thoughtfulness, as if their lives depended on experiencing every nuance of flavor in each molecule of food. I found them adorably self-serious, hilariously grave, like Red Skelton's painted clowns, if those clowns wore striped sailor shirts and smoked Gauloises.

I caught my mother's eye and smiled at her, ashamed of letting my horndog instincts take my attention away from her pain and sorrow. "At least you don't have to go through another divorce now," I said.

Irene looked startled and Amanda ignored me, but my mother immediately laughed. "Oh, God, it would be awful."

"What a pain in the ass that would have been. Can you imagine trying to find an apartment in this market?"

"Not to mention the emotional trauma, the legal complications—"

"Now Leonard's stuck with you forever," I said, and we smiled into each other's eyes.

"Poor man," she said.

Twenty-seven years before, we'd run out of gas at dusk on a cracked, desolate section of highway in the Sonoran desert. I, eight years old, had been instructed to wait with my little sisters, doors locked, windows cracked an inch for air, while our mother hitchhiked to Ajo, a town twenty-odd miles up the road. By the time she returned, morale was at an all-time low. Despite my efforts to keep everyone distracted with twenty questions and license-plate-counting games, Amanda had managed to convince the now-sobbing-inconsolably Lola that our mother had been kidnapped and murdered by the driver of the red sports car who'd stopped to pick her up, and that Emma wasn't really Lola's mother at all; Lola was adopted, and her real parents had been emotionally retarded, just like her. And the hand brake wasn't set, so the VW bus was about to roll and go out of control and bump through the desert until it blew up, killing us all.

The sight of our mother getting out of a blue sedan, seemingly unscathed, gas can hanging with reassuring heaviness from her hand, struck us all dumb with relief. Not only did she have gas, she carried a bulging paper bag that said "A&W" on it. "Dinner," she announced. As she filled the gas tank, we fell on the food, which was ambrosiacal, unbelievably delicious.

"When you think about it," I'd said after we'd eaten, "if we hadn't run out of gas, we would never have found the best A&W in the world."

"That's called a silver lining," my mother said with the gnomic authority of her forebears, who'd invented such aphorisms in an attempt to reconcile their contradictory, incontravenable urges toward asceticism and prurience, altruism and greed, waste and conservatism, all the bifurcated tines of bare forked man. "And every cloud has one."

What she should have said was "What do you know, you little Pollyanna faggot?" but no matter. My lifelong pact with my mother, a mutual agreement that it was both admirable and expedient to put a positive spin on misfortune whenever possible, with extra points for black humor and self-mockery, had just been sealed.

5 | PRIVATE LIVES

After dinner, I saw Emma and Irene into a cab and said a chilly good-bye to my sister. Ted was home now. I wanted to rush home and seize him in my arms and drag him off to bed. Whose bed? Mine, of course; we always slept in mine. I hadn't cleaned up my apartment, I realized then. Usually, I made at least a couple of cursory swipes through the muck with a shovel, metaphorically speaking. This time, for some reason, I had neglected to make a single preparation: I hadn't tidied up or laid in a supply of postcoital refreshments; I hadn't changed my sheets. If this was due to any foreboding, I wasn't aware of it; it simmered in the way-back of my mind, where I always tried to keep things I didn't want to know.

Instead of going home, I walked over to the Village East and bought a ticket for the eight o'clock showing of *In the Outback*. It didn't start for forty minutes, so I got a newspaper and went to a bar a few blocks away from the theater and sat on a barstool. The bartender cocked his ear. "Absolut on the rocks with olives, please," I said. He nodded and headed down the bar; I watched him to make sure he didn't give me Stolichnaya by mistake, which had a perturbing milky aftertaste. This bar looked like a lot of others I'd been in: smoky, low-ceilinged room with wood paneling and a pressed-tin ceiling, neon beer signs in the window, scuffed linoleum on the floor, the ascending rows of bottles doubled by the mirror behind them. Four stools down sat an old man; I'd seen him before, in those other bars that looked like this one. After his initial glance at me, he went back to staring into his glass of beer, taking a pull from it, wiping his mouth and staring again, as if all his faculties were trained on figuring out how many more gulps he had before it was gone. "I'll take another," he said without looking up, pawing at the change on the bar near his glass. The two guys in the back were playing a wordless game of pool; the balls clacked with a silky, well-oiled sound. The bartender set a glass on the bar in front of me, took the money I gave him, and sauntered back to the cash register.

I unfolded the *Times* and glanced at it. I already knew without looking what was in there: gunshot wounds, strip malls, clear-cut rain forests, fundamentalists, dirty oceans, syndicate-run garbage transfer stations, toxic waste, scary stories about how the earth was a creaking, falling-apart old whirligig spinning into the wild black yonder. But I read it anyway as I drank my drink. Then I left the bar and went back to the theater, where I watched the movie with hundreds of others, all of us staring up at Ted's image together. His face could have been a computer-generated composite of the best features of several Hollywood studs throughout the ages. This recycled-grade-A-parts quality made him simultaneously excitingly glamorous and reassuringly familiar, like the boy next door if you happened to live on a movie set. I would have bet that the entire audience, men and women, gay and straight, old and young, wanted him in one way or another, whether or not they would all have admitted it. I was the only one here, as far as I knew, who had actually had him. But this cinematic Ted Masterson was someone I didn't know and didn't want to know. He was completely different when we were alone together. To me, in private, he made mocking, black-hearted fun of everything he represented and espoused in public, the political posturing of his fellow Hollywood actors, the cookie-cutter corporate-spawned focus-group-generated screenplays, the hypocrisy of an industry that supported homosexuality in theory but punished it in practice. And yet he had chosen this hypocrisy. It wasn't about the money, he had stacks of money. He needed to be famous; I assumed he kept coming back to me to remind himself that he still had a soul, but I didn't know for sure.

By the end I was gritting my teeth, even though I had already seen the movie twice, so I'd known what to expect. Brock Martel was an old-fashioned two-dimensional good guy. He embodied principles: truth, justice, conservationist ecology. The villain was a corrupt politician spearheading a diabolical plan to turn peaceful, scenic family-run ranches into oil fields; Brock Martel chased him on horseback through the outback, followed him in his tiny sports car into Sydney, which the director had turned into a penumbral city of film noir fog and shadows rather than the sunny, light-hearted metropolis I'd always imagined it to be; finally hero and villain leapt from their cars and danced around violently together under a streetlamp, karate-chopping each other. Thanks to Yoshi, who had clearly trained Ted well in martial arts fakery, the hero was the one who walked away from the fight.

Laughing slightly at my own weird distress, I made my way out of the theater with the crowd onto the nighttime sidewalk, into a cool, wet night. Second Avenue was almost deserted; most of the storefronts I passed were dark behind metal gates and bars. I peered into darkened bodegas and diners, Laundromats and beauty shops and newsstands, small ground-floor enterprises, plain little storefronts and kiosks. Second Avenue was one of the few places in Manhattan that hadn't been overrun yet with corporate chains; it felt old-fashioned and peaceful, but its little family-run businesses were as frangible as tigers and coral reefs in their threatened natural habitats. The look-alike herds of Gaps and Banana Republics and Starbuckses moving en masse into the city gave me a jangling, horror-struck anxiety, the sense of some national blight-at-large encroaching, the real America I'd hoped never to have to inhabit. I knew perfectly well that flux was the natural condition of all things: cells divided and died, stars burned out, corporate baby boomers imposed their gutless, bland, Peter Pan aesthetic on everything on the entire planet, and so forth. There was nothing I could do about it, but I didn't have to like it.

I let myself into the house and stood in the foyer for a moment, listening to the sounds of the house. The living room was empty; the kitchen, I could see by the darkness under the door, was deserted, so Basia was probably in her room, which was behind the kitchen. I found to my surprise that I had stage fright: clammy palms, weak knees, speedy heartbeat. Would I have to deal with Giselle? Was Bretagne still awake? Would Ted be glad to see me? That was the real question, of course. The last time I'd seen Ted had been two months ago. He'd blown into town for two nights on his way to Europe; he claimed he'd come to see me, but I'd hardly seen him the whole time except for one furtive, oddly frustrating interlude very late the second night, when he'd come up to my bedroom after I'd fallen asleep, having given up on him. He'd crawled into bed with me, we tumbled around for a while, then he crept away again. Yoshi, meanwhile, had flounced around the house all weekend, licking his chops and purring. I wasn't stupid or naive; I figured I could see what was going on, but the fact that Yoshi might have designs on Ted didn't bother me nearly as much as the fact that Ted and Giselle shared a daily life, a house, a child. The ghost of La Rochefoucauld muttered helpfully in my inner ear: "Absence diminishes common passions and increases great ones, as the wind extinguishes candles and kindles fire." I felt a sudden surge of lust as powerful as thirst.

There was a light on in the library to my right. I rapped on the opened door and went in without waiting for a response. Ted stood in front of the fireplace. I was pleasantly surprised to find him alone. He turned and saw me, and his expression didn't change. "Hi," he said; he didn't come forward to embrace me, and I didn't go to him. Some invisible force field kept us apart.

"Welcome home," I said tentatively.

"Why weren't you at dinner? Where were you?"

"My mother's reading, then I ate with my family. I told you about it."

"No, I mean afterward. You weren't with your mother all night, were you?"

"What is this, an interrogation? I had a drink and then I saw a movie. I thought you might want to be alone with your family tonight. I've missed you, Ted."

He set his glass down. "It's so good to see you," he said contritely. I walked across the room and took his face in my hands and kissed him, clutching hanks of his rich, silky hair in both my fists, inhaling its spicy smell. He nestled the top of his head against the underside of my chin, his hands around my waist. I rested my hands on his muscled haunches, slid my palms under his shirt, and ran them up his belly and chest. We were both hard already.

"Let's go up to my room," I muttered.

He put his hands on my waist and held me at arm's length. "Look at you," he said tenderly. "You look terrible."

Surprised, I looked down at myself; I was wearing jeans, a black sweater, unobjectionable if ordinary black shoes. I looked all right, and no one else had commented on my appearance tonight, neither my mother nor my sister, who'd be sure to let me know if I looked sub-par.

He moved away from me and picked up his glass, which was nearly empty. As he took a gulp of his martini, it occurred to me that he was drunk.

"What do you mean, I look terrible?" I asked him.

He patted his own perfect stomach. "I should talk," he said. "Look at me! I'm a total sow."

"You look so hot, I could eat you alive," I said. "Come back here."

He submitted himself again to my embrace, but only barely this time; I felt him try to pull away from me, but I held him by the hips so he couldn't break free.

"Giselle's coming back soon," he said.

"So we'll make it fast," I said brusquely. "Look, I'm going to throw you over my shoulder and carry you upstairs if you don't go of your own free will."

He pushed me away with both hands on my chest, so firmly I had to let him go. He moved away from me, down the room, patting his torso and face and scalp as he went as if to demonstrate his point. "I'm serious," he said vehemently. "Look, I'm getting crow's-feet, I'm losing muscle tone, and I'm looking into hair implants; we've got to start doing whatever we can."

"I'd rather drink and ignore it," I said.

"Alcohol ages you as much as the sun," said Ted. "In Los Angeles I have a new health regime, you'd be very impressed. It's only when I'm with you that I let myself go." He sat down in one of the chairs by the fire.

"So it's my fault you've been drinking."

"Well, I was waiting for you to come home," he said.

I stared at him, laughing angrily. "What's happened to you? Has someone else taken over your brain?"

"It's not funny," he snapped.

There was a brief, fizzing silence.

I said cautiously, "Why exactly are we fighting?"

Ted looked at me, then looked away. "It's my fault," he said, his face still averted.

The blood thudded in my ears. My mouth was dry. "What do you mean?"

"I've been going through a lot lately," he said to the fire. "A lot of thinking. I've reached some difficult conclusions, Jeremy. I'm not sure how to tell you, but it's time."

"You're dumping me," I said incredulously.

He looked at me, startled. "God, what an awful way to put it. We just need to clear the air, that's all."

"Okay," I said. "Go ahead."

"Aren't you getting tired of having to be separated all the time, and sneaking around? I would be if I were you."

"I think sneaking around is hot," I said breezily, although I was shaking with anger and fear; I was damned if I'd collude with him in this bullshit. "I don't mind our separations; I get a lot of work done. We've been through this, remember? I've always accepted this arrangement."

He gave an elaborate sigh. "But not forever, not as a whole life, a relationship," he said with a pained, actorlike furrow in his forehead. "It's not fair to you."

"I'm a big boy, I can take care of myself." I went over to the liquor cabinet. "Ready for another drink?"

"Oh," he said distractedly, as if I were an importunate host and he a guest too polite to refuse. "Why not." I had gone into a state of mild shock; I mixed the martinis automatically, glad to have something to do, and to have a stiff drink in the offing. I piled ice in the shaker and poured in a hefty dollop of gin (I considered vermouth a pollution of good liquor), then agitated the shaker with the rhythmic aplomb of a maracas player, shaking it over one shoulder, then the other, amusing myself any way I could in the midst of disaster. Then I poured the ice-frothed liquid into two martini glasses, plopped three olives into each, and handed one to Ted.

I sat in the chair next to him. "Ted," I said, trying not to sound pleading.

"I was so sure you would understand," he said. "This is stressing me out so much, I can't sleep at night. There are rumors. It's only a matter of time."

I felt a jolt of guilt: Benito's, Gary O'Nan. But that had been just a few hours ago; it couldn't have reached Ted's ears yet, that was impossible. And in all this time, I had told only four people about my affair with Ted: my mother and sister, Max and Felicia, all of whom I trusted to keep my secret. None of them had told anyone else as far as I knew. Yoshi had probably guessed, but I was sure he wouldn't tell anyone. He had his own stake in preserving Ted's secret, I was sure. No one had ever seen Ted and me together, except maybe his bodyguards, but they'd signed legally binding agreements not to reveal any details of their jobs; if they couldn't be relied upon to be discreet, that wasn't my fault.

"What rumors?" I asked. "Who could possibly know anything?"

"Maybe I'm just being paranoid," he said, "but people have been hinting; it's in the air. You know how you can sense it when people are saying things about you."

"Then it might be time to just come on out," I said. "You'd have to make some sacrifices, but it would be worth it."

"But for what? What's in this now for either of us? We hardly ever see each other."

"We could see each other every day if you wanted to."

"Why, when I've finally got what I've wanted all my life?"

I had no answer to this, or, rather, I had no answer that Ted would have found acceptable. "How will you live with yourself?" I asked as mildly as I could, as if I were merely curious and this had nothing to do with me.

"I'll find a way," he said. It was difficult for me to believe that this was the same Ted who had once, drunkenly, wearing nothing but socks, recited King Lear's mad-on-the-stormy-heath soliloquy, "Blow, winds, and crack your cheeks!" in Ronald Reagan's cheery, senile wheeze, waving inanely at an imaginary audience.

"You were awful in that movie," I said.

"What?" he said, caught completely off guard.

"What a piece of shit. You used to be so much better than that."

"You mean the movie was awful?"

"Your performance."

He laughed, but it sounded hollow. "Are you getting me back for calling you fat?"

A hot black ball of fury slammed itself into my chest and exploded. "I'm not fat."

"We could both stand to—"

"You're not fat either, you look exactly the same as ever. It's just L.A. making you paranoid and puritanical and narcissistic like everyone else out there. Should I move out tomorrow?"

He stared at me, looking pale and distressed, but, I thought, secretly relieved. "Jeremy," he said. "You don't have to move out. I just can't—I can't live a double life any more. But you're welcome to live here as long as you want."

"Oh, fuck you," I said, and snorted with bitter, half-hysterical laughter. I couldn't stop. The cold gin warmed my innards and loosened my brain. "You're chickening out."

"That isn't at all the point," he said pleadingly. "You're not listening."

"Tell me the point."

"I'm married," he said urgently. "I have a daughter. It used to be worth it, but now it's not. I know that sounds harsh, but you made me say it point-blank."

I felt as if I hadn't inhaled for a few minutes. I drew a deep, jagged breath; the oxygen went immediately to my head and cleared it somewhat. "Where is your lovely wife tonight, by the way?"

"She met some friends for a drink after Bret went to bed. She should be back any minute." He stood up, carefully placing his empty glass on the coffee table in front of us. "I have to pee," he said. "I'll be right back, don't say anything interesting while I'm gone." This was an old joke between us, but I didn't smile. How dare he refer to our past life now?

I sat numbly in my armchair and stared at the fire, trying to ascertain what, exactly, had just happened here. Ted's presence in this house felt intrusive and unfamiliar. I had become proprietary about this room; I'd spent far more time in it than he ever had. The burning wood snapped as flames bit their way through and turned it to ash.

Ted returned and stood by the window with his hands in his pockets. "I hope there won't be bad feelings between us," he said in the unhappy but self-assured tone of someone who'd always had his way, all his life, and was used to having people do exactly what he asked of them.

I resolved never to let him see that he had broken my heart, assuming my heart was really broken. Just then, I felt numb, horny, and angry, but those feelings were easy enough to hide under a veneer of proud indifference. I could act too.

"I don't see how that can be avoided," I said.

"I wish it could," he said, running an aggrieved hand through his hair, which hadn't thinned at all as far as I could tell. "I'd hoped, after all we've been through, that you would understand."

"Did you," I said.

"I was thinking maybe—financially. God, it sounds so crass and I don't mean it that way. I want to set things up so you never have to—"

"I don't want your money," I said. "You'll just have to trust me. Although of course there's no guarantee that you can, is there? 'I was Ted Masterson's Gay Love Slave.' 'Ted's Dirty Little Secret—Male Lover Tells All.' "

"Please remember that I have a daughter," he said tersely.

"I'm impressed," I said. "I never realized you were such a devoted father."

"It's amazing what parenthood does to you. It makes you want to be better than you are. For the first time in my life, I know what it means to put someone else before myself. I've grown up, I guess." He flashed me his puckish, self-deprecating grin.

"Won't you miss me?" I said, hating myself for asking but unable not to.

"Well, of course I'll miss you," he said with a ruefulness that seemed involuntary and maybe even genuine.

Suddenly, things felt a little more familiar between us. "I wish you didn't have to be so noble and hypocritical."

"Noble and hypocritical," he repeated, laughing wincingly. He sat in the chair next to me, but he didn't take the hand I held out to him, so I let it fall onto the armrest of my chair.

There was a sound behind us. We turned, swiveling our heads in tandem so Giselle saw our faces between the chairs, backlit by the fire.

"Hello, boys," she said in her silvery-metallic voice. "Mind if I join you for a nightcap?"

"I'll make another pitcher of martinis, that all right with everyone?" said Ted in a voice I didn't know, a husbandly, hearty, manly-man voice. He stood up and headed over to the bar. "Did you have a good time, honey?"

Honey. A look flew between them, a look I would have missed if I hadn't been paying strict attention. I sat up straighter in my chair.

"It was okay," she said as she ruffled her hair with both hands, slid out of her sweater, and slung it and her bag over the table by the door. "Brr," she said, coming into the room to greet her devoted husband's old friend and longtime employee, "it's getting chilly out. It's great to be here. Like real fall. Jeremy, hi, it's so good to see you again, it's been what. Five years? Wow."

I stood and allowed her to buss me on both cheeks, making an effort to buss her back but managing only to stir the air by her cheeks because of the angles of our heads. We seated ourselves; she took Ted's chair, perching on the edge of it and rubbing her hands together in the warmth of the fire. She smelled expensive, and she looked amazing. Her hair fell in artful, luminous, golden fronds around her wide, firm-jawed face. She wore a long-sleeved, form-fitting black silk dress with plum-colored tights and chunky-heeled black leather boots. Her face sparkled and caught the light as if tiny bits of glitter or mica had been spread evenly over her skin.

"How are you, Giselle?" My hands were trembling; I slid them between my knees.

"Great!" she said. "Just great. Things have never been better, actually. How 'bout you?"

"How's L.A.?"

"Oh, God, L.A.," she said with a wave of the hand and a jaded little laugh, both of which seemed to occur not as an expression of any genuine urge or feeling but as a reflex dictated by some imaginary, ever-present camera.

"L.A.," agreed Ted with a laugh that was a deeper echo of hers.

They'd excluded me from their life in L.A., so I had nothing to say to this. Also, I sensed a flash of something telegraphed between them again as fast as an electrical pulse.

She was saying to me, "It's been such a crazy summer, Ted's probably filled you in."

"No," I said in my homo voice. "Do tell."

She delivered what I immediately gathered was a practiced monologue about the movie industry or, at least, the attitude toward it she had taken it upon herself to manifest, a darkly charming flippancy concerning the pitfalls, labors, negotiations, and machinations of playing a character in front of the cameras. *Catch as Catch Can* had been filmed almost entirely in London; she loved making movies in London, it felt so authentic, as opposed to soundstages in L.A., which removed her from real life and made her feel sort of like a zoo animal. She loved watching passersby while she played a scene on a blocked-off street; when they recognized her, they would do a tiny double take, and then play it very cool. The English were so great that way. To them she was an actor, not a movie star. The premiere Monday night promised to be an enormous publicity event; her next film was due to start shooting in Maui the following month. I couldn't take my eyes off her. She was a refractive surface, a lake on a windy day, all surface motion and play of light that hid whatever depths lay below. So you wouldn't want to dive in headfirst without checking.

But under her skin-and-bones polish, her sleekly aggressive aplomb, was Cathy Benitez with her unfortunate perm and Valley-girl baby fat, going to the mall with her girlfriends, French-smoking menthols; occasionally, Giselle's veneer cracked to reveal an occasional dropped "g," a fleeting suburban gawkiness, a vestigial "so fucking what?" quirk of the upper lip. But these flaws were the key to her allure; they evinced the efforts of self-invention and also its success. She was quite a little masterpiece, I thought.

When I looked beyond her to where Ted was standing, bottle of gin in his hands, the knowledge of what was going on hit me in several stages—first, the immediate bolt of recognition, then a gradual soaking-in, and finally there it was, complete and undeniable, solid as a rock in my mind. I'd never quite realized how married they were. I'd assumed the whole thing was a phony, polite sham for them both. Suddenly, I felt clunky and dull. Ted was right, I'd let myself go a little in recent years.

Then Ted looked at me, sharply with a question in his eyes, or a plea. I felt a small surge of victory, but it burst and faded immediately: Telling Giselle everything point-blank went entirely against my nature. Ted must have been reassured by the blandness of my expression; as if he knew that he was safe for the moment, he turned his back on us to mix the drinks while Giselle prattled on. Turning to glance at the clock, I caught sight of Yoshi's little grove of potted orange trees at the far end of the room. They looked as fussily artificial as concubines hand-fed rare delicacies and rose water, perfumed and powdered and brought before the emperor. Their leaves were as shiny as waxed bell peppers. Their lurid orange fruit bent the thin boughs. "Right, Jeremy?" Giselle said, and I felt myself nod as Ted handed her a brimming glass.

I'd been a waiter at a theater-district bistro for several tedious years before I'd hooked up with Ted. The night I met him, he was a cute little nobody playing the supporting lead in an off-Broadway play that was about to close. He'd just come out of a show and had wandered into Café Bonne-Foi alone for a late supper, and I had waited on him. He'd been in a chatty mood, and as it happened, I'd had a few things to say myself. I hadn't even been hitting on him. I hadn't realized he was gay, I'd been too caught up in what I was saying to think about anything so crass as getting laid. We talked about his play, which I'd seen and liked, and then I mentioned my own writing, which in those days was taking the form of plays.

One thing led, as it so often did, to another: He asked me to have a drink with him when my shift was over, and at a nearby piano bar, while the drag-queen singer warbled her way through her repertoire, we'd talked earnestly about the decline of the theater and our mutual love of Noël Coward. After several drinks I was sufficiently certain of our mutual attraction to say, "You're not gay, are you, by any chance," knowing full well he was and that he preferred to keep it a secret. Because I had divined this without being told and agreed to protect him from the outset, he had trusted me enough to sleep with me that night at my walk-up in the East Village, but it hadn't taken long for him to ask me to move in to the Gramercy Park town house he'd bought with part of his inheritance from his dead grandfather. I'd pose as his secretary or something, we decided, but back then it was all a lark because we had fallen, as the saying went, head over heels in love.

"Well, it's not as if they didn't warn you," Ted was saying to Giselle.

"Yes, but it took a couple of days of intense concentration—I mean, I really reached for those scenes—and then they're just thrown out? Come on."

"But all the work that gets thrown out gets used somewhere else. Remember the other day when we were talking about that? You reach into your deepest self and pull something out for one character, it goes on the floor, but the next time you're called upon to give that part of yourself, it's there, because you've done it before. Nothing goes to waste, Giselle, that's the most mysterious part; you're saved from wasting anything by the process itself."

"Oh, I know," she said in her flat, throaty California voice, "it's amazing. It's like, the hand of God has to be in there somewhere. It feels so spiritual sometimes, it gives me chills."

6 | COLD POINT

Soon afterward I said a transparently stiff good night to both of them without actually looking either in the eye, and then I escaped upstairs.

Up in my room, I stood in the darkness by the floor-to-ceiling windows, peering through the long white curtains out into the lamplit streets of Gramercy Park. Outside in the park the treetops swayed in the night wind, although I couldn't hear them through the thick glass.

I switched on the standing lamp, stood thoughtfully in front of the full-length mirror for a moment, then began to take off my clothes. Having no reason to be especially vain, I usually ignored my reflection unless I needed to make sure my hair was acceptable or my collar was straight, but now I looked at my naked self as objectively as I could. I was tall, dark-haired, strong-jawed, solid, and broad-shouldered, with a swimmer's slight padding of fat over defined muscles. I wasn't handsome, but I liked to think that I had a certain edgy comeliness on good days. My penis, although not extra large, was shapely and assertive, and could usually go whatever distance was required of it. But now, on what I was dismayed to recognize as the cusp of early middle age, my hair was graying just a little at the temples, my muscles were softening somewhat, and my whole body had widened slightly, had taken on a new maturity that I didn't entirely dislike but wasn't thrilled with either, because who would be? I put my hands on my hips and turned from side to side, surveying the new landscape, assessing the damage. My face was craggier; my forehead was becoming lined; I had crow's-feet, and my butt was sagging maybe just a tad, and I was getting the beginnings of what might turn into a gut someday if I didn't watch it. But I saw no reason whatsoever to call myself fat or old. In fact, if I'd met myself in a bar, I would have considered myself lucky to take myself home.

I put on a T-shirt and a clean pair of boxer shorts, and brushed my teeth, trying to remember the last time I'd done so. I stared into the piercing blue eyes of a mournful, shaggy, dark-haired, big-jawed Norwegian, with what on someone else I might have described as a humorously self-contained but sensual mouth. I looked so much like my father, I could have played him in a made-for-TV movie. My hair needed cutting; I'd missed a swath of stubble on the underside of my chin that morning. Other people washed their faces before bed as a matter of course, the same way they kept their nails neat and orderly, and threw away their underwear when it got torn or stained. Sometimes I felt as if I hadn't been properly brought up. Well, no wonder: I'd been raised in campgrounds and communes for the first twelve years of my life. When and where would I have learned basic hygiene?

I washed my face, as if to prove to myself that I knew how. My pale and flummoxed reflection blinked back at me.

I went out and picked up my phone and dialed.

"Hello?" said Wayne in his officiously lilting voice.

"Wayne," I said, "it's Jeremy. Is Felicia available?"

"She was right here a minute ago, but the sound of the phone sent her scurrying underneath her little rock."

"Give me the phone, you cross-eyed fuckhead," I heard Felicia drawl in the near distance, and then she said right into the phone, "Jeremy?"

I hesitated. "How'd you know it was me?"

"It's always you. What's wrong?"

"How'd you know something was wrong?"

"Don't get all suspicious, I'm not spying on you or anything, I'm just cutting to the chase because Wayne and I are right in the middle of doing something."

"I bet you are," I said smuttily. Wayne was a faunlike slip of a thing, as gay as a blade of grass. The idea of him and Felicia in bed together was ludicrous yet oddly compelling, if only because they were equally pale, bony, and asexual; it would have been like the coupling of two grasshoppers.

She sighed sternly. "Jeremy, I apologize profusely about earlier. I swear I'll never—"

"Ted dumped me," I said.

"Oh he did not," she said immediately in a shocked voice, which was all it took for me to burst into tears. "I don't believe it," she said after a moment.

"It's true," I sobbed.

"He must be insane, Jeremy," she said in a horrified voice. "He loves you."

"I don't think so," I said brokenly.

"What did he say?"

"He said he doesn't want his daughter to find out he's gay, so he's got to stop sleeping with me. Although I'm welcome to sponge off him for the rest of my life. I guess that's his idea of palimony."

She was silent for a moment. I could almost hear her brain ticking. "He must have decided it was too risky, that's all, but he can't possibly be happy about this."

"No, actually, I think he's fallen out of love with me," I said, and blew my nose into a hankie.

"Well, maybe you've fallen out of love with him but you just don't know it yet," she said soothingly. "Maybe you've outgrown him, Jeremy."

"No way," I said. "Really? You think so?"

"I think it's totally possible that your affair with Ted has run its natural course," she said. "I think maybe you're ready to move on, and maybe you'll be happier now that you're free."

For some reason, despite all the "maybes" and the fact that she'd been saying exactly the opposite earlier today, I was reassured by this idea. After we'd said good-bye, I got into bed and turned out the light, seething, bruised, but comforted enough to sleep.

I woke early the next morning and looked up at the ceiling. Here I was again, incrementally closer to death than I'd been yesterday. The days rolled by in a soothing, unstoppable, numbing rhythm. I had no desire to get up. Ted had dumped me. It was unbelievable that so much could have changed from yesterday morning to this one, but there it was. The rest of my life stretched away into the future on a bleak, bare road.

After a moment, a little blue flame leapt in my mind, and almost automatically, I fumbled among the books on my bed stand and pulled out my Wallace Stevens collection. After a while, I found "Sunday Morning" and began to read it, although I knew it almost by heart: late coffee and oranges in a sunny chair, a green cockatoo, complacencies of the peignoir, holy hush of ancient sacrifice. It pulled me in with a strong undertow, leaving thoughts of Ted on some stark, gravelly shore that receded into a medieval-style mist. By the time I reached the seventh stanza, the words had taken hold powerfully in my mind:

> *Supple and turbulent, a ring of men*
> *Shall chant in orgy on a summer morn*
> *Their boisterous devotion to the sun,*
> *Not as a god, but as a god might be,*
> *Naked among them, like a savage source.*

I felt a vertiginous rush, a desire to leap headlong into the poem and burst it open to reveal its shining innards. As my eyes unfocused slightly and the letters blurred, the words met my thoughts somewhere in the air between my eyes and the page where the whole poem hung, apprehensible in its entirety, and just beyond it an infinitely deep time-chamber only a split second long, the universe visible through the hairline crack of one poem. My brain tingled with a ski-jump swoop of exhilaration that lifted me just high enough to glimpse the whole of everything, through the words, just beyond my apprehension. Then it was gone, leaving the residue of a deep, shivery joy.

My fingers worried the page, curling it and ripping it out of its curl repeatedly with a soothingly destructive persistence until the telephone rang. I picked it up.

"Jeremy? Hi. I can't sleep." It was Amanda.

I looked at the clock. "So get up. It's eight o'clock."

"I sleep during the day."

"Then go to bed."

She sniffed loudly, then sniffed again.

"Do you have a cold?"

"Anyway, I'm just—whatever. Things aren't going too well at the moment. This thing with Leonard, that whole conversation last night, I don't know, it brought back all this old shit for me. Like the way Angus left us, and Lola's been in Australia all these years—we've never been much of a family. All this shit that's been going on with Liam—I miss Lola. I could use a sister right now."

"I'm sort of a sister."

She gave a short, unamused laugh. "So how was the romantic reunion?"

"Ted and I broke up last night."

"You did? What happened?" To my surprise, she sounded genuinely concerned. "Are you okay?"

"I will be," I said briskly, not wanting her pity. "But I need to get out of here for a day or two."

"We have an empty room here," she said.

"Here" meant a squalid Brooklyn apartment, home not only to Amanda and Liam, but also their freeloading long-term houseguest Feckin. But Felicia and Max and my mother would all demand one or another form of emotional currency in return for their hospitality, and unfortunately, I had nothing whatsoever to offer in that vein right now. I'd only disappoint them. Whereas I could buy Amanda and her Irishmen a bottle of whiskey and some token groceries, and they'd leave me alone. I considered the offer for a moment and decided I might as well accept.

"But it's your music studio," I said.

"I can live without it for a couple of days."

"You're sure?"

"Yeah, well, it's no palace, but sure. Listen, we have a show tomorrow night at Bombshell. Around midnight. In case you're bored. I'll put you on the list if you want." She said this offhandedly, but I suspected she wasn't saying this just to make conversation. She'd always made it clear without actually saying it that she knew how I felt about her music and preferred to perform without having to see me squinting skeptically and critically up at her. Apparently, she'd had a change of heart.

So this was Amanda's emotional currency; oh, well.

"Great," I said, trying to sound enthusiastic.

"You're better off without him," she said abruptly. After a brief, crackling silence she went on. "You deserve to be with someone who, you know. Admits you exist."

"What's going on with Liam?"

"Just the usual mind games and hostilities. Nothing really."

"That's my call waiting. Can I call you back later?"

"No, I'm going to try to sleep. You have a bed if you need it. And come to my show."

"Jeremy," came Max's voice as soon as I depressed the button and answered his call. "Did I wake you up? I couldn't wait till later. I just got home. I spent the whole night talking to the most amazing man. Amazing. Amazing. My socks are knocked off."

"Well, I just got dumped," I said.

"What?"

I told him.

"I'm stunned," he said. "It seemed like the perfect setup."

"For him, or for me?"

"What are you doing tonight?"

"Staying at Amanda's," I said.

"Let's go out to Brighton, we didn't go once this summer, it's our last chance. I'm so sorry you're heartbroken, sweetheart, but I'll cheer you with food and drink tonight, and incidentally tell you about Fernando, just to take your mind off Ted."

"Let me guess," I said. "He's got a gold cross around his neck, he reeks of Obsession for Men, he spends five hours a day lifting—"

"You might just be surprised for once in your life. Meet me at my place at five, we'll take a taxi, my treat."

"No," I said, "pick me up at Amanda's. It's on the way." I gave him the address.

"You could stay with me, you know, you don't have to go all the way out to Brooklyn."

"Amanda offered and I didn't want to hurt her feelings by saying no, although now that I think of it, she might have just been being sisterly, and now she's dreading my arrival and wishing she'd never opened her big mouth. I don't know where I'm going to live, frankly. I also need a job. I have nothing on my résumé, no recommendations, for the past ten years. What the hell am I going to do?"

"For starters, the night is on me. The rest you'll figure out in due time. Bye for now, time to work. I'll swing by at around six. Be ready, I'm not going up there and hanging out with those goons. I love you. It's going to be all right."

As I bathed, I monitored my vital signs and internal workings, avoided any thoughts that might exacerbate my wounds. I cried for a while like a little kid, sobbing noisily with my mouth wide open, my eyes and nose streaming. It felt good, very cathartic; I could see why my next-door neighbor Dina Sandusky went in for this sort of thing. When I'd finished I blew my nose, dried off, got dressed, made a pot of coffee, and drank it in the armchair by the front windows, looking down at the park. Juanita chirred and bustled in her cage. She knew better than to come anywhere near me right now. No one but a fellow mammal was capable of comforting the heartbroken.

After a while, I saw a scurrying figure dragged along by several four-legged beings that fanned out on their leashes to sniff, pee, bark, and explore, only to be jerked back in line. They pulled their charge along like a dog team with a sled. I could only imagine what invectives and threats he was subjecting them to today; unaccountably, I yearned to be among them, a yelled-at dog on a leash who knew exactly where he stood in no uncertain terms, just one of a gang, his only tasks in life to poop on the sidewalk once or twice a day.

I'd always taken Ted's public act for a front that masked the passion, sadness, intelligence, and abandon that I alone had been privy to. I'd loved the "real" Ted behind that handsome, charming, impassive wall. How could I not have taken him at face value all these years? After enough time spent tamping down his fires and denying them air, they had gone completely out. He was who he seemed to be through and through. Otherwise, he would have cracked long ago.

This revelation was infuriating and comforting in equal parts, a combination that necessitated immediate action. As I packed a duffel bag with basic necessities, I came across an old paperback collection of the short stories of Paul Bowles. I held the book for a moment thinking of a summer night a long time ago when Ted and I had stayed awake until dawn up here, lying on the rug on pillows, drinking Calvados and eating hard, meaty green olives, listening to Mingus and Monk. I read aloud a story called "Pages from Cold Point" about a sixteen-year-old boy named Racky who seduced his own father. When I finished, the beautiful, bloodless tale quivered in the air for a moment between us; Ted had looked at me through liquid, sleepy, amorous eyes and said, "Oh, Jeremy, God, you're the love of my life." And then I took him in my arms—he was so small compared to me, I cradled him, humming into his hair along with the music. We fell asleep entwined like that on the rug; the sun had nearly risen, the windows were wide open, the warm summer wind blew in. I remembered this perfectly; I hadn't invented it.

On my way downstairs, I said a silent prayer to Lord Muckety, the closest thing here to a household god, that I wouldn't see anyone between the stairs and the front door. But on the bottom step sat a kindergarten-sized girl who watched me as I descended.

"Hello, Bret," I said softly, as if she were a small dog with a reputation for biting.

"How do you know my name? Who are you?" she piped in a stern, sweet voice.

"I'm Jeremy," I said. "I know your name because your father told me."

"Do you work here?"

"I used to work here, but now I'm leaving."

"Oh," she said, getting up so I could go by. "Does Daddy know?"

"Yes, he does."

"Did he fire you?" she asked in a tone that implied that Ted fired people all the time.

"Yes, he did," I said solemnly.

"Daddy!" she shouted suddenly.

"What is it, Peachie?" said Ted, appearing in the dining room doorway in his bathrobe, holding a half-eaten piece of toast. "Where are you going?" he said to me, catching sight of my duffel bag.

"I was invited to stay at my sister's for a couple of days."

"He said you fired him," said Bretagne.

"He was joking with you, sweetie," said Ted, not missing a beat.

It was interesting to see him playing daddy with this self-possessed little owlet.

She looked at me. "Were you really?"

"I'm sure your father will explain it all to you some day," I said. "I've got to go now."

"Come on, Peachie, let's eat breakfast."

"I already ate my breakfast at seven o'clock," said Bret, trotting obediently into the dining room.

"Aren't you going to tell Basia you're leaving? She's planning on having you here for lunch."

"I'll let her know," I said briefly, without inflection. Then we looked at each other for a moment, our gazes colliding and glancing off each other. He followed his daughter into the dining room. As I slipped into the kitchen, I murmured bitterly to myself, "Ten Years in Love Nest with Closet Homo Star."

Basia stood on her footstool before the eight-burner range, scowling at some eggs bubbling in a cast-iron skillet. There was a brown burned-smelling haze in the air.

"Good morning, Basia," I said.

"I made special dinner last night," she said gruffly.

"I'm sorry I missed it, Basia. I had a sort of family thing last night, I thought I had told you. Actually, I'm going to stay at my sister's for a couple of days." I said it as if my sister lived far away rather than just across the river, and I was rushing to make a train.

The hair on my arms prickled slightly and the currents of air rearranged themselves: Yoshi, gliding silently into the kitchen behind me. "That smells delicious, Basia," he said, saying "dericious" almost unnoticeably. If he had been Japanese, it would have completely escaped my notice.

"I've been wondering something, Yoshi," I said, enunciating his name extra carefully. "Where are you from in Japan, exactly?"

I noticed that he kept his eyelids at half-mast to make his eyes look as narrow as possible, like a fat man sucking in his gut to look thinner.

"Move," said Basia brusquely. "No talking in here. Go!"

Yoshi didn't budge. Neither did I.

"I was born in Osaka," he said.

"Are your parents Japanese?"

"Why the inquisition?"

"We know so little about each other," I said with false earnestness. "And we live in the same house."

"You don't believe I'm Japanese?"

"I'm expressing interest in your cultural heritage."

He flared his nostrils a little at this, but instead of telling me to mind my own beeswax, he said with clipped hostility, "My mother is Japanese and my father is Dutch, so I was born Yoshi van Jeetze, a name I always hated, as I'm sure you can imagine. I legally adopted my mother's maiden name, which happens to be Tanaka, when I turned twenty-one. I grew up in Van Nuys, California, but I've traveled to Japan several times. I speak Japanese fluently and my cultural identity is Japanese."

"So you're American," I said mildly.

"Born in Japan," he said.

"And raised here. You're a half-Dutch Cali boy. I bet you never ate sushi as a kid."

"My mother," he said through clenched teeth, "made it all the time."

Basia went into the pantry, where she banged some things around to let us know passive-aggressively that she wanted us to bugger off.

"Oh, did she," I said. "Anyway, whatever. That's your business. I'm sure it helps in the martial arts world to seem authentically Japanese. I'm sure it did wonders for your credibility on Ted's movie set. And I'm sure you worked it all you could, because he's a total sucker for slippery slithery little Asian types."

"You seem to be sure about a lot of things," he said in a petulant suburban voice.

"Hey," I said, "you dropped your accent and suddenly I like you a little more."

He regarded me coolly, not deigning to respond to this.

"Do you have a black belt in anything?" I asked.

Half his mouth smiled, the other half compressed. He said tightly, "Why would I have been hired as a martial arts consultant on movie sets if I didn't know anything about martial arts? And now let me ask you something. Do you really think it matters, in the grand scheme of the infinite universe, where I'm from or how I talk?"

"Everything matters," I said as if I believed it.

We glared at each other like two little school-yard punks.

"Okay," said Yoshi promptly, "maybe I can tell you this without getting socked in the face, although please remember my black belts in karate and judo. The real reason Ted broke up with you was that I worked the slippery slithery Asian thing for all it was worth, and I threatened to stop sleeping with him unless he stopped sleeping with you."

Feeling as if he'd just ripped my abdomen open and shoved his fingernails into my spleen, I cradled my fist in my hand speculatively, wondering whether this urge to sock him in the face had arisen solely because he'd planted the idea in my mind.

"I think," I said in a hoarse voice I did my best to control, "I could have gone quite contentedly to my grave without knowing that, but if you feel better for having told me, well, bully for you."

"Out of here," said Basia, swashbuckling back into the kitchen, holding a bowl of onions. "I have patience today with nothing."

Yoshi, his face bland, his eyes shuttered, slipped through the swinging doors and vanished.

Basia's eyes glittered at me. "You too," she said.

"I'm going," I said. I wanted to smash every dish in the cupboard. There was a set of heirloom porcelain dishes in the hutch, I knew; it would have felt wonderful to fling it piece by piece at Yoshi's head, or at Ted's, whirling plates as decapitating disks, cups deadly projectiles, all of it crashing into shards, exploding, bursting apart.

Basia jerked her chin in the direction of the dining room. "That girl," she muttered.

"What about her?" I asked, puzzled, thinking she meant Bretagne.

"You don't know," Basia said harshly, as if she were telling me to wipe the grin off my face or she'd do it for me. "She's not nice, she's a very bad girl." Then she whispered, so fiercely I could smell her breath, which was medicinal and flowery, as if she'd recently taken a nip of violet water, "I was star once. I know what happens when you are star. You care for no one but yourself. It makes you very bad person. He will be sorry he married her."

What a skein of romantic yearnings Ted had spun here in the Heartbreak Hotel. "I agree," I said fervently. "He'll be very sorry, very soon."

"I try to warn him. He doesn't talk to me so much with her here. You have to tell him, as his good friend."

"Believe me, I tried," I said mordantly. "As his good friend."

"What did he say?"

"He didn't want to talk about it."

"He didn't listen to you?"

"Not at all."

"I'll spit in her eggs," said Basia.

I laughed bleakly.

She didn't smile back, and her mouth worked oddly; I had the feeling she was working up a good loogie, and the minute I left she'd hock it into the pan. Oh well, I thought: not my affair. Nothing I could do to stop her. People did what they had to do.

On my way through the living room I turned and looked through the arched doorway into the dining room. Ted and Bret had been joined by Giselle and a young woman I took to be the nanny. They made a good-looking tableau around one end of the old mahogany table, Ted at the head, his women surrounding him. I waved good-bye, but no one saw me.

I walked along the park and headed down Third Avenue. The day was warm and golden and smelled of dry leaves, but I walked heedlessly along, telling myself that Giselle was more of a dupe in all this than I was: She was married to him, and ignorant of who he really was, while I on the other hand knew everything, and was free.

"*Bon appétit,* Giselle," I muttered to no one.

"I love global warming," said Max. We were sitting outside at Cafe-Bar Moscow that evening, wearing sweaters but no coats, although it was mid-October. Since the last time Max and I had come here, the next-door Winter Garden had been appended to the whole operation, a step up, I supposed, but cheesy Slavic synthesizer-pop still blared from the speakers, there were still Beck's umbrellas overhead, their poles entwined with fake lilies, white fuchsia, and daisies. Lamb testicles "Farberge" and hickory-smoked eel were still featured on the menu. The only changes that I could see were that the floor was covered with Astroturf, the tables draped in teal, goldenrod, and peach linen.

"You won't love global warming when it turns into the next Ice Age," I said, but my heart wasn't in it. I'd recently learned, somewhat against my will, that Max's new love, Fernando Narvaez, was a forty-year-old Mexican painter he'd met at an art opening the night before. They'd sat all night on a porch swing in the roof garden of the Chelsea penthouse apartment where Fernando was house-sitting, looking out over the city, drinking Gibsons, watching the sun come up behind the water towers. "We didn't have sex," said Max, flushed and wide-eyed with the wonderment of this. "When we said good-bye the next morning, we shook hands."

"Are you sure he's gay? Maybe there's something he's not telling you. Maybe he's married."

He cut his eyes meaningfully at me by way of answer. "Do not compare Fernando to Ted," he said. "Don't even say their names in the same sentence. You're gun-shy right now and I frankly don't blame you, but this is different."

I'd always suspected that Max was jealous of my relationship with Ted on some level, so I had held my tongue whenever he went on and on about how selfish and vain Ted was, how he didn't deserve to suck the first knuckle of my big toe, how I was with him only because my father had been unavailable and I was repeating a familiar pattern.

"I'm not gun-shy, Max," I said. "I'm devastated."

Max looked up at the skeptical, hard-faced waitress, who was waiting to take our order. "We'll start with two hundred grams of Kremlyovskaya," he told her.

Her brief, bitter nod conveyed the distinct impression that this order was American and gauche, but whatever we might have ordered vodka-wise would have been, no matter what brand or how many grams we asked for. She stalked away. Max leaned back in his chair with a happy sigh. A warmish breeze blew in off the water; in the light from the setting sun the ocean looked like a shimmering bath. Toy-sized tankers and sailboats slid silently along, far away on the horizon. The broad, scuffed beach held a few late-season kite flyers and beachcombers. When the vodka arrived in a small sweaty-cold carafe, Max poured half of it into two small glasses and we drank it off, then he poured the second round, which we sipped. At first the vodka gave off an ammoniac vapor, but as it warmed, it turned peppery and robust.

Two plates of hot crepes arrived, each accompanied by a mound of coarse orange caviar. Then came bowls of hot borscht dense with tender meat, potato chunks, and lima beans. By the time the pelmenis came, we were full, but we wolfed down every slippery, nuggety beef dumpling, dipped into small paper cups of sour cream. We ordered another two hundred grams. When it came, Max fished out his multi-pill cocktail from his pocket, clapped all the pills into his mouth at once, and washed them down with a snort of vodka.

"L'chaim," he said, raising his vodka glass to the crowds of Russian Jewish émigrés out for a post-sunset constitutional along the boardwalk. For a moment we could have been at a Black Sea resort in the fifties, but this illusion was immediately dispelled by the appearance of a seven-foot-tall black stringbean of a guy in baggy pants and a bomber jacket, a tiny carved-face Chinese woman, then an old man with scaly skin, frog-like goiters, barrel chest, and bandy legs.

"It's funny," said Max, "watching all these Jews go by."

"Why is it funny?"

"It just is. I went to Hebrew school, I had a bar mitzvah, I thought I'd become a yeshiva bucher like my friend Avram. And I would have, I would be an observant Jew this minute if it weren't for Leviticus. What do I do with this? 'Do not lie with a male as one lies with a woman; it is an abhorrence.' He puts homosexuality on the same level as bestiality and incest: 'All who do any of those abhorrent things, such persons shall be cut off from their people.'"

"It doesn't say not to lie with a male," I said. "It says only not to do it the way you'd do it with a woman. That would be literally impossible, am I right?"

Max laughed. His stocky reddish-blond freckle-faced good looks, suggestive equally of soccer field and shtetl, were heightened by his electrified hormones and the anticipation of future bliss; his happiness was as unshakable as my churlishness. "Try running that line of reasoning past my father," he said. "Anyway, my point is that I have nothing against the religion except that it condemns me."

"Why don't you go to a gay synagogue, then?"

"One of those free-to-be-Jew-and-me places?" Max said, almost rising up from his chair in horror. "Those P.C. touchy-feely folksong 'temples'? You know how they do it? They bargain with God like they're at an electronics store. 'Oy-oy, God, okay, I'll fast on Yom Kippur but I can't keep kosher, with the two sets of dishes and the restrictions. If I'm not supposed to eat shrimp lo mein then why is it so good?' I don't think God wants to hear about it. I don't think he's open to negotiation. Either you're in or you're out, end of story. I sleep with men. I'm out. Call me old-fashioned."

"Okay," I said mildly. "Just asking."

"Just answering," he said testily, subsiding.

We leaned back in our white plastic armchairs and fell into a wordless waking doze, encased in our separate and incompatible moods. The sky was nearly dark.

"Should we order another round?" he asked after a while.

"No," I said. "Let's walk over to Coney Island."

"What's there this time of year?"

I waggled my eyebrows at him. "It's spooky," I said.

"I'm not sure you can handle spooky in your heartbroken state, sweetheart."

"Oh, so you've noticed that I'm heartbroken."

"You'll be all right." He gave me a sidelong glance. "I suppose it happens to all of us, sooner or later."

"Well, except you," I said.

"What makes you say that?"

"When have you ever been heartbroken?"

"You broke my heart," he said as he made a "check" motion at the waitress, who glowered at him. "But I'm over you, just like you'll get over Ted."

The news that Max had been in love with me was somewhat dubious, since I'd never seen any evidence of this, but I found it flattering nonetheless. After he'd paid the bill, we set off along the boardwalk, scuffing our feet, inhaling the breeze off the water. The rough, narrow boards were laid out in herringbone patterns that did psychedelic things if you looked down at them as you walked over them. I was suddenly almost giddy with a tipsy, cheerfully aggrieved euphoria. Possibilities for the rest of my life occurred to me—other men I might love, jobs I might get, neighborhoods I might live in. These ideas arose just long enough to thrill me with their potential, then vanished before I could panic about all the decisions I had to make to put them into effect.

Coney Island was dark and empty now, the stuffed-animal-hung booths shuttered, glittering lights turned off for the winter. The shrieking, lumpen summer hordes of teenagers had migrated to their winter haunts of video-game parlors and fast-food joints, and wouldn't be back to eat corn dogs and crash bumper cars until late spring. Instead of skull-pounding music, we heard low, inhuman moans, wind blowing through the metal struts of the Cyclone and the Wonder Wheel. On a ramp off the boardwalk, we ran into a couple of cute little Hispanic queers hanging out with their boom box. We flirted with them for a while, or, rather, with the idea of going under the boardwalk for a Doublemint quickie, something we hadn't done together in years. Max traveled everywhere with a supply of fresh condoms; he had slipped me two before sending me home with Frankie, and I knew he'd come through again now. But we soon got bored with the extended posturing and display these boys seemed to require as foreplay, so we waved good-bye to them, climbed down onto the beach, took off our shoes, and strolled along the sand at the edge of the waves, back toward Brighton Beach. The night was not warm enough for this, but our blood alcohol level numbed us enough to let us ignore our chattering teeth. We passed rocky promontories and broken pilings jutting wet and black from the moonlit water like scraggly rows of ruined teeth or tree stumps in a bayou. We raced each other then, sprinting down the beach until we simultaneously stopped short, panting and warmed through. Thoughts of Max's precariously dormant virus kept intruding, as they often did whenever we reached these heights of giddiness together, but for some ghoulish reason, this only heightened the fun.

"For some reason I just remembered," I said, panting, "this kid at the commune in Redding, where we stayed for a while. I can't remember his name, but he wanted to fuck me."

Max bent at the waist, rested his hands on his knees, and looked up at me over his shoulder. "A kid how old?"

"Nine," I said. "And I was seven."

"What did you do?"

"I said I would fuck him if he climbed the chinaberry tree and jumped onto the roof of the house and climbed down the drain spout. He did it. Then I told him I would if he dove into the water tank, which was freezing cold and supposedly dangerous, but he went right in."

Max stood up, having regained his wind, and we walked up the sand toward the boardwalk. "Then," I went on, "he broke into a house down the road and stole a blanket because I asked him to, and a couple of other things too, I can't remember what."

"A blanket," said Max. "Why?"

"It was cold there. I remember being cold all the time. It was wet and rainy."

"But he dove into the water tank? You must have been a very cute kid."

"He was no martyr," I said. "He finally told me to pay up, but the next morning my mother loaded us up and off we went, and I couldn't keep my end of the bargain. I couldn't even say good-bye. I would have gone through with it. I was scared out of my wits, but I'd made a deal. I still think about him sometimes."

"I never had anything like that happen to me when I was a kid," said Max with some irritation. "I was outwardly toffee-nosed and inwardly seething."

"You still are. You're the poster boy for schizophrenia."

"Do not joke about schizophrenia," he said priggishly. "It's a very serious disorder."

"You're such an ass," I said, and we laughed.

We put on our shoes and went to a nightclub up on Brighton Avenue under the elevated train tracks. Amid a shirred red satin ceiling and mirrored panels on the walls, a band of dumpy, tackily dressed, middle-aged, sexy men played synthesizer, drums, and accordion; an equally dumpy, tackily dressed, sexy woman sang in a thrilling, husky voice into a dildo-sized microphone. After another beaker of chilled vodka, Max and I ventured out onto the dance floor, jigged and vamped together at first cautiously and then with increasing enthusiasm. The atmosphere was wildly festive, post-Sabbath, but even so, we cut quite a rug. I caught Slavic scowls from some of the waiters, who stood in a thuglike lineup against the far wall, arms folded, pompadours cresting backward in frozen waves. When we got back to our table, we were immediately handed the bill by our waiter. We paid up and got the hell out of there.

"I'm Corey Flintoff," I announced to Max as we stumbled along the sidewalk under the elevated train tracks.

"And I'm Noah Adams."

"And I'm Nina Totenberg."

"Well, I'm Corva Coleman."

"And *I'm* Karl Castle."

"And I'm Linda Wertheimer."

I clapped the side of my head. "Shit, I've run out of names."

"And I'm Craig Windham," said Max smugly.

Idling at the curb was an enormous black sedan with a livery company's sticker on the windshield. We opened the back door and tumbled into the passenger seat, and told the driver where we were going. Without a word the driver put the car into gear and we were off. The car was like a rolling living room, plush and comfy; it smelled of ancient cigarette smoke and chemical pine air freshener. The heater was on; the radio was tuned to 1010 WINS, but so softly we heard only a soothing babble, while our driver, a retired ex-cop, kept us awake and alert with his Brooklyn-accented recitative about New York, which he talked about as if it were his mercurial, troublesome but irresistible wife of fifty years. We bounced off the BQE onto the weather-blasted asphalt of Williamsburg. The car floated along through the quiet and nearly deserted streets, rising and falling over the potholes and cracks as if it were a small boat on some narrow ribbon of ocean. The traffic lights turned green one by one as the car approached and slid through them without pausing.

When we pulled up in front of Amanda's, I got out of our traveling pumpkin and it continued on without me. I entered the tacky little vestibule of Amanda's building, rang the buzzer, then climbed the three flights to her seedy little apartment full of peeling linoleum and rickety furniture and ancient fixtures. She was in the kitchen when I came in, wearing a red silk bathrobe, her long black hair loose. She stood in the cold white air of the open refrigerator door.

"You hungry?" she asked. "I was about to raid the fridge."

It was two in the morning, but I was suddenly wide awake and ravenous. "What have you got?"

"We'll see," she said, rummaging around. "Have a seat. So Mom called me today. She was feeling a little better. Leonard had a good day, apparently. They took a walk in Central Park."

I sat at the kitchen table. A manic, tinny babble of voices came from the living room; I recalled from prior visits that Liam and Feckin liked to have the TV on constantly. On the table in front of me were a bag of Polish toffees, half a bottle of Ten High whiskey, butts bristling in a heap of ash in a Florida souvenir ashtray, an open pastilles tin with a Baggie of dope inside, beer-bottle caps, a lighter decorated with a bodacious blonde in a thong, two wrinkled old bell peppers, and a dog-eared fanzine called *Blunt*. I sat awkwardly in my chair, looking around, extremely conscious of being a guest here. She pulled from the white air of the fridge the remains of a roast chicken, a plastic container of green Sicilian olives, a sourdough loaf that had the chewy texture of a sponge and the odor of a clean baby's skin. She put it all on the battered metal table, shoved some things aside to make room for two plates. "Fuck Liam," she said loudly enough so that he could hear her over the TV. "I'm officially off my diet now. He can lose weight himself if he wants someone around here to be thin."

"You're too thin anyway," I said.

She wrinkled her nose. "That's not what he says. Sometimes I think he should go pick up girls in, like, Biafra or Cuba, one of those third world starvation countries."

We ate everything, leaving on our plates piles of limp rosemary-flecked yellow chicken skin, sucked-clean bones, sucked-clean olive pits, and a crust or two of bread. Amanda pushed her plate away and lit a cigarette, exhaling a stream of smoke that curled around the objects on the tabletop. I felt less like an intruder here now that we'd eaten together, some millennia-old tribal breadbreaking thing.

"Amanda darlin, throw me the matches, will you?" called Liam from the living room. Through the arched doorway, I could see him fingering a small heap he'd spilled from a Baggie onto a magazine, separating the seeds and stems out. Amanda tossed a book of matches, which landed at his feet.

Feckin sat next to him on the couch, plucking at a battered old guitar, squinting through the fog of cigarette smoke that swathed his small, ferretlike head. He smoked constantly and joylessly, and seemed to exhale more smoke than normal smokers did. His chain-smoking seemed so much a physical part of him that it seemed insensitive or at least futile to be bothered by it, like wishing someone with a speech impediment would speak correctly, or someone with chronic gas would hold it in.

"Oh yeah, this is a great show comin up here," Liam said. "They go on dates and then they come on and say, 'He's not my type,' 'She's too ugly,' and they're all feckin losers who can't find a date on their own."

"They should get a feckin life," said Feckin.

"Losers," said Liam.

I looked at Amanda, who looked back at me expressionlessly.

"How can they watch that shit all the time?" I said.

"Do you *ever* watch TV?"

"Not really," I said.

"Admit it, Jeremy, you hate pop culture."

"No, I don't," I said. "I only hate shit."

"Does that include my music?"

I paused. I was thrown for a loop. "Why do you think that?" I asked cautiously.

"I asked you on the phone this morning to come to my show and you practically choked."

"I did?"

She looked at me and sniffed. "You haven't come to a gig in years. The last time, you left afterward without saying a word. What am I supposed to think?"

"It was two in the morning, and you were backstage."

"You've got a point there," said Liam, but whether he was talking to me or someone on TV wasn't entirely clear. I glanced in at him; he was slumped shirtless on the couch. Spider legs of black hair sprang from his shoulders. His skin was luminous in the dim light, the cool, starchy white of the flesh of a potato, the white of chill, damp low-ceilinged row houses, cabbagy sooty air, borderline malnutrition, guilt.

"This one here," said Feckin smuttily, "this fat black girl here, I'd give her a toss." He took a big gulp of whatever was in the cup he held, washed it noisily around his mouth before swallowing it. He had a primitive, dissolute face, a fuzz of white-blond hair on his hard skull, thick horn-rimmed glasses, and a waiflike body. His accent was so thick, he often sounded as if he were speaking some language other than English. His real name was Declan McIntyre. He was Liam's boyhood friend. He had been staying with them now for ten months and showed no signs of going elsewhere. He slept on their couch, drank their whiskey, smoked their pot, watched their TV, and never went out; he even got them to go on cigarette runs for him. Their apartment had taken on during the course of his stay there the loamy, dark, loungy air of a hibernation cave, the accretions of a static life, a life on hold: Cigarette butts lay crushed in a mound in a pool of whiskey on a plate on the coffee table; his seldom-washed body smelled like some hearth dog, warm and moribund; his very indolence emitted a psychic odor, a sense of entitlement, self-romance, negative interestingness, as if by doing nothing at all, by sponging off his friends, by languidly denying forward motion, he set himself apart from the pack. He was the antihero of his own hermetically sealed world, the nondrama that unspooled only in his own mind, in which he couldn't be held accountable for anything he said or did. That Amanda and Liam hadn't asked him to move along was naturally their own fault, but their friendship with him was obviously predicated on their willingness to tolerate him as he was.

"Ech, you're so full of it," said Liam, shaking his big, shaggy head with its black-Irish mat of hair. "You potato-eating bugger."

"And what does that make you?"

Amanda had picked up the lighter and was examining the blonde on it, who had stretched her little thong up around her waist to outline the cleft of her crotch. She flicked the flame to life and held it to one of the green peppers until its flesh began to scorch. I could tell by the set of her face that she was not going to speak until I did.

I said earnestly, "Amanda, believe me, I'm really looking forward to hearing you guys tomorrow night."

She pulled another cigarette from her bathrobe pocket, lit it, and inhaled. "Don't do me any favors," she said, squinting. She was getting crow's-feet, I noticed with a pang. My little sister. "Just so you don't run away like a scared bunny afterward."

"A scared bunny," I repeated, laughing uneasily, beset by a somewhat dismaying image of a large, white, pink-eyed creature darting for the safety of its lettuce patch. Apparently, she'd struck a nerve.

After sunrise, I got up to get a drink of water. Through the kitchen window the sky was a low greenish-yellow smudge; according to the sunburst clock on the wall, it was just past seven o'clock. The slice of Manhattan I could see through a hectic grid of clotheslines and power lines looked small, dirty, and exhausted. I heard truck gears grinding a block away on Metropolitan Avenue, then the high, churning roar of the engine pulling its load away from the light. Right before I'd woken up, I had been dreaming that I was trying to escape from an unseen but menacing attacker; my stubborn mule of a body wouldn't budge no matter how hard my mind flogged it. I felt as if I were moving my dream-legs through taffy or sludge while my mind raced on ahead.

Going back along the hall, I saw that Feckin had passed out on the couch with his boots on. His bony ankles showed fishbelly pale between his pant cuffs and his boot tops. He lay under his overcoat with his face buried in a pillow, his nose squashed, his hand dangling off the side. His snores were soft, without aggression, little percussive grunts and sighs. Naturally, he preferred the seeming transience of sleeping on a couch to installing himself in the bourgeois confines of a bedroom, for which he'd have to pay rent, thus becoming just another ordinary working guy.

I lay awake in the absolute darkness of Amanda's windowless little studio, waiting for morning, sure I'd never go back to sleep. The room smelled of her perfume. I imagined her in here, sitting on the futon I was lying on, picking out chords, humming melodies, turning her little tape recorder on and off, cursing when a string broke. The room was filled with cassette tapes and pieces of paper with scraps written on them; I thought about turning on the light again and examining these clues to my sister's inner life, about which I knew almost nothing, but then I realized that I didn't want to know the humid, earnest little phrases Amanda had snatched out of the ether and written down, the insipid aphorisms that had floated up from the magic eight-ball window in her head. Just before I fell asleep I realized I was falling asleep and almost jerked awake again, but a surprise riptide pulled me under and I was gone.

I awoke at noon feeling hung over and wretchedly sad. Everyone else was still asleep, so I crept out and found some local hipster's recreation of an old-timey coffee shop. It had speckled Formica counters and table-tops, cracked leatherette booths and laminated menus, thick white crockery and pies turning in a case, but there was a self-conscious air of "authenticity" about it all that made it impossible to relax here; customers and waitstaff alike were on display just like the pies, almost all of them well under twenty-five and as aggressively, ethnically anti-beautiful as a magazine fashion spread. I sat meekly in one of the booths and was immediately served a cup of coffee so strong it blasted the inside of my mouth. I ordered some eggs, then rummaged around in my canvas bag and pulled out the Lonely Planet guide to Turkey. I turned to the introduction, which informed me that "the mention of Turkey conjures up vague, stereotypical visions of Oriental splendor and decadence, of mystery and intrigue, of sultans and harems, of luxury and wickedness in the minds of most Western visitors. These outdated stereotypes quickly evaporate once the visitor arrives in the country."

Although I had never been to Turkey, I didn't need to go there to write authoritatively about it, thanks to the thoroughness of the Lonely Planet guide's descriptions. I had been using the book as a geographical and cultural aid to create my own version of Turkey the same way I conjured a fictional Angus out of blurry memories. In so doing, I shamelessly perpetrated these myths and even invented new ones; Angus's Don Quixote–like political beliefs sent him through a hookah-blurred paradise of mint tea, dusky girls dressed like Barbara Eden, incense-laden marketplaces and alleys, bleached-white towns spilling down steep hillsides to the Aegean. I also used Turkey as a metaphorical Biblical land in which my father played out his messianic delusions: Efes boasted one of the seven churches of the apocalypse, coincidentally or not. Marxist fanaticism was political in nature, but Christian in mood and texture; what was bloody revolution if not ultimately a kind of apocalypse? Both Christian and Marxist trajectories progressed from the violent destruction of all heathens and heretics to a gathering of all true believers into a perfect society of shared common property, transcendent common good, freedom from individual gain and egotistical self-interest. The primary difference was that there was no Messiah, but my Angus was trying to fulfill that role as well as he could, even down to his martyred end.

Whoever my father had been, the fictional Angus Heyerdahl was a scruffy guy with a self-administered haircut, piercing blue eyes, an elusive low-key affability that was entirely illusory. The first section, "Hangdog," began in California, when he cracked up and left everyone and everything he'd ever known and signed up as crew on a freighter to Istanbul, bringing with him into exile only his volumes of Marx, sleeping bag, tent and a few clothes, and the cash he'd taken from the commune's bank account, which he justified by telling himself he'd left them his house in return. He gave very little thought to the fatherless future to which he was consigning his three children; being a Marxist was the perfect alibi for the would-be absentee deadbeat dad, since family ties were considered completely irrelevant in the grand scheme of revolution and social equality; in fact, inasmuch as I understood the Marxist take on families, they weren't supposed to get in the way of your ideals at all, ever.

In Chapter Two, when Angus got to Efes, he established himself in a campsite in an orange grove in Selcuk, began what would turn out to be a years-long affair with Oya, the daughter of the campground's owner, lunched every day in the local kofte joint, where he quickly learned enough Turkish to argue with his newfound like-minded Commie cronies over beer and grilled lamb at night. To Angus, born and raised in Minnesota, this was paradise, and he had a great time kicking back in the sun during the brief hiatus before his idealistic pathologies re-emerged and subsumed him. In the middle section, "Heresy," he tried to reconcile his pure beliefs with the political realities of his exile as he rose through the ranks of Turkey's strong Marxist underground. Of course, there was no possibility of a happy finish to this novel; the only ending Angus would have approved of would have been a successful revolution and the establishment of a socialist government, but he was doomed by his archetypal messianic role. In the final, as yet unwritten pages of the final section, "Blood," I planned that he would overstep his bounds, piss off the wrong people, and be violently killed in a remote village by members of a fanatic Muslim religious group during the political unrest and civil infighting of 1980. His corpse would be left by the side of a dirt road to be eaten by vultures. On one level, this could be viewed as my private revenge on the bastard for ditching me, but it also made sense in terms of the book itself. Fanatics came to no good end and dogma got you nowhere: If that wasn't a major theme in this novel, then I was Marie of Romania.

After I'd polished off my greasy breakfast, I fished out a notebook and pen and got to work. It was interesting, writing in longhand, sort of like cutting grass with an old rotary mower. The physical effort it took was half the fun, gripping the pen and forcibly imprinting crabbed letters onto unyielding paper instead of fluidly tapping keys and watching ribbons of words stream silkily across a computer screen. I forgot where I was; it was as if I were encased and suspended in a temporal bubble like an egg developing in a sac. Ideas and words came into my mind and passed through it onto the paper, and meanwhile, outside, nothing changed, nothing happened.

In the scene I wrote, Angus tried to enlist the sympathies of a man named Akbil, the owner of a bakery who edited a Marxist newspaper and held a lot of sway in the political underground. This Akbil was a gigantic man with bulging forearms and a square head. When Angus asked him what he thought about the likelihood of establishing a Marxist government in Turkey, he expostulated in broken but forcible English that Marxism had to be introduced gradually through the system, not imposed from without by outsiders. Change happened in its own time; there was no forcing things. The individual had no power over the course of history. Angus countered that the recent activism and protests in the States had proved this wrong, and that the only way to freedom lay in fomenting a revolution through demonstrations, dissemination of information, and grassroots coalitions.

"And then what," spat out the baker, "then you have a new government and nothing changes."

After a few paragraphs, my pen began to move as if it were powered by electricity, and all I could do was hold on and watch it all unfold. I found myself hoping Angus would put this guy in his place, to argue back with his usual articulate confidence, but for some reason I was powerless to help him. Cowed by the other man's sheer size and superior volume and authentic Turkishness, Angus tried to interrupt the flow of spittle, but only stuttered, interjected, parried, and in the end shrank defensively into himself with a narrowing of his shoulders.

When I came to, it was early evening and I was blinking and dazed. That scene I'd written crackled and popped, and I was a hell of a writer, and so forth; such were the illusions afforded by inspiration, akin to what a new mother must have felt for her garden-variety baby. I left the diner and took a long walk through North Brooklyn. The sky overhead ran the gamut from a wild sunset in the extreme west to an intense pale blue in the far east, the whole thing clotted with clouds, stippled with blowing leaves and wheeling seagulls. Everything below it, down here, was man-made and corrupt, rusty, comical—spray-painted tags on sides of buildings, razor wire coiled along the tops of corrugated fences, stenciled letters on Dumpsters, blowing plastic bags—all knit together to make a flawed but teeming whole, like bird tracks, tree bark, and filigrees of lichen or bare branches in the woods. The Empire State Building was ice white at its uppermost tip, ice blue farther down the shaft, like one of those multicolored bomb-shaped Popsicles we used to get from the ice cream truck.

Angus wasn't the only fanatic in my immediate family. Every generation had at least one: My maternal great-grandfather had been a British-born hellfire-and-brimstone anti-Catholic traveling preacher, thumping his Bible in Presbyterian pulpits all over America; my mother's aunt and uncle had been avid devotees of the "clairvoyant philosopher" Rudolf Steiner; my sister Lola had been a member of a doomsday cult in Arizona for eight years before moving to Australia, where she and her husband now ran an emu farm. She wasn't a fanatic anymore, but she was still weird.

I'd been completely spared the believer gene; I didn't understand these people. All my life I'd been highly resistant to any strain of dogmatically imposed repression or abstraction; my intellectual white blood cells attacked ideological invaders and wiped them out before they could take root. The idea of trying to improve or change the human race as a whole seemed totally hopeless to me. I couldn't imagine making leaps of faith all the time as if my soul were a ballerina on ecstasy: If the purpose of my life were to transcend it, how exactly would I live it? And I'd always found the concepts of sacrifice and suffering extremely boring. Believers were wet blankets, wrecking all the fun and crying at the party, yapping on about how things should be, not about how things were. It wasn't enough for them to restrict their own pleasure; they had to spoil it for everyone else on earth too.

Had a gun been placed against my head with the insistence that I identify my deepest belief or else, I might have cast my lot with Matthew Arnold's call for sweetness and light on the one hand and true love on the darkling plain on the other, although I'd have had to leave his later social-reform ideas completely out of it, not buying into that sort of thing myself. As far as I could tell, even the most high-minded, well-intentioned, idealistic organizations devolved sooner or later into platforms for power-mad zealots and would-be pundits, fueled by empty rhetoric like everything else. The very thought of joining groups, even those ostensibly made up of "my own kind," ACT UP, Gay Pride marches, and the like, immediately made me itch to do something to offend them all and get myself kicked out. This attitude might have been a rational, intelligent stand against didacticism and cant, but it might also have been nothing more than my way of rebelling against my father.

I headed along Wythe Avenue toward Broadway. The street was almost deserted except for truck drivers unloading their cargo at docks, an occasional whore on a corner smoking and pacing and clutching her purse, solitary walkers-home. Off to the right, between rows of low industrial buildings on streets going off at odd angles, across the blue-black shimmer of the East River, I caught glimpses of Manhattan. Straight ahead above the decaying web of the Williamsburg Bridge, smoke billowed into the violet sky, drifting sideways to blur and obscure the tiny white lights on the struts. The juxtaposition of violet sky, black bridge, and gray smoke caused me to stop and stare for several minutes before I continued on my way to the subway. At the Marcy Avenue subway station I waited for a J train and rode it over the bridge, looking out the window at the lights and water.

I came up out of the subway, stopped at a pay phone, and called my mother's number.

"Hello?" she said in a wet, clogged voice.

"Mom," I said, "how are you?"

She blew her nose audibly. "Oh, never better. How are you?"

"The same," I said. "Ted and I broke up. I'm staying with Amanda, I don't know whether she told you."

"She did," said my mother. "What happened with Ted?"

"I don't want to talk about it right now. I just called to see how you were doing."

"Well, I don't want to talk about my shitty life either, which brings this conversation to a bit of a standstill."

"Are you going to Amanda's performance tonight?" I asked.

"I don't think so, I'm not in the mood for all that smoke and noise. I think we'll just go to bed early. Anyway, give her my love."

"Let me know if you need anything. Give my best to Leonard."

"I hope Ted offered to support you for a while until you get on your feet."

"I turned him down. Don't worry about me, Mom. I'm a little out of practice at making a living, but I'll remember how."

"I've got money if you need some," she said, "and you can always stay with us, you know, as long as you want."

I hesitated. "Do you need me to?" I asked delicately.

"Only if you want to," she said.

"But do you need me?"

She made an exasperated noise. "Jeremy," she said. "If I need you, I'll ask. I'm trying to tell you that you're welcome here as long as you'd like to stay."

"Okay," I said. "Thanks, Mom."

On Carmine Street I opened the door to Frankie's restaurant and found a small table near the back. A waiter, not Frankie, but probably his brother or cousin, handed me a menu and went to stand on the other side of the little room. When I put the menu down on the checked tablecloth, he stepped forward again and I named the things I wanted. He wrote on a pad, put the menu under his arm and departed, returned with a glass of ice-clogged water, a rattan basket with a small sliced loaf of warm, crusty bread wrapped in a white napkin, and a small monkey dish packed with butter so cold, I had to dig at it with my knife to get some out. It ripped the soft insides of the bread when I tried to spread it. There were few things more delicious than ice cold butter on warm Italian bread. A moment later Frankie's relative brought me a glass of a Chianti so deeply reddish purple, it looked like blood in the large bulb of a laboratory vessel. These were the rituals I cherished, the niceties and formalities I happily spent any amount of money to experience on a regular basis. Sitting in a room filled with tables and strangers, sipping a glass of something that warmed my stomach while I waited for the food I'd chosen to be brought to me, made my toes curl with a profound well-being. It made me feel cared for, cherished, nurtured, attended to.

A middle-aged couple came in, sat down, perused menus, ordered, drank wine. A family took possession of the large round front table. My salad arrived, chunks of crisp, cold iceberg lettuce awash in oregano-flecked olive oil and red wine vinegar. I sprinkled it with black pepper and devoured it, watching as the mother of the large brood unbuttoned her shirt and tucked her suckling infant inside it, his mouth clamped onto her breast. He kneaded her flesh with his tiny hand as he drank. I knew exactly how he felt. This salad made me want to knead someone's flesh with contentment. I sopped up extra oil with a small piece of bread and chewed.

My dinner arrived: veal parmesan with a side of garlicky greens. I tucked in. Looking toward the door with my mouth full of tender breaded baby meat, I espied Frankie, arriving for his night shift in a cheap leather jacket that looked a size too small for him.

He didn't see me at first. I was just one of a number of customers, not his. He disappeared into a back room, emerged a while later in a crisp white shirt and black bow tie. He cast a quick, practiced eye around the room. When it landed on me, he raised his eyebrows and unhesitatingly made his way over to me.

He stood by my table and gave me his hand to shake. "Jeremy, hey. How you doin'."

"Hi, Frankie," I said.

"Where's your friend Max?"

"He's around somewhere. How's it going?"

"Same old fucking thing. How 'bout you."

"Okay," I said, and we exchanged uncomfortable little grins. I started to ask him something else, then realized that the air between us was completely dead, and that Frankie and I had no further sexual business in this lifetime. He had work to do, and my food awaited me. "Well, it was good seeing you again," I said. "I'll take my check if you run into my waiter."

"In my flat in London you had to put coins in a slot in the meter to get your hot water," Liam was saying, perched on a barstool at Bombshell later that night. He jiggled his knee, jackhammerlike, talking in a fast monotone, as if he'd long ago sent the words to the cargo bay of his brain to await shipping out and had stopped thinking the thought itself long before he said it aloud. "Know what I did? I made ice cubes the same size as shillings, stuck them in, and they melted and were never seen again. That flummoxed the coin collectors for months. Never figured it out. Had free baths all that time."

"Well," I said dubiously, "good for you, I guess."

"Good for me," said Liam, "and bad for them."

Bombshell was in a basement near the West Side Highway on Fourteenth Street, a former meat locker turned nightclub. The low ceilings were still embedded with the tracks from the pulleys and hooks where wet, crimson carcasses streaked with fat had swayed toward whirring blades, refrigerated trucks. The dampish rough concrete walls had been painted a rich Day-Glo gold and hung with blown-up black-and-white cheesecake publicity stills of B-movie golden girls, Rockettes, flapper showgirls, Ice Capades skaters, and chanteuses. Tiny fringed lamps protruded from the walls; votives in fishnet-swathed glass jars on each small table gave off small wavering bursts of light. Two sets of risers behind the bar held a chorus of bottles, the real stars of this operation. The place felt like a fairy cave or the inside of a huge hollowed-out butternut squash.

From the dark, shadowy area beyond the winglike curtains on one side, the silent, pug-nosed Mexican bar-back came and went, carrying ice tubs and cases of beer. Karina Ventrix, the transvestite bartender, lounged behind the bar in a leather push-up bra that sagged on her flat chest, belted short-shorts over fishnets, stiletto thigh-high boots, and a blond pageboy wig. When she caught me looking at her, she narrowed her eyes at me. Drag queens never liked me. Although I'd asked to have it extra dry, she'd made my martini with so much vermouth, it had a greasy film on top. I didn't want to further alienate her by complaining.

"Hey, how do I look?" Amanda asked.

She was gotten up in a floor-length green brocade dress, dangling rhinestone earrings that sparkled in the candlelight, a paisley-shaped bindi on her forehead, eyeliner painted out to her temples, a fake black mole by her lower lip. Her glossy dark hair was twisted and pinned up, one spit curl pasted against her left cheek. She wasn't asking me, but I thought she wouldn't have been out of place in a Louis Quatorze display at Madame Tussaud's.

"You look way too good for him," said Karina the bartender with a jerk of her head in Liam's direction. As she did this, her wig slid slightly askew. I was interested to note, before she pushed it back into place, that her real hair was gray and sparse.

"Excuse me," I said to her. "I asked for no vermouth in this martini."

She looked at me. "That martini is as dry as you're going to get around here."

"Really," I said.

"Karina," said Amanda, "be nice to my brother."

"Well, sure," said Karina, "if he's really your brother. He doesn't look a thing like you." She dumped my martini into the sink and busied herself with the shaker.

"When I lived in Amsterdam," said Feckin, "I lived in a yurt in a squat in a burned-out Chinese restaurant with a feckin armchair stuck halfway up the staircase so you had to crawl around it."

"What is a yurt?" Amanda asked Liam.

"A Himalayan hut," he told her. "Big smelly tent made out of yak fur or something."

Liam and Feckin were, I'd flattered myself into deciding, flirting with me. They'd never paid much attention to me before, but all of a sudden now they were telling alternating competing stories, each of them trying to top the other in hopes of winning my—what? Hand in marriage? I wasn't sure what the upshot of all this was, except that they were both shambling drunk and clearly in search of someone on whom to work off all their pent-up energy. Liam's true love was obviously Feckin, not Amanda, and I wondered where Liam and Amanda's ménage would be without Feckin there to diffuse tension and distract the two of them from their fundamental incompatibility. I'd seen these unconsummated hetero-boy love affairs before. Liam and Feckin were so intensely bonded, sex was in many ways beside the point.

Feckin stubbed out his smoked-down butt and lit another cigarette. "This Jap friend of mine called Sawa," he said on the exhale, ignoring the smoke that swathed his face as impenetrably as a chador, "built the yurt from trash he hauled off the street. He ate garbage and old produce the stores couldn't sell. He knew exactly how many pigeons lived upstairs, and just how long he could live off them if it ever came to that. I met my wife there. She lived upstairs in a flat in the attic where the kitchen fire was covered in soot from a fire, and pigeon shit on top of that, with a big hole in the roof. Black-and-white room with the weather coming in. What a crazy girl. Ha! Suzanne, my sweet wife, wonder where she is now." He nipped some whiskey, held it between his lower teeth and the pouch of his inner lip to warm it, then swallowed it with a small toss of his head.

"Feckin's green card wife," Liam said. "His sweet nothin." He gave Amanda a smack on her hip. "I'm hoping to bag one of those crickets."

"Are you calling my sister a cricket?" I said in a bantering, guyish tone, but I was out of my depth here.

Amanda walked around the bar and helped herself to a draft from one of the taps; Karina didn't flicker an eye in her direction. Amanda was the artist in residence here, loosely speaking.

Liam took a drag of his cigarette from the far corner of his mouth and I saw a flash of a smile. "Isn't she a cricket, then." He had an overbite, crooked lower teeth crammed together and discolored by tobacco. His hands were bony and long-fingered, the knuckles of each finger tufted with black hair. He encircled Amanda's wrist with his hand, took her mug away with the other, and downed the beer she'd just poured in several gulps. Wiping foam off his upper lip, he told her, "Easy on the beer, you don't want to turn into a cow, do you."

"I'm already your cash cow. Get your own fucking beer, and get a job while you're at it."

"Well, sure," he said, "if I were legal." He winked at me. I had the feeling this conversation was ancient, and they were rehashing it only because they had a fresh audience. There didn't seem to be much heat or interest on either side, it was more like an empty ritual whose original meaning had long since fallen by the wayside.

A while later, Amanda took the stage with her band. They were called Radish Night, after some festival in Oaxaca, where everyone carved radishes into grotesque figures and displayed them, or something along those lines; it had been a while since Amanda had explained it to me, and I hadn't paid much attention. It was Sunday, midnight, but there was quite a crowd. This was a relief; I'd expected to be one of only a few willing to stay up this late to hear them, and I'd dreaded having to keep my expression bland and nonjudgmental, knowing my hawk-eyed sister would notice any mocking flare of the nostrils immediately. It was presumably a worknight for most of these people, but they were all crowding eagerly and expectantly in front of the stage as Amanda and her bass player noodled around, warming up while the drummer and accordion player meandered onstage, all four of them looking as tarted up as I remembered from last time. Maybe that explained their success: Four gorgeous girls with instruments, how could that fail? It almost never did, as far as I knew.

I dutifully fought my way toward the stage to stand crammed between several of Amanda's more heavily perfumed fans. I didn't want to be there, but when I thought about it, there was really nowhere else I would have preferred. I didn't want to be anywhere. My inner eye was suffused with staggeringly painful images from the other night. It had been dawning on me all day that I'd been frozen psychocryogenically the whole time Ted and I had been together; whatever had kept me with him all those years had also retarded my emotional growth. I had predicated a large part of my daily existence on certain assumptions about him, namely that he loved me, that I knew him, and that I could trust him, all of which had been revealed all at once to be facets in a house of mirrors constructed by Ted for his own protection and convenience, and no one else's. I had been allowed to enjoy my pleasant little illusions about him as long as he wanted me, but here I stood now, ground up and spat out by his inexorable, well-oiled machine.

Amanda, looking larger than life under the stage lights, nodded to her drummer, and they launched into their set. I braced myself for emotionally overwrought, postcollegiate, jangly alterna-rock, and vowed to find something to like about it, even if it was only that every song eventually ended. But after several bars I was shocked to find that I had a lump in my throat. Of all the mawkish things, the song was evidently about a kid who got lost on her way home from the store after dark. Amanda's voice sounded husky and sad; the song's narrator wandered through dark, unfamiliar streets, thinking that everything she'd ever known was gone and she might never find her way back to her own lighted windows. "A gypsy moth beating on windows," went one line.

But instead of making me wince, the song gave me the electric pricks of an acupuncture session. An olfactory hallucination washed around my skull until it hit my inner nostrils—the smell of sage on sun-heated rocks, that ticklish, intense burst—which brought back a sudden memory of waking up at dawn when I was eight or nine, all three of us kids shivering in the chilly air as we ate cold charred hot dogs and leftover canned chili while our mother broke camp, shoving everything in the back of the bus, firing up the engine, calling out "All aboard!" like a train conductor. Off we lurched, yawning and half awake, our windshield scraped by low pine branches, along a pitted dirt road to the highway. While Amanda and Lola began the vicious, journey-long struggle for legroom in the backseat, I opened the maps. Our mother made a habit of teaming up for safety with other traveling families, so we usually had a rendezvous arranged at another campground down the road. Puerto Penasco, Mingus Mountain, Big Sur, Mendocino, the Tetons, Aspen, Four Corners, Bryce Canyon, Point Reyes, Oak Creek Canyon— pine shadows shifting in afternoon sunlight on wooden picnic tables, cardboard boxes full of Space Bars and granola, the shriek of a tent zipper in the middle of the night when someone got up to pee, rock-ringed ash-filled fireplaces with sticky charred grates over them, the smell of upholstery stuffing in the midday desert sun coming out of cracks in melting vinyl in the front seat of the dusty, spattered VW bus, which had been red, and which we'd called the Rolling Tomato for reasons I'd forgotten but which I knew would come back to me if I let them.

"We're gypsy WASPs," our mother had told us as we looked out windows at subdivisions, tract homes, neat, clean children with dogs and bikes, on our way to sleep in the wilderness of canyons, mountains, beach. Our mother's tone implied that we were superior to these people because they had to live boring lives in boring houses with their boring families while we got to drive around in the Rolling Tomato, part of a freer, richer, more interesting world than they would ever know. But Amanda had told me, when we'd grown up and left all that behind, that more than anything in those days she'd wanted a bedroom with a pink ruffled canopy bed, Barbies, a vanity table, and a family with a father who worked all day and read the paper at night, a mother with a real hairdo who let us eat sugar cereal and watch cartoons. Once when we parked in a Safeway parking lot and a family in a station wagon pulled up next to us, the daughter, who was around Amanda's age, stared at Amanda in her too-short jeans, her tie-dyed T-shirt, the woven headband around her rat's-nest hair, and smoke-smudged face from last night's campfire, and Amanda had felt like dying of envy and shame.

The next song was in Spanish. I had no idea what it was about, but it stirred the short hairs on the back of my neck. Amanda accompanied herself with some sort of flamenco strumming while the accordion plunged and wheezed along. At the heart of the song was a buoyant sadness I was feeling just lovelorn enough to comprehend. I may have been a fool about the whole Ted thing, it seemed to say, but everyone was a fool, we were all in this together. At this rate I'd be a puddle of goop by the end of her set.

Just then I caught sight of Feckin lounging laconically off to one side, his half-smile flickering through the veil of smoke, clamping his cigarette firmly in place so he could keep his hands plunged into his trouser pockets to achieve the proper air of ironic distance. He caught my eye, quirked an eyebrow, and looked away. Teary-eyed, I fumbled in my pants pocket for the hankie I kept there, and encountered with my fingertips the rough edge of another mint from the restaurant the other night. Was I wearing these same jeans again? I was. I honked my nose into the cotton square, thinking of Frankie's funny, somewhat poetical cock, long and skinny and curved, and that funny little depression at the base of his spine, as if he'd been born with a tail that had been amputated.

Radish Night played another song, and then another one. Everyone in the audience except for Feckin and no doubt Liam, wherever he was, seemed to be suspended separately in a tensile force field, like scarabs in amber or pieces of fruit cocktail in Jell-O; it was hard for me to breathe through the fracas in my chest cavity. I was aware that the person next to me was dancing in a way I would ordinarily have found irresistibly annoying, throwing himself about in a spastic liberal-arts-college-boy frenzy, thrashing his head like a horse with a fly in its ear. He wore baggy suburban would-be hip-hop pants that showed the corrugated elastic of his boxer shorts. His sideburns had been carved so they ended in points in the hollows of his cheeks. To maintain them, he must have devoted a certain portion of his day to their upkeep and grooming, wielding his razor like a topiary gardener. The part of my brain that was still aware of such things recognized him as the type who went regularly to yoga classes in hopes of enticing lithe, trendy girls back to his over-priced Williamsburg loft for body massages and Japanese twig tea; I would have bet that he consumed huge amounts of sugar to make up for the lack of meat, caffeine, and alcohol in his diet. I always suspected for some instinctive reason that such boys had unusually well-formed stools, which for another instinctive reason made me despise them even more, even as I couldn't tear my eyes away from their silly dance-floor shenanigans.

But now this guy was my semblable, my brother, my fellow suspendee in Jell-O. To my surprise, I thought I understood how this music made him feel; the possibility that this was a gauge of how low I had sunk since being dumped by Ted rather than any improvement in Amanda's music since the last time I'd seen her perform did occur briefly to me, but I was in no mood to take my own bait. I was having a lot of trouble getting a deep enough breath. The air in here was hot, smoky, charged. I gasped once or twice for air, but my lungs wouldn't fill; my head felt light, then too small. Things kept zooming in and out of my field of reference, and for a panic-stricken, brain-shattering instant I thought I'd been spray-dosed with some fast-acting drug. I felt as if I were tripping, then all of a sudden the stage lights closed in on my vision with an explosion of white light. A long or short time later, I had no idea which, I found myself on the floor, waking from a deep sleep. Faces bent over me, and someone tapped my wrist firmly.

"He's all right, he just fainted but he's awake now," someone said over the music to someone else, and a pair of hands grabbed my armpits and hoisted me slowly, carefully to my feet. I was relaxed, unable to speak, completely trusting, as if we were all playing one of those slumber-party trust games my sisters had played in junior high. I was surrounded by kindly, faceless beings who patted me and zoomed in and out of my field of vision. I felt a little light-headed, but wide awake, as if I'd slept for hours or days. I gasped, inhaled deeply, kept inhaling, until the dizziness passed. The person behind me steadied me, hands resting warmly on my shoulders, until I had regained my balance, and then whoever it was released me and I stood, wobbly but upright, on my own. I'd never fainted before in my life. Now, as I passed from that black, mindless sleep to awareness, the music seemed even louder than before, so loud it penetrated the membranes of my cells and throbbed in each individual nucleus. Amanda was standing very still under the lights, without her guitar, singing empty-handed into the microphone with her eyes closed. She looked gigantic and gentle, a Statue of Liberty come to life.

When the set ended, I stood there, my ears ringing, too stupefied to applaud. Feckin had vanished, I guessed to the men's room to relieve himself of the five or so pints of ale Liam had bought him with Amanda's money. Where Liam had got himself off to I had no idea and didn't care. I fought my way back to the bar and slid onto a just-vacated, still-warm stool and ordered a vodka on the rocks. When Karina set it in front of me, I tossed it down, ordered another one, tossed that down too. I was starting to feel normal again. I watched everyone at the bar with avid curiosity. Expressions flitted lightly over candlelit faces, fleeting facial movements that were gone almost before I could identify the feelings that prompted them. We were such a curious bunch, we humans.

A while later, Amanda was suddenly there next to me. "Jeremy," she said into my ear, "you're still here."

I turned to look at her. She had that peaky look around her eyes that meant she was about to cry. "What's wrong?" I said, surprised.

"I'm so sorry," she said. "We sucked."

"You did?" I asked, suddenly even more dubious of my own reaction.

"Liam just told me backstage," she said. "I was out of tune on a couple of songs, the drummer fucked up an entrance, my voice cracked a couple of times. I've got to quit smoking. Fuck, I feel like going home and slitting my wrists. I need a bagel, I'm starving, will you come with me?"

We climbed the stairs to the street. The night was cool and overcast. My face was pelted by tiny pricks of water that felt heavy as mercury, ominously acidic on my cheeks, as if the flecks of rain were freighted with toxic waste. The sidewalk was obstructed by Dumpsters big as water buffalo, overflowing with collapsed cardboard cartons. As we passed an open industrial doorway, we were blasted by a wallop of diesel exhaust from a panel truck idling there, being loaded by shouting men pushing box-laden dollies. Amanda clutched her wrap around her narrow shoulders, her face downcast. Words kept firing up on the launch pad of my tongue, then fizzing out at takeoff.

"Liam is not necessarily your best advocate, Amanda," I said finally.

She sniffed. "Whatever. He's honest."

No, he's threatened by you and dependent on you, and because of that he treats you like shit to keep you in your place, I wanted to say, but I'd learned the hard way that telling someone the truth about their loved one, no matter how good your intentions were, always backfired messily and horribly upon the truth teller.

"I thought you were great," I said.

She laughed and looked at me sideways. "Come on, tell me honestly."

"I just did."

"Really?" she said skeptically but with immense relief.

We went into Dizzy Izzy's and stood in line behind a devastatingly skinny guy in skin-tight peg-leg jeans, a leather vest, shiny pointy-toed lizard-skin boots, and a blue skull tattoo on his moth-white biceps. Amanda looked him up and down and flicked a sideways laughing glance at me. We ordered the same thing, toasted everything bagels with a scallion schmear, and a few minutes later were handed twin hot mini-bundles wrapped in wax paper. We took them outside and stood under a blank marquee down the street, watching a parade of cabs jouncing their way to the West Side Highway, their chassis sparking blue as they hit the same deep pothole, one after another.

"You'd think there'd be a collective evolutionary development among cabs," I said, "sort of like the hundredth monkey."

"What?"

"Never mind."

She swallowed her bite and held her bagel poised, ready to take another bite the instant she stopped talking. "Maybe they're more like dogs marking trees, squirting brake fluid into the same potholes."

"Maybe," I said.

"You're surprised I knew what you were talking about. You think you're the only one in the family who's ever read a book? I went to college, you know."

"Sorry," I said.

She sniffed.

"Amanda, why are you always sniffing?"

"Hey, that's Sebastian Philpott, isn't it?"

"Where? I just ran into him the other day. I can't believe it."

"Across the street. Oh my God, look at him, he looks exactly the same as he did in high school."

"Some people might take that as a compliment."

She laughed. "Hey, Sebastian!" she called, and waved him over.

He came bustling toward us, his doughy face alight. "Hello!" he called. "Jeremy, good to see you again! Amanda!" He was dressed like a film noir private detective or a vintage flasher: trench coat, fedora with a dripping brim. His glasses were fogged with his pleasure at seeing us, as if he generated his own personal weather system.

"How's the porn industry treating you?" I said.

"Like a king," said Sebastian joyfully.

"He made a fortune off his own magazine," I told Amanda. *"Boytoy."*

"Fascinating," said Amanda. She sniffed.

I hoped Amanda wouldn't say something snide to him; I didn't want his feelings to be hurt. I wasn't sure why, but I felt protective of him.

"And how have you been, Amanda?" he asked in his stiff, courtly way, as if he'd been mocked so many times, he was impervious to it, but perennially hopeful that someday it would stop.

"I'm okay," she said breezily. "My band played tonight. We blew."

"You have a band? Let me know next time you play. I'll be sure to come." He produced a business card from his hat brim, which he handed to her with a slight inclination of his oversized head. "You must be following me around, Jeremy," he said to me.

"I was going to say the same thing to you."

"Call it serendipity, maybe; I'm still desperate for writers. So call *me,* Jeremy, as soon as you can." Sebastian extracted another card from the brim of his hat and handed it to me. It was damp from the rain, or perhaps from the cloud of precipitation he generated.

"Okay," I said, taking it. "But I think I have the first one you gave me somewhere."

"I've got to be on my way now, I have an appointment." He winked at us. "An assignation, as they used to say. It's extremely good to see you both. What an unexpected pleasure. Good night, and please be in touch." And off he trundled along Fourteenth Street.

"He's just going home to abuse himself," said Amanda, dropping the card into the gutter. "He doesn't have a date. No way. Who'd go out with him?"

"Why are you so mean to him?"

She gave me a look. "Are you sticking up for Sebastian Philpott? Jeremy, that guy is such a weird loser, I can't believe he's still alive, I can't believe no one's pulverized him into a bloody pulp."

"He's nice," I said weakly.

"Man." She shook her head so her earrings caught the glare of the streetlamp and glittered like miniature disco balls. "You need to get out more. You're going to rot in that attic."

"I don't live in that attic anymore, you may recall," I said. "I'm homeless and broke now. Actually, in a way I live with you." I was scrutinizing his card, which said, "Sebastian Philpott, *Boytoy,* Editor in Chief and Impresario."

"You're not really going to *call* him, are you?"

"I need a job," I said, sliding the card into my pocket.

"I need a drink," she said with a sigh. "Come on, Liam probably thinks I ditched him. Let's go burst his little bubble."

"What did you think of the movie?"

"What I want to know is, who is her trainer? I do a hundred doggie kicks a day and my butt doesn't look like that."

"She probably got implants."

"Or lipo."

"Or both."

I turned around to behold two women exchanging sharklike smiles. One had a cap of wet-looking short dark red hair. The other's hair, jet-black, equally sleek, was worn twisted and pinned to the back of her head. Large shawls draped below their bony, bare, ballerinalike clavicles, the ends tucked into the crooks of their arms. They glistened with a well-tended and voluntary malnourishment that probably allowed them to feel as if they deserved so much more than whatever they already had, and therefore justified all their draconian bitchiness. When the redhead caught my eye with a laserlike, hunting-dog inquiry, I helpfully projected as much faggotry as I could at such short notice; without any visible reaction she flicked her eyes past me, scanning for more viable prey. Her friend, whose gaydar was clearly more technologically advanced, hadn't even bothered to glance my way.

When their nostrils flared in tandem, a look across the room in the same direction gave me an unobstructed view of Ted and Giselle, making their entrance. I was plunged back into my gangly, hormonal freshman body, gazing hot-eyed at the prom king.

"I'm back," said Felicia, appearing beside me. She had gone to "powder her nose" fifteen minutes before; I had almost forgotten about her.

"Hello," I said, staring blindly into my drink as a flurry of pain swirled through me like microscopic shards of burning ice. None of my decisions and epiphanies over the last few days had done anything to diminish this reaction to his proximity, a burning intensity at the cellular level no rational thought could block or control.

"You're going to be all right," murmured Felicia, watching me closely. I'd had a friend like her in high school too, a beautiful, fucked-up rich girl who'd used me to shield her from the very straight, unattainable boys I lusted after. Back then, she'd been named Pamela, Ted was Brian, and Giselle was Diane, but it didn't matter that I was almost twenty years older now and the cast had changed.

"I'm not going to be all right," I said.

"Buck up, buccaneer," she said, sliding her cold hand onto the back of my neck. My spine immediately lengthened in response, and I stood very straight and tall in spite of myself.

"I don't think Giselle's butt is so great," I said.

"Of course it isn't," said Felicia soothingly without missing a beat. She had gone into full-out Florence Nightingale mode. She patted my own tuxedoed butt. This "event" (a word I could no longer use without quotation marks, even mentally, given its smarmy catchall overuse in corporate lingo, car commercials, weather reports, and culture-vulture slang) was black tie, so I'd borrowed Max's tux, which was a passably okay cut and fit, but by no standards a dashing or imposing one. However, Felicia had recently enjoyed an artificial mood elevator that enabled her to say anything at all, no matter how preposterous, in hopes of helping me through this.

"Why did you let me come to this thing?" I asked her.

Her eyes were hot little black holes, sucking in everything she looked at with a tiny cosmic whoosh. She looked viciously beautiful. The two magazine sharks bristled in my peripheral vision; Felicia was every bit as balletically bony and haughtily attired as they were, but she was on the edge and hypersensitive, while they were circumscribed by convention. She was in tremendous psychic pain; they needed no opiates to get them through the day. They just wanted husbands, but Felicia was beyond such pedestrian female pursuits. This was Felicia's take on things, at any rate, and for once I was inclined to buy into it. Just then I loved her the way a drowning rat loves a piece of driftwood.

"You were very clear about it on the phone last night. Your pride demanded that you put in an appearance. You said you were a Norskehoovian lutefisk-eating aquavit-swilling iceberg, so you could take anything."

I burst out laughing. "I did not say that."

"Hewdy-hewdy," she said. "You're going to miss me when I go into rehab, admit it. I'm turning myself in tomorrow."

I looked into her hard, shrinking pupils, alarmed and excited. For some reason I didn't care to examine, my immediate visceral instinct was to talk her out of it. "What?"

"It's gone far enough. You were right. It's getting old." She nudged me. "It's Norskehoovian-iceberg time."

"Giselle," I said crisply. "Ted."

"Jeremy! Felicia!" Giselle looked simultaneously steely and luscious in a strappy, shimmery peach-colored dress. Her face had been made up to be photographed from afar; her eyes were drowning in mascara; her skin a celluloid-ready surface. I couldn't look at Ted.

"Oh, Teddy," Felicia was saying. "You were never this cute in college, it's not fair."

"You always say the right thing, Felicia," said Ted, laughing, tossing his head.

Double Eurotrash air kisses, girls kissing boys and each other—mwah mwah, mwah mwah, mwah mwah. Women were so small and oddly shaped and soft, I thought as I kissed Giselle, my hands resting lightly on her shoulders so I could maneuver my way around her head. They were so unlikely, such a dubious proposition. Their skin gave so easily; their shoulder bones felt so brittle and frightening. How could Ted have sex with this one? Ted offered me his hand to shake with an earnest, forthright smile. I was tempted to lick his palm or shove his hand into my pants. "Hello, Ted," I said instead. "How are you doing?"

"Very well. How's your sister?"

I was thrown, just for a beat. Amanda; I was staying with her. Ted's face was a mask of friendliness I saw right through but could do nothing to shatter. Did I imagine the resigned little sneer he gave my martini glass? Impotently, I twisted my fingers around its stem and sucked in my stomach, despising myself and him equally. "She's great," I said.

"Are y'all having fun in New York?" Felicia drawled, dripping honey all over everyone.

"I love New York," said Giselle. "I keep begging Ted to move here for a little while, that house is just standing empty. I can't believe we never use it."

Felicia's hand, which had found its way into the crook of my elbow, gave me a little squeeze. "And how's your adorable little *daughter*?"

"You can see for yourself, she's here with her nanny, getting spoiled rotten by the film crew. They worship her. She'll turn into a horrible brat if we're not careful." Giselle was clearly delighted by this. She no doubt wanted her daughter to have everything she herself had lacked as a child.

"Giselle," Felicia said, "you were just great in that movie. I hope you win an Oscar. You certainly deserve one for that performance."

Giselle's glance slid almost imperceptibly and probably unconsciously to me in anticipation of my expected assent, which I was too consternated to deliver on cue, but she covered for me expertly. "Thanks," she said. "It was pure fun to work on that movie. We all had such a blast together, it was like being at some totally fun boarding school or something. Ben and Dan are my favorite—oh, there they are, I'm going to go over and say hello. See you guys in a minute?"

She went off in a dazzling shower of flashbulbs that sounded like the popping and whirring of giant mandible-wielding insects.

"Where's Yoshi?" I asked Ted pointedly.

"I imagine he's around here somewhere." Ted skated his gaze smoothly around the room.

"I'm going to the bar," I said, getting bored with this bootless little game of Ted baiting. "Can I get anyone anything?"

"I'll have one of whatever you're having," said Felicia.

Ted shook his head.

Gary O'Nan stood at the bar, lurking raffishly in a white flannel suit, one hand in the pants pocket, the other holding a drink. His face resembled an iguana's, all slitty eyes and toothy lazy hungry grin, but his expression sharpened when he caught sight of me, as if he'd been lying in wait for me and I'd walked right into his trap when he'd least expected it, before he'd even set it. Standing right next to him, camera slung around his neck, bending his head to listen to a tiny, yappy, sharp-beaked old lady in a pale green dress who bore more than a passing resemblance to my pet bird Juanita and whose face I recognized from the charity benefit photos in the Styles section of the Sunday *Times*, was Phil Martensen.

"Hello," said Gary to me, making it sound like a question. "Jeremy, right?"

"Gary," I said as I held up two fingers and my martini glass to the bartender. "Absolut, very dry with olives and a twist," I yelled over the noise.

The bartender, a big, burly fellow in suspenders, took my glass from me and busied himself.

"Nice cruisewear, Gary," I said.

He raised his eyebrows. "How did you like the movie?"

"Giselle is so talented," I said blandly.

"Isn't she."

We sized each other up in silence for a beat or two.

"Your friend Felicia Boudreaux and I go way back," he said then. "Our grandfathers were *friends*, wink wink, if you catch my drift."

"She mentioned that the other day when she ran into you."

"Did she?" He looked flattered. "Would you mind if Phil and I joined you? I'd love to meet Ted Masterson. I gather he's a friend of yours? Felicia mentioned something at Benito's the other day."

"Come right along," I said, as excited and alarmed again as I'd been when Felicia mentioned rehab, the way I always felt at any unexpected turn of events. Gary tapped Phil on the arm and motioned to me and then to Ted; Phil gave a brisk nod and disengaged himself from his chatty little bird. We waited until the bartender and I had negotiated the transference of two brimming glasses, and then we made our way together over to the spot of floor occupied by Ted and Felicia.

"Felicia," I said, I hoped suavely but feared uneasily, "you remember Phil, of course, and Gary, né Carstairs. Ted, this is Gary O'Nan. Gary writes the gossip column for *Downtown*."

Felicia's eyes widened at me and she shook her head slightly, a quick, emphatic interrogation that meant "What the fuck are you doing?" I gave a quick little hapless shrug that said back, "What could I do? He followed me," and raised my glass slightly to her. With a half-smile I couldn't read, she took a sip of her drink.

"Of course," Ted was saying. "Hello, Phil. Gary O'Nan, I recognize the name, good to meet you."

"How flattering," said Gary. "I'm an enormous fan of your work. *In the Outback* is one of your best."

"That's not what Jeremy told me," said Ted without looking at me. "He thinks I was terrible in it."

"You're kidding," said Gary with a laugh, turning to me. I blinked at him. "Well, friends can be hard on each other."

Was it my imagination, or did he emphasize the word "friends"? I decided it wasn't my imagination. Phil had uncapped his lens and trained it on the four of us, focusing smoothly.

"This martini is perfect," I said, licking my lips. "No one ever talks about the role of the olive in the martini. A martini is only as good as its olives."

Flash went Phil's camera with a click and a mechanical whir.

"Really," said Gary.

"Vodka all by itself has no character. It's inherently bland, it needs that pungent peasanty taste to complete it. The sex, the earth, the dirt, the guts."

"What about the vermouth?" Gary asked blandly.

"No vermouth," I said. "It's the postmodern martini. The martini without the bullshit."

Felicia laughed, her hand steadying my elbow. Phil's camera exploded again.

"Actually," I went on, looking straight at Ted, "it reminds me of the fairy tale where the Cordelia prototype tells her father, the Lear prototype, 'I love you like meat loves salt.' Not understanding, he banishes her. He finds himself at her dinner table years later, only he of course doesn't recognize her. She knows him, though, and deliberately serves him meat without salt. One taste, and he realizes his tragic and horrific mistake. 'I did her wrong,' he says."

"I think I remember that story," said Felicia.

"I've never heard that story," said Ted.

"Sure you have," I said, still looking him straight in the eye. "It's a classic fairy tale."

"I never went in much for fairy tales," he said, looking stonefaced back at me.

"If it were me," I said conversationally, "I would say, 'I love you like vodka loves olives.' "

"I always wondered," said Felicia, "why Cordelia didn't just say it straight out instead. 'Daddy, I adore you with all my heart,' or something like that. Why did she have to be so cryptic about it? Why didn't she defend herself when he kicked her out? Smile, everyone, he's taking another one."

We all flashed our teeth at Phil, who hit the trigger and shot us.

"That's a good point, Felicia," Gary said with a sneaky grin. "Although there wouldn't be much of a story then."

"But really," said Felicia, "if you have something to say, why not just come right out with it? I disagree that there wouldn't be a story. There's plenty of drama in straightforwardness. I'm tired of all these suppressed emotions."

"I think innuendo has its place," said Gary.

Ted's face was as impassive as mine. I felt as if we were playing a high-stakes game of poker and I'd just raised the bet much higher than he'd expected me to, but he was determined not to flinch or lose his cool.

"And years after I was banished," I went on, "one day when he came to dinner at my house without knowing who I was, I'd serve him an empty martini, and realizing his tragic and horrific mistake, he would fall into my arms."

"But why the twist?" said Felicia, sticking her index finger into her martini and pushing the scrap of lemon peel around the glass. It looked like a tiny yellow fish being pursued by a thin pink shark. "We never drink them with twists."

"Well, tonight it seemed appropriate," I said.

"The twist in the tale," Gary said with a glint in his eye. "I'm a Gibson man myself."

"What's the anemic little pale crunch of a pearl onion," I said scornfully, half drunk on adrenaline, "compared to the pithy, salty, meaty olive, the way it rolls around at the bottom of the glass and permeates the whole drink?"

"*Au contraire,* the onion provides both the oily sheen and the underlying bite. No need to sneak in a twist if you want a little tang. A Gibson is the perfect drink."

I was starting to warm to this Gary O'Nan. "Which garnish camp are you in, Ted?" I asked. "Whose team are you on here, the olives or the onions?"

"I try not to drink at all these days," Ted said. His face looked tight and pale, as if it had been rubbed with ice.

"Well, let's see. The other night you were drinking gin martinis with olives, no twist. My friend Max, on the other hand, is a Gibson boy, but he'll do olives if you blow in his ear."

Felicia snorted. "He'll do anything if you blow in his ear."

"Not if *you* do," I said with liquid homo insinuation.

"I'd better go check on Bret," said Ted abruptly, looking at his watch.

"Of course," said Gary, "your daughter. She's so cute, I've seen so many pictures of you all together. You really are the most gorgeous little family. Is it true, the rumor that you and Miss Fleece are in the process of adopting a son?"

"I don't know, I haven't seen anything about it yet in the gossip columns." This had clearly been intended as a jocular parting line, but it came out sounding almost hostile.

"Well," said Gary warmly, not missing a beat as he offered his hand to Ted, who shook it. "I'd be delighted to mention it if you two need some encouragement. It was a great honor meeting you, Mr. Masterson, I've been hoping to meet you for years."

Ted acknowledged all this effusion with a semi-gracious inclination of his head, then pushed his way through the crowd, as far away from me as he could get. Phil bustled in his wake, looking like a determined basset hound.

"Apropos of what I overheard at Benito's the other day," said Gary swiftly in a low voice. "Just say yes or no: You two were an item, and he just dumped you. Am I right?"

I stared at him, unable to stop the horrified delight I felt from spreading across my face. "I have no idea what you're getting at," I said. "And it has nothing to do with his live-in quote-unquote gardener, no matter what he claims."

"Yoshi," Felicia said, grinning foxily.

All three of us spontaneously laughed out loud.

"Okay," Gary said excitedly. "Let me just think aloud for a moment, then, since no one else is saying anything. How does this sound? 'WHICH in-the-closet, very married male A-list action-flick hero, recently attending his movie-star wife's premiere in New York with their five-year-old daughter in tow, dumped his live-in boyfriend of—' How long were you two together?"

Felicia and I looked at each other.

"Jeremy, how long have we known each other?"

"God, what's it been now, ten years since Ted introduced us?"

" '—ten years, whom he dropped for his live-in Japanese gardener, all of which is unbeknownst to his superstar wife?' "

"Why not just give everyone's real names?" Felicia said. "Why all the secrecy?"

"Now now," said Gary. "I believe I'm the gossip columnist here. Blind items can be even more scandalous than names in bold type, depending on the story. Well! Our discussion of cocktails has made me thirsty. I'm going to go get myself another Gibson."

I felt giddy and freaked out and violently famished. "Is there anything to eat at this party?"

"There were a couple boys in vests with trays earlier," said Felicia, waving good-bye, "but I can't see where they went."

"Let the rumor mills begin their terrible swift turning," said Gary, waving good-bye.

"Felicia!" I hissed at her when he'd gone, and clutched her arm. "What made you back me up?"

"Did I mention I'm going into rehab tomorrow? Well, that was the new me, backing you up."

"Oh, my God, Ted is going to—"

"I've had it up to here with precious fake Ted and his precious fake wife and his precious fake daughter and that whole deal. Frankly, he makes me sick, and he treated you wrong and that makes me sick too. Giselle will survive, she's indestructible, she's made out of krypton. You're the one I love, Jeremy, and don't you forget it."

I felt a surprised, warm, goofy urge to laugh hysterically. "You're so full of it."

"Let's get the hell out of here. Let's go to a dive bar."

I glanced at her. "Does rehab include drinking? Please say no."

"I don't have a *drinking* problem," she said.

"Thank God. I was starting to worry."

"I'm just tired of wasting time," she said. "I'm turning forty in three years, and meanwhile all the other girls my age are getting famous for peeing on quilts and misspelling words in blood on maxi pads and hanging it up in galleries. I can't sit by and let this happen. It's time to throw my hat in the ring. I have a plan."

We claimed our coats, went out to the street, and walked along in silence in our premiere finery.

Gripped by a sudden surge of giddy fear, I stopped and stared at her. "Felicia," I said, "what just happened back there?"

"It's not entirely clear. Listen, are you still hungry, or do you just want to drink?"

"I won't be able to eat for days."

We went into a bar called McGee's, bought a couple of vodkas on the rocks from the baggy-faced leprechaun of a bartender, and took them over to an empty booth. I had a terrible feeling at the base of my skull that as long as I was with Felicia I was safe, but the moment I was alone again I'd writhe with horror like a slug doused with salt. What demon had possessed me back there? Whatever it had been, it was gone now, and in its place was a cold hollow demon-shaped space gradually collapsing in on itself.

Felicia said in an annoyed tone, "Gary O'Nan was blowing smoke up your ass with that poofter rumor about my grandfather, you know. Granddad was faithful to Gran all their fifty years together."

"How did you know he told me that?"

"He would," she said darkly. "Do you think he's gay?"

"I don't know," I said. "He's southern. I can never tell with southern men, just like black and Italian men. But he has that sadass, as you pointed out. Gay men try not to let that happen."

She brightened. "Really?"

I stared at her. "Are you *interested* in him?"

"I can't date a gossip columnist. And anyway, I'm sure he's gay."

"He probably is."

The bar was quiet, ecclesiastical. Inside the jukebox, brightly lit behind glass, was an open book with enormous stiff pages. Pink neon lights chased themselves through tubes around the jukebox's shoulders, reflecting diffusely on the wooden tabletops of the booths. The benches we sat on were as hard as pews and shaped like them, and coasters littered the tables like enormous wafers; the whole place had the same odd mixture of tackiness, grandeur, and supplication as a church, with framed photos of wrestlers and baseball stars like saints' heads on the walls, icons and relics—pennants, moose heads, neon beer-signs—above the bar, and the bartender himself, benevolent and all-knowing, dispensing succor and absolution. A vase of fake pink tulips sat by the cash register. Smoke rose slowly, incenselike, from an ashtray on the bar.

I swiveled my head around and looked at Felicia. "Did you and Ted ever sleep together?"

"No way."

"Come on, Felicia. You can tell me now."

"You know we didn't," she said, "that was our deal."

"I don't know what I believe about him anymore."

"Believe me," said Felicia. "About everything. Admit it, I was right about him all along."

I pressed my cold, wet, sturdy little glass against my eyelids, first one, then the other. My face was on fire; underneath this conversation, the knowledge of what I'd just done was building inside me, bubbling and heating up.

"I just exposed Ted," I said.

"Well, of course you did, darling. And it's about time."

"What did I say, exactly?"

"You said: 'I love you like martinis love olives,' " she said sardonically. "Now, what kind of a line is that?"

"I was delirious."

"That's what happens when you try to be something you're not. Not you, Ted." She looked hard at me. "Now we're going to change the subject. I want to talk about what I'm going to do in rehab with all those addicts and drunks saying 'I admit that I do not have the power to resist temptation,' or whatever the hell the first step is. What's the first step? See, I don't even know that much, and here I think I'm going to learn all twelve."

I looked at Felicia, squinting a little, trying to imagine her sitting on a plastic orange molded chair knee to knee with people in an institutional room. She was already starting to slip away. Her face was pale in the light from the small round lamps overhead. She had delicate smudges of purple pigment under her eyes. Her hair, which tonight she wore loose and straight around her shoulders, looked colorless in the washed-out light, and her skin was as flat and white as a Japanese dancer's. In her expression was the inward, deliberate stalwartness that I associated with the faces of very old people, the determination to go ahead with what was necessary and not crumble or complain. What choice did she have, really, if she wanted to go ahead at all? I was relieved that she was quitting, of course, but nevertheless it struck me as a kind of defeat.

PART TWO

On a January afternoon, I wrote the ending of *Angus in Efes*. The past months had been spent paring the thing down from a bloated thousand-page whale to a sleek four-hundred-page shark, and once I'd done this, all that had remained had been to kill Angus off in cold blood at long last, after all these years. All day I had wrestled with the description of his corpse's dismemberment by savage beak and claw, its dispersal through fast-moving avian digestive systems, then its gradual bespattering over the Turkish countryside and back into dust. I had plenty of birdshit on hand to help me get the description just right, but this was helpful only in theory.

I was sitting at an old wooden desk I'd found on the sidewalk, at the computer I'd bought with money earned churning out pulp for Sebastian Philpott's porn magazine. In the kitchen, my roommate, Scott, was making popcorn; I clattered the keys in a syncopated rhythm, with the space bar adding a nice thumping backbeat to the frenzied explosions of corn kernels against the lid of the air popper. Writing Angus's death scene was somewhat anticlimactic after all this buildup and foreshadowing. I scraped my chair back a little and squinted at the screen. I didn't like what I'd written today very much; it reminded me of a florid passage in second-rate magic realism.

I stared out the window for a while as a "commentator" nattered on to the NPR audience about her kooky family. Why did so many of these performance artists and regional storytellers seem to have squeaky voices, speech impediments, or accents? This one, a chirpy Appalachian lisper, had all three. Outside, the sky was a sun-shot, hellish blue. Water towers perched atop buildings looked like oversized potbellied stoves on spindly legs, and shaggy, unwieldy cartoon animals on cliff tops, and rickety jerry-built rocket ships, and other improbable things. In an apartment across the street, a man sat in front of a mirror with a white towel around his neck, lifting hand weights over and over and over. Watching him both soothed and irritated me, as did the NPR commentator.

I deleted a word and substituted another one, moved a sentence, added and deleted a phrase, gradually removing all traces of magic, leaving only the realism.

Suddenly, just like that, I had finished my first novel.

I looked askance at the computer screen for a while. Then I scrolled through the manuscript with the sinking feeling that I'd been missing the real point the whole time I'd been writing the thing, envisioning this so-called "real point" as a red-hot pinpoint right in front of my eyes but too intense and concentrated and searing to look at directly. I was cheered and reassured when a midwestern associate professor came on with his review of a new Balinese folk-rock album with musical excerpts: traditional instruments, augmented by a synthesizer and drum machine. I never ceased to marvel at these reviewers' unilateral, tireless enthusiasm for every world-music release, earnest new novel, and offbeat indie film. It gave me hope and bugged the shit out of me, simultaneously.

I heard the soft rustle of hot popcorn being tipped into a bowl. "Jeremy?" Scott called in his fluted voice. "Want some popcorn?"

"No thanks," I called back through my cardboard-thin door, striving to keep my own voice a good octave beneath his. I'd moved into the smaller of the two bedrooms in his apartment with grave misgivings nothing had made me relinquish yet. Scott was so young, so sunny, so pretty, so at ease in the world of gyms and grope bars and brunches and summer shares, smiling and slithering through his Chelsea days with a casual confidence I'd never even managed to learn to fake, let alone truly feel. He worked in an art gallery; he had a boyfriend as pretty as he was; he took courses at the New School and spent summer weekends in the Hamptons. He was twenty-three years old. I was desperately attracted to him. He made me feel for the first time in my life like a dirty old man, feverishly clattering out stroke stories for *Boytoy* at my dingy gray computer keyboard in my sweaty little blue-lit cave while he swanned blithely around the living room, knotting his silk tie and running a comb through his hair, which was vehemently copious, sun-kissed, and fragrant. Whenever I stood near him in the kitchen, my nostrils flared, inhaling the smell of Agree shampoo or some more au courant, salon-only elixir that cost twenty times as much as Agree but had that same smell of corruptible innocence.

I went out to the living room. The small apartment smelled of hot fluffy corn, but there was not one whiff of butter. Scott ate no fat. He was sitting on the sleek black leather couch, leaning back, one leg slung over a skinny chrome arm, his throat elongating as he tossed kernels into his open mouth. Juanita sat perkily on his forearm, sharing his snack. Squanto may have been bughouse, but Scott had nothing to lose.

Our apartment was decorated in Early Aspirant (by Scott, of course; I had virtually no furniture besides the secondhand futon bed and computer I'd bought and the bookshelf, chair, and desk I'd found on the street). He frequented flea markets and apartment sales. He had spent every cent of his disposable income on a Jazz Age chandelier, a mod multiarmed metal standing lamp, a kidney-shaped coffee table, a faux-zebra armchair, a velvet and mahogany fainting couch, a geometrically interesting hutch with a glass front behind which his collection of vintage glassware was displayed (never used, except by me on the sly; Scott didn't drink alcohol), a rug with brown zigzags on a red background which Scott had boasted was the best deal he'd ever found but which to my admittedly untrained eye looked like Charlie Brown's shirt, and a few big sit-upon pillows so painstakingly, obsessively embroidered, they might have been originally intended for the sultan of Brunei's summerhouse. Our apartment was therefore crammed full of a hodgepodge of different eras and clashing colors, but this place wasn't intended to be anything more than a storeroom. He planned to arrange these things brilliantly some day in his real apartment, the one he was going to buy as soon as he could afford it. He sipped mineral water and nibbled salad in restaurants; he visited his older, wealthier friends at their summer shares (who were no doubt thrilled to host this lovely boy), thus avoiding having to pony up for one himself; he owned a small amount of classic clothing he took extremely good care of; his gym membership was free because his boyfriend Matt was a personal trainer. All of his energies were directed toward having a beautiful home. "I grew up in a trailer park in Gary, Indiana," he'd told me once, "and I ain't never going back. I mean, I'm never going back." This was the sort of detail that made it almost unbearable to spend too much time around Scott; he was a walking compendium of the classic Boy Scout virtues and some others besides. He was modest, brave, unassuming, diligent, generous, kind, honest, clean. He was perfect. Quite literally, he had no flaws that I'd ever been able to ascertain, and I'd looked long and hard. The smallest, meanest, blackest corner of my heart harbored a healthy loathing for him. The rest of me felt otherwise, but this sliver of dislike was just enough to enable me to make a nice living from churning out one scenario after another about a delectable young blond being despoiled by a series of lecherous old sodomites like me.

I perched on the very edge of the fainting couch; I was afraid it would make him anxious to see me inflicting wear and tear on his precious things before he'd begun his real life with them, so I always made an ingratiating show of gingerly apology whenever I came into direct contact with any of them.

We sat that way for a moment. Scott, who seemed to be completely comfortable in his own skin, never seemed to feel itchy, as I did, at protracted welling periods of no conversation between two people in a room. The way I felt around him seemed to be a mirrored reverse of my adolescent awkwardness, which in truth had held a kind of power. His youth made me painfully aware that I was, in the current market, date-stamped to show my limited shelf life to anyone who cared to examine me, but at the same time I viewed him with a kind of condescending envy: He didn't know yet what lay in store for him, but I did.

"I just finished my novel," I said as the silence threatened to become uncomfortable for me.

The idling blankness behind his eyes brightened and began to whir, as if he were a freshly recharged battery-operated thing. "How does it end?"

"My father gets killed by Muslims and eaten by vultures."

"Could you put mine in there somewhere too?"

"What would you like me to do to him?"

Scott laughed. I caught a glimpse of pink gums, broad flat white teeth, a clean tongue. The pit of my stomach went dull with lust. "I don't know. Something really bad. I'm sure you'd write it perfectly."

I wondered, not at all for the first time, whether he was toying with me, whether his perpetual friendliness was a big act. Did he make fun of me to his friends, recount my bumbling attempts to befriend him, imitate my reluctance to sit on his furniture? Abjectness and a surfeit of solitude had made me uncharacteristically and painfully unsure of myself. Lying alone on my bed, listening to Scott and Matt laughing together in Scott's room, I often thought I heard frightening overtones of fun-poking at me. Sometimes when I was talking to Scott, explaining at some length my failed relationship with Ted or describing my former life, I thought I saw in his face a veiled pity, a stifled yawn. I had no idea, really, what Scott thought of me, assuming he paid any attention to me at all beyond the fact that I paid my rent, which wasn't cheap, on time and in cash.

I stood up. "I'm going out," I said briskly. "Do we need anything?"

"Birdseed, I think."

I glanced toward Juanita's magnificent Victorian palace of a birdcage, gilt ribs bowing upward to meet in an arched cupola, with perches, a little doll-sized house with windows for her to peer out of, a mini-fountain she loved to splash around in. Juanita seemed to have accepted Scott as her new owner from the moment she understood that this splendid contraption was hers to live in and that he had provided it. We were out of birdseed because, although I was technically responsible for providing it since she was technically still my bird, I'd passive-aggressively neglected to lay in a fresh supply when the old one ran out because this served her right for switching allegiances when I needed her most. Anyway, she was gorging herself on popcorn at the moment, so any guilt I might have felt at having my faults as a pet owner made manifest was allayed by a fresh surge of resentment. She got to eat popcorn out of Scott's hand.

"Birdseed," I said. "I'll be back later on."

"Bundle up," he called sweetly as I rooted around for my wallet in the pockets of the various pants on my bedroom floor.

Outside, I moved fast. An aerial view of me would have shown me scuttling at the speed of an important beetle. The wind came at me vehemently, as if a giant fan had been set up to blow directly at me over a skating-rink-sized piece of dry ice. The disk containing the fresh porn I'd just written for Sebastian, which I couldn't help thinking of as a semen sample in a test tube, was zipped into the inner pocket of my coat.

I stopped into a liquor store, where I slipped my hard-earned money through the slot in the bulletproof glass and received in exchange a bottle of Laguvulin. Outside again, I escorted it along in its brown paper suit, tucked into the crook of my arm like a little homunculus, my heavy, headless friend.

Seventh Avenue broadened and slowed as it went through the Village and became Seventh Avenue South, which was so wide, an entire row of buildings could have been built along one of its sides and there would still have been plenty of room for the traffic. Tacked onto a midsized skyscraper in the middle distance was the perky red neon Travelers Insurance umbrella, aggravating all its neighbors with its nighttime glow, reminding passersby that into every life a little rain must fall, and if we didn't pay our premiums, it would pound down on our bare heads and drown us.

I had finished my novel. It now had an ending, however provisional and crude. At the back of my head, steering me like a rudder, was this slightly uneasy knowledge. Now there was nothing for it but to send it to an agent; semiliterate hacks did such things all the time, so I could too, although I wasn't quite sure how the whole thing worked.

When the buzzer let me in, I climbed the old wooden staircase of Felicia's building, since her elevator was currently lodged at the twelfth floor, according to the lit-up dial above the doors. I climbed the golden, burnished, bouncy boards, as wide across as I was tall or wider, gently grooved from decades, possibly centuries, of feet. The stairwell had the glowing, neutral, well-worn splendor of elegantly shabby old hotel bars in foreign countries I'd been in.

Wayne answered the door. "Well well," he said with his usual air of laconic anomie, but something seemed off; the skin around his eyes and nose looked peaky and red, and the little fillip of dead-white hair that usually crested over his forehead was drooping, as if he hadn't had the wherewithal to deal with it this morning, or it with him.

"How are you, Wayne?" I asked, following him into the loft. It was extremely hot in here. I shed my coat.

"Me?" he said with a self-deprecating little scowl. "It's Mademoiselle Boudreaux you should be worried about. Maybe you can cheer her up, I've tried everything. I ordered in some chicken noodle soup, I made hot chocolate—"

"Where is she?" I asked.

"Bubble bath," he said, and scuttled to the far end of the loft, where he seemed to be making a big mess with various items from an art supply store.

I detoured over to the kitchen and twisted the top off the whiskey and poured a good slug into two designer glasses that looked like old-fashioned jelly jars. When I knocked on the bathroom door I heard a little cough I took as an invitation, so I opened the door and went in. I saw a pair of pale knees protruding from slightly flat foam in the bathtub. I couldn't see her face, which was hidden by the toilet alcove wall. "Felicia?" I said tentatively.

"Jeremy!" Her knees disappeared, the water heaved gently. Steam rose from the surface in wispy funnels. "What on earth are you doing here?"

"I made it past the three-headed watchdog," I said. "I solved the riddle and he had to let me pass."

"You're mixing up your Cerberus and your Sphinx," she said. "You might as well come and sit on the toilet seat and talk to me."

"Okay," I said with a surge of cozy, sociable happiness, and perched on the plushly cushioned toilet seat. She had created quite a little nest for herself in there. An empty cup and bowl were on the tiled floor by the tub. She was leaning back against an inflatable pillow, her face glistening and rosy, her hair tied up in a scarf. She rearranged the bubbles to conceal most of herself. They made tiny popping noises.

"Hello there," she said.

"It's like a sauna in here."

"I like it hot," she said. "It makes my bones feel warmer."

"I've missed you, Felicia," I said.

"Quite frankly," she said, "you haven't missed a thing. I have never felt so hellishly depressed in my whole life. My therapist wants to put me on Prozac, but I said no more drugs, I'm going to tough it out."

"Good for you," I said. I handed her one of the glasses of whiskey. "I brought you something to warm your insides. I thought we could drink to rehab."

She handed it back to me. "I can't anymore," she said. "I quit all that, remember?"

"Wait a minute," I said, staring hard at her. "I thought you said you didn't have to stop drinking because you didn't have a drinking problem."

"Drinking defeats the purpose of the program," she said impatiently. "Alcohol is a drug like any other."

"No wonder you're depressed," I said. She didn't laugh. "That was a joke, Felicia," I added. I set her untouched glass on the floor by the other dishes and took a swig of my own.

"So," she said, "what are you up to these days? Are you still writing pornography for that creepy guy you knew in high school?"

"Yes," I said with the queasy anxiety I always felt when I thought about Sebastian. "He pays me a lot of money."

"Hang on," she said. "I'm getting out. Avert your eyes, please."

I closed my eyes while she sloshed her way out of the tub. I heard busy toweling sounds, then the slick whir of roll-on deodorant, and then she said, "All right, everything's tucked away in the bathrobe. Let's go sit on the couch and throw spitballs at Wayne."

"I thought you loved Wayne," I said.

"Adore," she said, making a face. "He's been getting on my nerves so much lately, I'd fire him if I just could face training someone else. But the way I'm feeling these days, all I really want to do is sleep. Let's see what's on TV."

We boarded the leather couch, which enfolded us in its billowing depths. I reached for the remote control and switched on her grand old console TV, which had been retrofitted with cable technology, and therefore had crisp, clear reception and something like ten thousand channels to choose from. It throbbed to wavering life, then resolved itself into a close-up of a raven-haired girl with shining red lips and dark wet eyes saying something in Spanish, then a shot of a barrel-chested lad with lips like twin earthworms and a wavy, forceful coif so perfectly sculpted, it could have been made of plastic, like Ken's hair.

"Oh," said Felicia, "my favorite novela. She's going to leave him for his crippled twin brother, I just know it."

"Do you speak Spanish?"

"Not a word," she said. "I invent plots to go with the dialogue. You'd be amazed how often I'm right."

"I already am," I said ruefully.

"Oh, because I told you Ted was a selfish, heartless person just like me? See, it's a gift. Now watch, she's going to slap him, you can tell by the way her eyes are narrowing like that. Watch. I knew it!"

After a few minutes of this, I flicked my way through a sitcom whose laugh track sounded as if the studio audience contained a number of hyenas and gibbons, several car commercials of identically enormous SUVs churning through pristine rain forests, a seventies movie where the men sported bell-bottom-shaped sideburns and the women had waterfall hairdos and false eyelashes, a cheesy, overwrought hip-hop video, and finally a movie starring, to my amazement, Ted.

"Oh my God," Felicia and I said in unison, and looked at each other, laughing.

"Look at him," I said. "He looks so young."

"He was so cute," she said wistfully.

It was one of his early movies, a not-bad romantic comedy about a psychiatrist who fell in love with a suicidal patient. Ted was completely unconvincing as the psychiatrist, but he was so cocky and high-spirited, it didn't matter that he'd been miscast. I nipped at my glass, refilled it, nipped some more.

Gary O'Nan's little item had duly appeared in *Downtown* shortly after Giselle's premiere, only it had turned out to be not so little after all. Other gossip columnists had naturally pounced on this like vultures on Angus; a wild inferno of gossip had then spread through the industry, attracted the notice of the mainstream press, eventually and inevitably reached Giselle herself. Throughout this furor, I'd turned down requests for interviews, offers to sell "my story" to tabloids, rags, glossies, and up-scale magazines alike, shielded my face from the occasional clued-in paparazzo, evaded a couple of reporters intent on getting me to say something, anything at all, so they could quote me in whatever update they were concocting for their columns.

Eventually, as always, their rabid attention moved on to fresher scandals, leaving me reeling a little in its rocking, fluffy wake. The overall public reaction was on the whole supportive of Ted, but it wasn't primarily the public whose reaction Ted had feared. Just before Christmas, Giselle had filed for a legal separation; Ted's parents had no doubt been told or read about it or heard or found out as well. Of course, I felt a certain amount of compassion for him, but most of all I also felt empty, neutral, numb, as if the slate had been, in some indefinable way, wiped clean. I didn't know much about Ted's reaction to any of this. As far as I knew, he hadn't given any interviews. He'd effectively disappeared from the public eye, and I didn't blame him. He and I hadn't spoken since the night of the premiere.

"You know what?" Felicia said suddenly. "I miss him."

"Me too."

"I know you do," she said, her voice syrupy with the newfound empathy she'd picked up at rehab camp.

"I'm not pining for him, Felicia," I said. "That's not what I meant. I've moved on, I just miss his company sometimes." I turned the TV off and looked out the window at the early darkness. "He was a lot of fun."

"Are you taking care of yourself these days?"

"What do you mean?"

"When's the last time you got your hair cut?"

"I'm growing it out," I said. "It's warmer that way."

"When did you last go to the dentist?"

I didn't answer; I couldn't remember.

"See, I knew it. Wayne," she called imperiously, "don't you have a dentist appointment tomorrow?"

Wayne was across the room in a splotch of lamplight on the floor, making something that involved Scotch tape, many small squares of colored paper, and a lot of bending over. He stood up, rubbing his lower back. "At ten," he said. "Just a checkup and cleaning; I shouldn't be long."

"Well, you'll have to reschedule. Call and tell them your slot has been filled by Jeremy Thrane, and make a new appointment for yourself."

Wayne contemplatively fingered his sagging forelock, darting glances around the loft like a cornered rat. "Felicia," he said after a moment, "it's my dentist appointment."

"Well, I know, but you're giving it to Jeremy. He needs it more than you do."

"Don't, Wayne," I said. "I can make my own dentist appointment."

"But you won't," said Felicia. She wrapped herself more securely in her red flannel bathrobe and collapsed against the couch cushions as if being pinned there by gale force winds. "You guys, cooperate with me here, don't be such a pair of pills. Wayne, make that call and give Jeremy the information. And Jeremy, ten tomorrow, don't you dare oversleep."

Wayne and I exchanged a look before he stalked off to get the cordless phone from the kitchen counter. A moment later I could hear him muttering to someone I surmised was the receptionist.

"What's got into you?" I asked her.

"This is a hard time for me," she said. "A transitional time. I'm learning how to be in the world again. Remembering how to manage daily life on my own. And for some reason, it helps to think about someone else for a change. Listen, are you eating enough fruits and vegetables? I've got a juicer now, I could have Wayne whip you up a—"

"That's okay," I said. "Wayne's done enough for me today. Anyway, I'm going over to Sebastian's for dinner."

"I'm worried about you," she said mulishly.

I regarded her with skeptical amusement. "You are? You haven't returned my calls in three weeks."

"I know," she said without apology. "It's just one of those daily things, using the telephone as a clean and sober person. I haven't quite mastered that skill yet, but I think about you a lot. I would have Wayne call you and tell you, but I know you can't stand him."

Wayne and I exchanged another brief look from across the room. He had finished his phone call and was once again taping the colored squares of paper together.

"Have you heard from Ted since Giselle kicked him out?" I asked, trying to sound casually curious, like an old friend without an agenda. "Where is he living now?"

"I have no idea," said Felicia. "I called him from rehab same as I called you, to, you know, apologize for my bad behavior and all that. I haven't spoken to him since I got out. I don't think he's very pleased with either one of us. He seems to think I had something to do with that gossip column, but where he got that idea I haven't a clue. He said there was no apology I could make that would atone for what I'd done to him. No, he's not feeling too warmly toward us at all. Do you want a glass of water or something? You're sweating."

"That's because it's stifling in here! Why don't you turn down the heat? And it's so dark."

"Are you too hot over there, Wayne?" she called.

"Not really," came his snotty little voice.

"And you have enough light to see what you're doing?"

He pretended not to hear this.

"I feel sort of bad about Ted," Felicia went on. "We shouldn't have done that, Jeremy, it was wrong. He was our friend. I'm resolving my trust issues right now; my therapist thinks I pushed Ted away preemptively, before he could push me away, because I have abandonment issues from when I was a little girl and my parents would go on those long trips without me. I tried to explain all this to Ted when I called him, but I don't think he heard me at all."

"We did nothing wrong," I said firmly. "We were overheard, remember? Gary knew everything. We just filled in a couple of blanks for him, that's all."

She plucked at the sleeve of her robe, unraveling a little thread and worrying it with her thumbnail. "Well, I see it differently now," she said.

"Is that why you've been avoiding me?"

She gave me a coy look from under her eyelashes. "Come on now, Jeremy, don't be like that. I haven't been avoiding you."

Filled with a sudden, overwhelming need to get out of there, I looked at my watch and saw that I wasn't due at Sebastian's for almost an hour. "Whoa, it's late!" I said. "I'd better go. I just dropped in for a minute, I didn't mean to stay this long."

"Really?" she said contritely. "Come again soon. I'll make you a fresh juice. That's one of the touchstones I use to help me leapfrog through each day. I need them right now. A bubble bath every afternoon, that's another one."

"Some other people might use a job, grocery shopping, paying bills, those sorts of things," I said.

"I know," she said. "And you know what? They're lucky; I have to find my own touchstones and it's not always that easy. I don't care how spoiled that sounds, it's true."

Wayne handed me a slip of paper as I was leaving. "The appointment was for X rays too," he said poisonously. "Upper and lower."

"Sorry," I said. I tried to look apologetic, but a triumphant smile stole over my face instead; I couldn't prevent it, although I had no idea what it was doing there.

I bounced down the stairs, plunged into the ice-blue evening and walked down Church Street to the tip of Manhattan with the wind blowing my coat against my spine. I stood for a while by the railing along the Battery promenade near the ferry terminal, looking out over the water at the freighters and pleasure-cruise ships strung with lights. After a while, without premeditation, I sat on a chilly bench, cradling the whiskey bottle in the crook of my arm, and began to sing as loudly as I could, since there was no one around to take me for a drunk or a lunatic, in a soulful baritone that sounded almost exactly like Angus's: "In Dublin's fair city, where girls are so pretty, 'twas there that I first met sweet Molly Malone. She wheeled her wheelbarrow through streets broad and narrow, crying 'Cockles and mussels, alive, alive oh.' "

My father had taught me the lyrics to this and a lot of other old, mostly forgotten songs; he'd learned them all as a boy, up in the attic in his family's house outside of St. Paul. He'd found a box of his grandfather's old glee club sheet music and gradually memorized the songs, learning them note by note. Knowing this told me both everything and nothing about him.

"She was a fishmonger, and that was no wonder, her mother and father were fishmongers too. They wheeled their wheelbarrows, through streets broad and narrow, crying 'Cockles and mussels, alive, alive oh.' " During the late sixties and early seventies, my father and his brotherhood of other crazy Marxist lawyers, Ed and Murray, had hung out in San Francisco jazz clubs. I imagined them hunkered together around a table, buying each other rounds of whiskey and beer till closing time, then smoking joints in the car on the way to the all-night bowling alley. "She died of the fever, and nothing could save her, and that was the end of sweet Molly Malone. Now her ghost wheels her wheelbarrow, through streets broad and narrow, crying 'Cockles and mussels, alive, alive oh.' " I probably would have liked my father a lot if I'd known him, despite everything, and he might have liked me too: Maybe that was the crucial thing I'd left out of my novel.

At twenty to seven, I headed into the wind and walked back up to Sebastian's building, which was just three blocks west of Felicia's. I arrived exactly on time, almost to the minute. My saliva had frozen on my lips and the bulb at the end of my nose was a shining, multifaceted red jewel I could have snapped off and had set in gold filigree and hung around my neck.

"Jeremy!" Sebastian cried when I emerged from the elevator, which gave directly into his foyer since he occupied the entire top floor. Warm air enveloped me immediately, invitingly, not stiflingly like the air at Felicia's. I gave myself over to it as if to an embrace.

"I'm so glad you're here," he said, beaming. "Let me take your wraps." One of the things I had to like about Sebastian was his inability to hide what he was feeling; in spite of myself, I found it heartwarming to be greeted with such frank enthusiasm by my putative employer. He hooked my coat and scarf onto a peg in the entryway while I stowed the whiskey underneath; Sebastian didn't drink hard alcohol. "I hope you're hungry. I'm making corn bisque and crab omelets."

"That sounds good," I said, suddenly ravenous.

"I opened a bottle of Cabernet, it's been breathing for twenty minutes and should be ready to drink about now, but if you'd rather something a little more, oh, I don't know, what do I know about wine? The man at the store said it was good, and so I laid in a case or two."

"Cabernet sounds fine," I said with a straight face. I'd learned the hard way that Sebastian disliked being laughed at for his habit of apologizing for his generosity. He didn't say so, exactly; he just retreated momentarily into an affronted silence that lasted only until his natural earnest ebullience reasserted itself.

He ushered me to the low divan by the fake crackling electric log in the fake fireplace and seated me, then disappeared for a moment. The prospect of a glass of Sebastian's costly, exciting wine cheered me so much, I wanted to clack my heels together in a little jig, but I stayed still, and waited quietly.

"Here you are," he said as he handed me a glass. "If you don't like it, just say so and I'll open something else. But before we get down to it, why don't I just run your new work upstairs."

"It's in my coat pocket," I said. "Let me get it, just a sec."

He was already halfway to the foyer. "No, no, that's all right," he said, reaching into my coat.

"The inner pocket," I told him resignedly, swallowing my annoyance. In an odd way, Sebastian's pushy largesse felt less genuinely considerate than Felicia's frank selfishness.

"I'll take a look at it after dinner," said Sebastian, coming briskly down the stairs. "Something to look forward to." He sat on an ottoman with his usual ungainly decorousness, crossing his legs at the ankles and slumping his spine. "How is the wine?"

"It's good," I said, an intentional understatement.

He dipped his tongue into his glass, then made a series of little wet nursing-kitten sounds. He looked like a big cartoon boy; his face was as soft and featureless as a boiled lima bean, his body as squishy and formless as a pastry tube. He lacked the sarcous density that would have lent dignity to his passions and enthusiasms. Tonight he wore a navy-blue turtleneck and baggy brown corduroy trousers. His chestnut-brown hair sprang in wiry clumps from the bald spot on the crown of his head.

"Oh!" he said suddenly. "The hors d'oeuvre plate. I'll be right back."

He set his glass down, disappeared, then came back bearing a hexagonal black lacquered tray. I knew this tray well. He hauled it out and loaded it with little bits of color-coordinated food every time I set foot in his place. Tonight it held small mounds of gherkins, pickled beets, green olives, red-dyed pistachios, green grapes, and tiny teardrop-shaped tomatoes.

"Now," he said, settling himself again on his ottoman, "tell me what you've been up to! And then I want to talk about something else. I have a surprise for you."

"I finished my novel today," I said.

"To you, then!" He held his glass high in the air. I lifted mine a little, and we drank. "Will you send it to your agent?"

"I don't have an agent yet. I have to find one."

"But I thought—the script I just read was—"

"That's my movie agent," I said, "and anyway, that script is a piece of—"

"A masterpiece! I finished it this morning. I read it in one sitting; I could not put it down."

"Well, thank you, that means a lot to—"

"That's my surprise!" he said. "I'm going to bankroll it. What do you call it, produce it. I spoke to your agent today about it. The ending is so beautiful—" He stopped, staring intently at me, so intently I couldn't look away from him, or squirm.

"I—well, thanks," I said, caught mid-munch on a salty little gherkin. "You don't think it's too weird and absurd? And pointlessly kinky?"

"First of all, not one of those qualities is even remotely negative, in my opinion. And second, no! It's not too anything, it's even better than your writing for *Boytoy*, and that's saying a lot. I always admired your writing; even back in high school I knew you were marked for greatness."

Back in high school he had acutely embarrassed me with his unasked-for admiration. Now, twenty years later, with money he'd made from his porn rag, he was planning to produce a script I'd written in a week. In some odd way, this struck me as perfectly appropriate.

I cracked open a pistachio with my teeth and put the lurid halves of its shell on my knee for lack of anywhere better. Sebastian leapt up, fetched an ashtray from the marble mantelpiece, and set it on the floor by my foot. As he did so, I felt a brief unconscious fear that he would try to touch me in some way and braced myself, but without a glance in my direction he returned to his ottoman. I relaxed and dropped the nutshell into the ashtray, which was shiny, pink, and swan-shaped, and could have been the genitalia of some theme-park Disney character.

"Well, that's what I think, anyway, for whatever my opinion is worth," Sebastian added somewhat stiffly without looking at me, as if he had discerned my mental recoil from him and was wounded, not by the implicit rejection, but by my lack of trust in his utter propriety where I was concerned. "I know I'm not the most literary man on the planet, but I know what I like, and it's stood me in good stead all these years."

"Another toast, Sebastian." I lifted my glass. "To bachelor bliss."

Sebastian looked startled for an instant, as if he'd been expecting me to say something very different, then said somewhat lugubriously, "To bachelor bliss, then." When he leaned over to bash his wineglass against mine, he almost spilled some on the old Persian rug. He got tipsy implausibly fast, after several sips in fact, which led me to think he was highly suggestible, so the smell and taste of alcohol induced a psychosomatic giddiness in him.

I noticed that he was looking at me searchingly.

"Are you all right, Jeremy?" he asked suddenly.

Now it was my turn to be startled. "Why is everyone asking me this?"

"You seem sad," he said simply. "About everything in general, or something in particular, I don't know which it is."

I considered this for a moment; my instinctive urge to say something flippant met a stronger reluctance to deflect this attentive empathy, a too-rare commodity these days. The past few months had been filled with soul searching and scrambling for me, two highly incompatible activities. My mother was understandably taken up with her own troubles; Max and Fernando had vanished into a cloud of torrid eroticism; Felicia was sequestered with Wayne and her touchstones; Amanda had just returned from a protracted tour with her band; Ted was gone.

"Maybe it's both," I said in a rush. "I have a feeling lately. It's hard to explain; it's as if I'm not living life to the fullest, not making the most of my time on earth, swimming in the top six inches of the ocean, if that makes any sense."

"You're lonely," he said. "Of course it makes sense."

"I am lonely, it's true," I said. "But you know, I've never been lonely before, even when Ted was gone for months at a time. Somehow my solitude was always infused with him even when he wasn't there."

"Yes," said Sebastian. "I can see how that could be the case."

"I don't like this at all," I said. "In spite of all my daily activities, I'm bobbing along up here, nothing is forcing me to go deeper, or I don't have enough ballast. I know there's a whole other world down there; I can feel it, but I can't get to it."

"You're referring to your bachelor bliss, aren't you, and it isn't bliss at all. It manifests itself as an internal problem, a depression, an emptiness, but really, the ballast you're talking about is wholly external."

"Maybe," I said skeptically, wondering how he always managed to worm out of me my deepest, more fiercely guarded feelings. No one else had this effect on me, not even Max or Felicia, my two oldest and closest friends. I supposed it was because Sebastian's own complete lack of guile made it seem futile to try to mask any feelings of weakness out of pride or fear of exposure, so I had nothing to fear from him. Or maybe my newfound loneliness was making me say and do things I wouldn't ordinarily have done.

"You are in mourning, Jeremy," said Sebastian. "It'll pass, with time."

"But this feeling also has to do with getting older, the sense that there's only limited time left in my life to do the things I want to do." A distressingly plaintive note had crept into my voice; I forced myself to stop talking. This sort of disclosure was not something I normally allowed myself to make even to myself. Self-pity, I had found, fed on itself; it was host and parasite rolled into one.

"We think we know we're going to die someday, but we don't really," Sebastian said crisply. "It's like final exams in college. We're never really prepared for it, no matter how old we are when it happens, and meanwhile we fritter away our study time." He brushed his hands on his trousers and stood up. "Would you like to move to the dining room and eat our supper? I'll just whip up the omelets, and then we'll be all set. Now, I used canned crabmeat, I hope you don't mind; the crabs at the fish market looked a little seedy, and the canned stuff is not bad. Come sit at the table while I cook."

I followed Sebastian over to the far end of the loft where the kitchen and dining area were, and sat at the table while he went around the island and got down to business, pulling things out of the refrigerator.

"I'm serious about your script," he said, cracking eggs into a red bowl and poking them with a whisk to break the yolks. "I know you think this is idle chatter, but I mean business."

"Well, I hope you won't blame me when it turns out to be a losing proposition."

"Ah, but it's not going to be a losing proposition," he said as he flicked a pat of butter into the hot omelet pan.

"I hope you're right."

The air filled with the rich, melting smell that had been so patently absent from my apartment this afternoon. Sebastian poured the beaten eggs into the pan with a sizzle of fat, then busied himself opening the can of crabmeat. "Do you like capers?"

"I do."

"You'll find some in your omelet, then. I think it goes extremely well with crab."

I watched him occupy himself at the stove for a while. Poor Sebastian. Whether I liked it or not, he and I were the same kind, sensitive plants who felt everything very strongly, our lily-white hands clasped to our frail chests, earnestly importuning: "Lord, I do fear/Thou'st made the world too beautiful this year/My soul is all but out of me. Let fall/No burning leaf—prithee, let no bird call." My old neighbor Dina Sandusky was another such teabag who hadn't steeped quite long enough in the pot. So was Felicia, and so, come to think of it, were all the people I tended to attract, except Ted. In a science fiction movie, our species would have been depicted as gelatinous quivering forms with two giant rubber eyeballs on springs, gaping mouths with oversized taste buds, extruded bundles of nerve endings, our primary functions gustatory, aesthetic, contemplative, and emotional. What good were we? Maybe we served as processing plants for the psychic by-products of commerce, politics, advertising, technology, the excess emotions of Type-A super-achievers with no time to deal with such useless things themselves; their raw passions and inchoate yearnings left them and found us, blew across our inner landscapes, strummed the aeolean harps of our rib cages, caused seismic tremors in our brain pans.

"Why are you so nice to me, Sebastian?" I asked in a rush of claustrophobic irritation.

He kept his back to me. "Why do you think?"

"Maybe you need someone to fuss over," I said snidely. "Maybe you're the one who's lonely."

"Do I fuss over you?"

"A little bit, you do."

"How so?"

"You do things for me all the time, even though I don't ask you to, and I give you nothing in return. I've never cooked you dinner, for example, and you pay me much too well for the trash I churn out for you. It makes me uncomfortable. Are you planning to call in your chits anytime soon, or what?"

There was a long silence during which he fussed at the stove with the spatula, added things to the omelet, stirred something in a pot. I started to think that I'd hurt his feelings. I was clearing my throat to halfheartedly apologize, when he set a bowl of golden, savory-smelling soup on the table in front of me and said, "I'm not going to tell you what you seem to want to hear, which I suppose is something along the lines of 'I need you as much as you need me,' which of course is true, but what an utterly ridiculous thing to have to say aloud to another adult. It should be obvious. When did you become so suspicious of others? Now eat your soup."

"Aren't you having any?"

"I'll sit down in a minute. Don't wait, I hate it when my guests let their food get cold out of what they think is politeness. It's not polite, it's silly. Eat."

Guests? Who were his other guests? I tasted the soup. It was velvety and rich, with a smoky, subtle array of flavors under the robust potato-and-corn base. "What's in this?" I asked.

"Oh, let's see, Worcestershire sauce, a bay leaf, a pinch of fresh thyme, minced celery and leeks, a drop of Tabasco, white pepper. But the secret ingredient is Mrs. Dash, although it's not a secret anymore now. I'm putting some in the omelet too." He set a cutting board with a fresh loaf of bread and a knife on the table, and a plate with a hunk of cheese. "Help yourself."

I felt a bottomless hunger at the first taste of the corn bisque. I polished it off before Sebastian sat to eat his own soup, then swabbed out my bowl with a hunk of the bread. He refilled my bowl as soon as he saw it was empty. "I like to cook for enthusiastic eaters," he said.

"Who else do you cook for?" I asked, trying not to sound insultingly skeptical.

"My other writers," he said as he slid half an omelet onto my plate and sat across from me. "My friends." He looked at me through the candle flames wavering between us. The points of fire gave his eyes strange, lionlike glints. He tasted the soup, nodded, and poured us both more wine.

"You don't know this," he said thoughtfully, "and you may be shocked to learn it, but as it happened, I was an extraordinarily beautiful boy. Until puberty, that is. Older men fawned over me, and boys my own age vied for my attention. Gay and straight, they all wanted to be my friends. I was golden, especially by English standards, a little Adonis."

"You were?" I kept my tone perfectly neutral, with some effort.

"Then my thyroid began to fail, and my entire physiognomy changed. If I hadn't been so sick, and so devastated by my sudden ugliness, I would have found the experience fascinating, from a biological standpoint. It coincided with our move to the States. I turned thirteen, learned to jerk off, became interested in practicing my new skills with other boys, but horrifyingly, at the same time, almost overnight, I turned into a gargoyle. I also found myself in a strange country where the children were well built and healthy, had perfect teeth, and could be very, very cruel. Much more so than in England, where everyone looks a little queer, by which I mean odd."

"Didn't the medication help?"

"Oh, well, I take it every day, of course, but it does nothing for me aesthetically. I wonder, now, how much of it had to do with inevitable genetic predisposition and how much was the disease. In any case, my adolescence was—" He quirked his lips. "Well, you knew me then, you saw how it was for me. You were the only person in the school who didn't make my life a living hell. We each had to keep our distance from the other for obvious self-protective reasons, didn't we; in a school like ours it was preferable to go it alone than to band together and risk being branded beyond doubt. But I sensed that we were kindred spirits, even then, and as it turned out, I was right."

"Well," I said, deeply uncomfortable.

"And although you must have known, because it was so painfully obvious," he went on, "I was obsessed with you in high school."

"I didn't know," I said in a panic, "don't worry about it."

"No, not obsessed exactly; that implies a neurotic attachment that goes beyond the rational. The truth is, I loved you."

I looked away from him. I didn't see what he was hoping to accomplish here.

"I felt I understood you," he went on as if he couldn't stop now that he'd launched into this soul-baring speech, as if its momentum were fueled by the uncorking of the energy it had taken to keep all these feelings inside him. "A silent sympathy, if you will. I never hoped for anything in return. So when you ask—" He covered his face with both his hands and rubbed it hard, then looked at me again and said, "When you ask me why I 'fuss over you,' as you put it, that is the reason. I see no reason to hide this from you anymore; anyway, it's no doubt become fairly evident."

I put my fork down on my plate carefully. He wasn't wearing his glasses, I realized. It gave his face a naked look, made his eyes even more pronounced and gave them an eerie incandescence, like a leprechaun's or a bobcat's.

"I'm not as foolish as I may seem. I know you lived with Ted Masterson for ten years and may still be in love with him. I know what I look like. I have so much to offer you, but I expect nothing from you, believe me. I won't call in my chits, as you put it; that would imply that this has all been a strategic game on my part, and I assure you it's nothing of the sort."

I gulped some wine, then forced myself to meet his luminous, intent, rapt, bulging eyes. I could hear my own heartbeat in the immense silence. His loft was a shadowy, cavernous space; we were huddled together in a pool of light. The gigantic multipaned windows that ran the length of one wall reflected our small, wavering patch of light, our two pale faces; beyond the reflection, superimposed on it, glimmering lights from faraway buildings, a dense water of clouds, the slow twinkling crawl of a passing airplane or satellite in the hard, cobalt sky. I swallowed. "Well," I said glumly. "Thank you for telling me. I'm flattered."

"Adolescent love is a strange phenomenon. It's like no other love I've ever experienced, it's hard-wired into my brain. Did you love someone in high school?"

"Yes," I said reluctantly.

He waited, watching me over the rim of his wineglass.

"I did," I added. I looked at my watch, just a flick of my eyes.

"May I ask whom?"

"Well, it doesn't really matter who," I said, embarrassed. The silence grew; he didn't look away from my face. His expression was gentle and accepting. "Okay—it was Brian Heydorn," I blurted out finally, trying to laugh.

"Brian *Heydorn*!" He looked disappointed. "But that's so obvious, Jeremy."

"He was beautiful," I said. "Probably the most beautiful thing I'd ever seen in my life. It's hard-wired. If I met him today, even if he were a potbellied, bald used-car salesman, which he probably is, I'd still faint with joy if he laid a hand on me."

"I would faint with joy," Sebastian said quietly, quizzically, "if you laid a hand on me."

I cringed. "Have you been in love with other men besides me?" I asked him through the lump of dread in my throat.

He laughed, a little sadly. "Of course I have. I'm not a hermit or a virgin. I've had three relationships, as you Americans call them."

"You're an American, Sebastian; you've lived here most of your life."

"One ended in early death," Sebastian went on as if I hadn't spoken, "the second in an amicable separation, and the third in anguished heartbreak." He paused, looked off into the middle distance, then recollected himself and said briskly, "Have you finished your supper? Can I offer you some coffee? No? Come upstairs with me now. We'll have a look at the work you've done, and I'll pay you for it. I've got a pear tart for dessert, and some Calvados I've been saving."

Upstairs in the office, staring at the light-gray computer screen with its slowly pulsing cursor, Sebastian read aloud my first-person description of sex with a character who resembled my roommate Scott in every particular, down to the waxed skin around his nipples and the cute little pout of his lips when he was thinking; I'd pounded it onanistically onto my keyboard as I watched Scott stripping to the waist, just back from a recent bout at the gym, then toweling his hair, shirtless after his shower.

Sebastian read this new scene out loud, enunciating as perfectly as if he were reciting Shakespeare, with a fruity British accent. My *Boytoy* style was modeled on the crisp, declarative, manly, Hemingway-colored prose of adventure stories, those heterosexual male-bonding outdoorsy against-the-elements fantasies: But of course, instead of ice climbing, bear wrestling, or sailing through a hurricane, my male heroes wrestled each other, mounted each other's bucking bodies, and rode out the storms of their raging passions. The style adapted itself beautifully to gay sex, if only because it had always been about gay sex. I had simply, or so I imagined, stripped the masks and opacities from it, and shown it for what it was.

I stood awkwardly by in the gloom, waiting for Sebastian to finish reading, afraid my scene would ignite his unrequited yearning and cause him to embarrass us both in some way. My own words sounded unbearably silly to my ears; I hoped my novel wasn't equally hackneyed, but greatly feared that it was, or worse.

"This one isn't the best I've done," I said when he finished. "I wrote it in a hurry. I've been working so hard to finish my novel."

"It's wonderful, Jeremy," Sebastian said, without looking up from the screen. "In fact, I have to confess that I read your stories for my own—pleasure. I find them doubly erotic simply because you wrote them. I read them and think of you."

"Whoa," I said. "Please don't tell me that."

"I apologize," he said mournfully.

"You have to admit it's a creepy thing to say."

"Of course. I overstepped my bounds, I see that."

"I'd better get going," I said.

"Your money—"

"You can pay me another time."

"I was sure you'd be flattered," he said with anguish. "I meant it as a compliment."

"Oh, I think it's very flattering," I called over my shoulder on my way down the stairs. "Thank you, Sebastian. I'll let myself out." I went to the entryway by the elevator and fumbled my hands into the sleeves of my coat. "Thanks for dinner," I called up to him. "It was delicious."

"I'm sorry," he called from the top of the staircase. "I didn't mean to disgust or repel you, it's the last thing I wanted, believe me."

"I believe you," I said.

As I stepped into the elevator, I expunged from my brain a gloom I decided was purely circumstantial and associative; it belonged back there with Sebastian, and not with me, so I left it hanging in his entryway. My mind washed of dolor, deliberately focused and calm, I went out. The sky let down whirling snow like a breast giving milk in one of my mother's poems. I ducked my head and hurled myself into the wind tunnel of sidewalk as snowflakes hurled themselves at me kamikaze-like out of the pinkish, glowing darkness. Snow was so rare now, a throwback to an earlier era, back when winters here were harsh and cold. On my way to the subway station I hummed my way through "The Foggy, Foggy Dew" and "Clementine." It was Angus's Dead-Girl Song Night: She died of the fever and nothing could save her, she fell into the foaming brine, and the only only thing that I did that was wrong was to keep her from the foggy, foggy dew. These songs and the snow inspired the same kind of jittery nostalgia: Both were emblems of lost eras, but whether they had been better eras than this one was doubtful. I didn't miss my father any more than I missed blizzards, but, like all lost things, the memory of them had a certain poignant resonance, if only because they were gone.

Early the next morning, I got out of bed and went to the kitchen to make a pot of coffee. Scott must have gone to Matt's; the apartment was empty. While the coffee brewed, I poured some of the sunflower seeds I'd bought on my way home last night into the dish in Juanita's cage. She immediately got down to serious work on them, cracking and nibbling and dropping empty seed husks, every now and then cocking a suspicious eye at me, as if she were wondering what the hell I was doing watching her; didn't I have anything better to do?

I wandered back into the tiny kitchen and put together a sandwich of headless sardines lying snugly alternated, top to bottom, between two pieces of rye toast, anchored in place with a thick layer of mustard. When the coffee was ready, I breakfasted in my room, sitting on my bed while I ate, listening to Ted Hawkins and looking around at the half-folded shirts tumbling out of stacked milk crates, boxes of books, an old boom box on the floor with a pile of cassettes.

Scott invested all his money in permanent artifacts, things of beauty and style he would have forever; I spent mine on ephemera, food and drink, nights out, creature comforts that only made me fatter and taxed my liver and brought me closer to death. I didn't care about things and never had. A forty-dollar bottle of something good pleased me more than a forty-dollar vintage lampshade, even though one was gone in a week and the other could some day be handed down to Scott's adopted Chinese daughters, who were also part of his long-term plans.

When Ted Hawkins sang his first line, I felt a goose-bumpy happiness that lasted for the rest of the album. When it was over, I flipped the cassette and listened to Nick Drake. I closed my eyes and gave myself over to the warbling, melancholy music, a roiling tributary that fed right into the river of sadness I was floating down. Both of them, Nick with his princesses and Ted with his green-eyed girls, their pristine guitars, yearning lyrics, pure voices, perfectly suited my mood this morning, this almost pleasurable dread of a dominatrix of a dental technician who would soon assault me with her powerful forearms and stainless-steel torture tools and half-hostile injunctions to floss, come in more often, brush more thoroughly. The anticipation of the sound of that pointy, picklike scraper in my skull as it dislodged calcified chunks of tartar and caught on my tender blood-rich gum tissue was enough to curl my toes. But if I didn't go to Wayne's damned dentist, I would never be able to visit Felicia again as long as he worked for her. He had fulfilled his end of the deal. If I failed to uphold mine, he would lord this over me every chance he got.

I flipped through my old Norton anthology until I found Yeats, purveyor of bee-loud glade and pilgrim soul, then adjusted my spine against the wall for a pre-dental anodyne of his serpentine, earthily mystical wisdom. I settled on "Crazy Jane Speaks to the Bishop," and after a moment, my eyes began to boggle slightly as they tried to pluck each word from the page and pin it to my brain.

> *"Fair and foul are near of kin,*
> *And fair needs foul," I cried.*
> *"My friends are gone, but that's a truth*
> *Nor grave nor bed denied,*
> *Learned in bodily lowliness*
> *And in the heart's pride.*

> *"A woman can be proud and stiff*
> *When on love intent;*
> *But Love has pitched his mansion in*
> *The place of excrement;*
> *For nothing can be sole or whole*
> *That has not been rent."*

My loins thus girded with the morning's neuralgic brew of melancholy song, the faint fishy aftertaste of breakfast, four ibuprofen tablets, and Crazy Jane, I arrived ten minutes late for my appointment and landed shortly thereafter in the frightening chair with a steadily beating heart and a resolute smile.

"Hello," a youngish woman said on a singsong as she entered with a brand-new chart and clipped the paper bib around my neck with the little metal fastener that looked like a pair of toothy alligator jaws. "I'm Lorraine. Let's have a quick look at your teeth before we get to work. Let's see . . . my goodness, it's been a while."

"Five years," I said. "Maybe six."

"You've got a lot of tartar in here."

"I don't have insurance," I said in a feeble attempt to fling myself on her mercy. "I scrimp and save to come as often as I do."

"I know, don't get me started, the medical system in this country. But for your own good you should try to come twice a year. Think of it like—do you smoke?"

"No."

"Oh, good for you. I'm up to almost two packs a day and I'd smoke more if I had time. Well, like coffee and a bagel, then. Try putting two dollars a day in a jar." Lorraine had a husky Long Island–accented voice, dark eyes, warm hands. I liked her for all these things and also for her air of breezy candor, which I hoped would translate into gentleness with my gums.

"Maybe I'll try that," I said, leaning back and closing my eyes, settling into the mint-green vinyl-covered chair. The air smelled faintly of drill-burned teeth, antiseptic soap, and fluoridated mouthwash, a smell that made my gums ache gently. I had forgotten how comfy these dentists' chairs were. This one had excellent neck support and spinal curvature so every square inch of my body was met with perfectly calibrated tensile resistance. I felt like an astronaut ready for takeoff.

"Open wide," she said a moment later, her masked face hovering above mine, mirror and sharp tool in her Latex-gloved hands, which were poised over my mouth. I opened my mouth wide until my lips stretched and I got a sharp crick in my jaw. The protracted picking and scraping that followed was neither entertaining nor pleasant, but it bothered me less than I'd expected. The ibuprofen protected my nerve endings, and the words "nothing can be sole or whole that has not been rent" ran in a semiconscious stream through my sub-brain in Nick Drake's voice and protected the rest of me, and pretty soon Lorraine was handing me a little paper cup half full of blue fluid and saying, "Go ahead and rinse out, and then we'll polish you."

As I spat bloody tissue and chunks of tartar into the sink, she fitted her drill attachment with a little round pad, and soon she was buzzing it all over my teeth, which made me want to giggle uncontrollably, or sneeze, and made my eyes tear up from a joyful surge of relief, almost euphoria, but there was an interpersonal component I couldn't identify at first. I lay trusting, limp, my head cradled in her arms, my ears very near her breasts in a comical echo of the pietà. What was this feeling? I'd had it before, I remembered it clearly, I associated it with spring, excitement, sex, promise, anticipation of something soul-stirringly, violently wonderful.

This burst of pheromonal giddiness, yes, I remembered now, it was associated with the very existence of another person, an urge to fling myself headlong about the room. Falling in love, that was the feeling. "Love has pitched his mansion in the place of excrement." My body, quite independently of my heart or brain or any real circumstances beyond the ticklish scrubbing-bubble action of this little brake pad of a tooth polisher, seemed to think that I was falling in love, and so my brain was synthesizing the proper biochemical drugs. "For nothing can be sole or whole that has not been rent." And suddenly Ted's face filled my mind. I almost heard his voice. I felt almost as if he'd just walked into the room.

"Sorry, am I hurting you?" Lorraine asked, dabbing solicitously at my eyes with a Kleenex.

"No, not at all," I stammered. The sudden image of Ted had sparked a neuron-firing shower of almost unbearable intensity. Ted, I thought again, and like magic it happened again, a fresh explosion of cranial fireworks, light particles like a chrysanthemum's petals bursting and floating downward through my mind's dark sky. "Learned in bodily lowliness and in the heart's pride." My unconscious mind had apparently realized that Ted was single, free, out of the closet, available now in a way he never had been before as long as I'd known him, and it was now bringing this to my startled attention here in the dentist's office, as a message attached to the tooth-polishing machine. "Fair and foul are near of kin, and fair needs foul . . ." This was humiliating and sad, in equal parts; I was no better than Sebastian, clinging to his own stubborn, idealistic love for someone who didn't care about him. If I imagined that Ted would even speak to me now, let alone acquiesce with any enthusiasm to whatever romantic reconciliation I was evidently yearning for at the very bottom of my heart, I was bughouse.

But there. At the thought of the utter futility of a reconciliation with Ted, throughout my body blasted a wild jolt of exaltation that spread to the tips of my toes, fingers, nose, penis, lips, tongue, then contracted and concentrated itself into a fiery ball of powerful hunger.

"Now let's take a couple of X rays," said Lorraine, and then came the lead apron draped over my chest, those hard white folded cardboard rectangles wedged painfully between my cheeks and gums, the undetectable bursts of radiation. When that was over, the dentist came in, took a cursory gander at the inside of my mouth, and looked at whatever information Lorraine had for him, then scribbled something in my chart as he told me I needed to replace all my old amalgam fillings with porcelain ones, and I should make another appointment to come back soon. Then he went unceremoniously away.

"Okay, Jeremy, you're finished," said Lorraine.

I scrambled to my feet, took the floss and toothbrush she handed me, and wandered out to the waiting room in an exalted funk, where I paid for her ministrations in cash at the little window and retrieved my coat from the closet.

When I got home, there were four messages on Scott's answering machine, and they were all, as it turned out, for me. I stood and watched Juanita dip her little fluffy head repeatedly into her water bowl and then run her beak along her wings, first one, then the other. The first message was my mother, inviting me to dinner that night, the second from my sister Amanda, saying that she was running late today and would meet me at four instead of three, the third was from my movie agent, no doubt to inform me that Sebastian was sniffing around my script with big dollar signs in his eyes.

The fourth, to my chagrined discomfiture, was Sebastian himself, who said in a drenched, breathless voice, "Jeremy, it's Sebastian, and I'm calling because I owe you for your work. And I wanted to apologize again for my ill-advised . . . admission last night, I meant it only as a compliment, a tribute to your writing. I hope you'll forgive me." There was a pause, then he added, "Speak to you soon," in a low murmur.

"Freakazoid," I said, stabbing the erase button.

I fell into Scott's vintage armchair and watched Juanita go about her speedy, lightweight day. I yawned, then twisted the top off the bottle of whiskey, which I'd left here last night after a nightcap before I went to bed, and took a swig of liquid peat. It burned its way through my chest and spread to my gut, my liver, my spleen, and eased my fierce postpartum emptiness, the cold, sunny waning afternoon of my first day with no novel to write. Felicia and her touchstones suddenly seemed poignantly understandable. I felt like going to a leather bar and finding myself a hot little whelp I could bend to my will and then send on its way, out of my life. The only trouble was that most of the people I met in those bars were too boring, vain, and needy to bother with for longer than five minutes. Necessity was the mother of invention and idle hands were the devil's instruments: I was going to have to start another book right away, or I might as well join Felicia in her hothouse.

Then, before I could censor them, into the negative space in my head flowed, with the whiskey, various sensory memories of Ted. I was assaulted by the taut line of his profile, his pent-up long-withheld ardor the first time I touched him after a long time apart, his abrupt laughter when I teased him, that night when he'd said, "God, Jeremy, you're the love of my life." As my memory's pitiless lens zoomed in on the particulars of this night, the in-love-with-Ted euphoria resurged: the two of us entangled like kids on my rug, sated with sex and olives, Monk and Bowles, the wind at sunrise blowing through the open windows. This memory had become a touchstone of sorts for me in recent months. As hard evidence that Ted had loved me, it seemed a bit thin, but I bought it anyway.

My mother's phone rang several times, four, five, six, before Leonard picked up and said "Yes?" in a clear, collected, normal voice.

"Leonard, it's Jeremy. Is my mother there?"

"She just ran out to the store. Can I have her call you when she gets back?"

"She invited me over for dinner tonight and I'm planning to come, but she didn't say what time."

"The usual time, I guess," he said vaguely in that impatient way he had that had always nettled me, because it made me feel as if trivial things like dinnertime were too far beneath his august physicist's notice to be treated with anything but offhanded surliness.

But now he had Alzheimer's, so I couldn't justifiably say something borderline-pissy in return the way I usually did. "Okay, I'll come around seven, then," I said. "You'll remember to tell her?" Immediately, I wanted to kick myself in the head; I hadn't meant it the way it sounded, as if I didn't trust his spongy brain to retain the information. I would have said it six months ago without thinking twice.

"Well," he said, "I'll try. But you might want to call back later just to be sure, or you could just show up. Either way, I know she'll be very glad to see you."

"Although you yourself will be deeply dismayed," I said.

"That's right," he said with a little chuckle, and we hung up. I almost liked my stepfather whenever we shared a wry joke about our fundamental incompatibility, our one isthmus of common ground.

I heated a can of lentil soup, then took my lunch to my desk, where, in less than an hour, I had reworked the last paragraph of *Angus in Efes* to my immediate and probably wholly temporary satisfaction. Right away, before I could change my mind, I turned my printer on and loaded it with paper, then began the tedious, busy process of tending to it while it spewed forth inky pages one after the other. Just when I began to breathe easily, thinking it might have spontaneously recovered its youthful energies, it jammed or took two sheets at once, and then I had to hit Stop and fix everything. My printer was wheezy and whiny, and slurped its thirsty way through expensive print cartridges, but it was all I had. So, like anyone cohabiting with a decrepit elderly person in a long, slow decline, I had learned to accommodate its quirks and appreciate its efforts.

As the printed-out stack grew on my desk, I made little penciled corrections here and there and tried and failed not to despair over how wretchedly dull, improbable, and stilted the thing was. The whole time I'd been writing the book I had felt hampered by the little I knew about my father, his rages and limitations and political fanaticism. My belief in his ultimate failure to realize his most deeply held objectives had informed every word, every scene. I wanted to shove it into the garbage. Instead, I swaddled the whole thing in an enormous padded envelope, diapered with a cover letter I'd written yesterday, and put on my coat.

The phone rang as I was looking for my keys. Without thinking, I answered it. "Hello?"

"Jeremy," said Sebastian. "Did you get my message?"

"I got it," I said tersely, wishing more than anything that I'd screened the call or that I could just hang up now before either of us said another word.

"Listen. I don't expect you to want to talk to me." He waited for me to deny this, and when I didn't, he went on in a rush. "First of all, do you know the Song of Songs in the Old Testament? 'Oh, give me the kisses of your mouth, for your love is more delightful than wine.' "

"For now the winter is past, the rains are over and gone," I said in an impatient singsong. "Milk, olives, honey, wine. I am the rose of Sharon and the lily of the valley. Gazelles and stags. A swarthy girl and her shepherd."

" 'Oh, give me the kisses of your mouth,' " Sebastian said determinedly. " 'For your love is more delightful than wine.' Now I'm going to put the phone down and put the speakerphone thing on, and then I'll play this song for you, and you can hang up, but I hope you'll listen. I know this is completely off the wall, and I know you think I'm daft. I don't care. This is important."

I sighed audibly, but I didn't hang up.

There was a clunk, which I assumed was the phone being set down on some hard surface, and then I heard a guitar strumming. A couple of strings sounded out of tune. I closed my eyes and clenched my fist around the phone. Would I hang up, or would I listen to this? I didn't know yet. The strumming resolved itself into a chord, which became another chord, and I sensed some rhythmic intent in all of this, so apparently the song was off and running, and this was the intro. It was all fairly bouncy and upbeat; I guessed I was in for a folk standard, but I didn't recognize it yet. Then Sebastian's voice came in, sweet and high, far more tuneful than I'd had any reason to expect: "When I was a young man and never been kissed, I got to thinking over what I had missed. I got me a girl, I kissed her and then, Oh Lord, I kissed her again . . ." The tempo slowed, major shifted to minor, then Sebastian's voice again, "Oh, kisses sweeter than wine," and the song suddenly turned haunting and melancholy. "Oh, kisses sweeter than wine."

"Sebastian," I yelled into the phone.

Immediately, he stopped playing and said, "What is it?"

"What are you doing? Why am I listening to this song?"

"Just listen. There are only five short verses, it'll be over before you know it and then you can get back to whatever you were doing. Trust me, there's a point to this."

"Can't you just tell me the point instead?"

"No," he said. "Ready?"

I made an impatient sound that he interpreted as assent, because the strumming started up again and he launched into the second verse, in which the narrator proposed to his girlfriend and she accepted, then came the chorus again, and then apparently their farm prospered and they had twins, kisses sweeter than wine again, and then they had four kids who got married and suddenly our hero was, Oh Lord, the grandfather of eight, Oh, kisses sweeter than wine. Sebastian was right, the song was short, I'd give him that.

"Last verse," Sebastian called out, then came the major chords, then the verse, which went "Now that we're old, and ready to go, We get to thinking what happened a long time ago. We had a lot of kids, trouble and pain, But, Oh Lord, we'd do it again."

His voice broke on the last word and he stopped for a moment or two, as if he were trying to collect himself. He cleared his throat. "Sorry," he said. "That line always gets me."

Then he strummed the minor chord that heralded the chorus and sang, his voice a little wispy with emotion, "Oh, kisses sweeter than wine, Oh, kisses sweeter than wine." He decrescendoed on the last word the way songs ended on albums, as if this were a recording and there was a sound guy in a booth, twiddling the knobs and making it trail off.

Then he came back to the phone and said, "Jeremy."

"What."

"I'm so glad you're still there." There was a silence; I could hear him breathing through his mouth into the receiver. "I won't ask whether you understood; it's enough that you listened and that you heard it. Thank you."

"You're welcome," I said. The temptation to giggle was as strong as an oncoming sneeze. Somehow, I suppressed it.

"Of course I read your work for my own pleasure," he said. "I can't help responding to it viscerally, because of how I feel about you. You can think that's pathetic and unhealthy, or you can be flattered and amused. It's entirely up to you, of course."

"Can we please just not talk about this anymore? If you'll send me a check for what you owe me, we'll call it even."

"What?" he said, stricken. "You're not going to write for me any more?"

"Maybe not. It might be better if I don't."

"Well, if there's anything I can say to change your mind, please tell me. In the meantime, of course, I'll send you a check."

There was another silence, this one a lot longer.

"All right," he said. "I have to spell it out, just so I'll know there was no misunderstanding. When we're old men, after years and decades together, after trouble and pain, I want us to be able to say, Oh Lord, we'd do it again. I know you don't love me now, but then, you're still getting over Ted. But some day?"

"I doubt it. I'm not really the marrying kind."

"You were married to Ted."

"That wasn't marriage," I said bleakly. "I've got to go, I have to be somewhere."

160

"All that matters," said Sebastian, "is growing old with someone. It doesn't really matter whether or not they're the perfect mate for you at the beginning, because there's really no such thing. I think that comes with time. What matters is those years together."

"I disagree," I said. "Staying with someone out of some misguided sense of loyalty strikes me as a tragic mistake. We only get one life. I do anyway, I don't know about you."

"You've forgiven Ted for breaking it off with you, then?"

"All I'm saying is that I would rather be alone than settle for someone."

"Well, I'd like to take back my participation in that toast you made. I hereby reverse the wineglass, unclink it from yours. Bachelorhood is not blissful. To wedded bliss, Jeremy, or united bliss. We are a mating, pairing-off, two-by-two kind of animal, and I've chosen you."

"That may be," I said hollowly. "I haven't chosen you though. That seems like something of a stumbling block."

"All I ask is that you think about what I've said."

"Well, all right, but I don't know what good it'll do. I have to go."

I hung up. Out the window, water towers stood against the sky, solitary and shaggy and comical and sad. I pocketed my keys, picked up my package, and went out into the blistering air and made my shoulder-hunched way to the post office. I stood in the long line, which advanced slowly, giving me plenty of time to change my mind. But when at long last I reached the window, I dutifully mailed my ambitious progeny first class to Hope Gladwell of the Piers Blandon Literary Agency, chosen from the yellow pages solely on the strength of the resonance and charm of those names. I had called Hope's assistant yesterday morning and received permission to send it, and so there was nothing now to stop me from doing so. That was, I gathered, how these things were done.

At four o'clock I walked into the Old Town Bar. Amanda was already there, sitting in a booth facing the door, looking into a small mirror with a disgusted expression on her face. I took off my coat and sat across from her.

"Hi," she said tonelessly without looking away from her reflection.

"What's wrong?"

"Every time we go on tour, I come back with a pizza face," she said.

"I fucking hate it. It's no mystery—we eat greasy food, don't sleep enough, smoke and drink too much, and breathe exhaust on the interstates. I've lost weight, though, don't ask me how, so Liam doesn't care if I'm covered with pustules. As long as I'm thin." She put her mirror away.

I took the menu I was handed and glanced up at the waitress. "What are you drinking, Amanda?"

She sniffed. "I'll have a glass of water and a cup of coffee."

"Make that two of each," I said. I scanned my sister's face; her skin looked fine to me, if a bit pale. "Are you going to Mom's later for dinner?"

"Quit looking at me like that," she said. "You're making me feel even uglier. You're going to Mom's tonight? She didn't invite me."

"Why not?"

"I don't know." She sniffed again. "She told me Leonard's getting worse. She said he'd gone out shopping and forgot where he lived. A neighbor brought him home."

"Oh, poor Mom."

We were silent for a while. Our coffee and water arrived.

"I'll have a vegetable plate," Amanda told the waitress.

"I'll have a bacon cheeseburger and fries," I said. "Mom's going to serve some healthy low-cal low-fat thing," I told Amanda. "I need sustenance."

"Listen," Amanda said when the waitress had gone. "I have something to tell you. You have to promise not to tell Mom tonight, I want to tell her myself, in person, next time I see her."

"Why don't you come have dinner up there with me?"

She cut her eyes at me. "I don't want to, actually. Things have been sort of weird between Mom and me since I got back from tour. I don't really know why, there's just this tension between us. I feel like she's mad at me."

"For what?"

She lit a cigarette, inhaled deeply, and examined the burning end, stalling. "Well," she said, exhaling smoke, "maybe it's because I called her one night from the road, I think we were in Cincinnati. I was probably drunk, I don't remember, and I was exhausted. I was so mad at her though. I started thinking about how she raised us. Being on the road brings it all back. We had such a fucked-up childhood. Anyway, I think I came at her sort of hard, and it was totally out of the blue. She didn't know how to respond. She was crying. She said right before we hung up that she wished she could go back and do it all differently but she can't, so maybe we can try to work things out as adults. Which I thought sounded good, but she's been so distant since I got back."

"You know how she is," I said. "She hates confrontation. It freaks her out. And it must have been really hard to hear that, especially since there's nothing she can do about it now."

"Well, yeah." She took another lungful of smoke and blew it out in a rush. "Okay, you're probably right, but that's not what I wanted to talk about."

I waited; she didn't say anything. She seemed increasingly brittle and nervous the longer we sat here; I had the feeling that if I probed too hard, she might shatter. Her face looked tense; her eyes were skittery and unfocused. When she looked like this, it meant she was on the defensive about something, but I couldn't imagine what it could be.

"Are you mad at me for something I did when we were little?" I asked with wary provocation after a moment.

She laughed a little too hard. "No," she said. She hesitated, then blurted out defiantly, without meeting my eyes, "Liam and I are getting married."

"Oh," I said. "Well, that is news."

She leaned back, trying and failing to seem calm and sure of herself, shooting a look at me to gauge my reaction.

I took a sip of coffee and wiped my mouth on my napkin.

"Aren't you going to congratulate me?" she asked with pleading indignation.

"Congratulations," I said. "It just took a minute to sink in."

"I'm not pregnant," she said. "If that's what you're thinking. And it was officially romantic. He went down on bended knee the night I got back. He told me I was the love of his life and gave me this." She extended her left hand so I could see that there was indeed a gold-looking band bearing a tiny but inarguably authentic diamond on the appropriate finger. "The words 'green card' didn't come up once. We love each other, Jeremy. I know you don't believe me because we treat each other like shit most of the time, but it's true, we do."

"And you said yes."

"I cried."

"What did he do while you were away on tour?"

"He got a job," she said proudly. "He's tending bar at this new place that just opened in Williamsburg, right near where we live. This ring is all paid for; he saved his tips."

"So why haven't you told Mom yet?" I asked.

"Because," she said. "I thought if I told you first, then you could be prepared to stick up for me when she asks you what you think."

"What makes you think she's going to ask me what I think?"

"Because you're like her little oracle. She splits your head open and reads your brains like chicken entrails whenever anything happens."

"Chicken entrails," I repeated, laughing. "She does not."

Her eyes glinted. "Come on, Jeremy, she does too. She always has. Whenever I cough or sneeze, she has to find out how you feel about it."

"You're just being paranoid, Amanda." This was my older-brother trump card; I had always, from the time we were little, been able to make my sisters question their versions of reality by asserting my own. The indisputable authority of having been around longer was one of the perks of being the oldest. "You always think everyone's talking about you."

"Well, maybe I just wish you were," she said. "Then I'd feel like you gave a shit."

"Of course I give a shit," I said. "Listen, Amanda, I have to ask this, as your older brother, it's sort of in my job description and I'm asking precisely because I do give a shit. I just wonder, are you completely sure about this? It wasn't just the heat of the moment, the joyful reunion and all?"

"See," she said disgustedly, "this is exactly the reaction I was dreading. God! You act like I'm fourteen! Like I can't think for myself!"

"First you say you wish I gave a shit, and then you get pissed off when I do. If that's not fourteen-year-old behavior, I don't know what is."

"I just, I don't know. I want you to get what I'm about, is that so

164

hard to understand? I wish you got why I'm doing this without my having to explain it. You have this idea about Liam that isn't true, he's not what you think he is or why would I still be with him? Why can't you give me the benefit of the doubt? You think I'm that pathetic?"

"Why does it matter so much what I think?"

She stared at me, dry-eyed and seething, chewing on her lower lip; I looked back at her impassively, my heart pounding. We had just reached our classic stalemate, the end of a familiar, worn-out conversation. We had to retreat from the edge at this point, or we'd fall into a bubbling lava pit. For a split second I thought we might actually be about to go for it, but our food arrived, and we immediately turned our attention to our plates, half glad for the distraction.

"So will you walk me down the aisle?" she said suddenly through a mouthful of carrot.

"Give you away?" I said. I was suddenly all choked up for some reason. "With pleasure," I said with an attempt at a light, teasing laugh. "It'll be a relief to finally get rid of you. When's the wedding?"

"June, probably," she said. "We don't know where yet."

"Look, Amanda," I said through the lump in my throat, "you have to call Mom and tell her. I can't necessarily be trusted to keep this a secret. Call her before tonight."

"No, you tell her. Go ahead. I'd rather you did it."

I couldn't suppress my pleasure at her trusting me to be the go-between. "You should tell her," I insisted. "She's your mother."

"I'll think about it," she said. "But, man, I've been dreading her reaction. I hate it when she gets all cheerful and brave and openly accepting when you know inside she's just freaking. I wish she'd just come right out and disapprove sometimes. It would be such a fucking relief."

13 | A RABBIT AS KING OF THE GHOSTS

I had some time to kill before I was due uptown at my mother's, but didn't feel much like seeing Scott when he bounded in from his wonderful day, so I decided to walk around for a while to help digest my lunch. The streets were refreshingly frenetic. Traffic honked and roared and squealed, I was jostled and elbowed as I dodged oncoming people and wove my way past slower pedestrians, sped along empty stretches, bottlenecked in crowds, bobbed through stalled traffic. I threaded my way through Union Square, over and down to the East Village, up Broadway to Union Square again, and up Park Avenue South. This herky-jerky wandering lulled my mind into a meditative calm.

I was somewhat surprised when I found myself in Gramercy Park outside Ted's house, staring up at the fourth-story windows that had once been mine. They were dark except for glinting reflections from the streetlamp below. Chelsea was just across the island from Gramercy, but my new neighborhood felt far, far removed from here, years and miles away instead of blocks and months. This was the first time I'd come back since I'd left. I was amazed to see the house again; it looked as if I'd never lived here. There was the heavy door, there were the mullioned windows, there was Dina Sandusky's boring husband Cory on the couch in the house next door.

It was Thursday, the night Basia went to Astoria, where her fifty-year-old portly Greek gentleman friend wined and dined her and (I surmised, but of course didn't know for sure, because she never would have told me) took her to bed in the house where he still lived with his ancient mother, and afterward paid for her homeward taxi. It was also the night Yoshi went God knew where, probably to some yoga center to pose ostentatiously in drawstring pants and a muscle shirt.

The blinds were pulled down in the library, but light showed around their edges, and after a moment I saw the silhouette of a man cross the room. Yoshi must have stayed home from the ashram to avail himself of my old haunt; no doubt he'd taken over the chair where I'd once spent so many pleasurable hours daydreaming by the fire, book on my knees, martini glass in one hand. Yoshi didn't drink martinis or read, and as far as I knew, he didn't daydream; what the hell did he think he was doing in there? Maybe he had moved up to the attic after my departure. I would have bet anything he'd slithered right up there the minute I'd cleared out. I'd left all my furniture, my bookshelves, even the cans of soup in the cupboards. At the thought of Yoshi using my stuff, hatred swept over me. I wanted to pee in his orange trees, poke him in the eye with his own chopstick.

But when the man crossed the room again, I recognized Ted's erect bearing and the way his hair foofed up in front. I stood there in the cold, looking up at where his silhouette had been, feeling like a jilted Peeping Tom, a lovelorn Little Match Boy, but I saw nothing more. Realizing after a while that my feet were frozen through, I went around the corner to the warm darkness of Pete's Tavern. I asked the bartender for a pint of ale and carried the brimming glass over to an empty booth, where I took my increasingly besmirched and tattered paperback copy of *Jude the Obscure* from my coat pocket and held it open in front of me to the last page I'd dog-eared. For the first ten minutes, the letters might just as well have been cigarette ash or cockroach droppings; the ale slipped down without my even noticing where it went or that I was drinking it. Then I realized that the sentence I was reading had some actual bearing on the thoughts that were preventing me from advancing on to the next sentence, and the one after that: "Hers," meaning Sue's, the woman Jude was in love with, who had just married another man, "was now the city phantom, while those of the intellectual and devotional worthies who had once moved him to emotion were no longer able to assert their presence there." Recognizing that my own city phantom might rise up and take over my consciousness, I forced my turbulent emotions to be given over wholly to the book and was immediately very glad I had. Thomas Hardy's dark, skeptical, hard-nosed sobriety enthralled me. Jude's problems took me so out of myself, I almost forgot where I was; he struck me as a better man in every way than I was, and Hardy an infinitely better writer.

At six-thirty, in a funk, I put the book back into my coat pocket. Half an hour later I was on the Upper West Side, turning onto my mother's street, a tree-lined block of buildings full of rambling, grand, book-and-plant-filled apartments bought for almost nothing thirty, forty, even fifty years ago by "lefty" writers and composers, now middle-aged or elderly, who'd raised children there, held consciousness-raising and Communist Party meetings, started grassroots campaigns and circulated petitions; now they read the *Nation* and *Tikkun*, half-glasses perched on their noses, drinking herbal tea out of hand-crafted mugs, looking up occasionally to admire the tapestries and carved masks they'd brought back from Bali and Turkey. My mother and Leonard lived in just this sort of apartment.

In the doorway of my mother's building, lying near the double glass front doors, was a used condom. The sight of that shed membrane with its soft ring of a mouth made me feel itchy and curious, like a dog sniffing at another dog's spoor. I felt a twinge of indignation: rutting in my mother's doorway, the nerve, the lucky dogs. "And love has pitched his mansion in the place of excrement," indeed. As I rode the elevator up, I realized I had just gone longer than I could remember having gone in years without pitching my mansion, so to speak. Frankie had been the last, in October. This was an unacceptable state of affairs that needed to be addressed and mitigated immediately.

My mother came to the door with a pot holder in her hand, looking harried. "Oh, good," she said, "you got my message."

"He didn't tell you?"

She gave me a look, but all she said was "I'm so glad to see you."

She turned and I followed her down the long, dark hallway lined with small lithographs, etchings, oils, watercolors, and photographs, all given to Emma by her artist friends. At the end of the hall, which had doors all down its length leading to rooms on either side—their bedroom, a guest bedroom, Leonard's study, Emma's studio, the bathroom, a storage room—was the gallery of rooms joined by French doors or archways, the dining room, kitchen, living room, and library, which contained two old couches, several high bookshelves, and an old black-and-white television set. Sitting on one of those couches, I was dismayed and annoyed to see, was Irene Rheingold wearing half-moon glasses, sipping something out of a hand-crafted mug. I would have bet a hundred dollars was peppermint tea. Leonard sat glowering as usual on the other couch, leaving me little choice but to join him there, since I preferred to sit next to almost anyone on earth but Irene.

"Do you need any help, Mom?" I called, tossing my coat onto an empty chair.

"There's nothing to do, really," came her voice from the kitchen. "You can help Leonard entertain Irene while I finish up in here."

I looked dubiously at Leonard, and then at Irene, who was leafing through a book; it seemed to me that Leonard was ignoring her and she was entertaining herself, but what did I know?

"Jeremy," she said, simpering in her self-important way, "this is a cult memoir I was just asked to review for the *Voice*. It's the story of a woman who was in a group remarkably similar to your sister's, a doomsday cult out in Montana. And it's absolutely fascinating."

"I bet," I said. What I meant was, I bet no matter what this ex–cult member said, she was assured of Irene's unalloyed approbation, and if she happened to be handicapped or a lesbian, she would receive the kind of accolades due, in my opinion, only to Shakespeare. Irene, as a privileged liberal who got to enjoy a smug sense of moral upperhandedness along with every other imaginable kind of security, couldn't imagine how anyone who suffered from a minority status, mental illness, addiction, poverty, single motherhood, handicaps, or worse could bear it, let alone write books about it. Her blanket awe at the literary efforts of the disadvantaged betrayed an elitism she would have been absolutely shocked to recognize in herself.

My mother emerged, handed me a glass of red wine, and vanished back into the kitchen.

"This is from her letters home, which make up the second section of the book." Irene gave me a penetrating glance to make sure I was listening with the attention this book deserved instead of drooling and staring into space. Then, my evinced degree of interest evidently having passed muster, she read aloud in a purse-lipped, hushed voice, " 'My dearest mother, I write to you in all urgent sincerity. The lake of fire will consume you all if you do not come with us back to Eden and finally to Him. Please come with us! I cannot leave you behind without trying my utmost to fight for your very souls! Please tell my sisters, those poor lost sheep gone astray, to come back to their shepherd, to come with us to Him.' "

"Baa," I said, and took a gulp of wine. Next to me, Leonard gave a very small snort, audible to me only.

"Just think," said Irene, "of her poor family. I find it very moving how impassioned she was, how convinced she was doing the right thing, but this must have been so painful for them to read."

I'd heard identical self-righteous judgments expressed in letters Lola had written to our mother; these hadn't stopped, although she'd been out of her cult for years. Her personality had been distinguished since birth by a didactic earnestness, a detached remoteness that bordered at times on semi-autism, with a dash of mulish arrogance thrown in like Angostura bitters. Our mother, accustomed to the relative obedience of Amanda and me, had found Lola, her baby, intractably pigheaded in her resistance to any point of view but her own, and given up. The only other disciplinary choice would have been slapping her silly, which Amanda knew didn't work because she had tried it, only to find Lola as stolidly unresponsive as a tortured patriot. She had always done whatever her inner voice told her to do; Joan of Arc's older siblings must have felt something similar to what we had felt for Lola. When, fifteen or sixteen years ago, she had joined a little raggedy band of weirdos living in huts by an abandoned mine in the mountains in Arizona, waiting for the Messiah and practicing the most stringent forms of self-denial, no one had been surprised. The surprise was that she had left under her own steam, and that she now led a relatively ordinary life in Queensland. I wondered what all those emus made of her.

"Her family probably thought she was nuts," I said, "and wished she'd keep her opinions to herself."

" 'In Eden,' " Irene read on without giving my remark the dignity of a serious answer, " 'a dazzling screen spread over the earth, a scrim and shield between darkness and light. Our consciousness was unbroken, there was neither sleep nor waking, but one constant state of being. To go forward is to go back. Our loss is too great a burden to bear, the terrible solitude of humankind. I ache for you, for your own separation and alienation from Him. A great healing must occur and a destruction of the old ways for the loss to unbend, for the fabric of human time to fold on itself and collapse like a dying star into a knothole, and pull us through. I am prepared and silent, I will receive God, that most difficult and terrible path that leads to perfect oneness and joy.' "

I cleared my throat.

"Her language has such fire," said Irene, "like old-time religious oratory. It's quite formidable. Like outsider art in prose. She writes very well."

"Not that well," I muttered. "Fuzzy-headed crap."

"Dinner is ready," said my mother, appearing in the arched doorway.

My mother wasn't much of a cook, but because she was my mother, her cooking never failed to comfort and nourish me. Tonight she'd brought to life a low-fat, high-fiber, antioxidant-rich menu from the Alzheimer's cookbook she'd bought after Leonard was diagnosed: several huge broiled slabs of some bland, nontoxic, farm-raised fish, a massive platter of black, shiny, dauntingly chewy wild rice (something I secretly felt was suitable for consumption only by ruminants, who had both means and motive for eating such time-consuming, unrewarding stuff), and steamed broccoli unsullied by butter or salt, both of which I fetched from the kitchen and availed myself of liberally. Even though this wasn't my idea of a fun meal, I managed to empty my plate of two helpings of everything. When I was finished, I leaned back in my chair, tongued a wild-rice hull from a tooth, and stifled a belch out of consideration for regional etiquette. The tapered white candles in their candlesticks had burned halfway down so the flames were at eye level, giving each of our faces a kind of reverse nimbus; the air between our faces fizzed with light.

"The theory is, simply put," Leonard was saying, "that even though we live in an eleven-dimensional universe, we can't detect the presence of those other seven dimensions directly." He had been remarkably lucid throughout the meal. "They're curled into an incomprehensibly tiny seven-dimensional ball of string, as it were, at every point in the universe. If I do this"—and he waved his hand through the air—"I'm moving my hand not only through our four familiar space-time dimensions, but also through those other seven dimensions, coiled at the subatomic level."

I discovered then that for the past few minutes I'd been absently fondling my stomach, which lay like half-risen bread dough over the waistband of my jeans; I'd been running my thumb over a two-inch-thick roll of flesh, pinching it, rolling it between thumb and forefinger. I straightened in my chair and it disappeared as if by magic; maybe it melted into those other dimensions. This lecture was bringing back some of the panicky agita of my high school physics class, when I'd been completely unable to grasp even the most elemental rudiments no matter how I applied myself.

"Why seven?" I asked. "Why not two or eight or thirteen?"

"Good question!" he almost shouted. "And the answer is this: Because quantum effects render all theories in other dimensions anomalous, the superstring theory works only in ten or eleven space-time dimensions. The eleven-dimensional model is the only one that unifies all five string theories. It's called M-theory: 'M' for mystery, or mother, or membrane, or matrix. My own pet name for it is 'mulligatawny,' but I'm alone with that. It's purely hypothetical at this stage. The cart's way before the horse."

"But how do you know it's true, then?" I asked.

"Well," he shot back, eyebrows twitching vehemently, "because it's too beautiful not to be. It unifies every theory; it reconciles quantum and cosmic laws. Particle physicists all over the world devote their careers to contributing an equation, a further hypothesis. No one will be able to carry out experiments to test this theory for a long time; at the moment we're all sort of like the medieval cathedral builders."

"Amazing," said Irene.

"Or like cult members waiting for the Messiah," I said with a hint of raillery in her direction.

"Nothing like it at all," said Leonard curtly.

"Oh, Emma," said Irene. "How could you bear having a daughter in a cult all those years?"

"She chose it," said my mother. "Just like she chose to move to the other side of the planet. There's never been a single thing I could say to that girl. She came out of the womb with her own agenda."

"Heartbreaking," Irene breathed melodramatically. "She was lost to you all those years."

She hadn't expressed much concern when Lola had actually been in the cult, but here she sat, eating my mother's food and sniffing around for material to use in her review. Irene had always seemed to consider the honor of her own company adequate and even abundant recompense for the indulgences and favors she accepted as a matter of course from her friends. My mother had nursed her through a hysterectomy a couple of years before, but I would have bet anything that Irene would find a convenient excuse to weasel out of doing anything to help her with Leonard. Although she had known Amanda and me all our lives, whenever we went out to dinner with the Rheingolds we were expected to pay our own share even though Emma always treated Beatrice. And the Rheingolds had plenty of money; it wasn't about money. Thinking about all this, I wanted to pull her stupid long silver hair.

"Why do you keep talking about this?" I asked her through a surge of resentment. "Are you digging for dirt to use in your review?"

Leonard gave me one of his inscrutable, saturnalian smiles.

"Goodness, no," said Irene, her hands fluttering near her face like an autistic child's, her jaw twisting in a way she probably imagined was self-deprecatory and charming, but which made her look unbelievably weird, "why would I do that?"

"I really have no idea," I said in my homo voice, my face expressionless.

"Oh, stop it, Jeremy," said my mother. "If she wants to ask questions about Lola to help her with her review, what on earth is wrong with that? Anyway, it's flattering," she said to Irene, "that you're interested. It happened so long ago, I haven't thought much about it in a while."

Irene said promptly, her brow furrowed in sisterly empathy, "Did you fear for her life at any time, Emma?"

"Well, of course I did, but as far as deprogramming went, I felt a moral dilemma. I've always believed that it's wrong to push my own beliefs on my children. I've tried to let them do their own thing, as we used to say; I even thought about letting them choose their own names at one point. Remember that, Jer?"

As she said all this, the spirit of the sixties sprang from its lair and I saw in my mind's eye a bunch of young, half-naked adults, among them my mother, passing a joint as they lay around on dusty velveteen couches and armchairs; nearby, we kids lay sprawled on the rug, watching dust motes float in the sun, feeling skittish, bored, not quite sure what we were supposed to be doing.

"I remember that phase," I said. "My first choice was Boycott, which I thought was a kind of grape. It was either that, or Pow, because Amanda wanted to be Mia."

"It's good I decided to keep the names you had," said my mother with a laugh.

"I think that's a bunch of caca," said Leonard. "Kids don't know anything. I would have hired a deprogrammer and yanked her out of there."

"Don't start again with how I should have raised my children, Leonard," Emma said in the prickly way she had whenever she was criticized.

"I'm not," he said. "I'm telling you what I would have done with a daughter in a mind-control situation. I told you the same thing then, and I haven't changed my mind."

"Well, it all turned out all right," said Irene. "You were an absolutely wonderful mother, Emma."

"Thank you," said my mother huffily.

"You were," Irene said firmly, as if her saying so put an end to any discussion.

"Well, thank you," my mother said again, and they nodded at each other.

"How do you think we should have been raised?" I asked Leonard with real curiosity.

He looked at my mother. "I'm not sure I should get into this," he said. "I don't want to offend the sensibilities of the bohemian faction over there."

"Oh, go ahead and tell my son all the things you think I did wrong," said Emma. "They're all grown up now; the die is cast, the damage has been done."

"Thanks a lot," I said, laughing.

I waited for her to reassure me that we'd turned out just fine as far as she was concerned, but she was looking at Leonard with a startled, frozen expression. When I glanced over at him, he made a strangled sound and pounded his fist against his forehead as if he were trying to jar something loose in there. "Goddammit!" he roared.

Emma leapt up and put her arms around him and said soothingly, "Leonard, I'm right here, it's okay."

"Leave me be," he said, pushing her off him. He stood and paced around the room. The unlit chandelier overhead trembled slightly with each step he took; the tiers of crystals winked with reflected candlelight. "I can't think with all this noise!" he said harshly. "Everyone just shut up. Shut up."

"Should we go now, Emma?" Irene asked with pained compassion.

"Should we?" I echoed skeptically, thinking our leaving was probably the last thing my mother wanted.

"Oh, no," she said, "no, you two, don't go, he'll be all right, he'll calm down in a minute."

"I will not be all right and I will not calm down. This is so fucking disgusting!" He stood by the hutch and looked wild-eyed at my mother, grasping clumps of his hair in both hands. "You have no idea how disgusting."

"I know," she said, smoothing her palms down her thighs and then making a this-is-the-church, this-is-the-steeple thing, slowly wringing her hands. She had made those same gestures when I was little, when either of my sisters had thrown a tantrum, or wouldn't speak to her, or got hysterically manic. Seeing her do this now, I quailed with an ancient protective exasperation. "He gets so upset these days," she said, not lowering her voice or looking away from him. "His emotions are so fierce now, so sudden, almost out of nowhere. They always were, of course, but lately it's like hurricanes compared to thunderstorms."

"I can hear you perfectly, Emma," he announced in a loud, harsh voice.

"I know you can. I'm explaining to Jeremy and Irene so they know what's happening."

"Do not," Leonard said, "treat me as if I'm—as if I'm, you know what. You know what you're treating me like, Emma."

They both looked startlingly old all of a sudden, my mother and Leonard.

"A child?" she said. "Insane? What?"

"Why are they here?"

"They came over for dinner," my mother said.

"I haven't had dinner."

"We just ate."

"You ate more than anyone, Leonard," I said, hoping to strike a jovial, lighthearted note.

"You don't even know me," he snarled at me.

I stood up and backed away from him, out of the dining room, and went down the hall to the bathroom. I stayed in there for a while, leafing through a three-month-old issue of *Health* magazine, wondering how much of the information therein had since become outdated. I was feeling somewhat tense, and so I accomplished little in there besides learning that a diet rich in prunes and green tea would keep you alive forever. When I emerged, my hands washed with my mother's unscented oatmeal soap, my hair combed with her carved wooden comb, Leonard was sitting at the table, and I could hear the rattle of dishes as my mother loaded the dishwasher in the kitchen. Irene was nowhere to be seen. I glanced at my stepfather.

"So," he said. "This isn't much fun."

"It must be awful."

He made a stab at a smile, baring his teeth at me. "Emma!"

"What is it," said my mother, hurrying into the dining room, holding a sponge, her face pinched.

"Is there any dessert?"

"What do you feel like?"

"I'd like some ice cream if we've got any left," he said.

"I'll get it," I said, and went into the kitchen and leaned against the counter. My mother came in behind me and shut the swinging doors.

"Where's Irene?" I asked.

"She went home. She said to tell you good night."

"She went home?"

"She said she needed to get some work done tonight."

"Oh, right," I said irritably. "Her all-important review. She couldn't even clear the table. Not that I cleared the table either." I slid over to the sink, took a glass from the drain, filled it with water, and took a sip, avoiding my mother's intent gaze.

Leonard yelled from the dining room, "Emma! Did I ask for some ice cream?"

"You did, but you can wait a minute," she called back in a sharp, high voice. She compressed her lips and rolled her eyes at me.

"Have you looked into getting a nurse?" I asked. "A health care worker?"

"I'm not ready to have a stranger here all day," she said. "Leonard would bite the poor guy's head off. We'll manage, don't worry. How have you been, Jeremy? I've hardly had a chance to talk to you all night."

"I'm doing just fine," I said. "Have you heard from Amanda lately?"

She sighed. "She called just before you arrived tonight and told me her news. What is she thinking? Why? Do you have any idea?"

Here it was, the head-cracking and brain-entrails reading. "They love each other, I guess," I said with sober authority. "She says there's more to Liam than meets the eye, and she hopes more than anything that we'll be happy for her."

"I don't know what she sees in him, frankly," said my mother. "Maybe she thinks he's her only chance. She wants babies, she's thirty-three, I understand that, but it's terrible that she doesn't have more faith that someone better will eventually come along."

"What did you say when she told you?"

"I didn't know what to say. I was shocked. I couldn't hide it. She was extremely hurt. She started to cry and asked if I'd rather not come to the wedding."

"Oh, God," I said. "You two."

"I apologized, she apologized, we both cried. I said I was happy for her if this was what she truly wanted, and she said of course I'll be invited to the wedding. But anything could happen between now and June. I'm not buying my mother-of-the-bride dress just yet."

"Don't you think she's capable of deciding whether or not she really loves him?"

"Well, no, I don't," said Emma. "Look at all the mistakes I made. Frankly, I don't want any of you to have to go through what I went through. I don't think Amanda's making the right decision here, but I can't tell her or she'll blow up at me again. I have to handle her with such kid gloves. I always have. Anything I say is the wrong thing. Can you talk to her?"

"I already did," I said. "She was dreading having to tell you because she knew you'd disapprove but wouldn't tell her."

She blew some stray hair out of her face with a quick upward whiff. "You're very lucky you never have to be a mother," she said with a grim laugh. "That's all I can say."

There was a crash in the dining room, then we heard Leonard say, "Fuck it all to goddamn hell."

"We should bring him his ice cream," I said.

"And whatever else he needs for the rest of his life," she muttered, opening the freezer. "How do all those other spouses do it, the ones who are so uncomplaining and supportive when their loved ones turn into two-year-olds?"

"I bet they all want to kill them," I said.

She laughed loosely, with an edge of hysteria. "I'm laughing to keep from screaming," she said.

"Don't hold back on my account," I said.

"Don't worry," she said.

A little later, as I walked down Broadway, a nonoptional imperative radiating from the pit of my stomach informed me that I was going to call Ted. With no internal protest, I sought a working phone booth. Most of them had empty wires dangling, their receivers ripped off by vandals, or had been craftily mutilated by some homeless guy so the quarter stuck in the slot, presumably so that same homeless guy, watching from a shadowy doorway, could retrieve it as soon as the schmuck who'd tried to make a call moved on. The first plausibly intact telephone I found ate my quarter; I called the operator and was assured that the quarter would be deducted from Scott's next phone bill. The second intact phone's receiver smelled as if it had been sprayed with noxious bacteria or put down someone's pants. The third, like Goldilocks's porridge, was just right; the receiver smelled fine and gave a dial tone, my quarter clunked into the slot, and each number I dialed registered as a beeping tone in my ear. At last, Ted's line purred twice in my ear before someone answered.

14 | PRIDE AND LOWLINESS

"Haro."

"Yoshi," I said with plummeting confidence, "it's Jeremy." I pictured him standing by the telephone table in the living room in the black tank top he wore to lift weights, prancily flaunting his long, flat stomach, repugnantly apple-round biceps, and sweat-free flesh. Ugh. My hand was slippery on the receiver. "May I speak to Ted, please?"

"I don't think," said Yoshi pointedly, "Ted wants to talk to you."

"I think that's for Ted to decide. Will you tell him I'm calling, please?"

After a brief but eloquent silence, he said, "Just a minute."

Not a sound. I waited. Minutes later, I inserted a nickel at the request of a female automaton. The phone lady shut up and went away for a while, then returned to request another nickel. I did as she told me, much as I would have rolled up my sleeve for a shot at a nurse's command; she had that same impersonal authority, and I needed all the guidance I could get here. Obviously, no one was going to come to the phone, but I waited, hanging on to the receiver, shivering and sweating. My excited nervousness gave way suddenly to a slash of fear through my sternum that left an electrical depression in its path, a damp sense of foreboding.

Then I heard footsteps, faint at first, then louder. Then a crackling sound, someone picking up the receiver, and then Ted said coldly, "What do you want, Jeremy?" right into my ear.

"Ted," I stammered. "I didn't think you'd come to the phone."

"And why is that?"

"After all the pain and trouble I've caused you."

"You can't even imagine how much," he said. "I'm interested to hear what you think you've got to say to me."

"I'm not calling to apologize," I said. "What would be the point?"

"What's the point of calling, then?"

"I'd like to see you," I blurted out. "Have a drink."

He made an exasperated sound. "How did you know I was in town?"

"I didn't," I lied. "I just hoped."

"You just hoped," he said as if he'd seen me lurking outside his house earlier, as if he could read my mind. "Do you imagine we'll just say hi, shake hands, have a nice friendly chat, let bygones be bygones?"

"No!" I said, although this was exactly what I had hoped. "I just wanted to talk about what happened. Face-to-face."

"You wrecked my life," he said, the words shooting out as if they were cold bullets. "You caused the end of my marriage, and you ruined my career. My parents are only now beginning to recover from the shock. My daughter—"

"Is she okay?" I asked tentatively.

"I just wonder," he said. "What did I say or do that warranted that degree of retaliation, to make you think I didn't have your best interests at heart? I told you I loved you like a brother, I made it clear that you were welcome to live in my house for the rest of your life. I did absolutely nothing wrong to you except decide not to sleep with you any more, and that was my right."

"I know," I said wretchedly as a man behind me cleared his throat. I glanced over my shoulder and saw a boulder-sized black guy in a down jacket and watch cap, scowling at me. He had a round, perfectly smooth face; he couldn't have been much older than seventeen.

"You going to be long?" he asked in a tone that said the only possible answer was no.

I put my hand over the receiver and hissed, "Yes, I am," then turned around and cleared my own throat aggressively so he'd move on.

"You probably also know," Ted was saying, "that you were one of the best friends I've ever had. I trusted you with my life. Felicia too."

"I know," I breathed. I wanted to climb through the phone and hurl myself at him, pin him to the ground and eat him raw. I couldn't help it, it was a biochemical phenomenon expressed by some formula: The strength of his indifference to me was inversely proportional to my desire for him, or something like that.

"She called me recently from rehab to make amends," he said. "Can you imagine anything more ironic? First it was the drugs talking, now it's the treatment."

"Yeah," I said, laughing a little, "she called me too. It seemed completely contrived. She apologized for things I don't even remember her doing. She sounded like she was reading from a script."

"She's a horrible actress," said Ted.

"You know," I blurted out, my heart constricting with hope, "Gary already knew about us; I didn't tell him anything and I didn't contradict him. That's all."

"Haven't you ever realized that not everyone has to know everyone else's business?"

"Are you still sleeping with Yoshi?"

"What?"

"Faggots think they own the fucking city," the kid behind me muttered. "Just 'cause they're *gay*."

After a charged pause, Ted said very quietly, "What did you say?"

"Come on, Ted," I said, outraged apprehension prickling along my scalp as the guy's down jacket rustled and his exasperated, raspy breathing sounded in my ear. "Surely you can admit it now."

"Giselle is divorcing me, she's going to get custody of Bret, my parents are beside themselves. Whether I'm sleeping with Yoshi is not really the point."

"Please deposit five cents for the next three minutes," said the phone lady.

"Hold on," I said urgently. "I have another nickel right here."

"Oh, come on, get off the phone," said the black guy.

I shoved a nickel into the slot; for a couple of seconds the line jangled and whirred, then opened up again. "Hello?" I said several times. "Ted!" But there was only a humming silence, then a click, and finally a dial tone.

I replaced the receiver, sagged against the Plexiglas wall of the booth, and closed my eyes, wrapped my fingers around the little rungs of the metal shelf and held on to keep from sliding down to the pavement.

"You done in there?"

My antagonist and I stared at each other for a moment. His eyes were dark and hard. I don't know what mine looked like. "Oh, get a cell phone," I muttered.

"*You* get a cell phone," he said right back.

For the next few blocks I bumbled along the sidewalk, "I did him wrong" resounding in my head so loudly, it was indistinguishable from a splitting headache. But I hadn't done him wrong, I'd been accidentally overheard in a restaurant and had subsequently been unable to deny Gary O'Nan's sneaky innuendo; Ted had convincingly painted me as the wrongdoer and himself as the helpless victim, but I had been unable to set him straight because my desire to have sex with him again had rendered me temporarily stupid, and now my frustrated anger was mutating into guilt because it had no external outlet, so I had no alternative but to turn it on myself. That was the source of this headache, not guilt.

As I puzzled my laborious way through this maze, I almost bumped into several people, almost stepped on a tiny dog in a sweater on a leash, almost knocked over a deli fruit bin. A garbage can zoomed into my field of vision and I crashed into it. Then I veered off the curb into the gutter and held up an arm at the oncoming traffic. Almost immediately, a taxi shot across two lanes and squealed to a halt, idling less than a foot from where I stood. I opened the door, slid across the heated seat, shouted my address into the air between the back and front seats, then collapsed with my temple against the steamy window, writhing slowly, consumed with a self-loathing so noxious, it felt like an internal pit of acid. All was supposedly fair in love and war. "Nothing shall be sole or whole that has not been rent."

"Wait," I called out to the driver, and then I heard myself giving him Sebastian's address. For the remainder of the ride I watched the low tunnel of traffic lights through the windshield and gulped breaths of heated, strawberry-scented air, floating in a limbo of anticipation, not even trying to pretend to myself that this sudden change of plan was anything but selfish. I wanted Sebastian to pour me a glass of wine, offer me a chair by his synthetic fire. I wanted to sit there like an exalted king on a pedestal, basking in his deep, yearning adoration.

"Hello," said Sebastian when I had paid the driver and got out of the cab, found another working phone booth, and located a quarter in my pants pocket, "Jeremy, where are you?"

I heard voices in the background, laughter, music. "Right downstairs from your place. Are you having a party or something?"

"No, not really a party, just a few people over. Would you like to come up?"

"No, I don't want to intrude—"

"Oh, you certainly won't be intruding," he said with a little laugh. "Some of these people are big fans of yours. See you in a few minutes?"

"No, I couldn't," I said like the scared rabbit my sister had accused me of being. "I was just passing by. I'll see you another time."

"Do come up," said Sebastian firmly. "I'll unlock the elevator for you. We'll be so happy to see you." He hung up, leaving me to either scurry back to my warren or brazen it out. As I walked the two blocks to his building, I was beset by a horrible image of Sebastian in a black Speedo, fondling a male blow-up doll, listening to a tape marked "generic party noise" all by himself.

But when the elevator doors slid open, I was bathed in simultaneous gusts of warmth, cigarette smoke, cologne, candlelight, conversation, jazz, and laughter. I heard the festive sound of a champagne cork being popped. A tiny brown dog, yapping with frantic fury, hurled itself out of nowhere at my legs. I looked down to disengage it and saw its teeth bared in a cute parody of ferocity, its eyes bulging like Sebastian's, but instead of brimming with overeager friendliness, these eyes were almost white with the need to kill me. Its hairless, tan-colored, projectile-shaped body trembled with murderous appetite.

Sebastian rushed out of the same nowhere the dog had emerged from, like spaceships uncloaking or coming out of warp. "Chad!" he cried. "Chad, that's our friend, that's Jeremy!" He bent down and whisked the Chihuahua off my calves and tucked him, still yapping, under his arm. Then he kissed my cheek and smiled for an instant into my eyes to show me that he hadn't taken my rejection to heart, and he hadn't given up on me in any way. "Jeremy, I'm so glad you came, I wasn't sure you would. Come and meet everyone."

"I've already met Chad," I said uneasily. "I'm not sure I want to meet anyone else."

"Isn't he horrible?" Sebastian said cheerfully. "He's not mine, thank God, he's Peter's. He seems to think he's a Doberman guarding a junk-yard. Well, we all need our little illusions about ourselves."

"We do," I said inanely.

"Jeremy, these are some of your readers. Gentlemen, meet Jeremy Thrane, the real man behind the pseudonymous and wildly popular Blaze Cinders."

I found myself drawn into a circle of sleekly handsome young men. "Hello," I said, bewildered. Someone handed me a flute of champagne; instinctively, I took a big gulp, which fizzed in my sinuses.

"Blaze," said a chesty redhead with tortoiseshell glasses and a trim little gingery mustache, "it's so good to meet you in person, I feel like I already know you. You write the *hottest*—"

"He knows," said Sebastian imperturbably. "Anyway, he just dropped by for a moment, so don't monopolize him. I'm going to get those canapés out of the oven, I'll be right back, and then, Jeremy, let's you and I go up and have a little tête-à-tête."

"Do let's," I muttered, not sure what I thought of this inexplicable and unprecedented transformation of Sebastian, and for that matter his loft, since last night. Fat beige candles bloomed with light everywhere— on the mantel over the ersatz fire, along the windowsills, on the floor by the couches, on the dining room table, up the spiral staircase. Tall brown porcelain jars bristling with peach-colored tulips sat here and there. A gigantic woven tapestry I'd never seen before hung on the far wall; at first glance it looked like a rocket ship flying against a complicated dec-orative background, but on closer inspection I saw that it was an erect penis, stylized but distinctly phallic.

"Do I know you?" asked a smirking little black guy with a glint in his eye.

"He's Blaze Cinders!" bayed the redhead. " 'Adventures in Sodom.' My favorite *Boytoy* writer, bar none."

"Well, I've hung up my shingle for now, I think," I said. "But thanks."

"What do you mean?"

"I'm retiring," I said apologetically. "I've decided to move on."

"No! I have to know what happens to Brett," said a peach-faced, muscle-bound lad with a slight lisp I suspected was entirely manufactured. "You can't just leave us hanging. Does he or doesn't he let that older guy take him to Europe?"

"See, you can't quit now," said someone else, laughing. "You've got us all hooked."

"I'll think about it," I said. I was feeling oddly shy. These young boys seemed so sure of themselves, so mindfully self-possessed; I remembered how I had felt at their age, as if my skin were too large for the rest of me, or too small. They all appeared to be around the same age as Scott, with an equal denomination of erotic currency.

"I'm Peter, by the way," said the redhead as he offered his hand, which I shook. "I don't think you've ever been to one of these things before."

"No," I said, "I haven't. I didn't know Sebastian had things, actually."

"All the time! Sebastian's parties are the best! This is just the warm-up period, don't worry, the real event starts once we're all nice and liquored up. He has the *best* champagne."

"Pig in a blanket?" Sebastian asked at my elbow. "Baby carrot with sour cream dip?"

"No thanks," I said. "Sebastian, I never knew you threw parties."

"I would have invited you to all of them, but I didn't think this sort of thing was your cup of tea," he said apologetically.

Then I got it, or at least I thought I did. "What?" I said on a rising note as my cod began to stir on a rising note of its own. "I write *pornography*, Sebastian. Or rather, I used to."

He gave me an odd look. "I think you've misunderstood," he said, handing the tray to a swarthy lad with a low-slung slouch I had been unconsciously admiring. "You'll see. Come on upstairs and we'll talk about whatever you came to talk to me about."

As a matter of fact, I was feeling a certain inclination to stay downstairs and mingle. "Oh, it wasn't really anything very—" I began, but he had started up the spiral staircase, picking his way through the burning candles. I made my way up the stairs behind him. Below us, the young men stood in a loose-knit clump, talking, laughing, occasionally raising their glasses at one another.

"Sit," Sebastian said to me, patting the sofa next to him. I sat down, and there we were, Sebastian and I, knee to knee in the *Boytoy* office, in the near darkness of refracted candlelight from below.

"By the way," said Sebastian, "I spoke to your agent again and convinced him that I'm completely serious about producing this film. We're discussing terms now. By which I mean money."

"That's great," I said vaguely.

"But this isn't what you're here to talk about. Go ahead."

"I called Ted from a pay phone tonight. He wasn't exactly glad to hear from me."

Sebastian leaned back against the couch cushions. "Poor Jeremy," he said with a tenderness that made me ashamed of myself.

"I don't know what made me do it. I wish I hadn't. If I were the histrionic type, I'd probably want to drown myself."

"Don't drown yourself," he said, smiling. He reached a hand over and placed it firmly on the back of my neck and rubbed the base of my skull.

His hand was warm; my neck muscles were tense. I didn't flinch when he sat up and braced the heel of one hand against my spine as he worked his way down my spine with the other, vertebra by vertebra.

I cleared my throat. "Anyway, I called to ask him if he'd have a drink with me. He was beyond scornful. He despises me."

"You still love him," Sebastian said soothingly. His fingertips were splayed on either side of my spine, kneading away, making my head flop forward slightly with every thrust. He leaned forward, stilled his hands on my back, and kissed the back of my neck.

"It doesn't matter how I feel," I said. "I can't have him. He doesn't want me and never will, but I can't help wanting him anyway even though it defies all logic."

"I understand," he said in my ear.

The half of me that wanted to push him away and run downstairs was easily and immediately vanquished by the half of me that was too needy and demoralized to resist any sympathy, no matter where it came from or in what form. I leaned against Sebastian, and he rested his head against mine, his hands on my shoulders. A gale of laughter blew up from downstairs.

"It's time to start the proceedings down there," said Sebastian. "For the first time, I wish they weren't here."

"How often do you have these orgies?"

He laughed. "These what?"

"What is this all about?" I asked, nettled.

"It's a support group," he said soothingly. "It's meant to be a normalizing, nonjudgmental, open-minded gathering where we all feel absolutely free to share our fears and our most shameful secrets."

"Oh," I said. "How long has this been going on? Are you the leader?"

"I'm one of the original instigators. I met Peter and Joseph on Fire Island a couple of years ago, and one night we found ourselves naked in a hot tub together, all talking honestly for the first time in our lives about ourselves. After a while we confessed our secret insecurities about our penises. I won't be betraying anyone if I tell you that Joseph thought his was too small, and Peter thought his was too crooked. The point is that it felt unimaginably good just to say this to each other, it literally changed the way we felt about ourselves."

"What did you think was wrong with your—with you?"

"It's all right if you're uncomfortable at first, saying the word 'penis.' It's not an easy word to say with a straight face." He massaged my back again as he talked, less vigorously than before, more ruminatively. "I was afraid all my life that my penis was too big. People laugh when I tell them this. I mean it quite seriously: malformed, grossly oversized, weirdly gigantic. I imagined that it stuck out whenever I wore pants that were even slightly tight, which is why I favor a baggy style of trousers. Gym class was excruciating for me. Bad enough to be an obvious fag, you don't want jocks thinking you're getting a hard-on around them, they'll beat you to jelly."

"I never noticed you sticking out in gym class, Sebastian."

"You never looked," he said. We laughed. "Anyway, Peter and

Joseph and I agreed to get together every so often just to talk, and then came Bill and John and Wallace, who had plenty of shame and fear of their own, and they brought other friends, and we decided to get together here every other month to have a party and then sit around and say whatever is on our minds without fear of judgment or mockery. We all feel immeasurably better about ourselves, thanks to these parties. You might have noticed a certain phallic theme in the food and decor. We call these evenings 'penis parties' as a sort of joke on ourselves."

There was a long silence then while he karate-chopped me from the base of my skull to the base of my spine. I had nothing to say. His hands on my back were comforting and invigorating. The babble of voices downstairs removed the pressing need to talk that complete silence would have engendered.

"Are you feeling better?" asked Sebastian.

"Thanks," I said. "I am."

There was another long silence. He slid his hands under my shirt and rested his warm palms against my kidneys. I had a hard-on so painful, I thought it would detonate if anything touched it. It throbbed and twitched in my undies like a tree branch in a gale.

"Jeremy," he said falteringly, "I would love to touch you right now, to give you pleasure."

I was silent.

"Please don't say no. It's a gift. Meaning that nothing, absolutely nothing, is expected in return, except that if I faint with pleasure, I hope you would revive me."

I cleared my throat and said, "I'll try."

With a happy little groan, he slid a hand around to the fly of my jeans and undid it, then knelt between my legs and unloosed my cock, grasping it as it sprang from its trappings. I gazed at his downy, shining bald spot, his doughy, shapeless body, hunched unprepossessingly there on the floor.

He pushed me gently backward so I reclined against the couch pillows. "You have a beautiful penis, I knew you would," he whispered, then took me into his mouth.

I stared up at the ceiling in a state of vague, passive, empty apprehension.

Afterward we went downstairs together, Sebastian leading the way. I smiled steadily at everyone as I said good night, but as Sebastian helped me on with my coat, I couldn't look at him.

"It's all right," he said as I stepped into the elevator, but I wasn't quite sure what was all right or how he knew. I went home and stayed up very late finishing *Jude the Obscure*. I knew I was supposed to pity and admire the brilliant, fey, emotional Sue and deplore the hussy Arabella, but I got so impatient with Sue's principled equivocating, I almost threw the book across the room a couple of times; meanwhile, every time Arabella appeared, I smiled inwardly with relief. If she and Sue represented the two sides of woman, as I suspected they did, I infinitely preferred the amoral, scheming side to the neurasthenically cerebral one. My favorite scene in the book was the all-night whiskey-fueled card-playing party Arabella threw to get Jude drunk enough to remarry her. She was doing him a kind of favor, in my opinion, no matter how he felt when he sobered up and realized what had happened. She had rescued him from the swooning tragic Sue, from thinking too much, from abstraction and dithering, and offered him instead a bluntness on which to dull his pain. Hers was an oddly Zen kind of love; coarse and limited and cynical though she may have been, she took him for what he was and offered her whole imperfect self in return. I wanted to take him aside and explain this to him, but there was nothing for it but to muddle on with my own life instead.

PART THREE

"Maybe I'll play the part of the bakery truck driver myself," Sebastian said to me one evening in June. We sat at an outdoor café in the West Village; he was treating me to a dinner I'd accepted because I hadn't felt like cooking, and was in need of some company. "I was a child actor, I think I've mentioned. At eleven, I played Mustardseed in a West End production of *A Midsummer Night's Dream* and was told I had quite a gift."

"Mustardseed," I said, laughing. "You could play the truck driver as well as anyone, I bet. How hard could it be to act in a movie anyway?"

"Oh, no," he said, scandalized. "Film acting is a delicate and difficult art. I wouldn't presume to think of doing so myself except that I was on the stage. You never forget how to act, it's like riding a bicycle."

"Oh, please," I said, scowling at the waiters gossiping by the bus tubs, the gay young blades wafting by in springtime twosomes on Macdougal Street, and my dinner, ginger-sake-glazed swordfish with some sort of gourmet glop that looked like thick porridge but was touted as toasted-rice polenta. "Movie acting is like falling off a log, not riding a bicycle. The camera does all the work for you. You don't even have to memorize your lines all at once. My pet bird Juanita could do a passable Lady Macbeth on film, given enough takes."

In the patchy squares of dirt between street and sidewalk, saplings had burst undauntedly into leaf once again. Although the air glittered with industrial particulates under a burning haze, these small young living things had put forth an unusually healthy-looking bunch of greenery this year. These leaves fluttered in the breeze like pennants on the tips of the bayonets on the losing side in a battle, their fruitless, dubious bravery a comically poignant metaphor for every living thing under the sun, from paramecia to redwoods to me myself. The sight of those fresh leaves twirling on their stems in the polluted air should have buoyed me up, sprung a little eternal hope in my human breast, but they served only to make me feel weary. We all hewed to the ways and habits of our kind, fought to flourish at all costs, even though it hastened our collective end.

In early February, thanks to Gary O'Nan and in spite of the blank decade on my hypothetical résumé, I'd managed to wangle a job as a copy editor for *Downtown* magazine, a job that not only provided me with a low but respectable income, it dispelled forever all the naive notions I'd ever cherished about office buildings as steamily erotic settings for men's room quickies. Long ago, I dimly recalled, I'd been a self-sufficient loner cozily enjoying a leisurely pot of fresh-brewed coffee every morning, high and secure in my sunny aerie. Now I hit the snooze button until the last possible second, leaving just enough time to leap from my bachelor's grainy sheets to jam on some clothes and gulp the dregs of Scott's coffee, now lukewarm and bitter, before running out the door. I spent my shockingly long days in a windowless cubicle, squinting at articles about the openings of "hot" new clubs, trying to render them error free, even readable, without compromising the vision, so to speak, of the author. On my way home in the evenings, I stopped for groceries and made dinner for myself alone in Scott's kitchen, listening to music, drinking cheap but potable wine.

In March, Ted had, with much media fanfare, announced his return to the theater. He'd bought a run-down loft in the meat district and started his own small company. Their first play, an all-male gay-themed romantic comedy, had just opened to mixed reviews, but every drama critic in the city was raving about Ted's courage and determination in returning to his theatrical roots. "Disproving once and for all Fitzgerald's famous axiom about American lives," gushed one, "Ted Masterson has launched himself into his own inspiring and triumphant second act." This had appeared, appropriately enough, in *Downtown*, the very publication responsible for ringing down the curtain on Ted's first act. I had read this particular column only because I had copyedited it. In fact, I'd debated changing "axiom" to "saying" or "quotation," just for the hell of it, but had passed my pencil over the piece with an unusually light hand. I'd wanted as little to do with it as possible.

On March 31, the day before April Fool's Day, *Angus in Efes* had been officially taken on by a literary agent named Howard Fine, at which point it began a do-si-do into and out of the hands of a slew of editors, all of whom so far had deemed it unpublishable. Someone would buy it eventually, Howard assured me, and lacking any better alternative, I did my best to believe him. But each rejection upset, enraged, and depressed me even further, and although I tried not to dwell too much on them, it was becoming increasingly difficult not to panic. Howard worked out of his house in Bronxville and seemed to have no other clients besides me; he was the third literary agent I'd sent my novel to. I'd got his name from Sebastian, who knew his brother. He had called me less than a week after I'd sent my manuscript to him and offered to send it around on my behalf with an enthusiasm that surprised and flattered me; I suspected in my darker moments that Sebastian had paid him to represent me, but this was absurd.

While my novel was banished at every turn like Gloucester's good son in *King Lear*, my cynical bastard of a screenplay had connived its way to incomprehensible success. In mid-April, Sebastian had officially bought the rights to *The Way of All Flesh*, which provided me with enough money to carry me for a while. But, in a burst of uncharacteristic prudence, instead of quitting my job at *Downtown* and living on this windfall until it ran out, I spent a chunk of it on health insurance and socked the rest away in a savings account, where it sat collecting interest, rainy-day money, mad money, my hedge against drudgery and privation. Meanwhile, the machinery of crew, locations, and casting was set in motion; the role of the pedophile-necrophiliac undertaker was given to Rick Thomas, the former star of a couple of 1970s cops-and-robbers flicks, who was currently down on his luck and desperate to get back into movies. His headshot showed a compellingly furtive, world-weary desperation; he was a little baggy around the edges, as if his skin had gradually collapsed inward over the years. His eyes were authentically pouchy and bloodshot; the end of his nose was flaking. He looked like exactly the right person for the job.

I had had no time this spring to start another novel. Rather, I'd had time in theory, but the combination of waiting for *Angus in Efes* to sell and working in an office all day made me want to spend all my leisure hours goofing off, as if I'd entered some sort of holding pattern in which the passage of time would have no real consequence until something big happened to resolve matters one way or the other. On the one or two nights a week when I went out with friends, I made sure to drink enough to give myself a good solid hangover the next day; the hours in the office went exponentially faster when I was only partly conscious. Instead of reading Victorian novels or poetry, I filled many of my solitary evenings at home with Scott's TV. Sometimes I watched straight through from dinnertime sitcoms to the local news at ten to *Star Trek: Voyager* reruns, to which I'd somehow become addicted. *Voyager* was an old-fashioned naval romance with a corporate-utopian twist I was able to overlook due to the enthralling special effects and imaginative plots. I admired Captain Janeway to a degree that perplexed me. I couldn't decide who was hotter, Commander Chakotay or Lieutenant Paris; it depended on my mood, but I was deeply torn. Luckily, I had no other romantic prospects to speak of, so I had plenty of time to consider the question.

Sebastian, on the other hand, had been happily coupled since February, when he'd finally accepted the fact that I would never return his love and, with his usual swift pragmatism, promptly installed in his loft the chesty redhead Peter along with his cute little mustache, his murderous Chihuahua Chad, and his crooked but perfectly normal penis. Now, no matter where Sebastian went, the psychic protoplasm of his connubial bliss went with him.

"Have you had your meeting yet with the guy from the production company?" he asked, looking up from his plate of fontina-porcini-basil ravioli in butternut-squash puree. In his eyes was the gleeful excitement he couldn't contain whenever he talked about anything to do with the movie biz.

"It's tomorrow afternoon," I said, rolling my eyes.

"Will you call and let me know how it goes?"

"I don't know why you're so hot on the movie industry, Sebastian.

It's like a big corporate-run high school. Producers are the student-council treasurers, directors are the class presidents, and casting agents are like those kids who tried to get other kids to do things but never did anything themselves, they just hung out by their lockers all the time. Actors are football players, starlets are cheerleaders. Rock stars are druggy rebels and screenwriters are nobodies like we used to be."

"But this time around I'm not a nobody." Sebastian gave me a shy, happy smile. "Even the launch of *Boytoy* wasn't this much fun. It's worth every penny I'm spending on it, even if I never see any of it again."

"You won't," I said.

"I don't understand why you're so negative about all this. Aren't you even a little bit excited? And you're not a nobody either, I don't care what you say about screenwriters. Maybe you'll change your mind at the premiere. I guarantee you'll get star treatment there."

"I hate premieres," I said.

"Oh, Jeremy," said Sebastian with fond amusement. He often assumed this tone with me now that he was no longer in love with me, as if I were a long-cherished ideal he'd outgrown, which I was. "Most screenwriters consider their work their lifeblood, but no one wants it, so they languish in development jobs till they're put out to pasture or promoted. You wrote a fantastic script without even trying. Almost no one does that. You should be proud and happy."

"Maybe so," I said through a mouthful of environmentally irresponsible but undeniably delicious fish. "But imagine George Eliot's opinion of my script. Picture Matthew Arnold at the screening. And what do you think Thomas Hardy would make of the scene where Michael Jackson goes on about how sweet his little boyfriends are when they play with his pets, and how he loves to watch them, and why is that so wrong? They'd be glad they were dead, that's for sure."

"What have they got to do with this movie?" said Sebastian with a sidelong gleam of amusement. "Anyway, they might think it was a lot of fun."

"I doubt that," I said. I wiped my mouth and added casually, "By the way, have you read my novel yet? It's all right if you haven't. I'm just curious."

"No, I haven't had time," he said. "I'm looking forward to it."

"Don't worry about it," I interjected, "really, no rush, I was just asking because—"

"I'm taking it along when Peter and I go to Tuscany next month. I have no time to read anything but contracts and proposals until then."

"Oh," I said, hating how vulnerable it had made me to expose my work to the eyes of anyone at all, even Sebastian, who was historically guaranteed to deem it genius. It made me feel as if I'd grown a whole new trembling, pink, fragile, raw vital organ, but instead of being safely inside my abdomen with all my other organs, this one was external and visible, and possessed the capacity to move around independently of me. Often I lost track of it, and then would remember with a jolt of ice-cold shock that I didn't know who was assessing it at any given moment, who was prodding and jabbing it, who was diagnosing it as diseased, malfunctioning, deformed. I lay awake at night, going over random paragraphs in my mind, alternately wretched and ecstatic. Recalling certain overly flowery passages, I burned with shame, wondering miserably how anyone could ever want to publish such a thing, but a moment later the memory of a powerful scene or fortuitous turn of phrase almost caused me to levitate with a vengeful urge to lop the heads off those witless editors. It was a masterpiece, it was a piece of crap; I was a cockroach, I was a demigod. It was all very unnerving, and paranoia-inducing in the extreme.

"Howard's not having much luck selling it," I added dolefully. "Are you sure he's a reputable agent?"

"Well, he sold Allan's computer manual for a huge amount of money. But as I told you when I advised you to send it to him, his track record with literary fiction is a complete cipher to me; I recommended him only in order to provide you with another option. Poor Jeremy. This whole thing must be so trying for you."

"It is more trying than I ever imagined it would be," I said with an abrupt, frustrated gesture, accidentally dinging my fork against my wineglass; everyone at the tables near us turned to look, as if I were about to make an announcement. "What I'm most terrified of," I went on in a subdued voice, leaning over the table, "is that there is nothing else. I don't have a Plan B, as you producers say. This is it. And Howard reads those rejections to me as if they were letters to Dear Abby, as if he had no idea whatsoever how humiliating and suicide-inspiring it is for me to hear them. But what's he supposed to say? He's doing his best; it's not his fault. I can't take much more of this," I concluded passionately, then took a big bracing gulp of wine.

Sebastian reached across the table and patted my hand. "Someone will buy your novel," he said simply. "You'll succeed as a writer. I've always known it, Jeremy."

"I hope you're right," I said in a slightly calmer tone. "Maybe I shouldn't have tried to write a book about someone I barely know who was so important to me. Maybe it was doomed from the start."

"Something just occurred to me," said Sebastian. "Isn't your father a lawyer?"

"He was once; I don't know whether he still is."

"The American Bar Association might have some information on him. You could call and ask them. If you want to find him, that is."

"That's a thought," I said through a rush of startled panic. "Listen, my friend Felicia is having her first opening on Saturday night. It's in TriBeCa, from seven to nine; I was wondering whether you'd like to go with me."

"Saturday night," he said. "I'd like to go, but I can't stay long. Peter and I are having dinner with friends. You're welcome to come along."

"I'll probably go out with Felicia afterward. I haven't seen her in ages, so I imagine we'll have a lot to catch up on."

"I thought all the galleries had moved to Chelsea," said Sebastian.

"It's her NA meeting place," I said.

After dinner, as we said good night on the sidewalk, Sebastian took his new cell phone out of his bag and turned it on. "You turned it off for me?" I said, touched and amused by his willingness to forgo almost two hours' worth of deliriously urgent movie talk in favor of my churlish sniveling. I was almost certain I wouldn't have done the same for him. I headed uptown into the delectable violent night, walking fast so I'd get home in time to hear the theme music to *Star Trek*, which I enjoyed singing along with in a hammy falsetto on those nights when Scott stayed at Matt's house.

The next day, I slumped over my desk in my cubicle, embroiled in an article called "Pooper-Scooper Soul Mates: The Dog Run Singles Scene" by Bianca Mantooth, a formerly trendy downtown writer whose last few books had sold poorly because they were shallow and badly written. Her earlier books had been too, but back then she'd had cachet; she had been a celebrity, so the artlessness of her writing had seemed fresh and hip and real. Now she scribbled barely literate musings on torn-out notebook pages crinkled and stained with spilled Cosmopolitans, which then had to be typed into the magazine's editing program by someone else; she likewise submitted her expense accounts on cocktail napkins, which I knew because my cubicle was right across the aisle from Melanie's, who worked in Accounting. *Downtown* was exactly the right milieu for Bianca; her level of literacy was right on par with that of the staff writers, and her astonishingly banal insights into city life fit right in with all the gossip and shameless pandering. In fact, she was one of the most kowtowed-to *Downtown* columnists, which might have been connected to the fact that she was rumored to have slept with the editor in chief back in the club-hopping eighties. Whatever the reason, I had to be extra careful with her copy; I couldn't query a statement like "It's worth getting dogdoo on your Pradas to hang with the Frenchies and Jack Russells at the dog run" without thinking very hard about it, because, although in my opinion it should have been "dog-do," I knew these misspellings of hers were intentional, meant to enhance her childishly arch style, and querying them would only piss her off. I had learned this the hard way with the word "sintelating." "Get a clue," she'd scrawled impatiently over my politely evinced skepticism as to the English-language existence of such a word. "It's spelled FI-NE-TIC-LY. Like, a joke!"

I had a low-level headache and needed a nap. I should have drunk more last night; half-assed hangovers did nothing to alter my sense of reality the way really sintelating ones could, rubbing off all the sharp edges from experience, sealing me in an invalid cocoon of cheerful relaxed semiderangement that allowed me to pretend to be someone else for its duration, someone happy-go-lucky and frivolous and somewhat dim. It was raining, I knew, although I was nowhere near a window and couldn't see the streaks of dirty water sliding along the panes, or the gray minicloud enveloping the skyscraper I sat in, or the lighter gray billows of steam rising from manholes in the street below, or the black bobbing umbrellas jabbing and jostling in their ongoing, pointless territorial combat. Even though I couldn't see any of it up here in this climate-controlled warren of laminated surfaces under fluorescent light, I could feel it; the barometric pressure put me in a restless, slightly worried mood for no good reason, and the humidity made my fingertips feel as if they'd soaked in soapy water all morning.

Rosa, the secretary in the cubicle on my left, was gabbling nonstop in ticked-off Spanish, I assumed into the phone, I assumed to some wheedling shithead of a boyfriend, but I didn't know for sure. From the cubicle on my right came the vigorously enthusiastic wet clicks of Frederick, my fellow copy editor, flossing his teeth. I fell into a waking coma. After ten minutes, I resurfaced from my trance, slapped a stickie right by the word "dogdoo" and penciled, "change to dog-DO? As in, 'dogs DO that'? 'DOO' is not an English word." Of course, Bianca would just stet it in her usual hissy-fit fashion and I'd be right back where I started. The copyediting department was made up of frustrated literary writers, namely Frederick and me, who resented the free and easy liberties these hacks took with the language of Wordsworth and Dickens. If we could have forced them to butcher, instead, some lesser but related language, Esperanto or pig Latin, for example, we would have. My relationship with Bianca Mantooth in particular was sort of like that of the dog owners in her story to their pets: Although I knew myself to be of a far superior species, I was duty bound to clean up after her. But if she objected to being pooper-scooped so diligently, she could take it up with Daphne, my supervisor, a beady-eyed, potbellied old crosspatch who never missed an apostrophe, lived in Queens with her sister, was afraid of no one and nothing on earth, and always stuck up for her own.

My phone rang. I picked it up and said, "*Downtown* copy," which I'd hit upon my first day on the job as the way I liked to answer my phone. It sounded like a snappy thing a beat cop would say into a walkie-talkie. "This is Jeremy."

"Hello, *Downtown* copy," said Max. "What's the four-one-one?"

"I should have let it go to voice mail," I said. "I'm in no mood."

"What mood are you in?"

"The mood when anyone cheerful makes me want to kill myself."

"I'm turning forty tomorrow," said Max. "I'm not cheerful. I'm calling to ask a huge, friendship-straining favor of you."

"This might not be an ideal time for that."

"I have no other time, I've got to have an answer right away, in the course of this phone call." He clicked his tongue against his teeth, gathering steam for his pitch. "I know it's short notice, but I just this minute decided. I want my parents to know the love of my life before they die. They don't have to know he's the love of my life, but I'd like them to have met him. So I'm having a very small birthday party at their house tomorrow night, and I would love it if you would come."

"What do I have to do with any of this, exactly?"

"Oh, bubeleh," he said in his deepest, faggiest, most syrupy voice, "you're the love of my other life. And also, you've always said you wanted to meet them. It's Shabbat, so you have to get there in time for sunset, which should be no problem, since it's June."

"What time will this party be over? Are you allowed to drive me to the train on Shabbat?"

"You can stay over. There's plenty of room."

"I don't know," I said, nettled that in all the years Max and I had been friends, he'd never invited me to his parents' house, and now all of a sudden this interloper he'd known all of six months was the star guest while I was hauled in as third wheel. "I frankly don't see why you need me there."

"Beside the fact that you're one of my oldest and dearest friends," he said, "I need you there as a buffer so they don't notice the red-hot love hormones flying between Fernando and me. And I asked my mother to make her brisket."

For years I had been subjected to drool-inducing descriptions of Rivka Goldenberg's melt-in-your-mouth brisket that simmered all day in a thick and redolent broth, her crisp golden latkes with homemade applesauce, her unbelievable chopped liver, with just the right amount of schmaltz, so crumbly, so rich.

"I can't stay till sundown on Saturday," I said. "I have to be back in time for Amanda's wedding rehearsal at four."

"So Rita will drive you to the train whenever you're ready to go," he said. Rita Monteferrante had been the Goldenbergs' live-in housekeeper for most of Max's life. I'd never met her either. "She'll pack you a lunch for the train," he added entreatingly.

"All right," I said wearily. "I'll do it because it's your birthday, but you know exactly how I feel about this kind of charade. You're going to owe me."

"Anything," he said. "Bless you."

"What should I bring?"

"You could bring some kosher wine," said Max. "Also, don't forget, it's baseball season, so we'll be watching the game before dinner."

"Oh," I said, immediately concerned. "That's right. The game." If Fischl were half the Yankee fan Max had made him out to be, the game would no doubt be rife with land mines onto which I feared I would almost surely step with unthinking remarks that betrayed either my complete ignorance of the game or worse, my frank attraction to one of the players. Fernando could get away with not knowing the rules of baseball; he was a foreigner.

"Don't worry," said Max firmly. "I'll pick you up at the train. Just call and let me know which one you'll be on."

After we'd hung up, I dialed Information and asked for the number of the American Bar Association. Then, without pausing to think, I dialed the number I'd been given. As it rang I waited, hardly breathing, doodling endless figure eights on the margins of Bianca Mantooth's copy, until someone picked up.

"I'm trying to locate a lawyer named Angus Thrane," I said. "He was once based in San Francisco, California, a long time ago. I'm not sure where he is now. I thought you might have his whereabouts on file."

"Can you spell that last name, please?" the woman who'd answered on behalf of the American Bar Association asked in her warmly melodious voice.

While I waited on hold, I was treated to a Muzak version of some song that had played every other minute on KRIZ and KUPD when I was in junior high, in Phoenix. I couldn't place it right away, but it had been Amanda's absolute number-one favorite song for about three weeks. She'd performed a dance routine to this song in one of the Thrane family extravaganza revue shows my sisters and I had occasionally foisted on our mother and Lou when we had nothing better to do with our Saturday afternoons. In a purple leotard and metallic-thread leg warmers, Amanda, bony and flat-chested and all of eleven years old, had lip-synched and slithered around the living room. Just as I recognized the song as "You Light Up My Life" and began to gag, the Muzak was cut off abruptly with a beep.

"Hello?" came the dulcet purr of the American Bar Association lady.

I fully expected her to tell me to stop bothering her, this was highly classified information and I was wasting everyone's time. But instead, to my stupefaction, she gave me the street address and telephone number of a man named Angus Thrane, a retired attorney who had practiced in San Francisco but now lived in the San Juan Islands in Washington State.

"The San Juan Islands?" I asked skeptically. I hadn't pictured my father in the Pacific Northwest. The climate was all wrong for him. He needed to be somewhere hot and severe and uncompromising, like the Middle East or the Arizona desert. "Are you sure?"

"Well, that's the information we've got on him," she said. "Can I help you with anything else today?"

"No," I said in a dazed voice. "No, you've helped me so much already. I can't thank you enough."

I hung up. Then I stood by my desk, gazing into space, flexing my hands with gingerly curiosity to see whether I'd been altered biochemically somehow in the past three minutes. I looked down at what I'd written, stared at it until all the letters and numbers swam and merged and blurred. Shaking myself back to consciousness, I folded the piece of paper and put it into my pocket, forgetting it was supposed to stay here with the rest of the dog-do story.

When it was time to go meet Josh Turnbull at the offices of Waverly Productions, I stuck my head into the airspace of Frederick's cubicle. He clutched a pencil over a typewritten page of single-spaced lines of irregular length, from which I surmised that he was laboring over his own poetry while Daphne was in a meeting. His desktop was rubbled with pink eraser detritus. A floaty tendril of longish hair hovered above his scalp, waggling gently with the motion of his head like a phonograph-needle arm as he scanned his work.

"Frederick," I said gently when he didn't look up. "Sorry to bother you."

"Jeremy!" He snapped to attention. He was stoop-shouldered; his skin had an indoor, defeated cast, as if he shaved too much and rarely went anywhere exciting. "What brings you to these parts?"

"I'm not feeling well. Can you tell Daphne I've gone home when she gets back from her meeting?"

"Consider it done," he said. "Nothing serious, I hope."

"No," I said. "Just under the weather."

"I hear you," he said, moving his hands in a squidlike motion between our heads to demonstrate the wavelength we shared. "I've been feeling that way for twenty years. Always happy to cover for a comrade."

"Thanks, Frederick."

I began to edge away, but not fast enough.

"You know," he continued, stretching a rubber band pensively between his fingers, "you'd think they'd be happy to see us go home when we're sick."

"You would," I agreed swiftly, but I was caught.

"But they want us here anyway. Sick or dying, they don't give a fuck. The fundamental axiom of the copy editor's life is that we can't afford a life, which is good, because then we'd know what we were missing." He tossed the rubber band onto his desk.

I edged my elbow up to the top of the cubicle wall and rested my weight against it. Had Frederick been the type who thrived on academic striving and political intrigue, he might have been a professor, but he wasn't, so he vented his pedagogical instincts on any random person who wandered into his sphere of influence. These impromptu diatribes were his outlet, along with reading his poetry at spoken-word slams and open-mike bookstore readings.

"It all goes like clockwork," he said with nasal vehemence, "as long as we can manage to buy enough food to keep us strong enough to work. But when we get sick it's our loss. No insurance, no benefits, no paid sick days. If we died, they'd just wheel us off to the dustbin and install another drone from the supply closet." One corner of his mouth turned up in a mocking little half-smile as he talked as if he were kidding, but I knew otherwise by then, so I didn't laugh the way I might have several months before. "But we forget this, conveniently for them, because we're lulled by our steady little paychecks going drip, drip, drip like Chinese water torture into our bank accounts."

I cast a casual eye at the clock on the wall and saw that it was getting late. "Good metaphor," I said. "If you have direct deposit, which I don't."

"It's a corporate gulag, my friend," he said. "Make no mistake about that. The absence of natural materials is a deliberate assault on passion and intellect. These soft chairs, the filtered air, the free soft drinks in the kitchen, all these denatured creature comforts are symbols of death in life." He rapped his knuckles with a series of dull thuds on the particle board separating his cubicle from mine. "It's hollow and flimsy and fake, but it might as well be razor wire. Before you know it, you're fifty. I'm fifty, for example, as of last week. But you! You're still young enough to get out alive. You've still got juice in you, you've still got hope."

"I'm not that young," I said, "and at the moment—"

"Go," he said, waving me off. "Run while you can. Go! Don't come back!" He scratched his head, not because it itched, I suspected, but because he was trying to contain his excitement at the idea of my busting out of there.

I went out to the elevator, boarded a downward car, and watched the descending numbers light up as a swooping sensation rose from the pit of my stomach to my inner ear. The lyrics to "You Light Up My Life" presented themselves cloyingly; I pushed them away. Then I walked out into the wet street without an umbrella, without a raincoat. By the time I'd gone half a block, I was sopping wet. An uptown bus veered precipitously into a stop just ahead; without thinking, I climbed its stairs, presented my Metrocard, and grabbed hold of the overhead pole just as the driver wheeled sharply back into the traffic without checking to see who might have been in his way, then muscled the bus up the avenue as if he were too enraged, bored, and homicidal to care who got hit in the process. I swayed and bobbed with the herky-jerky forward momentum, periodically checking our progress through the steamy windows.

A man bumped against me at a sudden stop. When I looked at him, he smiled. "Sorry," he said. He was a standard-issue brown-haired guy in his mid-thirties, like me. The lines at the corners of his eyes fanned out, crinkled; he looked both amused and sympathetic, and it struck me that he was intelligent. This made me trust him immediately, as if intelligence were a moral quality like integrity or loyalty, even though I knew perfectly well it wasn't.

I smiled back at him and couldn't stop. I felt priapically turbocharged and giddy from the sudden, swift, unexpected possession of the information in my pocket.

"That's all right," I said. Our bodies were warm against each other. His face glowed in the milky air; our identically wet hair suggested hot showers, swims together in pools beneath waterfalls. We both seemed on the verge of laughing, and held our gaze. Tiny signals flashed between us, bursts of photons that penetrated my bloodstream, caromed between platelets in hot saffron bursts. Here he was. I took a deep breath to say something else to him, I wasn't sure what. The force of my inhalation seemed to draw him in closer, so near that my exhaled words could have passed from my lips to his ear like a kiss.

Just then the bus stopped again and people got on and off, jostling me and forcing me to retreat farther along toward the rear of the bus. My lungs leaked their cargo in an inaudible little puff. In the new configuration, when the bus started up again, the brown-haired man was wedged into a pole-hanging crowd with his back to me. We had been separated by a short, pushy woman whose fat little arm shot assertively skyward in front of my face to grasp the pole. She had floury hands, as if she'd been rolling pizza dough; I wanted none of her. I tried to telegraph a silent message to the back of his head, but he didn't turn around to meet my eye again, and got off at the next stop. His retreating raincoat, tan and slightly dingy, blended into the crowd of identical raincoats and vanished. The bus lurched on, dim and cavernous as a warehouse.

Now, all of a sudden, my father was in the San Juan Islands. His whereabouts were no longer unknown, he was no longer dead or abroad or lost or a figment of anyone's imagination. He had been there all along, just a phone call away, which also meant that he could have found me at any time. I wasn't listed in the phone book and neither were my mother or sisters, but the Rheingolds had lived in the same apartment on Eighty-ninth Street since the early sixties and had had the same listed telephone number all that time. Angus had known them; the Rheingolds and Thranes had gone camping together, visited each other, had friends in common. As far as I knew, Angus had made no effort to contact them; he hadn't cared to learn whether we'd survived without him, how we'd all turned out. This made the whole question of contacting him slightly more complicated. But I had absolutely nothing to lose, I told myself as I climbed down the bus steps onto the relative safety of the pavement. I'd already lost him.

An elevator as big as a bathroom took me to the eleventh floor of the Marks Building. The receptionist sat at a desk under spiky black letters that said "Waverly Productions." Her hair was in an impeccable, shining bun that accentuated her deerlike head; her glistening eyes were focused unblinkingly on me. For the split second it took for the elevator doors to shut behind me, she and I assessed each other thoroughly and decided we were not kindred spirits. "I'm Jeremy Thrane," I blurted out then, crossing the bare expanse of creaking, buffed hardwood floor, shedding water like a dog. "I have an appointment with Josh Turnbull at three-thirty. I think I'm a little early."

"Have a seat," she said coolly. "Can I offer you some bottled water? Coffee?"

"No," I said, "I'm fine. Well, okay, some water would be great. If it's not too much trouble."

"It's no trouble," she said with bland disdain. She leaned over from the waist like a dancer to open a cube refrigerator on the floor, then handed me a small, cold, wet plastic bottle and gestured to a pair of black leather armchairs under a potted ficus. As I sat damply in one and twisted the lid off the bottle, she picked up her telephone, pressed a button, moved her lips without making a sound, and hung up. "He'll be with you shortly," she said to me, then resumed her motionless, expressionless position, staring at the elevators in readiness to greet the next arrival, as if she'd hit some internal reset button.

My eyes began to water; it had been dark outside, but the windows up here let in inexplicably bright light. I noticed a distinct smell of celery, a sharp, thin odor that could have come from the barely dry plaster on these spanking-new walls or vapor from the recent varnish on the floors. Or maybe it was the receptionist's perfume; it suited her. Then I was seized with a sudden attack of flatulence that I was unable to discharge freely in the proximity of the snooty bunhead. As the time ticked by and Josh failed to materialize, the temptation became increasingly overwhelming to get out of there, release my excess gas, then get myself a grilled cheese on rye and a bowl of tomato soup at a diner somewhere.

Just as I was about to bail, I heard a male voice saying my name. I parked my half-drunk water bottle behind a leg of my chair, then stood up and shook the hand I was offered. Josh turned out to be a tall blond guy in a pair of crease-free blue pants and blindingly clean white Oxford shirt. I followed him down a short hall and into a room filled with couches and low tables, where we sank into facing couches at the same time. Then a young Chinese woman came in through a door I hadn't noticed and perched smiling on the arm of Josh's couch, pad and pencil at the ready. She had shiny shoulder-length hair and wore a straight pink skirt and a blouse that was the feminine version of Josh's shirt. Same buttons, even: expensive-looking mother-of-pearl discs.

"This is my assistant, Mai Lin Chang," said Josh.

"Hello," I said.

"It's really great to meet you, Jeremy," she said back. To my surprise, she had a strong southern accent.

"Thanks," I said.

There was a pause as we all looked with bright, expectant smiles at each other.

"So," said Josh abruptly as if he'd just remembered that he was in charge of this meeting. "Jeremy. We loved your screenplay, I'm sure your agent told you. Your dialogue is very smart, lots of punch and emotion, and the plot is wild. Hilarious. That undertaker is quite a character. Very dark, very original, and in spite of everything, very funny."

"Thanks," I said. The flatulence had gone away somehow, magically, although I hadn't farted as far as I knew.

"Why don't you tell us a bit about yourself? Where you're from, what else you've written, what you're working on lately, that sort of thing."

To my private chagrin, I heard myself deliver a sincere, detailed, operatic description of my childhood whose establishing themes were "peripatetic" and "bohemian." I presented myself as a bookish, introverted lad, reading until late at night in my sleeping bag with a flashlight, writing stories and memorizing poems at campground picnic tables. For some reason, as I talked I felt the left side of my mouth lift in Frederick's mocking little half-smile. As briefly as I could, I whisked them through my liberal arts college career, my move to New York, my recent decade of singleminded work on a novel. They appeared to listen as attentively as children at a library story hour, although they might secretly have been mulling over what they were going to say to me when I finally shut up. "In a nutshell," I said finally, "I never thought I'd be anything but a writer."

"Are you working on anything else at the moment?" Josh asked. "Any other finished scripts in a drawer somewhere?"

"Well, as I said, I recently finished my novel," I said bravely. "It's about an American Marxist in Turkey in the seventies who tries to ignite a revolution but gets assassinated by Muslim fundamentalists. It's currently being sent out by my literary agent." There was a brief, odd silence. "Howard Fine," I added quickly.

"Okay," said Josh, his enthusiasm undiminished. "By all means, we'd love to see it. But no scripts, no treatments, that kind of thing?"

"No," I said. "Sorry. I'm really just a novelist."

"We have a book we're developing right now?" said Mai Lin. "An amazing memoir by a teenage survivor of incest called *Walking Under Bridges*."

She handed me a book, which I held in both my hands and squeezed as if I were testing the ripeness of a melon at the supermarket. I wasn't sure what else they wanted me to do with it right now, since we were having a conversation and I couldn't very well read it. I checked out the author photo on the back flap and saw a swath of honey-blond hair, a fresh, angelic, freckled face.

"We'd be very interested to hear what sort of ideas you'd come up with, scriptwise," said Josh. "We have a feeling you could be just right for this material, since you handled the theme of incest with a light touch in your screenplay, which is not an easy thing to pull off."

"Thanks," I said.

"The author has a great sense of humor," said Mai Lin. "We're looking to develop a script that frankly shows the horrible things that happen to her, but without painting her as this destroyed little victim."

"If anyone could do it, we think you can," said Josh.

"Absolutely," said Mai Lin.

They smiled at me and waited for me to respond.

"Well, I'd be happy to read it," I said, wondering if this were true, and deciding it might as well be.

"That would be so great," said Mai Lin. "Take it home, take a look at it, and let us know what you think. We are so excited," she said, looking over at Josh, "to see what you come up with."

"We're really excited," said Josh. "This could be big. This could be really big. I don't want to get ahead of ourselves, Jeremy, but we're excited about you in particular and in general. We think you've got that something, that combination of originality and insight and humor that's so rare, it's like gold. Reading *The Way of All Flesh* was literally like being a prospector who's been panning for months and coming up empty, and then suddenly, boom, he hits a mother lode. Mai Lin and I were jumping up and down, that's how thrilled we were to discover you. Most screenwriters are cookie-cutter, jaded, by the numbers. They don't reveal anything of their souls, they write for a market. You're an artist, if you will. You're exactly what we're looking for."

"Gee," I said, smiling, trying to seem unfazed but deeply flattered in spite of my skepticism about these people. "Thanks."

"And while we're on the subject of the future," said Josh. He looked at Mai Lin. "Should I bring this up yet?"

"Sure," she said. "What the hey, it's all part of the mix, right?"

"Just off the cuff, Jeremy," he said, his blue-blue eyes glowing interrogatively at me, "what's your gut feeling about relocating to Los Angeles?"

I slid my eyes to the door, then back to him. "Los Angeles?"

"I know this is premature," said Josh. He spread his hands on his knees, palms up, nothing to hide, all his cards on the table. "But we wanted to just run the idea by you, all completely hypothetical on both sides, but something to keep in mind in the eventuality that this project works out the way we hope it will."

"We would really love to have you on our team?" said Mai Lin. "But you couldn't stay in New York, unfortunately."

"Aren't you based in New York?" I asked carefully. I didn't necessarily want to sound accusatory, but I had a sneaking suspicion they were trying to pull some kind of bait-and-switch on me; suddenly, I felt the uneasy antennae-prickling alertness of the gull.

"Well, we just opened this new office here?" said Mai Lin. "Right. But this New York office is primarily for the purposes of interviewing, recruiting, that sort of thing. Like this meeting right now. All the real work gets done in our L.A. office. We're actually just here for the week for meetings with—well, with people like you."

Josh's eyes narrowed thoughtfully; he leaned forward to rest his elbows on his knees, his hands clasped loosely. He fixed me with a warm, frank smile. "Waverly is a very close-knit group, Jeremy," he said earnestly. "And it's based in L.A., as Mai Lin just told you. We're small, we're pretty new, and we work very closely together on our various projects. We really like our writers to be in-house. They work in open offices around a central atrium, where there are conversation pits, with modular couches and conference tables for workshopping and discussions."

"Sounds really great," I said with a smarmy enthusiasm I couldn't disguise or suppress. It did sound really great; I just couldn't buy it at face value.

"It's an amazing way to run a production company," Josh said energetically. "It's Stuart's original vision and impetus, of course."

"He means Stuart Waverly," interjected Mai Lin. "Our founder and CEO."

"He's galvanized a lot of like-minded people in the industry," Josh went on without missing a beat, as if they'd rehearsed this many times, "who feel exactly the way he does, and convinced us to come on board. So when I say 'we,' I really do mean all of us, from Stuart on down. We're trying to be a community rather than a corporation, if you will, and we hope our films will reflect this. We're looking to get back to the roots of what was great about American movies in their golden ages, the forties and seventies: We want original scripts by great writers to be shot by brilliant directors, and we want to cast the most interesting, genuine

actors, not golden-calf idols. We want to create art. We think the world's
ready for us."

"We think it's starving for us!" Mai Lin chimed in.

Their smiles were dazzling.

"Are you trying to recruit me into a cult?" I blurted out before I
could censor myself.

They looked at each other. Mai Lin wrinkled her nose and Josh raised
his eyebrows.

"I'm sorry to be so impolitic," I went on apologetically. "But I'm not
a joiner or a believer in any way. I'm a very bad prospect for this kind of
thing."

They burst simultaneously into merry peals of laughter.

"That's hilarious," said Josh. "This is exactly one of the reasons we
want you to work with us. We need that sense of humor. The fact that
you're not a joiner is a plus, believe us. We're none of us joiners; that's
why we work for Waverly, because we can be individuals there. We don't
have to toe any party line."

Mai Lin was still giggling. "Oh my God! I can totally see why you
said that though. Like, we're all happy and we have this whole, like, philosophy and all, and a quote-unquote leader, and all this talk about community." She grinned at Josh. "He is so funny," she told him as if he'd
just walked into the room and she was catching him up. "Jay and Cindy
would just eat him up. Two of our writers," she said to me. "Former New
Yorkers. Most of our transplants live in a small community of bungalows
in Santa Monica, near the beach."

"Your transplants," I said.

"Waverly owns several of these houses," said Josh. "We lease them at
very reduced rents to our staff. There's one for you if it works out, and
you want it. They have avocado and lemon trees in the yard, patios with
barbecue pits, most of them are within walking distance of the Pacific
Ocean. We have lots of parties, we socialize, anyone who relocates has a
built-in life waiting there."

"Jeremy would have loved that beach party last month," said Mai
Lin.

"He would have seen Jay and Cindy at their best, that's for sure,"
said Josh.

"Those wisecracks were flying thick and fast," said Mai Lin. "I was laughing so hard, I almost choked on my hot dog. That kind of laughing where you don't want to laugh so you don't miss a word but you can't help it."

"If the Algonquin writers had been transplanted to California and the present day," said Josh, "they would have felt right at home at that party."

They both turned simultaneously to me.

"Sorry," said Josh. "We get carried away sometimes, you know?"

"Sure," I said, feeling an odd compulsion to reassure him. "I can imagine."

"But you don't have to take our word for it," said Mai Lin. "We can't really convey what it's like. You should come out and see for yourself."

"Not to be intrusive either," Josh said, "but we gathered from your script, and from what your agent told us, that you're gay, am I right? I am too. Quite a few of us at Waverly are."

"But not to pressure you!" said Mai Lin. "Oh my God, we never pressure anyone, we're really and truly not recruiting you into any kind of cult." She giggled again. "We're just trying to paint an accurate, complete picture for you of a really truly special, wonderful place to live and work."

"The upshot of all this is, Jeremy, we know you'll do great things with your talents, and we hope you'll decide to share them with us. What more can we say?"

"Thanks," I said quizzically. There was a suspiciously warm feeling in my chest I tried and failed to quell. "This is all very flattering."

"We really, really appreciate your taking the time to come today," he said, then he and Mai Lin simultaneously stood up. A beat later, I stood up too. They escorted me to the elevator, flanking me like a pair of vice cops. I pressed the down button, then the three of us stood while I waited for the car, somewhat awkwardly after the ebullient meeting we'd just had; we were strangers, after all, and we'd said everything we had to say back there in the conference room. I had no idea what Josh and Mai Lin were thinking, or what they really thought of me. I glanced over at the floor by the chair I'd sat in; the water bottle was gone. I didn't turn to catch the eye of the receptionist, but I could feel her cool gaze on the back of my neck as we all stood there facing the closed elevator door; for some reason, I felt a sudden affinity with her, as if our unspoken but honest dislike trumped any manufactured affection this pair of Californians could throw at me.

When they heard the little ping as the car arrived, as if a spell had been broken, Josh and Mai Lin suddenly resumed their effusive informality, wished me well, told me how great it had been to meet me and how much they looked forward to our next meeting, and shook my hand firmly. Finally, just when I feared the doors would close and the elevator would go away and leave me stranded there in their affectionate clutches, they released me and I was free to board the vast white empty car and ride back down to the street in humming silence.

The rain had stopped. A warm, humid wind blew up the avenue, carrying with it lightweight plastic lids, Chinese restaurant menus, ATM receipts, and a flurry of handouts advertising dry-cleaning services and manicures. I plucked a pink square of paper off my pants leg and scrutinized it briefly, wondering what else those House of Nails places were selling. They couldn't possibly make a go of it on manicures alone, could they? According to the flyer, a deluxe mani-pedi with all the trimmings was only ten dollars. That didn't seem to add up to a whole lot of revenue.

When I got home, I let myself into the empty apartment and went straight to the kitchen, where I made a cheese sandwich with mayo on rye bread and poured a glass of tomato juice, a quick, cold substitute for the diner lunch I'd envisioned earlier. I wolfed it all down, standing at the counter, then went into my room, took off my shoes, flopped onto my bed, and was asleep within five minutes.

When I woke up, my room was flooded with sunlight and I felt wide awake and energetic. It was almost six-thirty. I was supposed to meet Amanda and Emma at seven to shop for Amanda's wedding shoes and, in the process, buy Max some kind of a birthday present, although I had no idea what to give him. I'd been somewhat roped into this expedition; Amanda had pleaded with me the day before to come along and protect her from our mother, whose enthusiasm for the future groom had apparently not substantially increased in the duration of their months-long engagement.

As I walked down toward the West Village, it occurred to me that I was being pressed into service in this helpful capacity quite a bit lately; maybe I should start a business, "Extra Man, Inc." or "Third Wheel Ltd." I was feeling handsome and devil-may-care and refreshed after my nap; my meeting with Josh and Mai Lin had given me a shot in the arm I hadn't been aware of at the time. I began swaggering a little, eyeing all the men who passed me with some of the sexual confidence I'd felt when I was with Ted. As we approached each other, I caught the eye of a ravishing black youth with sparkling eyes who carried himself like a prince. As his eyebrows lifted a fraction of an inch, my stomach felt flatter, my arms magically more powerful, my aura irresistible. As he passed by me he looked away and was gone forever. But coming toward me in a great unending phalanx were other men, young, old, sexy, odd-looking, chubby, svelte, every race and ethnicity and range of intelligence, on and on, a never-ending army walking up the avenue. I continued on my way, undaunted and hopeful, looking at them all.

As I opened the door of the Cedar Tavern and stepped inside, sunlight nipped at my heels and was shut out to wait for me on the sidewalk. As my eyes adjusted, I saw that the dark old room was populated by the usual locals and a smattering of tourists acting casual in hopes of being mistaken for locals; the giveaway was the way they surreptitiously but hopefully checked the door when I came in just in case I might be a famously hard-drinking painter or writer from the mythic past. Anyone who'd ever spent time here in recent years knew how futile an exercise this was, and had ceased to bother; that whole species had either died out or gone into hiding.

Amanda and Emma were waiting for me right where they'd said they'd be, in a booth near the back, half-empty martini glasses in front of them. "Howdy, gals," I said, plunking myself down next to my mother. "Been here long?"

They were unable to answer. Their foreheads were lowered almost to the tabletop; they clutched their stomachs, and their faces were contorted. High keening noises came from their grimacing mouths.

"Ahhhh," said my mother, wiping her eyes. She gave a few weak little bleats of diminishing laughter, shaking her head.

"What's so funny?" I asked indignantly.

My mother patted my hand. "Girl talk," she said. She and Amanda grinned maniacally at each other. From this I surmised that they'd been laughing at me, or, quite likely, laughing at men in general, and pinning it all on the first one they saw. And even though I sympathized, I resented being made the butt of the joke. Men hadn't exactly been doing me any favors lately either.

Amanda said with moist eyes, the aftermath of uncontrollable hilarity hovering around her mouth, "What are you drinking?"

The prospect of a drink usually made me feel festive and lucky, but at the moment it just gave me a headache. "Nothing, thanks," I said. "I'm tired of drinking."

"How about a martini," she said. "Vodka, olives, no vermouth, right?"

"No," I said. "Not a martini. Surprise me. I want something new and unexpected."

She gave me a thumbs-up and headed for the bar.

"It's just gallows humor, really," said my mother. "We're both in states of near hysteria right now; we were just trying to channel it in a positive direction."

"Why are you hysterical?"

"Well, it might have something to do with the fact that Amanda's wedding is on Sunday," said my mother. "And as for me, Leonard had a bad spell this morning. He accused me of taking his keys and hiding the book he was reading because he couldn't find either one. He gets so accusatory; it's hard to remember sometimes that he isn't himself any more."

"Why don't you get a nurse?"

"Well, this time Irene came over to help me."

"She did?" I asked, amazed.

"Well, she would have come right away, but Richard needed her to listen while he played through the concerto he's performing with the Philharmonic next month; apparently, he's got some new interpretation of it and he's very nervous about it. So she couldn't get there for about an hour, and by then Leonard had calmed down."

"You should call me next time. I'll get there as soon as I can."

"I would, but Irene lives just two blocks away."

I rolled my eyes. "You'd rather wait an hour for her than half an hour for me?"

"She's just so focused on whatever she's doing at any given moment," my mother said soothingly. "She loses track of time."

"Whatever," I said. "I know you'll defend her no matter what I say about her."

"I was trying to work on the wedding poem I'm writing for Amanda and Liam," said Emma, "but Leonard upset me so much, I couldn't concentrate at all the rest of the day. I hope I can finish it in time. I'm getting worried; it's so rough now."

"What's it about?" I asked.

"My first wedding, the day I married your father," she said. "The way my mother looked at me after the short ceremony that changed me, like a spell or enchantment, from her daughter into Angus's wife. I hope the fact that the marriage ended badly isn't a downer, considering the occasion. It's supposed to be about mothers and daughters, not the beginning of my first divorce."

"That reminds me," I said, "I have something to show you really fast, before Amanda comes back. Don't tell her. I want to give it to her at the wedding." I took the piece of paper out of my pocket and handed it over.

Emma put on her reading glasses, unfolded the paper, and started to read Bianca Mantooth's copy, ignoring what was penciled in the margin. "Purebred dogs are the new silicone implants, the must-have fashion accessory of the new millennium," she read in an excited but uncomprehending voice. She looked up at me. "You're giving her and Liam a dog? I don't think they—"

"Look at what I wrote in pencil. There."

"Angus Thrane," she read aloud before she knew what she was reading. She went silent and stared at the information, then looked up at me again, then glanced over at Amanda, who was talking to the bartender. She stared at the paper again. "Where did you get this?"

"I called the ABA."

"The what?"

"The American Bar Association. And they gave it to me just like that."

"Did you have to say who you were?"

"No."

She shook her head. "My God. You could have been a vindictive ex-con he put away, or a stalker, or worse."

"Or his long-lost son who's tracking him down."

She laughed. "Have you called him yet?"

"I just got it this morning. I want to give it to Amanda and Lola before I do anything. When does Lola get here?"

"Tomorrow night," she said. She looked at the paper again. "Angus Thrane," she said grimly. "That bastard. All this time. And he's probably still as selfish and full of himself as he ever was. If I ever saw him again, I think I would strangle him with my bare hands."

We looked at each other, each of us thinking our separate thoughts about Angus.

"Here you go," said Amanda, setting my glass in front of me. "What are you reading?"

"Nothing," I said, taking the paper from my mother, folding it up, and putting it back into my pocket. I took a taste of my cocktail, which was cloudy green, tasted like toothpaste, and was so sweet, it curled my tongue. "What the hell is this?"

"It's a grasshopper," said Amanda.

"You got me a *grasshopper*?"

"Is it awful?" Amanda asked, laughing. "I was trying to surprise you. It's not easy."

I took another taste. "This is an old-lady drink, Amanda."

"Hey," said my mother. "What's wrong with being an old lady?"

I tried another sip. "It's not bad once you get used to it. Try it."

"Ecch," said Amanda. "Hey, Jeremy, how was your meeting today?"

I told them I'd asked Josh and Mai Lin if they were recruiting me into a cult. They found this uproarious; their martinis were almost gone, which might have explained why. For some reason, they found the idea of my living in a bungalow in Santa Monica even funnier; I laughed along with them, although I was still half considering the idea, or at least mulling it over in the back of my brain.

"The question is," I said, "what's the catch? It can't be as flat-out wonderful as they say it is."

"Of course not," said Amanda. "Nothing ever is. They probably work you to death, or steal your best ideas and don't give you credit."

"How much will they pay you?" asked my mother.

"No idea," I said. "It's not customary to discuss salary until they make a concrete offer and we start talking terms."

"Listen to you," my mother said fondly. "You sound so savvy."

At this, Amanda and I flicked a glance at each other so quickly, no one else could possibly have noticed, not even our mother, who was gazing at both of us with misty-eyed, vodka-enhanced affection. When it was my turn to buy another round, I fetched three grasshoppers from the bar. Emma lifted hers and offered enthusiastic toasts to marriage, then to Amanda's wedding, and finally to Liam himself. As we hit our glasses together for the third time, I was afraid we might break them with the vehemence of our collective goodwill.

"Your shoes, Amanda," Emma said, remembering suddenly.

Amanda waved the thought away. "I'll just wear some old ones."

"No, you need new ones to get married in," she said. "Let's drink up and find you some. It's only eight; the stores will still be open."

We left our three empty greenish glasses on the table and went burbling off to SoHo, where Amanda hit upon a pair of strappy, golden, pointy-heeled shoes at the second store we tried, exactly the sort of fairy-princess things she might have chosen as a little girl for her Barbie, if she'd had one. As she teetered around the store, stopping by every mirror to gaze at her feet, my mother and I exchanged a look, and then she got out her wallet.

On my way home, I stopped into a drugstore and bought two greeting cards, one a poetic, embossed wedding card, onto which I planned to copy Angus's address and telephone number, and the other a manly, jokey birthday card. I was at a loss for actual birthday-present ideas that wouldn't strike the Goldenbergs as suspiciously gay, but a gift certificate from a sporting goods store seemed like a nice, butch sort of present, not too intimate, not too emotional. I knew Max would actually use it, since he belonged to a gym, so I wouldn't be wasting my money. When I'd done all my shopping, I stopped into a bar a block away from where I lived, which I'd never been to before. I was there for a few hours, and made a passel of temporary new friends, none of whom seemed interested in going home with me, but when I thought about it I found I wasn't all that interested in taking any of them home either. I had a fine time anyway. I felt witty and attractive and magnetic. My shirt looked extremely good on me, I noticed in the mirror behind the bar; I described my illustrious future at Waverly Productions, my job lolling in the atrium on a couch, spouting ideas, and impersonating a latter-day Dorothy Parker at beach parties after work. Everyone seemed to find this extremely fascinating, judging from the fact that I didn't have to buy myself a drink all night.

The next morning I woke up with the kind of hangover that made me feel as if I were made of fine crystal. On my way to work, every jolt of the subway vibrated in my head with a high, clear ringing sound. The skin on my face felt tissue-thin and crackling. My eyes seemed to have become slightly too large for their sockets; when I blinked, my eyelids scraped against my eyeballs with an almost pleasant friction.

"Feeling better?" Frederick asked solicitously when I showed up at five after nine with my shirt half out of my pants and my hair uncombed.

"Much, thanks," I said robustly, unfolding Bianca Mantooth's missing page, erasing Angus's information, and restoring it to its manuscript.

"Good," said Frederick. "Bianca Mantooth called Daphne after you left yesterday. She's stopping by the office this morning to say hello to Simon."

Simon was the editor in chief. His office was two floors above ours. "Oh," I said, inspecting my coffee cup to make sure there were no dead bugs in it. "Lucky day for Simon, I guess."

"She also said she wanted to see you," Frederick said. "She wanted to make sure you'd be here."

"Me?"

"That's all I know," he said sympathetically. "There's a fresh pot of coffee in the kitchen; I just made it."

I went to the men's room, where I relieved my bladder of the remains of the pint of orange juice I'd downed on my way to work, then fetched a cupful of coffee from the kitchen and brought it back to my cubicle. I sipped it slowly, letting my eyes rest on the laminated brown surface of my desk, whose interesting light-and-dark swirly patterns convincingly mimicked the natural whorled grain of wood. Frederick was probably right; this place was very likely an evil corporate minimum-security prison, and I the urban, noncriminal equivalent of an incarcerated piece-worker, but I enjoyed having a reason to get out of bed early every morning and somewhere to go all day. The work was easy, and the editors left the copy editors alone; they were young and fabulous, and we were old and weird, so they didn't waste their precious time trying to befriend us. My cubicle was cool in the summer and warm in the winter. My wastebasket was emptied every night. The bathrooms were spotless and generously stocked with toilet paper, soap, and paper towels. And whenever I wanted, I could get almost any kind of food delivered quickly and cheaply. This morning, for example, the astonishingly inexpensive Western omelet with rye toast and side of hash browns I ordered from a nearby deli arrived piping hot in twenty minutes in a tidy Styrofoam container with napkins, extra ketchup, and tiny salt and pepper packets. It seemed I had found another comfortable cage for myself. Maybe I liked cages; I suspected that Frederick, for all his grousing and muck-raking, did too.

The hours crept by; the morning ended. Everyone straggled off to forage for food. I left at one o'clock, as I always did, and spent my lunch hour hunched over a prepackaged California roll and a Styrofoam cup of reconstituted miso soup at a Japanese fast-food hole in the wall, reading *Walking Under Bridges*, which wasn't nearly as bad as I'd expected, and was even funny in places, as Mai Lin had said it would be. I envisioned myself walking barefoot across my new backyard in the smoggy Santa Monica morning sun to pick a ripe avocado for my breakfast. The idea didn't entirely repel me, although it was hard to picture what I would do after I ate the avocado and put on my shoes; I drew a blank when I tried to imagine sitting at a conference table in the Waverly Productions atrium with my fellow transplants, earnestly discussing story arc and character motivation. Arc and motivation struck me as completely spurious storytelling devices, invented for the purposes of writing from a formula, developing a protagonist from point A to point B to point C, three acts and you're out; I had considered none of this when I wrote *Angus in Efes*, for example, but maybe that was my problem, and I could learn otherwise.

After lunch I went back to my cubicle for the languorous midafternoon lull, when all the editors gathered in each other's offices to backbite and kibitz and discuss which lucky hot spot to grace with their collectively fabulous presence tonight, and Daphne disappeared as she did almost every afternoon, I suspected to take a nap on the couch in the ladies' lounge. While she was gone, Frederick flossed his teeth and whistled tunelessly and shot rubber bands into the air; Rosa's usual hum of low-level pissiness curdled into almost-intelligible invectives and snarls. I thought I heard a "pinche cabron pendejo" and a little later, "Chingate! Me vale madre! Vete al carajo"; her boyfriend, I gathered, was not going to propose to her no matter how inventively she threatened him. I put my feet up on my desk and checked Scott's answering machine, but there was nothing there for him or me. I made it through another twenty pages of *Walking Under Bridges* before one of the miniskirted gazelles wafted by on the air-conditioning, deposited some fresh copy on my desk without a word, and hightailed it back to her rarefied domain.

At ten minutes before three, I sensed a sudden twittering disturbance of the atmosphere of the editors' offices, several notches up on the excitement scale from the usual manic fizz they generated on their own. Then I heard a throaty female voice asking for me. One of the twenty-five-year-old male mannequins said with disdain, "I think he's somewhere over there," which I assumed was accompanied by a pissy little flap of the hand in the direction of the ghetto in which I was a socially impossible nonentity.

First I caught a burst of perfume that smelled like the essential distillation of a way of life I'd never know; it was probably called "Envy" or "Better Than You." A second later, I found myself looking up into a theatrically chalk-white face surrounded by a glossy, curling mass of hair the color of cherry soda. I hadn't yet had the pleasure of meeting Bianca Mantooth; our months'-long, ongoing, semicontentious relationship had been conducted to date entirely on paper. If this were indeed Bianca rather than her older sister, then her byline photo had been taken a number of years earlier. The flat white powder, a stark and stylish makeup choice for a woman ten years younger, had on Bianca an unfortunate tendency to accentuate the fine spiderweb of wrinkles that crinkled from each eye and the curved lines on either side of her mouth. I could also tell that in a few years she was going to have a forehead-crease situation unless she staved it off with Botox injections, which she probably would.

"Jeremy?" she said.

"Bianca," I said, standing up and offering my hand, which she shook with the tips of her smooth, thin fingers. "Nice to meet you after all these months."

Frederick's usual finicky bustle of activity had suddenly stopped. I didn't blame him; I would have been eavesdropping as avidly as he was if the situation had been reversed.

"So," she said sharply, parking her streamlined tuchus on the edge of my desk and looking around my cubicle, "this is where my deathless prose gets butchered."

"Butchered?" I said with a woefulness I hoped sounded sincere. "I truly hope you jest."

I suspected that she was here to see for herself what a dork I was. I had decided to play along with her preconceptions, quote Shakespeare, or at least pepper my dialogue with a "methinks" and a "shan't" every so often, since "There is a willow grows aslant a brook" or "Is this a dagger that I see before me, its handle toward my hand?" seemed unlikely to arise naturally. I hoped these archaisms would give her a vindicated glee that would cause her to go away feeling delighted with the world in general and herself in particular, and maybe then she wouldn't be such a pain in the ass to work with.

"I'll just say it," she said. "You're a troublemaker, Jeremy. I can't write a sentence without you coming down on me for being an illiterate airhead. I can read your mind, I know what you're thinking when you go over my stuff—this chick never went to college, she can't write her way out of a paper bag, why does she get to be the rich famous writer while I'm just an underpaid copy editor?"

"I'm paid all right, actually," I said disingenuously.

I heard a muffled snort from Frederick's cubicle as Bianca tucked her leg up underneath her, minxlike, and slithered into a more comfortable position on my desk. She settled her back against the cubicle wall I shared with Frederick, then tossed a handful of her tresses over one shoulder to unleash another daunting cloud of perfume. "You know what? I'm thinking of getting a rubber stamp that says 'stet,' that's how sick I am of having to write it everywhere. But you never give up, do you? You really believe in yourself, don't you? You think this is *Pygmalion*, and someday I'll learn to use proper English if you keep badgering me. Right?"

"Yes," I said. "I have to admit, I wish you would. It would make my job a lot easier, not that that's any concern of yours."

"You're surprised I know about *Pygmalion*, aren't you? I bet you thought I only knew *My Fair Lady*."

"Not necessarily," I said. "People know all kinds of surprising things."

"Well, I appreciate your efforts on my behalf, but I happen to know exactly what I'm doing. You know and I know it's not textbook; but it's what they want." She gestured toward the editors' offices. "They represent the person I'm writing for. Not you, darling. And it's a little insulting to me, frankly, that you seem to think I don't know any better."

"I stand corrected, it would seem," I said mildly.

"The English language has been changing and evolving ever since it began," she said. "Let me guess: You cringe at the use of 'impact on' or 'reference' as a verb. You want to scream when someone says 'off of.' "

"Not to mention the catch-all overuse of the word 'event,' " I said. "All the world's a corporate boardroom these days, it would seem."

"I bet my whole stack of chips they'll all be taught in the next century as correct usage in grammar classes by sticklers just like you, committed to defending the greatest language on the planet against people like me. What you forget is that it's the people like me who've made it so great, people who aren't afraid to break the rules and shake it all up."

"You and Shakespeare," I agreed.

"We're the fresh winds of change, the creative forces of evolution." She stood up and offered me her elegant fingertips again. I was tempted to proffer my own fingertips but gave her a real handshake instead.

"It was a pleasure to meet you," I said formally.

"Keep your mind open, Jeremy," she said with affection. "You might learn a thing or two from me, wouldn't that be a shock."

She was gone before I could assure her that it might not be a shock at all, but that was probably just as well.

Frederick's mournful, sallow face loomed into my field of vision, rising like a full moon over the top of our cubicle divider. "My friend," he said, one pontificating forefinger in the air, as if checking the direction of the wind, his hair pasted with sweat to his pate like seaweed on rocks at low tide, "that is one ill-informed and arrogant female, although her calculated appeal is not altogether lost on me. Where exactly does she get off, telling you how to do your job? I might have put her in her place if she had said those things to me. I might have pointed out that I was hired by Simon, the same Simon who writes her paychecks, to render comprehensible her so-called deathless prose."

"I think she might have said that ironically," I said.

" 'Breathless' is more like it," he went on as if I hadn't spoken. "Or depthless." He gave a ghoulish honk at his own wit. "I might have added that breaking the rules of grammar and usage and spelling is all very well if you're Bianca Mantooth, but it wouldn't do much for a black inner-city teenager trying to escape fast-food minimum-wage slavery, or a Hispanic or Chinese immigrant who doesn't want to be stuck behind a sewing machine for the rest of his or her life." He scowled with monkish fervor. "I could say a great deal more in this vein, but I don't want to make you feel any more hapless than you must already feel."

"It's okay," I said. "Don't worry about me, Frederick. As far as I'm concerned, she won fair and square. You have to pick your battles. It's only *Downtown*; if she wrote for *The New Yorker*, it would be a very different story, but she never has and never will."

"I hope not," he said skeptically. He inhaled deeply through his nose. "I hope not. Although their standards have sunk execrably low in recent years. They're not the paragon they once were. What a strong smell she left behind her. Like a persimmon grove, if there is such a thing. Or an opium den." He inhaled through his nose again as if he held a glass of wine and was identifying its bouquet. "Incense, exotic fruit, a lot of spice and something else, something tarry and dark and unspeakable . . ." He gave me a look of piercing yearning as his head sank from view, back down to his eraser-rubbled desk, his rubber bands, and dental floss.

17 | GREAT NECK

"For now the winter is past," I thought sleepily, my head lolling against the cracked leatherette headrest, "the rains are over and gone." Sheets of rain washed over the train windows, blurring the suburbs that rolled past as the train made its way through them. I'd left work early again, pleading a recurrence of yesterday's illness, and caught the train that left Penn Station at 5:29, laden with my packed overnight bag, a dozen white tulips for Rivka and two expensive bottles of kosher red wine, which the white-bearded expert at Warehouse Wines and Liquors had assured me was "as good as any comparably priced nonkosher wine." I hope white tulips weren't nonkosher or symbolic of death or something; I hadn't thought to ask Max, I'd just bought them on a whim on my way to the station. Judaism, it seemed, was a formidably exact science, and not for the faint of heart.

On my lap was *Walking Under Bridges*, which had devolved from its rather promisingly knowing, fresh, and snub-nosed beginning into an all-too-predictable and familiar catalogue of horrors, without either the leavening of insight or the undergirding of rage. The tone vacillated between arch cuteness and flat-footed affectlessness, as if Shirley Temple and Lolita had taken turns at the word processor. About a quarter of the way through, I'd caught myself actually suspecting that this girl was just trying to cash in on the public appetite for this sort of thing, and had quite possibly invented the whole raped-by-her-father deal out of cynical wholecloth. I hadn't been able to read a word since. How I'd turn this pathetic little diary into the light, witty screenplay Josh and Mai Lin seemed to expect of me was a total conundrum. Why they required it to be light and witty at all was even more baffling.

Max had gone out to Great Neck this morning. His clients had all had to suffer through their neuroses and tics without him for a day; fleetingly, I imagined them all licking doorknobs and slashing their wrists and crying in the fetal position while a wine-drunk Max blew out his birthday candles. But could you blow out birthday candles on the Sabbath? Anyway, by the time the cake emerged, it would be well past his usual quitting time. And if I hadn't been filled with trepidation about the ordeal ahead and in need of mental distraction, I wouldn't have given two figs about any of this.

I was often mistaken for a straight man when I wasn't trying to fool anyone, but on the rare occasion that I was required to pretend, I would inevitably catch myself swishing my wrist or cocking my hip or lisping slightly, none of which I ever did normally. Then I'd wonder whether anyone had noticed, then decide no one had, then realize that someone was looking at me speculatively. The collar of my white shirt was already damp; my hands were clenching and unclenching in my lap. Oh well; at least I didn't have to pretend to be Jewish.

Fernando was due in well before dark, as I was, and might even have been on this train with me, but he and I hadn't arranged to meet up and travel together, the simple reason being that the few times we'd met we'd vaguely and irrationally disliked each other, so riding the train separately meant having to spend that much less time pretending to get along for Max's sake.

Goddammit. I would never have asked this of Max. He had such a sense of entitlement sometimes, it was unbelievable; maybe that was the result of being the only child of doting parents. The tormented only child of clutchingly doting parents. I had never seen any pictures of Rivka and Fischl, because Max didn't display any in his apartment, so I envisioned them as two birds of prey holding Max between them in their claws.

Their fully grown fledgling was at the train station by himself to meet me when I disembarked at precisely 6:05. He stood under an enormous red umbrella, wearing a seersucker suit.

"Happy birthday, Jay," I said as I walked toward him. His yarmulke was embroidered with the Yankees logo; I felt a flutter of nervousness.

"Mr. Gatsby to you," he said back, taking the bag of wine from me with one hand and parting the folds of the paper cone of tulips with the other to peer in at them. "White tulips," he said neutrally. "Isn't that a little limp-wristed?"

He put the umbrella over my head, and we made our way up some stairs and across a catwalk to the parking lot.

"What should I have brought instead?"

"Maybe carnations or daisies, you know, those dumb butch flowers."

"Sorry," I said testily. "Should I just throw them away?"

"Oh, stop it, I'm just kidding. I've been jumpy all day. You, I'm not worried about. But Fernando. He's already there, by the way; he's making conversation with my father in the den."

"Why are you worried about him?"

"Because he refuses to understand that he can't kiss me in front of them," said Max, who sounded a lot more smug than jumpy about this. "This morning as I was leaving he said, 'I might not be able to restrain myself for an entire evening.'"

"How hot-blooded of him," I said, annoyed.

"You look nice," he said with a sidelong glance at me.

"Thank you," I said dubiously. I was wearing a beige linen suit Max himself had given me as a hand-me-down when he decided he'd had it long enough. It was wrinkled already from the train ride, and fit me strangely, since he was shorter and stockier than I was.

We had arrived at the parking lot. As we approached a charcoal-gray car, one of those ugly new machines that looked like high-tech running shoes, Max took a key chain out of his pocket and aimed it at the car; the alarm gave a shrill yip. I got into the passenger seat, and we were off, rolling at a stately geriatric pace through the streets of downtown Great Neck.

"Mommy," said Max, turning on his blinker two hundred yards from the nearest intersection, "said to stop at the store and pick up olives and some crackers, even though you wouldn't believe how much food there is already."

Apparently, grown Jewish children said "Mommy" as a matter of course, but every time he referred to his mother that way, I jumped as if he'd suddenly put on a diaper.

"Did she make her brisket?"

He rolled his eyes. "Ecch," he said, "you'll die when you walk in the house. I hope you're hungry."

I'd never seen Max on his home turf before.

"Are you kvelling, Max?"

"You won't be making fun when you sink your teeth into that meat," he said, finally executing his left turn. "How is your movie deal coming along?"

"I had lunch with some big studio cheeses yesterday. They want my soul on a platter. They want me to move to Los Angeles and join their wonderful community."

"What? Are you thinking of going?"

"Well, I don't know. First I have to write a treatment for a screenplay for them based on some memoir by a teenage girl who aborted her father's baby. They seem to think I'm some kind of specialist in kinky incest, based on my screenplay."

"That's great," he said. "Jeremy, I'm so proud of you."

"Max," I said, "it's not great. Screenwriters are hacks; screenplays get mashed to lowest-common-denominator porridge. Oh, God, the thought of it. If I fall into that black hole, I'll never get out alive. I'll sit in that bungalow and scratch myself into a pile of dead skin on the floor and blow away."

He slid the car into an illegal parking place and turned off the engine. "Has your agent heard back from any of those editors he sent your novel to?"

"As a matter of fact," I said, "he has."

Max turned in his seat to look straight at me. The seat belt cut into his cheek, but he didn't seem to care. "What did they say?"

" 'Dear Mr. Fine,' " I said in the voice of a snooty, know-it-all editor, " 'I fail to share or even understand your enthusiasm for Jeremy Thrane's tedious piece of crap, *Angus in Efes*. Best of luck placing it elsewhere. May we venture to suggest a vanity press? Sincerely, and so forth.' They could hardly bring themselves to be polite about it, that's how unbelievably bad they thought it was."

"What do they know?" he said indignantly, but his protest didn't ring wholly true.

"Be honest," I said. "Have you read the copy I gave you yet? And if so, what did you think?"

The windshield wipers greased the windshield with rain for several thumping cycles before he answered. "You know I'm no literary critic," he said lightly. "I thought the book was well written and imaginative. I'm not sure about the plot, but what does plot matter in contemporary novels, isn't that right? But if you're doomed to be a rich and successful Hollywood screenwriter, I don't see why that's such a tragedy."

"I worked on that novel for almost ten years," I said. "The screenplay was nothing."

"I thought it was hilarious," he said "But your novel is very good too. It's just maybe not as commercially viable, but what do I know? Wait here and guard the car while I run in and get the groceries."

While he was gone, I stared at the fire hydrant right next to the car; I contemplated his diagnosis of my literary future and decided not to discuss it further with him.

"Okay, I have two questions for you," I told him when he returned with a bulging plastic bag. "How did we meet and all that, when they ask me, and what do I say during the game to fake a degree of familiarity with the great American pastime?"

"The truth: We met at Charlie's wedding," said Max blithely, "and as far as the game goes, I have no idea why you're so worried about this. You played baseball in school, it'll all come back to you."

"What will come back to me is standing in left field, praying to God, who I suddenly believed in, that the ball wouldn't come near me."

"It's all going to be fine," said Max soothingly. "My parents love you already, don't worry, they'll do all the talking. All you have to do is look at Bar Mitzvah pictures, listen to all their stories about what a brilliant child I was, and eat five big helpings of food and try for a sixth. And do not, Jeremy, whatever you do, blow my cover if anyone refers to my ex-girlfriends. Jessica was the lawyer, Debbie was the medical student, Lisa was the actress. All very nice but extremely busy Jewish girls who unfortunately could never make it out here to meet my parents. You got that?"

A few minutes later, on a street Max called Synagogue Row, which was lined with one huge, hideous mausoleum after another, he pulled into a driveway in front of a rambling white one-story house surrounded by old trees. He turned off the engine. "I forgot to ask," he said. "How's your love life these days?"

"Oh my God," I said. "There's no time to tell you the whole story, but I picked up this guy the other night, about a week ago."

"Do tell," he said. "We can wait a minute before we go in."

"I went to the Dugout at four in the afternoon, and there he was at the bar, this seedy-looking but sort of hot little delinquent type. We started flirting, I bought him a beer, he asked for another one, we got a little drunk. He said he was into partying, he mentioned he'd been a go-go dancer, he'd been in prison. Whatever, I didn't pay too much attention, you know how it is when the hormones are in full throttle. He asked if I wanted a date." I paused. "Define 'date' for me, Max."

"Oh, no," he said. "I hope this isn't going where I absolutely think it is."

"I took him home to my little room, where he gave me highly efficient if belabored head. Afterward he sprawled there on my bed, smoking a repellent cheroot sort of thing. By this time, the endorphins had worn off and I was thoroughly sick of him and was trying to get rid of him, and that's when things got hairy. He demanded money. He thought he'd made that clear at the outset."

"Did you pay him?"

I said dourly, "Well, he sort of mentioned at that point that he'd been in Sing Sing for murder. Actually, the way he put it was, 'I was in a fight with this dude and I did what I had to do. I'm not proud of it but I did my time.' Then I gave him whatever I had in my wallet, which was around sixteen dollars. He tried to intimidate me into going to the ATM, but that turned out to be fruitless because I wasn't budging because I hadn't agreed to this, I'd been tricked, so to speak, so he finally left. Then a while later I noticed my new CD player was missing."

Max tsk-tsked, giving my shoulder a gentle, consoling shake. "If it had happened to me, this story would be hilarious."

"For some strange reason, I find that sort of comforting," I said.

We got out of the car and made our way, huddled together under the umbrella, to the house, carrying the flowers, wine, and groceries. To my mind's eye, we could not have looked more overtly homosexual, mincing over the wet grass, our trouser legs swishing, our steps small and geisha-like. I started to laugh to myself, then stopped when the front door opened and a woman looked out at us through the screen door. I caught a glimpse of cheekbones and blond hair.

"Welcome," she called as we came through the rain toward her over the sopping-wet, acid-green lawn.

"Mommy," Max said, "this is Jeremy."

If Max hadn't told me that his mother was almost eighty, I would have guessed she was sixty, tops. She had a foxy urban face with a wide curved mouth, a long elegant nose, and a chin-length blond wig, which I knew all the Orthodox Jewish wives wore because their real hair was too enticingly erotic for anyone but their husbands to lay eyes on. She was tall and leggy, about the same height as Max. She wore a man's white Oxford shirt over a long, straight black skirt that fishtailed out slightly at the bottom.

"Hello, Mrs. Goldenberg," I said, handing her the tulips.

"Who?" she cried, looking over her shoulder. "Call me Rivka, please, you make me feel like Maxie's grandma. What are these? White tulips? Oh, you are wonderful. Wipe your feet and come in. By the way, Jeremy, my hearing aid is crapola tonight, so shout if you have anything to say to me."

We wiped our feet on the black rubber mat and then followed her into the brightly lit white-carpeted house, down some steps, through a silent, shrouded living room and along a hallway lined with pictures of Max at every stage of his development from birth onward. "My walk of fame," he muttered behind me. I caught sight of a picture of him at age fourteen or so, wearing a suit, looking for all the world like a three-dollar queer; how was it that parents didn't instinctively guess these things? Well, people saw what they wanted to see, that was the only plausible explanation I'd ever come up with.

Rivka turned and took my overnight bag from me. "You'll be in here," she said, placing it just inside the doorway of a room we were passing; I hoped I would remember which one when the time came to toddle off to bed. We continued on to the huge kitchen, which smelled as good as Max had promised it would and was actually two Siamese-twin kitchens joined by a big island in the middle, with opposing, identical sets of cupboards, stoves, refrigerators, sinks, dishwashers. The left half was all activity, steam rising from pots on the stove, dishes in the open dishwasher, vegetables in a colander; the right half was gleaming and quiet and perfectly clean. A bay window looked out to a dripping, lush little garden; I caught a glimpse of someone I assumed was Rita crouched on the ground between the rows out there, draped in a black poncho, picking small round red things that looked like strawberries and putting them into a basket on her arm. I set the bag of wine and the flowers on the countertop. Max began to put the groceries away.

Rivka stood in the left-hand kitchen with her hand on one cocked hip, the other flat on the counter next to a cutting board dotted with little bits of cut-up ingredients whose identity I couldn't ascertain but which filled me with excitement. "Now, who wants a drink? We have vodka, gin, whiskey, rum, and rye." She took three tall drinking glasses out of a cupboard.

"Rye, please," I said eagerly. I'd never had rye, but everyone in noir novels drank it, the guy in *The Lost Weekend*, Marlowe in the Chandler novels, all those small-time shysters and down-at-heels grifters.

"What was that?"

"Rye," I repeated loudly as she trained her eyes on my lips.

"Fernando and I will have vodka," said Max.

She put a few ice cubes in each glass. She filled the first one to the top with brown liquid out of a bottle that looked about forty years old and handed it to me. Even by my standards, this drink was huge. She poured the same amount of vodka into the other two and handed them to Max.

"She isn't really trying to kill us," said Max under his breath. "She doesn't drink hard liquor; she has no idea. She pours seltzer and milk the same way. Come on, let's go in the den."

I took a sip of rye. It tasted exactly as I'd expected, like fermented wood chips with a whiff of formaldehyde. I took another, bigger sip and trotted along behind Max as he bustled down the hall to a dark room at the end. Fernando sat on a brown leather couch, looking perfectly at home and at ease, one ankle slung in manly fashion to rest on the other knee, his arms stretched along the back of the couch, his head leaning comfortably against the wall. Sprawled on a green vinyl reclining chair was the most obese man I'd ever seen, or one of them. The chair was slung all the way back. He lay on it with all the resplendence of a lotus on a lily pad or a monument on a pedestal. His black yarmulke looked comically small; a gray beard covered his many chins with the uniformly shallow fuzz of lichen on rocks. He was more thing than man, more substance than flesh; the chair cupped and sustained him. I darted a glance at the TV screen to see whether or not the Game had begun yet, and was relieved to see that it hadn't.

"This is Jeremy, Dad," said Max.

"Hello, Mr. Goldenberg," I said, raising my glass at him somewhat awkwardly. "How are you, Fernando."

"Hello, Jeremy," said Fernando with an inexplicably amused expression on his thick-lipped, intelligent face. I had to admit, he was pretty hot; maybe I disliked him because of the cellular taboo I felt against being attracted to my friends' boyfriends. Why he didn't like me was anyone's guess, but I chalked it up to the logical truth that a certain percentage of people I met just wouldn't. I noticed that he was wearing a yarmulke. Max had told me I didn't have to wear one if I felt uncomfortable about it, so I'd accepted this as a way out and hadn't given it much more thought. Well, he was Max's boyfriend and I wasn't. I touched the top of my bare head with my fingertips as Max handed him his drink and sat on the couch a good distance away from him; I slid into the armchair near the television set.

"We started the parsha discussion already since we're not going to shul tonight," Max's father said in a hoarsely breathless voice. "We're up to the grasshoppers, the fruit, how to read Torah."

"Welcome to Hebrew school, Jeremy," said Max. "Dad, maybe we could save the devar Torah until after you say how nice it is to meet Jeremy, you've heard so many good things about him, and how was his train trip, that sort of thing."

"Is that what I'm called upon to do?" Fischl wheezed. "Is that polite?"

"Don't worry about it," I said, gulping my rye, which was going down surprisingly well. "No pleasantries necessary. What part of the Old Testament are you talking about?"

I had tried to sound light and conversational, but they all looked at me as if I'd committed an incredible faux pas.

"We call it the Torah," said Max gently. "God wrote the Torah, whereas a bunch of different guys who weren't even eyewitnesses wrote the Christian Bible, which they call the New Testament to differentiate it from the 'old' one, as if they were in any way comparable."

"I see," I said hesitantly, not wanting to offend anyone any more than I already had. "God actually held the pen, or whatever it was, the chisel? How did that work? How do you know?"

"That's the point," said Fischl. "Exactly. The spies went into the Promised Land and what did they find? They found giants! They went looking for danger, why?"

"What part of the Torah is this?" I asked.

"It's in Numbers," Max said to me; then, when I looked blankly back at him added, "Okay, really quick: God tells Moses to send some of his men to scout out Canaan, the Promised Land, which he's told them will soon be theirs. They come back with fruit so big, they have to carry it in wagons, which seems promising, right? What a great place. But they tell stories about terrifying giants, the Canaanites, who made them feel as small as grasshoppers. When the other Jews hear this, they start kvetching and moaning that they'd rather go back to enslavement in Egypt than die by the Canaanites' swords. Big mistake: God strikes the spies with a plague for their cowardice, and condemns the others to live the rest of their lives in the wilderness. No Promised Land for them if they're going to be so whiny about it. But they disobey; off they go to Canaan without the Ark and without Moses, and of course they all get hacked to bits by the Canaanites."

"That's harsh," I said.

"That's nothing," said Max darkly. "For the Jews that's like a little spanking."

Fischl stirred in his chair, which caused tectonic tremors under his rumpled white shirt. "What is the first commandment?"

"You will love God," said Fernando in his accent, which on NPR would have been accompanied by a chicken.

"That's right," said Fischl. "And Torah is like the Promised Land, we are spies sent in to scout out the truth. Our midrash is what we bring back. If we read believing that Hashem wrote every word we read, we are rewarded with the delicious fruit of truth." He gasped for a moment, catching his breath. "If we read without faith, we see only according to our fear. We see giants everywhere, and we're too scared to understand."

"Hashem is God," Max told me.

"I knew that," I lied. I was beginning to feel a nice warm glow in my chest from my drink. "But weren't the spies right? They got killed by the Canaanites, so their fears were justified. They were grasshoppers after all."

"They died because they had no faith." Fischl looked at me. "What is sin?"

"Sin," I said, thinking fast, since my feelings about sin were essentially quite positive, "is going against the word of God. Hashem."

"There are six hundred and thirteen commandments. It's impossible to follow them all, I mean physically impossible, even if you did nothing else. Why? The Temple no longer exists. We can't make burnt offerings there the way the Torah tells us to. Why do I wear this ridiculous garment coming out from under my shirt in these tassels?"

"Those are tzitzit," said Fernando, "and you wear them to remind you of the commandments."

I stared at him. Teacher's pet, I thought balefully. How the bejeezus did he know this? Had Max primed him?

"Because I can't remember them all the time," said Fischl. "The heart covets, the eyes seek out, according to Rashi. 'And not explore after your heart and after your eyes after which you stray.' Feelings are deceptive, what we see is illusory. Hey, the game's starting. Maxie, go tell Rita the game's on."

"We can't ask Rita to turn up the volume," Max said to me as if he were my tour guide, and as if he enjoyed this role. "All we can do is tell her that the game is starting. If she chooses not to take a hint, there's nothing we can do."

"Except fire her," said Fischl.

"Well, I could turn up the volume," I said, feeling quick-witted for the first time since I'd arrived, "or Fernando could, he's closer."

"Fernando can't," said Max, "he's Jewish."

"You are?" I asked, staring at Fernando, who blinked limpidly at me as if to imply that it was racist of me to assume that because he was Mexican he couldn't also be Jewish, but he had expected nothing more; he was used to it.

"Mexico City has twenty-three synagogues," he said, pronouncing "Mexico" the American way, which I was pretty sure wouldn't have flown on NPR.

"I didn't know that," I answered, smiling with false apology.

"Remind me, Jeremy," said Fischl with some urgency. "What were we just talking about before?"

I thought for a moment, then got up and turned up the sound on the television. A sports announcer's voice gabbled hysterically away.

"You like it that quiet?" said Fischl and Max in doleful unison.

I turned it up, sat down again, and stared glumly at the men on the screen, who wore those cute billed caps and tight, cozy outfits that looked like foot pajamas. After a while, I began to cheer up a little; baseball players' big round butts, bellies, and arms were very much to my liking. I took another pull of my rye and was astonished to discover that it was almost half gone. My pinkie was sticking out faggily; I clamped it onto the glass with the rest of my fingers and did a quick check to make sure Fischl hadn't noticed.

"Ha!" Fischl yelled a moment later as the Yankees did something organized and coordinated, startling me out of my reverie about the shortstop, an adorable fellow with a relaxed, serene, joyful stance.

It was too bad the Goldenbergs weren't allowed to know that Fernando was their son-in-law, because it seemed that in addition to being a Jew, he was a baseball fan. "Good one!" he shouted, and Max clapped his hands once, loudly, as if to cement their shared jubilation. I had no idea what had just happened. I was intrigued by but wholly ignorant of the significance of all the hand gestures the catcher made in his crotch. Nothing much seemed to be happening at any given time; clearly, baseball had a numerical structure and precise rules that played themselves out on the diamond in an inexorable temporal flow, but it seemed that the more you knew about it, the more complex and arcane it all became, and, judging from these exclamations from Max, Fischl, and Fernando about things I didn't even see, the more exciting. The aerial view of Yankee Stadium reminded me in some obscure way of the synagogue service

I'd once let Max drag me to: During the service, some people yakked to each other while others davened to beat the band. There seemed to be no holier-than-thou piety involved: The more you participated, the more you seemed to get out of it, but no one seemed to judge anyone either way.

I noticed then with some amusement that Max and Fernando were sitting as far apart on the couch as they could get, with a whole chaste cushion between them. The air between them was suspiciously neutral. They neither slapped each other five nor kept up a riffing, boisterous running commentary the way two straight male friends would probably have done.

"Hello, boys," came a loud voice from the doorway. It belonged to a wiry woman with a black bouffant I identified immediately as Rita. "Am I too late for the kickoff? Oh, I see you found another Shabbos goy for the evening."

"That's me," I said.

"Lucky you," she said, and grinned at me. She was gap-toothed, which according to the old-wives'-tale canon meant, I seemed to recall, that she liked sex.

"This is my friend Jeremy Thrane," said Max. "Jeremy, this is Rita."

Rita set a tray on the coffee table near Fischl. He immediately palmed a handful of something and tossed it into his mouth with the fluid delicacy of a circus elephant eating peanuts with its trunk.

"Then you," Rita said, turning toward the couch with a puckish glint in her eyes, "must be Fernando."

She knew, I thought with a jolt of pleasure. She knew exactly who Fernando was. Had Max told her? Of course he hadn't. She must have guessed everything somehow.

"I am pleased to meet you, Rita," said Fernando, rolling the "r" in her name and rising to his feet to shake her hand with old-world gravity. "Fernando Narvaez."

"I'm very pleased to meet *you*," she said significantly. "Oh, Jeremy," she said, turning back to me, "it's not sundown till around nine. They're just being lazy. They start as early as they can every Friday."

"We're training him," said Max. "Gotta get him with the program right away."

"You," said Rita, swatting Max's head, "are the worst. The liver-wurst. And, Fishy," she said to Max's father, "don't look so innocent. Jeremy, watch out or they'll have you wiping their noses and God only knows what else." With an abrupt honk of a laugh, she disappeared.

"Oh no!" Fischl howled through a mouthful. "What is this, Little League, what a bunch of pansies, they're throwing like girls!"

Max and Fernando and I avoided each other's eyes. "Where's the bathroom?" I asked, standing up and setting my empty glass on a coaster on the coffee table.

"Closest one is downstairs in the basement, first door on your left," said Max. "Want me to show you?"

"No, I'm sure I can bushwhack my way to it," I said, not quite sure what I meant by this, but gripped by a craven, unaccountable need to prove something to the fat man in the armchair. The bathroom was right where Max had said it was. I went in and turned on the light, which came on with the roar of an invisible fan. I hated those fans; they made me claustrophobic. What if the house caught fire while I was in here? I'd never hear them calling me until it was too late. I turned off the fan-light and peed in the dark. When I was finished, I zipped up, put the seat down, and sat there in the silence and darkness. I rested my cheek against the toilet paper roll and closed my eyes.

I realized in the post-urinal silence that I could hear Rita and Rivka talking as clearly as if they were in the room with me. There was proba-bly a heating vent in the ceiling that connected this room to the kitchen, because I could also hear the clang of pot lids. I didn't technically mean to eavesdrop; it just happened that their words started to make sense to me once I'd figured out what they were talking about, and there I was.

"So good-looking," Rita was saying. "Fishy seems to like him too."

"Well, as long as he doesn't know," said Rivka.

"Are you kidding me? He doesn't notice anything unless it has calories."

Rivka laughed. "Rita!"

They laughed together, in unison, at the same frequency, as if they'd laughed together before many times.

"Look at these strawberries," said Rita then in a completely different tone.

"I know, they're so small this year," said Rivka. "Next year let's go back to those chemicals."

"Okay," said Rita. "I guess I better set the table now. Should I put these flowers out too? Aren't they nice, they're so fresh."

"White tulips," Rivka agreed huskily. "Very classy. That Jeremy seems like a nice boy too. I wonder, do you think he and Maxie ever . . . ?"

"Rivka," said Rita, "get your mind out of the gutter for once, why don't you."

They laughed together again, and then their voices faded as they moved into the dining room.

I fell asleep. When I awoke I had a crick in my neck and the house was silent. I checked my watch; the glow-in-the-dark numbers said it was just after eight, which meant that I'd been asleep for fifteen minutes. Then I remembered that I'd been dreaming that the prostitute, Hector, was here too, sitting in the den upstairs, watching the game with the rest of us, a squat, taciturn bruiser with cigarette-stained teeth who could have squashed me like a bug if he'd wanted to. He'd leered menacingly at me, threatening me, while everyone else obliviously watched the game.

My inner voice suddenly began taunting me in a mewling singsong, "I'm so alone, I'm so alone," and then I thought, Well, it's true, I am so alone, and put my cheek back down on the toilet paper roll and began to cry, getting the paper all wet. I felt ridiculous, would have looked ridiculous if anyone had walked in on me; of course I was alone, everyone was alone, it was the price we paid for getting to have our separate skulls and individual perspectives and autonomous fields of operation. But why the hell wasn't anybody buying my novel? And how had I so totally misread Hector's cues? How could I have been so naive? And he'd stolen my new CD player, which had cost me a half hour of teeth-grinding conversation with a patronizing squid of a salesman at Radio Shack. I wouldn't have knowingly traded that CD player for any blow job, no matter how passionate and masterful it may have been, which Hector's had not been in any way.

I washed my hands and face and went back upstairs, where the rest of the night unfolded inexorably according to the three-pronged dictates of the rituals of Shabbat, birthdays, and houseguest entertaining. Rivka said Hebrew prayers as she lit the candles, her sophisticated face above the light, her cheekbones thrown into bas relief. Fischl chanted some Hebrew blessings in his out-of-breath tenor over the bread, the wine, his wife, and son, his legs miraculously supporting his body as he stood at the head of the table. Finally, the divine, amazing brisket was served, of which I ate three helpings and would have attempted a fourth if I'd been willing to rupture my stomach. After dinner, Rita brought in the nondairy birthday cake decorated with the too-small strawberries, whose candles she and I then blew out together before we opened Max's presents for him.

"Shabbos goys to the rescue once again," I said.

"We should get ourselves up in some superhero capes and tights," said Rita, laughing. "Sew a big red 'S.G.' on our shirts."

"Shabbos Goy!" I sang, and punched my fist in the air as if I were flying under my own power. "It's a bird!"

"It's a plane," said Rita, handing Max the card I'd brought for him.

"It's a gift certificate from Steiner's," said Max. "Jeremy, I need a new pair of running shoes, this is great. Thank you. I can really use this."

"That's what I was hoping," I said.

"New running shoes," said Fischl. "Good, you can wear them to Yom Kippur. The ones you wore last year looked terrible. I was embarrassed for everyone to see my son in these things. They were all thinking, Fishy's son is a doctor and he can't afford new shoes?"

"Dad," said Max, "don't you think they had other things on their minds on the Day of Atonement besides my sneakers?"

"No," said Fischl, his eyes protruding with the force of his opinion.

"Also," Max persisted, "do you ever wonder why we wear sneakers on Yom Kippur when the whole point of not wearing leather shoes is that we should be uncomfortable? Sneakers are the most comfortable shoes there are. It seems to me," he began, and then stopped, his cheeks ruddy with wine and nervous tension. "Well, anyway, there are other ways we follow the letter of the law but not the spirit."

"What other ways, Maxie?" Rita asked with sly curiosity.

For some reason, Fernando and I exchanged a cool, probing, not wholly unfriendly glance.

"It doesn't matter, really," said Max through a bite of cake.

"Can I ask you all something?" I said. "What do you all think is the correct spelling of 'dog-do'?"

Everyone stared at me.

"I know this is out of the blue," I said. "But it's related to what we were talking about, I promise. It has to do with this letter-spirit question."

"D-o-g-dash-d-o," said Fischl.

"Two o's," said Rita.

"D-o-g-d-o," said Max, "no dash."

"Let's see," began Rivka slowly, thinking. "D-o-g." Then she stopped, chuckling. "It's a trick question, that's what it is. There's no correct answer. That's Jeremy's point, I bet: It doesn't really matter how you spell it because it's not a real word."

"The question for me," said Fernando, "is what is dog-do."

Max poured more wine all around. "Here's my thing about the sneakers," he said. He'd recovered his equanimity under the cover of distraction I'd provided. "We keep doing something that goes against the letter of the law just because everyone around us does it too. Well, this year I'm going to wear rubber rainboots over bare feet to synagogue on Yom Kippur. My feet will be cold, they'll chafe, they'll itch, and I'll fulfill both letter and spirit."

"You'll look like a schmuck," said his father.

"I don't care," said Max.

"You're such a rebel, Maxie," said Rita affectionately. "I think you'll look very cute in your rubber boots going off to synagogue."

"I'm not doing it to be a rebel," said Max crabbily. "I'm doing it to make a point."

"Dog-do," I told Fernando, "is dog shit."

"I have no idea why you're talking about this at my birthday party," said Max.

"Because," said Fischl, "to agree to spell a word the same facilitates communication and understanding. We all wear sneakers to shul because the Talmud says no leather on our feet for Yom Kippur. It brings people together. It doesn't say to wear shoes that make our feet hurt, although that might have been the original idea, it says no leather. Sneakers are a very nice loophole for old yids like me who are in enough pain not eating for twenty-four hours, we don't need our feet hurting too."

"I disagree," said Max. "We understand the law by following the law. Following the law even more stringently is maybe to understand it even better. If you're going to do it in the first place, you might as well do it right."

"Right?" said Fischl irascibly. "What's right is wearing sneakers."

"But," I said, "let's say Max wears rainboots this year, and someone else sees him and thinks it's a good idea and wears them next year, and the year after that people at the next synagogue start wearing them, then it starts to be a whole new tradition, rainboots on Yom Kippur. Then someone else comes along and questions that, saying why not go even further, why not wear boards with thumbtacks sticking into the soles of your feet?"

Fischl smacked his lips loudly over an enormous bite of cake. "All I hope is that I'm dead by then."

"I can't hear a word anyone is saying," said Rivka, tapping her shrieking hearing aid. "This damn thing, I need a new one."

"You're not missing anything, Mommy," said Max loudly. "Everyone's making fun of me."

"No," said Rita, kissing him on the cheek, "we're celebrating your existence."

Around midnight, after the rain had stopped and the "grown-ups" had all gone to bed, Max and Fernando and I took a short walk around the neighborhood. When we were several blocks away from the Goldenbergs' house, Fernando pulled Max into the darkness under a huge, spreading tree. As I cooled my heels a few yards away, doing calf stretches on the curb, breathing the smell of wet lawns and staring into the misty, streetlamp-stained darkness, an odd and unexpected sadness gripped and squeezed my upper abdomen like a girdle. This piercing melancholy served the unexpected dual purpose of easing my overstuffed discomfort, so on the whole it was, like most things, a mixed bag.

As we started back to the Goldenbergs' house, I said, "Max, while I was in the bathroom I overheard your mother and Rita in the kitchen, talking about you."

To my surprise, Max was silent for a while, then he said without looking at me, "I don't want to know. Don't tell me."

"But you have no idea what—"

"Don't tell me," he repeated firmly.

"He means he knows already," said Fernando.

"How do you know what I was going to say?" I snapped at him. "How do you know he knows already?"

"I know Max," said Fernando. I felt a surge of testosterone in him as he said this, but I didn't back down.

"So do I," I said.

"Maybe not as well as you think," Fernando said clearly, looking me right in the eye.

"I say we go in and have a nightcap down in the rec room," said Max jovially, as if no one had said anything at all since he had made out with Fernando under that tree. "Let's open the cognac Fernando brought. There's cake left. We can play my old records, it's soundproofed. I used to have parties down there in high school. We used to take turns puking in the bathroom sink, we drank so much."

"The same bathroom where I overheard your mother and Rita?" I asked stubbornly.

"The same bathroom," said Max. "The one that keeps all secrets." He slid his hand into the crook of my arm and rested his other arm across Fernando's shoulders, pulling us both close to him so the three of us walked in lockstep together on the echoing, wet asphalt in the middle of the street.

After Amanda's wedding rehearsal at our mother's apartment, I set out into the warm, clear early evening, walking downtown toward TriBeCa; the address Felicia had given me was over ninety blocks away, but I needed all the exercise I could get after the brisket and birthday cake, the cream-cheese-lox-and-bagel breakfast we'd had this morning, and the leftover brisket on rye Rita had made me for the train. I was also feeling in need of some air and escape; Amanda's wedding rehearsal had been from start to finish a crowded melee of taut nerves, tears, and babbling voices. I had no idea how or whether anything we were doing would translate tomorrow into an actual wedding ceremony. The wedding wouldn't even be held at my mother's house, it would be on a pier in Chelsea. I'd barely spoken to my sister Lola, newly arrived from Australia with her husband, Fletcher, whom I'd never met before.

As I'd squired Amanda down the "aisle," otherwise known as the hallway, she was shaking a little, but whether with fear or emotion I couldn't tell. Her hand on my bare arm was sweaty and cold.

"It's not too late to change your mind," I told her under my breath.

"I think Mom's hurt that I didn't ask her to walk me down the aisle," she replied.

"It's not too late to change your mind about that either," I said.

"I want you," she said stubbornly, and my whole chest swelled with a strong, yeasty brew I identified as brotherly love.

A second later I handed her over to a virulently pale post-bachelor-party Liam, hulking in the library with the likeable oddball they'd hired to perform the ceremony, the best man Feckin, and Amanda's slutty bass player, whom she'd appointed as her maid of honor. We'd decided to forego the poems and songs that would precede the ceremony, so I had nothing else to do now but duck into the bathroom for a while. When I came out, a red-eyed Irish lass I'd never met before was waiting to get in, inspecting all the pictures along the hallway in the meantime. Then I went and hung out in front of my mother's open refrigerator door, purely out of ancient habit rather than hunger, not really even looking at anything, merely basking in the glow of the tiny bulb and feeling perfectly at home.

I felt someone breathing behind me.

"What the feckin Jaysus is kasha?" a voice I recognized said. "What's that green-lookin slime back there? Is that food?"

"Help yourself," I said, and went away to let Feckin inspect the yogurt and wheat germ and homemade stewed prunes a little more closely, in private.

A short time later, when the rehearsal was officially over, everyone went out to a nearby Chinese restaurant, but I got out of having to go along by mentioning Felicia's opening; if my mother and Amanda respected anything in the world, it was art of any kind. So I was set free, with plenty of time to walk the whole way down.

I ricocheted down Broadway, the great spinal aorta of Manhattan, its teeming core, from one familiar but eternally exotic landmark to the next, from the fruit and vegetable sidewalk bins at Fairway to Gray's Papaya to the lit-up jets of the Lincoln Center fountain, through the corporate-skyscraper corridor of Midtown; every time I took one of these extended hikes up or down Broadway, I fell into the same indefatigable, dreamy fascination with everything I saw that I experienced whenever I traveled in a foreign country. An invisible conveyer belt pulled me through the untawdry, Disneyfied but still psychedelic New Times Square, past the video screens and billboards that blinked and foamed and fizzed high above the theater marquees and chain hotels, down to the garish pink neon weirdness of the urban mall on Thirty-fourth Street, and on through the dark, third-world-country-atmosphered rug-and-jewelry district. At Union Square I crossed Fourteenth Street and picked up Broadway again on its little jog east, then whizzed down the chute of lower Broadway, past shops crammed full of NYU students, across Houston into SoHo, past shops crammed full of Eurotrash tourists, all of them in plate-glass storefronts at the bottom of solidly corniced and mullioned buildings that looked far too old and dignified to house these overpriced jet-set shoe emporia and overlit fly-by-night sunglass boutiques. As I approached Canal Street, my muscles loose, my feet pleasurably fatigued, my mind in a happy fog, I veered toward a deli and scanned the buckets of flowers lined up on the sidewalk near the door. At some point on my long trek, inspired by my mild success with those tulips for Rivka, I had apparently decided to buy Felicia a bouquet.

As the tiny, borderline-malevolent Korean woman behind the counter wrapped a bunch of tiger lilies in a sheet of flowered paper, I felt the hair on my arms stand up in a way I knew all too well. Turning to identify the cause, I espied Yoshi in the exotic foods aisle, staring at me with much of the dismay I felt evident on my own face. He was holding, I couldn't help noticing, a package of those pressed seaweed sheets they rolled sushi with. I knew what they were called but preferred not to even think the word for fear of somehow appearing to legitimize his whole Japanese affectation in any way and having this show in my face.

"Yoshi," I said, stifling a childish desire to call him "Sushi" instead and pretend I'd done it by mistake.

"Jeremy," he said without a trace of a Japanese accent. He looked paler than he'd been the last time I'd seen him. Maybe he'd stopped using Ted's tanning bed. He also looked puffier, less aggressively buffed and oiled, and he'd had that damn ponytail lopped off so his black hair was as bristly and short as a dog's fur. He looked better, if only because he looked less deserving of his high opinion of himself.

I turned back to the counter, received my change and the wrapped flowers from the scary little Korean lady, and would have happily left this unexpected reunion with my former housemate at this terse exchange of names, but he handed over some money for the package of nori and exited the store on my heels. It seemed we were headed in the same direction; we walked along in uneasy tandem for half a block. Finally Yoshi said, "It looks like we're neighbors again. I live a few blocks from here."

"I don't live in this neighborhood," I said. "Anyway," I added after another brief pause, "I thought you lived with Ted."

"I did," he said.

I considered letting the matter drop, but curiosity prevailed. "What happened?"

"I moved out."

"Why?" I asked, my heart beginning to pound slowly in a way that alerted me to the fact that this was something I probably wouldn't enjoy hearing but was powerless not to inquire after. I thought of a rat gnawing off its own limb to escape a trap.

"He was pathetic after you did that to him," Yoshi said with a faint sneer of triumph. "He sat around the house all day, feeling sorry for himself."

"I didn't do anything to him," I snapped.

"So anyway," he said. "I got fed up with him and found my own place. He wasn't pleased."

I said through a lump of bitterness in my throat, "You broke his heart?"

"Heart?" said Yoshi, giving me a look. "I insulted his pride. He thought I should have been more appreciative of what he'd given up for me."

I cleared my throat. The bitter lump didn't budge. "You mean me, I suppose," I said flatly.

"Your loyal silence," Yoshi said with airy unconcern.

"My loyal silence," I repeated, attempting wryness but sounding as if I were being lightly strangled. Yoshi and I hated each other, I had long since figured out, because we were attracted to the same man for completely different reasons, and therefore saw through and despised each other's efforts to attract him; what didn't entirely make sense was why Yoshi's efforts had triumphed over mine.

"Things happen," said Yoshi enigmatically. "We all do what we have to do." He paused on the corner of Grand Street. "I turn here," he said. "Take care."

"Oh, thank you, I certainly will, and you take care too," I said with heartfelt hatred, but he'd already headed off, so I wasn't sure whether or not he'd heard me.

I continued on my way in a welter of black-hearted rawness that slowly gave way to perverse satisfaction. No revenge I could knowingly have perpetrated could have achieved a more satisfying end. When Ted's life fell apart, just when he needed a true friend most, he was forced to recognize that he'd swapped me, the man who truly loved him, for a poisonous little snake.

I heard the opening before I saw it, a roar of voices through a door that opened directly onto the sidewalk on Walker Street. Through the doorway I saw people standing around in little clumps and immediately dreaded going in. Whenever I went to these things, I inevitably got trapped in intense but awkward one-on-one conversations with people who had even less reason for being there than I had, such as the artist's old college roommate or the gallery owner's out-of-town cousin or some guy who'd wandered in to pounce on an unsuspecting lamb like me to corner me far from the drinks table while he tried with smooth desperation to ascertain who I knew, how I could help him in his own art career, and what I thought of his idea for his new video installation. The fact that I knew no one in the art world and could converse with no interest or authority about video "art" seemed to be no deterrent whatsoever to such people.

I went in and threaded my speedy way to the drinks table like a race car in a video game, skirting all the obstacles without easing up off the accelerator and reaching my destination well ahead of schedule. As I waited for my glass of wine, I did a quick reconnoiter. Through the crowd I could see objects that would probably, on closer inspection, turn out to be the work Felicia was exhibiting. There was Felicia herself, over by the far wall. She wore a tight black wifebeater and looked considerably more substantial, healthily so, than she had the last time I'd seen her, which was over two months ago. Hovering just beyond her was someone I recognized vaguely from other openings, a wrinkled elf who used all her tragically limited powers to be mistaken for a twenty-five-year-old girl, aided by pink rouge, a belted minidress, and tights with go-go boots, her dead-black hair in two little braids. Coming toward me was a tall, intelligent-looking, alluring man who made my heart go pitter-pat but looked blankly at me when I caught his eye as if to say, "You can look all you want, of course."

"Here you go," said the guy who'd been hired to stand behind the table dispensing beverages, handing me a glass. My response to the ubiquitous bad red wine in plastic cups at gallery openings was almost

Pavlovian by now: I could feel the pounding in my skull the moment it was handed to me. I always supplied myself with one, though, and carried it with me throughout the "event" as a less extreme version of the cyanide capsules Second World War spies carried behind enemy lines; as a last resort, I could always gulp it down and announce that I "needed" another one, excuse me, nice talking to you.

It was very hot and loud in there. I wondered where Felicia had found all these people; last time I'd seen her, she'd hardly known anyone. Either she'd hired a bunch of out-of-work actors to impersonate art lovers, or she'd been extremely schmoozy since I'd seen her last, or these were all her fellow 12-steppers, reciting all their sobriety mantras under their breath and wishing they could have a real drink. Or so I imagined, based on the way I would have felt if I'd been they, since I had never fully understood the mechanism of addiction. Since my own habits were pleasurable rather than problematic, I had never seen any reason whatsoever to give any of them up, whereas for these people, an uncontrollable appetite for intoxication seemed to have necessarily mutated into an equal and opposite passion for renunciation. For a lot of them, it had probably been a matter of life and death. From what I knew of the process, though, they still identified as strongly as ever with whatever substance had controlled them, but now they avoided it as radically as they'd sought it; instead of drinking or snorting or shooting up to excess, they gathered ritualistically in groups, where they exorcised these demons while vicariously reliving their pleasures. It all seemed very romantic and obsessive in a medieval Christian sort of way.

"Jeremy," I heard someone say.

There was no mistaking that lugubriously snippy voice.

"Wayne," I said automatically, and turning, picked his pinched Dickensian guttersnipe's face out of the crowd.

"How are your teeth?" he asked with insinuating resentment.

"My *teeth*? Oh, the dentist."

"I think it's time for another appointment," he said. "It's been about six months since you took mine."

"Listen, Wayne, you know I went only because Felicia made me."

"I work for her," said Wayne. I took this opportunity to study Wayne's own teeth. They looked smaller than normal, but otherwise undistinguished. "I have to do what she says. But you're her friend. You could have refused."

"That's what you think," I said.

"They're looking a little yellow, you should watch that," he said. "There's a new whitening technique you might look into. Bye now." He slid off into the crowd. I decided to say hello to Felicia, look at her work, and get the hell out of there. If this thing ever ended, there would be plenty of people ahead of me in line for a postmortem chat with her, and I wasn't in the mood to pull rank, especially because I had no faith that it would get me anywhere.

Just as I was assembling my musculature to take me through these motions, I saw Sebastian across the room. I hadn't been sure that he'd come; he'd said he'd try to make it if he could. I drifted along the edges of the crowd until I arrived at his left elbow. "Hello, Sebastian," I said. "Sorry I'm late."

"Jeremy!" he cried, and kissed my cheek. "I just got here. Have you been here long?"

"Long enough to collect my ration of wine," I said.

"I don't think it has any alcohol in it," he said, looking with warning censure into his own plastic glass. "But maybe you got the real thing, I don't know."

I tasted my wine. "Damn," I muttered. "Do you want to go and get a real drink somewhere?"

"I'm due to meet Peter in half an hour," he said apologetically. "Shall we look at the show? Have you seen it yet?"

We fought our way through the crowd to a hanging blanket at the far end of the room, an enormous quiltlike tapestry.

"Oh, I see," I said. "It's made of heroin packets. She sewed them together."

"I don't believe they're sewn," said Sebastian, peering at them. "That looks like Scotch tape to me."

"Scotch tape," I said as a memory fell into place in my mind. "And I don't believe she taped them herself." Mercury made a silver square, Blood a red one, Money a green one, Time Bomb a white one, and so forth, like a real old-timey country patchwork quilt. The colors were opaque, delicate, almost Japanese-looking, like rice-paper origami panes;

the doubled facing pieces of tape provided a fingernail-thin transparent ligament between each one, holding them all barely but discretely apart. The huge, fragile thing undulated slightly in the air currents. It was beautiful, but I didn't like it at all; it gave me the creeps.

" 'Now I lay me down to sleep,' " Sebastian read off a small white card on the wall next to it.

"Felicia used to be a lot more subtle with her titles. And she used to be a painter. Where are the paintings?"

"Well," said Sebastian, looking around, "there don't seem to be any."

"Oh, that's right," I said, recalling that the invitation had said "Dreaming in Installments: a multimedia installation by Felicia Boudreaux." I took another gulp of grape juice and was immediately, briefly plunged back into some remote corner of my childhood. "It's a multimedia installation, that's why there are no paintings."

"You brought her flowers," said Sebastian. "How thoughtful of you."

I looked absently down at the bouquet I held in my other arm. "I called the American Bar Association," I said. "Like you suggested."

"Oh, tell me!" he said, turning a little pink with excitement.

"They gave me my father's current address and phone number. All I had to do was ask. He's in Washington State, near Seattle."

"Have you called him?" he asked avidly, his eyes as wet and bulging as freshly shucked oysters.

"Oh my God," I said, "what a terrifying thought. Now that he's so close."

"Yes," he said, his face inches too close to mine. "Yes, I can well imagine how terrifying. But you must do it, Jeremy; you'll never be satisfied until you do."

"What's that thing over there?" I said. My eye had been caught by something as the press of bodies momentarily thinned around it. It was ridiculous to expect to see any art at an opening, I knew perfectly well, but since this was the work of an old friend, I had to make the effort to view each piece in its entirety instead of hanging back and glancing at whatever snippet was revealed by the shifting crowd.

"That thing" turned out to be a life-sized, Felicia-shaped, faceless mannequin with white-blond hair in a chopstick-fixed chignon. Long, shiny needles poked out of its flesh-colored skin at neatly spaced one-inch intervals so the whole surface bristled dangerously. Two syringes had been plunged into the nipples and another into the crotch. All three were half full of fluid the color of fresh blood. "A Higher Power" this one was called. It, too, was coldly beautiful, but beyond that it had no resonance; it meant nothing except that drug addiction was sexy and dangerous and all-consuming, which everyone already knew.

"Good heavens," Sebastian said. "This is absolutely wonderful. It's quite original, don't you think? Powerful and effective."

"I suppose," I said queasily, wondering with disappointed skepticism what this enthusiasm said about Sebastian's praise of my own writing.

On the next wall was a series of fifteen or so photographs hung behind one long, thick sheet of clear Plexiglas bolted to the wall. Felicia's expressionless face filled the entire frame of each shot. They were all identical except that in each successive one her eyelids drooped more and more over her clear green eyes. In the last one, they were closed.

Sebastian bent slightly to examine the typed card. " 'Land of Nod.' "

"Oh, for God's sake," I said. "Let's go see what all the fuss is about over there."

A crowd was gathered around three pedestals on which, I saw when I was close enough, were carefully constructed dioramas of Felicia's loft itself, her bathroom, bedroom, and the main open space, including tiny reproductions of her paintings on the walls. There was the bathroom sink with its spoon, candle, and Chinese jar of packets, there was Felicia on her bed with her dress hiked up to show her flanks, a syringe in her hand, and there was her living room couch, upon which sat— "That looks like me," I said with horror. "Sitting there on the couch. It looks just like me; look at the face." I stared at the thing, coldly curious. So that was what I looked like. Not bad; not bad at all.

"How flattering, Jeremy, she's got you in her show."

I wasn't sure yet whether or not I was flattered by this; actually, I was pretty sure I was creeped out. That particular day hadn't been among the better ones of my life. And the expression on the little Jeremy's face was the same tragic-lemur blend of sadness and archness I'd once admired in the expressions of the people in her paintings. There I sat on her couch like a lonely exile, a solitary dreamer, a man who didn't know what he was missing. The tiny Felicia, on the other hand, bore an expression of ardent anticipation, her eyes half shut and her neck arched as if she were about to be penetrated by a lover.

"There seems to be an audio component to this display," said Sebastian. "Look, they're all listening to those earphone things."

Dangling from each pedestal was a cluster of headsets. I picked one up and put it to my ears; Sebastian did likewise. I heard my own voice, and then Felicia's.

"What am I, Felicia?"

"You're a slut," she said coldly.

I gasped aloud.

"Okay," my recorded voice went on insistently, "but it's not the same thing at all. Your choice is willfully self-destructive and mine isn't and that's a real difference, no matter how you want to justify it. I take care of myself. I'd never ask you to stick me in the ass with a syringe, for example."

"You didn't have to," she said with a tiny catlike yawn. "What kind of intervention was that, Jeremy? Was that the best you could do?" There came the sound of coughing, then several thudding sounds: She'd choked on her own laughter, I'd thumped her on the back. "I'm sorry," she said then, "but that was the most pathetic little confrontation I ever heard."

"I've got to go," I said.

"Jeremy, come back here and get your sense of humor," she called. "I think it's under the couch or somewhere."

Footsteps, then the sound of the front door being unlocked.

"Don't go," she said. "Don't leave all mad at me like that. I won't be able to get any painting done today, I'll be too upset."

"I have to go," I said. "I'll call you later."

"Give Ted my love," she said; had she really sounded so lonely at the time?

There was a brief hiss, then a click, and then the whole thing apparently started over.

"I'm not going to do this for you, Felicia," I heard myself say. I sounded petulant and irritated.

"Please," she answered breathlessly.

"No," I said. "I can't even watch."

Footsteps resounded and died away. There was a pause; breaking the silence was the faint hiss and honk of faraway traffic, and then a long, slow exhalation; it sounded as if the microphone were right by Felicia's mouth. Then I heard footsteps, then came a pause.

"Sorry about that," Felicia's airy voice said.

"I've got to go."

"Jeremy. Accept my apology."

"This whole thing is bullshit. You started doing it because you liked the idea of yourself doing it. Now look at you."

She laughed. "I don't have to answer to anyone."

"That's hardly the point, Felicia. Think about it."

"Oh, fiddle," she said. "I want to be a drug-addicted neurotic semirecluse. You want to be what you are; it's the same thing, Jeremy."

"What am I, Felicia?"

"You're a slut."

"Okay," I said (had I really sounded so earnestly self-righteous?), "but it's not the same thing at all."

I took off my headset, then Sebastian's. He didn't resist; he merely blinked at me and stooped slightly to read the card.

"It's called 'Hitting Bottom,'" he said. "Clever, don't you think?"

I looked at him. "Did she plan this? I can't believe she did this to me!"

"But you come off heroically," he said, perplexed.

"In what way, exactly?"

"You told her the truth."

"But she knew all along," I said. We were shouting, trying to be heard over everyone else who was trying to be heard. "She planned this whole thing. She set me up."

"I might be flattered," said Sebastian, "if it were me."

"I always knew she was like that," I said insistently, "totally out for herself. But as long as I thought she was on my side and we were in it together, I didn't care. It didn't matter."

A couple of the people around us looked curiously at me, then at the diorama, then back at me again.

"She meant to go into rehab all along," I said directly into his ear, lowering my voice. "This had nothing to do with her decision. This is fake. She's fake. She probably got addicted on purpose."

A flashbulb went off in my face. I was briefly blinded by twin slippery gold-black starbursts wherever I looked. When they faded, I recognized Phil Martensen, aiming his camera, about to shoot me again.

"What the hell are you doing?" I asked him, directing all my rage at his unassuming silhouette.

He came out blinking from behind his camera. "We're covering the opening for *Downtown*," he said blandly. "Gary's writing a feature on Felicia. You're a friend of hers and of some interest to readers due to recent events."

"Because of the whole Ted story," I said disgustedly. "Aren't your readers completely sick of him yet?"

"If you don't want your picture taken, of course I won't take it, but in that case you might want to step aside so I can get a clear shot at Mr. Philpott here, who I believe is the founder and editor in chief of *Boytoy*. Right? If he's game, of course."

"I don't mind in the least," said Sebastian happily. "I'm producing a script Jeremy wrote, you might mention that as well. Jeremy, do come and stand by me, don't be shy. Let's give them something to talk about." He smiled starrily at me, then at Phil. "I've always wanted to say that," he said, "but I've never had the chance before."

"I'll be over there," I said shortly, "talking to the famous artist."

"Well, she's not famous yet," said Phil, busily working his focus dials, "but give her a day or two."

Trembling with an intense emotion I couldn't quite identify, or possibly a welter of different emotions I might have been able to parse out later, in retrospect, if I cared to, I wended my unsteady way through the crowd, which seemed to have doubled since I had arrived.

Felicia was across the room, talking to several good-looking men. Gary, although not technically good-looking, was among them, holding a pen and a notebook, in which he was busily scribbling as if he were a real journalist instead of whatever he actually was.

"Hi, Gary," I said to him.

He looked up eagerly, but when he saw that it was only me, his enthusiasm faded visibly. He had been perfectly happy to see me at Giselle's premiere, back when I was a potential fount of gossip material for him, but now that I was a lowly copy editor at the magazine where he was a bona fide columnist, his attitude toward me had understandably altered.

"Hi there," he answered, and went back to whatever he was writing.

"Well, I wouldn't call it a feeling," Felicia was saying, her accent oozing enough southernness to incite another civil war, "since you don't really feel anything at all, that's the point. The Plexiglas over the photographs is meant to suggest a sense of imperviousness, the way it makes you feel, so invulnerable and superior. It's bulletproof, by the way, same as they use in taxicabs and liquor stores. The idea is," she added, laughing a little, "everyone sees right through it."

"They see through it," muttered Gary, writing busily.

"It's quite impressive," said a pouty-lipped faun with a pan-European accent; he sported a porkpie hat and a scruffy little goatee. I would have bet he was named Ronni or Rudi, one of those nicknames inexplicably shared by Eurotrash hipster dudes and preteen Valley girls.

Felicia's eyes flicked to mine as if she'd known all along that I was standing right there.

"Thank you," she said. "Jeremy!"

She detached herself from them all and sidled over to me and kissed my unresponsive cheek. She had to stand on tiptoe to reach it, because I didn't bend even slightly.

I looked into her face. Nine months ago she had been ethereal as a flamingo, but all that spooky beauty was gone; she looked much prettier now, younger, gleaming, and curvaceous, and as commonplace as a robin. Her bare arms were stringy with new muscle; her rosy flesh thrummed with a peppery buzz of ambition it could barely contain. She felt hot and solid and tough. I could feel how jacked-up she was. The whites of her eyes were so clear they looked unreal, and she smelled soapily clean, like a freshly bathed boy.

"Flowers for me? You sweetheart!"

As she embraced me, I experienced the strangest jolt of attraction I'd ever felt in my entire life. Fumes from the nonalcoholic wine I held wafted up to my nostrils, fruity and coarse; I breathed them in as if they were in fact an amulet against her palpable, audacious, boyish charms. I backed away from her.

"Actually, they're for someone else," I said. "I just came over to say hello and good-bye. I've meeting a friend."

"You're leaving already?" she said, slightly put out. "You just got here. Well, thank you for coming, and I'm so sorry I haven't been in touch. As you can see, I've been busy getting this together. But before you go, tell me, and be frank now, how do you like the show?"

I hesitated just long enough for her to notice. "It's okay," I said.

She looked at me, chewing her lip, waiting for me to continue. "I thought you'd have a lot more to say than that," she said after a moment. "Especially about the darkest moment of our friendship."

"Did you," I said in my homo voice. "Sorry to let you down. Good-bye, Felicia."

"Wait," she said. "I swear I didn't know at the time. I was taping everything in those days for something else I was working on. The recorder was on, that's all. When I heard our conversation, it seemed perfect for this piece."

"You had the recorder on the whole time we were at Benito's?"

"It didn't occur to me to mention it," she said.

"So you taped that whole conversation about Ted too?" I said, aghast.

"Well, I erased that," she said shiftily, suddenly looking away from me.

"You did not," I said.

"Wait a minute," she said. "What if you used me as a character in a novel, and repeated one of our conversations verbatim? Wouldn't that be exactly the same thing?"

I looked at her. She held my gaze; it reminded me of our shielding conversational technique, back when we'd protected each other from conversations like this one.

"No," I said musingly. "It really wouldn't be the same thing at all. You made an actual tape of my voice and made a replica of me with a stupid expression on its face."

"Is that what I did?" she gasped, half laughing. "Is that what you call it?"

"If I put you in a novel, I would give you a whole array of stupid expressions, and I would try to disguise you enough so no one but you would know it was you," I said. "I've got to go. Congratulations. I think you're going to be a big success."

She touched my arm as I turned to leave and said lightly, "Jeremy, my feelings for you are still exactly the same as they ever were. They haven't changed at all."

"Oh," I said, watching her expression, "but mine for you have."

I ambled up Broadway, enjoying the sweet, green, carefree smell of late spring that vanquished bus exhaust, garbage fumes, and dried urine. I hadn't said good-bye to Sebastian, but I didn't care. I didn't care about anything at all, at least not for the first two or three blocks. I cruised smoothly along in autopilot, meshing and interlocking like a cog with my fellow pedestrians in an intricate human machine, gliding past waddlers and dawdlers, hitting all the green lights.

But as I walked, my mood gradually darkened. As I crossed Canal Street, I suffered a piercing convulsion in my stomach that felt like gas, but wasn't gas, and found myself darting and bumbling erratically. Maybe I had been too hard on Felicia just now. Maybe I had overreacted, maybe she hadn't meant any harm with her damn diorama. Maybe the mini-Jeremy and the recording of our conversation had been meant as a tribute. And maybe my unwillingness to compromise my idealized, archaic insistence on authenticity weighed me down like a cargo of lead and sand while everyone else raced lightly on ahead, realizing their ambitions, finding mates, moving on to fulfilled and carefree lives, unhampered by useless pangs of conscience, uncircumscribed by all this superannuated deadweight I seemed to have mistaken for ballast.

A woman laden with shopping bags came charging toward me. I dodged to the right to let her pass, but she moved along with me, directly into my path. Then we both stepped to the left in awkward congruity, then to the right again. She rolled her eyes and said with brisk exasperation, "Stand still and I'll go around you," then veered around me and continued on her way.

I stood there for a moment and took a deep breath, considering my options, then went into a dark old-man bar, sat on a stool, ordered a vodka on the rocks. My drink came. I took a good long pull on it and then breathed deeply again. The bar smelled comfortingly of stale cigarettes and mold.

But this was just how I was; I couldn't be any other way. If I found myself alone in the world, at least I was alone with the knowledge that I had always tried to be true to myself.

Another pang clutched my innards. Why the hell wasn't anybody buying my novel? Maybe the whole exercise of being true to myself was one of the very things I clung to out of the misguided belief that anything so ponderous must be valuable. People who jettisoned such things seemed to be rewarded with money, love, success; everyone I knew seemed happier and lighter than I was. The common, shallow pool they swam in was cloudy and of dubious aroma, but it buoyed them, allowed them to bob carelessly around and bump against each other; its murk provided concealment, and its tepid-bathlike warmth invited them never to emerge into the air, which felt so much colder in comparison.

I took another gulp of my drink. Its warmth spread through my chest. I chuckled at the image of myself, sitting all straight and proud on my high horse, nostrils flaring at the whiffs of mediocrity and pretension drifting up from the darkling plain.

"To *The Way of All Flesh*," I said aloud as I toasted the air in front of me.

"Come again?" said the gentleman to my right.

"The movie I wrote," I said. "They're shooting it soon. It's already generating a lot of buzz, apparently."

He looked impressed, if a tad mystified. "Here's to it," he said, and we clacked glasses. I left a tip under my empty glass, picked up my flowers, and went out again into the warm, spring-scented evening. I bought a newspaper, opened it to the theater section, and stood under a streetlamp while I searched for the address of the Bankhead Theater, and once I'd found it, there was nothing for me to do but go there, to the far edge of the West Village. It was nine-forty; Ted's play had started at eight. By the time I got there, it would probably just be ending. I headed fast up Seventh Avenue South, secure in the knowledge that I was destined to stand at the stage door, waiting for Ted to emerge after tonight's performance, bouquet in the crook of my arm.

The fragrant, humid air felt drenched with life in all its forms and stages; new leaves, floating spores, human pheromones, geraniums in pots on fire escapes, earth exhaling and sprouting wherever it could. My skin osmotically absorbed this zing; although I was exhausted and my feet were sore, the air itself kept me going forward at a youthful clip. Light from streetlamps shimmered on the pavement like leaf-thin, ancient-looking, golden-bronze ice, so I half expected to slip on it as I walked through its irregular pools. Colored neon bar and bodega signs glanced off the mica in the concrete, looking like the thinnest smears of colored water, red and blue and green; the whole city was wet with light. Window squares shone from dark apartment towers with a yellowish aquarium glow. Airplane lights trundled far overhead through a pink sky, as blurred and slow-going as the lights of boats seen from the ocean floor.

I found the Bankhead Repertory Theater on a crooked cobblestone street in the meat district. The address turned out to be that of an old factory building. There was no sign of any theater on the premises beyond the small plaque near the buzzer that said "Bankhead Rep." I pressed it; there was no response. No doubt they paid no attention to it when there was a show in progress. It was now just after ten, so I guessed I didn't have long to wait until the audience dispersed; I would go up and knock on his dressing room door instead of waiting for him to emerge. I envisioned myself walking down a dark hallway toward a glittery star on a door that opened at my knock to reveal a small room strewn with costumes, bright bulbs burning around a long mirror, and Ted, his makeup smeared with cold cream, sitting at a long, cluttered counter. I had seen too many old movies, read too many novels, not to have such a scene spring full-blown into my imagination at the mere thought of the words "dressing room."

Just then the door buzzed, and without thinking I pushed it open. I climbed the stairs to the third landing, where I pushed open a heavy door marked "Bankhead Rep" in stenciled white letters. Immediately, I found myself in a hot, stuffy, brightly lit little antechamber filled with people, many of whom held plastic cups of bad red wine, most of whom were talking and gesturing with the up-with-people ebullience of theatrical hopefuls. Before I could chicken out, I pushed my way through them to a desk and said to the plump, dreadlocked girl sitting there,

"I'm looking for Ted Masterson. Can you tell me where to find his dressing room?"

"Well, they're all backstage changing right now. It's a total madhouse. Do you want to send him a message? I can tell him you're out here."

"Actually," I stammered, thinking fast, "I was hoping he would meet me for a drink. I'll be at Florent. My name is Jeremy Thrane. You promise you'll tell him?"

"Jeremy," she repeated. "Okay, I'll tell him." She wrote my name on a small slip of paper as I spelled it aloud for her, then she waggled it at me in farewell. I fought my way free of the rabidly peppy crowd and descended the stairs on shaky legs, then went along to Florent. I went in, slid onto a stool at the counter, and ordered a martini.

This was not the ideal place for a reunion. It was crowded and hugger-mugger; everyone could overhear everyone else's conversations. I had to pee very badly, but I didn't dare leave my post to go to the bathroom; what if he came in and didn't see me? He'd go away and I'd never see him again, I was pretty sure, and then I'd lose my momentum, my impetus, my determination to have it out with him once and for all, whatever was making me sit there, staring out the window, tapping my foot in apprehension.

Finally, when I was beginning to think my bladder would explode before I ever saw Ted again, I saw him in front of Florent with several other men. They stood on the sidewalk for a moment, talking and gesturing.

"Can I get another martini?" I said to the bartender. "No olives."

"Put it on your tab?" he asked.

"Sure," I said. My lips were trembling; my hand shook as I tried to raise my glass to my mouth. Ted came in just as his fresh, brimming drink was set on the counter. He came over to me, smiling warmly, which greatly shocked but didn't disappoint me. "Hello there," he said, sitting on the stool next to mine. "This is an unexpected surprise. Excuse me," he said to a passing waiter, "there are going to be five of us in a couple of minutes. Is it possible to get a table? Want to join us, Jeremy? They all went to get cigarettes."

He looked exactly the same. He wore jeans and a button-down shirt. He was freshly shaven; there was no sign of makeup on his face.

"I ordered you a drink," I said intensely, feeling like a crazy person, feeling as if I were about to sing an aria or get down on bended knee. He was so mild, so casual and unaccusatory, almost indifferent; this was not at all how I had imagined the tenor of our reunion to be. "Here," I said, and gestured to the martini.

"Oh, thanks," he said. "Actually, I was sort of looking forward to a beer, but—" He lifted the glass as if to toast me and took a sip. "Ahh," he said, "that's good, actually. God, I hate this place. The service is terrible, the food is worse, but I always seem to end up here. Did you see the play?"

"No, I missed it."

"Oh, too bad. It went without a hitch tonight." He took another gulp of his martini and set it down again. "I can get you tickets if you're interested."

"I've heard good things about it," I said. "I'd love to see it."

"You've heard mixed things about it," he said, "if you've seen all the reviews. But I'm not discouraged; it's gotten a lot of attention, and that's all that matters, especially when it's just our first play. We've sold out every performance."

"That might have to do with the fact that you're in it."

"Well," he said shortly, then smiled again. "You're looking good," he said out of nowhere; but his tone was impersonal, as if he were simply making conversation until his friends arrived.

"The screenplay I wrote is being produced," I blurted out. "A production company is hiring me to write another one. Have you heard of Waverly Productions?"

"I think so," he said.

"Well, that's them. They actually want me to move out to L.A." I laughed modestly.

"You? I can't see you there." He looked startled, even impressed, which gave me a strange mixture of regret and panic; I felt cheap for bringing it up, as if I were trying to prove something to him.

"Me neither," I said. "By the way, I was just at Felicia's opening."

"Yeah, I got something in the mail about that but I couldn't make it, obviously. I'll have to go check it out some time. How's Felicia?"

"Recovering," I said.

"Clean?" he asked with his familiar grin.

"As a whistle."

"The twelve steps in action?"

"Every man jack of them."

There was a brief pause, during which we smiled somewhat stupidly at each other. I realized that I'd been staring at him since he'd arrived. My eyes felt as if they were emitting laser beams.

"How's your drink?" I asked pointedly.

"Great," he said, his mind clearly elsewhere.

"Actually, I'm referring to—forget it." I paused, then added more loudly than necessary, with a flash of anger, "Guess who I ran into tonight."

"I give up."

"Yoshi."

Ted's left eye twitched slightly. "Yoshi," he repeated.

"I just saw him tonight, near SoHo," I said. "We walked together for just a block or two, so we didn't talk for long. He said he lives down there now."

"I wouldn't know," he said, glancing at the door.

"You threw me away for him," I said with cold, clipped fury.

Ted stared at me. "Can't we just let this go?" he asked with a small frown. "It's over. The damage has been done."

"Well, it all seems to have worked out nicely for you in the end."

"Assuming this is the end," he said. He took a tidy, conservative nip of his drink, then set his glass down carefully in the center of the napkin.

Just then his fellow actors surrounded us. Ted introduced me to them, but the inside of my head felt hollow and cold, and I immediately forgot all their names; they all looked identical to me, young, short, good-looking, with wide, smiling red mouths and an abnormal amount of social energy. I finished my martini and set the glass on the counter with deliberate care.

Ted stood up and put his arm around one of his fellow actors and kissed him on the lips. "Tony," he said, "you were fucking fantastic tonight."

"Baby," Tony said with a toss of his head, "you ain't seen nothin' yet."

The rest of them hooted in unison. "I think he has," said an apple-cheeked lad with a Shakespearean goatee. Tony nuzzled Ted's neck.

I stood up and tossed some money onto the counter, too much, but I didn't want to wait for change or stay there another nanosecond. Somehow I said good-bye to them all and made it out of there. I pissed in a doorway, then walked home, too sober to forget anything, wondering yet again, with a grim, frustrated fury that was becoming all too familiar, why not one editor in New York would publish my novel. Maybe I was doomed, as Max had said, to be a successful screenwriter. But as soon as I thought that, a small voice in the back of my head piped up, as it always did when I was on this mental hamster wheel, and said that all those editors were dunderheads who wouldn't recognize a good book if it bit them in the ass. But, said a louder and more compelling voice, maybe my book wasn't good at all; maybe it was just the kind of pretentious, overwritten thing I most deplored. No, said the smaller voice; it couldn't be.

This bootless internal argument continued until I got home. Scott was out somewhere, to my relief; I had been dreading having to have to make cheerful chitchat with him while I was in this mood. I took the tiger lilies out of their paper, put them into a jar of water, carried them into my room, and put them on my nightstand. Although it was still early, I took off my clothes, turned off the light, and flung myself onto my bed. The flowers, slightly bedraggled by now but still mockingly gorgeous in the white, glimmering half-light from the city outside, were the last things I saw before I fell into a deep and mindless sleep.

And they were the first things I saw the next morning, too, when I opened my eyes and let my vision adjust slowly to the new day. I lay there for a while, as the five gangly stems came into focus along with the velvety orange petals streaked with dusky purple. I got out of bed and made my slightly unsteady, sleep-drunk way out to the living room, where Scott and Matt lay entwined on the fainting couch, watching Juanita enjoy her new bell toy. It dangled from her perch and responded with a merry tinkle whenever she butted it with her head.

"Morning, fellas," I said as I reached a finger into the cage and withdrew her.

"Oh, don't take her," said Matt.

"Time for her calisthenics," I said heartlessly. "Maybe there's a bird show on the nature channel." I put her on my bare shoulder, where she sat without fussing or pooping while I made myself a big cup of coffee. I went back to my room and set her on the nightstand by the vase of flowers. She looked lovely there, diminutive and green. She cocked her head and watched me politely as I stood in the middle of the room, drinking my coffee and scratching a mosquito bite on my arm.

"Jeremy?"

"Come on in."

Scott, standing in the doorway, glanced at the grimy computer keyboard, rumpled bed, slovenly stacks of old scribbled-on drafts of chapters, discrete heaps of soiled clothes, and the astonishing array of food-caked dishes tucked handily here and there to double as repositories for my castoff toenail clippings should I find myself in need of them. The place where my new CD player had been was now a clean rectangle of shelf surrounded by a solid layer of black dust. Where did that black dust come from? New Jersey, most likely; it wasn't my fault it kept falling on everything, I had nothing to do with it.

Scott stayed where he was, which made me feel like Oscar to his Felix. "I've been meaning to talk to you about something," he said with a touch of nervousness. "I don't know how to break this to you, but here goes."

He took a deep breath. I cradled my coffee cup, bemused but intrigued. I had never seen him betray the slightest tremor of uncertainty; whatever news he had to impart was of secondary interest to me.

"Matt and I have been talking about moving in together for a couple of months now," he said. "We've been looking for the right place and it just sort of fell into our laps. It's available on July first, which means that I'd be moving out in a couple of weeks. But I've found you a replacement roommate. His name is Andy, and he's a very good old friend of mine."

"Andy," I said noncommittally. "Well, actually, I'm probably moving out in a month or two as well."

"Where to?" he asked with a startled flicker of disbelief.

"Los Angeles," I said.

"Los Angeles," he repeated with undisguised awe.

"That's right. So Andy will have the whole place to himself."

"Wow," he said a little enviously. "Well, I hope you're really happy out there." He hesitated. "Is Juanita going with you?"

I looked deeply into my pet's beady little eyes for a moment. "You can have her," I said then, divining and granting her fondest wish. "Consider her my parting gift to you and Matt. A housewarming present."

"We can have Juanita?" he echoed.

"Yes," I said briskly. "You can take her now. We've said our good-byes."

"Come on, chickie-chick," said Scott, extending a finger. She hopped right onto it and gazed up at him.

"Ciao," I said in a Eurotrash variant of my homo voice as Scott and Juanita went together to the living room to celebrate with their new roomie.

Oh, God, everyone in L.A. was going to be a Scott clone. With dread I envisioned myself squinting in the sun in an outdoor café beneath smog-bleached palm trees, staring glumly at a plate of vegan sushi and a glass of mineral water with a paper-thin crescent of lemon stuck among the ice cubes. I could already deeply relate to the predicament of that lemon.

19 | THE PILGRIM SOUL

That evening I found myself sweating in Max's old tuxedo next to my sister at the top of the gangway of a rusted-out boat called the *Skillet*. In its former life as an aid-giving ship, the *Skillet* had sunk to the bottom of the ocean; years later, it had been dragged to the surface, permanently docked next to a pier in Chelsea, and pressed into service as a floating pleasure palace. The sun had shone through a shifting mass of clouds. Amanda looked as beautiful as any bride who'd ever tied the knot: Her mass of black hair was pinned on top of her head with a wreath of dried roses; a few stray ringlets fell around her face. She wore a form-fitting cream-colored satin dress and her new gold fairy slippers.

The Radish Night accordion player hit the first notes of the wedding march.

Amanda and I looked at each other. Her eyes glittered with tiny shards of sunlight reflected off the river. I was swamped by a knee-buckling pang of love for her.

"It's show time," I said. My throat was tight.

She gave a small, delicate sniff, as if to brace herself, then wordlessly put her hand into the crook of my arm. I walked her down the gangway, onto the pier and down the flower-strewn aisle between rows of folding chairs, past a hundred or so of her and Liam's families, friends, former lovers, bartenders, and bandmates, all of whom stood up at once as soon as the music started and turned to watch our slow and stately procession toward and through them. I heard many gasps of "She's beautiful" and saw tearily smiling faces. We made our way to the makeshift altar, where my sister's bloodshot lug of an intended stood waiting for her in a white tuxedo, so clean-shaven his cheeks looked scalded. He looked completely freaked out, which I took to be a clear sign that this wedding was not just a cynical joke for him. Feckin bristled alongside him, restive and disreputable in a moth-eaten tuxedo as ill-fitting as my own, with a cherry-red bow tie and cummerbund. Gina, the bass-playing Jezebel of a maid of honor, wore a bloodred strapless ball gown that clashed with Feckin's accessories.

As I handed Amanda over to Liam, I looked him right in the eye, as a warning, then stepped back to stand next to my mother. Amanda turned her pale, somber face to Liam's as the music ended. When my mother gave my arm a little squeeze, I realized that something was supposed to happen now, and that something was me.

I cleared my throat and fumbled in my pocket, then plunged headlong into the first line of the Yeats poem before I'd even located the piece of paper I'd copied it onto.

> *When you are old and gray and full of sleep,*
> *And nodding by the fire, take down this book,*
> *And slowly read, and dream of the soft look*
> *Your eyes had once, and of their shadows deep.*

I knew the thing by heart but had decided not to recite it from memory, because then I'd have nothing to hide behind. I was only one third of the way through, and already I knew I'd chosen completely wrong, that I was attempting to foist my own notion of what should be read at a wedding upon my sister, whose face I was unable to see because I was looking only at the paper.

> *How many loved your moments of glad grace,*
> *And loved your beauty with love false or true;*
> *But one man loved the pilgrim soul in you,*
> *And loved the sorrows of your changing face;*

I wanted to do justice to the immortal words of the national bard of this small contingent of jet-lagged Irish people, but in spite of this wish, my voice had established itself in a singsong that proved to be devastatingly difficult to escape. I plunged on, rounding the track toward the finish line.

And bending down beside the glowing bars,
Murmur, a little sadly, how love fled
And paced upon the mountains overhead
And hid his face amid a crowd of stars.

After I said the last line, I folded the paper, shoved it into my pants pocket, plucked my handkerchief from my coat pocket, and mopped my brow, feeling overheated and abashed. Only then did I meet Amanda's eyes, and only then did I see that her face was streaked with dusky tears. Even I had heard of waterproof mascara; why hadn't she thought to lay in a supply before her wedding? I was blindsided by another wave of love for her.

A buxom Irishwoman, Liam's cousin or aunt, strummed the strings of a guitar, then began to warble a minor-key ballad narrating every hitch and snafu of the doomed love affair between a farm boy and an ordinary brunette from County Cork. After a couple of verses I caught the eye of my sister Lola, who sat in the front row next to Fletcher Barkin, her big-headed, strapping Australian husband. She and I quirked our lips at each other. This was the first time in fifteen years I'd exchanged such a look with her; I'd forgotten her wry squint, the twitch of her nose that said she felt just the way I did, and that she and I had once shared this half-amused sense of the strangeness of things. Just as quickly, we both looked away, as if we were amoebas sliding our pseudopodia toward each other, then retracting them the instant the membranes touched, as if the whole point of the contact had been to establish our mutual separateness.

Who was this blond, ruddy, emu-breeding fellow Fletcher anyway? He looked like a rugby player. Lola's marriage a few years ago had made barely a squiggle on my internal seismograph, or so I'd thought when I'd heard about it. But now it occurred to me that Fletcher was my brother-in-law just as much as Liam was, whatever that meant. If we'd all grown up in a small town in the Midwest and lived our lives within a mile of each other, we might have shared the familiar habits and jokes of men in a family together. Perversely, possibly because my woolen pants were itching me and I couldn't scratch myself because I was standing there in front of everyone, I wished all of a sudden that I belonged to this imaginary small-town family, an extended clan glued together by a shared disinclination to push the envelope, living next door to people we'd grown up with, sticking together through church bazaars, droughts, ice cream socials, drunk-driving accidents. I could have been the bookish bachelor, squiring the town's spinsters, widows, and divorcees to Fourth of July barbecue suppers. Whenever I arrived at one of my sisters' houses, my adoring nieces and nephews would have shouted "Uncle Jeremy!" and jumped up and down with excitement. It would have been a trade-off, but I could sort of see why some people did it.

Just then the ballad came to an end, and with it, these thoughts. It had been the minor key, that watery soprano; the moment the song ended, I started to choke with claustrophobia at the thought of such a life. My mother took her hand off my arm, which she had been clutching through the layers of my sleeves this entire time, and produced her own piece of paper, neatly typewritten and unfolded.

"This poem is called," she said in her ringing, clear, poetessy voice, " 'The War Bride.' It describes another wedding that took place in Berkeley, California, in 1963."

Without clearing her throat or fussing with the paper as I might have done, she then began to read. As always, she gave a slight intake of breath to indicate the line breaks, which gave the words a portentous weight they may not have had on the page. Rummaging around in my mental family-history archives, I gathered that this poem was concerned with the fact that Emma had married Angus to get free of her mother, and that Lucy had opposed the marriage with all the didactic vigor she possessed; this I gleaned from the series of old-fashionedly feminist images of which the poem was comprised, concluding with the lines, "The alchemy of the ring binds bird to beast and snaps/The cord around my neck/My veil bandages the wounded air/He plunders what she's spoiled. We all/surrender." I hoped this wasn't my mother's sneaky way of expressing her own disapproval of Liam and repeating history, but fortunately, neither Liam nor Amanda seemed to be listening, judging by their rapturous, dazed expressions, and everyone else appeared to be either crying or smiling, or both. I'd never been so glad before that everyone tended to space out when poetry was read aloud.

After my mother's poem, it was time for the real business of the wedding. The justice of the peace, a sane-looking man with a wandering left eye and a wart on his chin, discharged his duties briskly and without undue sentiment, as if hitching people were no more or less momentous than delivering the mail. After the bridal pair exchanged their plain gold bands, he said, "You may kiss the bride" as if it were a no-nonsense directive along the lines of "Sign here for this package." Liam planted his lips on Amanda's, and everyone burst into the spontaneous applause that always greeted this moment. Then we all flocked back up the aisle we'd so recently paraded down to stand in a line on the pier behind the rows of chairs.

There was a mass communal bustle for half an hour or so as the newlyweds and their families, me included, were assaulted by all the assembled in what I supposed was called the receiving line. Once everyone had exchanged hand sweat with me or kissed their lipstick off onto my cheek, I followed them all up the gangway, descended the stairs that led belowdecks, and wormed my way through the crowd to the ship's galley-cum-bar, using my leverage as brother of the bride to take cuts in front of all the lesser guests. It had been thirsty work, handing my sister over to that green-card–seeking rogue. The bar was in the middle of the ship, flanked on either side by narrow corridors leading back to the living quarters and forward to the defunct engine room and the catwalk over the hold, which now served as a dance floor. The portholes showed wavy views of the Hudson River.

"I'll have a vodka on the rocks," I told the grizzled old bartender who looked as if he could have been the captain, brought up from the ocean floor and resurrected along with his ship. He looked a lot like the vessel itself; his face was fretted with wrinkles and creases the way every square inch of the ship's innards was covered with rust.

He obligingly handed me a nice, stiff, three-fingered drink, and I climbed back up to the aft deck, I supposed it was called, although I supposed I could call it whatever the hell I wanted. I sat on a bench and watched people come two by two up the gangway. Toward New Jersey, the sun was staining the lowering sky with a toxic Crayola meltdown of coral, tangerine, amber, carmine, a lemon-custardy glow underneath, mirrored in the moving surface of the river, where the pulls and snags of the tide showed their patterned contours in flashes of contrast, dark on one side, light on the other. The wind off the river smelled of algae and oil and the promise of rain.

A tall young woman in a pink dress proffered a loaded tray. I took a goat cheese tartlet and ate it whole; Amanda and Liam's budget had allowed only for drinks and hors d'oeuvres, no sit-down dinner, even with the money Emma and Leonard had kicked in. They had democratically opted to invite everyone they knew and get them drunk and feed them snacks instead of whittling the list down to a select elite. A plump boy with a shock of red hair trundled behind the tartlet girl with a tray of champagne-filled glasses. In the glow of the sky they looked like chalices of molten gold with trapped air bubbles; they were so appealing, I downed my drink in a gulp and traded my ice-filled glass for a tall, slender flute of champagne. A chartered pleasure boat ablaze with strings of white-hot lights and emitting tinny music cruised by on its way downstream.

Suddenly, I became aware that the man sitting next to me was sending me signals I recognized. I turned and looked him in the eye. He was a younger, spiffier version of the groom.

"Hello there," I said.

"Hello yourself," he said in a brogue I found charming in spite of myself.

"You're a relative of the groom."

"His little brother Johnny."

"What a coincidence," I said. "I'm Amanda's brother, Jeremy."

"What does that make us, then?" he asked with a saucy grin. "Kissing cousins, is it?"

No, I thought to myself; it would be too creepy to have sex with someone who looked so much like Liam. "I think it's more like friendly relations," I answered.

"Ah," he said, raising his eyebrows.

The trouble with the whole innuendo game was that you couldn't suddenly decide to explain yourself point-blank. My next move was to soften my rejection of him with a dry bit of flattery, but I found my mind lazily slipping away from this conversation. He knew what I was about to say as well as I did, so I might as well spare us both the trouble.

Abruptly, I stood up and drifted up to the bow, where I found my sister Lola and brother-in-law, Fletcher, standing near the steps that led up to the wheel room.

"Jeremy, hello again," said Fletcher, extending a hand for me to shake. His palm was soft yet tough as suede and easily engulfed my own. He seemed nice enough, but there was something overly boisterous about him, something too breezy and ingratiating. Maybe it was an Aussie characteristic and my reaction was akin to the patronizing dismay Europeans felt for Americans, or maybe any brother would have been suspicious, meeting his sister's husband for the first time; all I knew was that this must have been much freakier for him than it was for me, coming all the way around the world to stand on a rusty boat drinking champagne with his wife's peculiar family.

"There you are!" said Amanda, flinging her arms around Lola and me and kissing us each on the cheek. "Come down to the pier for a family picture; the photographer just told me to round you up."

"Should I come along?" Fletcher asked.

"Of course, Fletcher, you're family too," said Amanda immediately, and we all trooped down to the pier to join Emma, Leonard, and Liam.

"Irene!" my mother called. "Over here!"

Irene Rheingold bustled along the pier toward us. She wore a red velvet embroidered caftan that looked like sofa upholstery and a necklace of large clay beads the general size, shape, and color of dog-do.

"I missed your ceremony," she called to Amanda when she came into earshot. "Something came up; but here I am now."

"Something came up?" I blurted out before Amanda or Emma could reassure her that they understood perfectly, she was so busy, it was so great that she could make it at all. "Did you have to go to the emergency room? Were you kidnapped? Did aliens abduct you?"

"Oh, you know how it is," she said airily.

"I saw Richard and Beatrice earlier," said Amanda. "They said you'd be late."

"Yes," said Irene, "good."

"What," I persisted, "could possibly have 'come up' that was more important than Amanda's wedding ceremony? You've known her since she was born. She's like your niece."

"Oh, shut your cakehole, Jeremy," said Amanda tolerantly.

"Amanda," Irene gushed, ignoring me completely. "You look so beautiful! Congratulations to all you wonderful, beautiful Thranes and Margolises."

"And O'Flahertys now," said Amanda.

"And Barkins!" said Fletcher.

"Line up, everyone," said the photographer, a stout, businesslike girl in a black schmatte. "The light is perfect. Quick, before the clouds cover the sun."

I sidled up to Irene and looked her right in the eye as if to say that she had no business whatsoever inserting herself into this photograph and she knew it. She smiled back at me with syrupy sorrow, as if to say that she was disappointed that I felt this way but didn't care to involve herself in my emotional troubles.

"Smile," barked the photographer.

We all smiled on cue together, smiled again, then again, changed positions, smiled again and again. When we were finished, Emma leaned over and cupped Lola's abdomen in her hand. "This one made it into the pictures too," she said. "I'm so glad."

I noticed with instantaneous, primitive bloodline-protectiveness that Lola held a glass of champagne; I had to restrain myself from snatching it away from her.

"What are you talking about, Mom?" I said indignantly.

"Well," Lola said, shooting our mother an impatient look, "we were going to announce it later, but I'm pregnant." She pronounced it "prig-nunt," since she'd picked up a strong Australian accent in all her years there. This was only normal, I supposed, but it never failed to startle me when my sister, whom I'd known since she was born, opened her mouth and talked like a person from another hemisphere.

"But you're drinking," I said.

"So?" she said mulishly, blank-faced; an ancient urge to smack her surged in me. "One or two glasses of champagne won't harm the baby."

"But how could you even take the chance?" Amanda said.

"It's my baby," said Lola.

"Our baby," said Fletcher, sliding his arm along her shoulders and pulling her to him. I thought I saw her stiffen and resist. I wondered briefly what the dynamics of their marriage were; if we had been a family where everyone stuck around and saw each other all the time, I would probably have been privy whether I liked it or not to Fletcher's half-drunk confidences on the porch after all the women had gone to bed. Or maybe not. In any case, I didn't know a thing about the adult Lola, her marriage, or her life. She could fill me in on details and anecdotes and feelings until she was blue in the face, but some things couldn't be explained, you had to be there; and similarly, what would I tell her about everything that had happened to me since I'd last seen her? How could we ever recover all the time we'd spent apart?

When the photographer began to herd O'Flahertys into photogenic configurations, Leonard plopped himself with a sigh onto a bench, looking around him as if he weren't quite sure who we all were, or where he was, or why. I could see from his bewildered expression that he was trying very hard to piece it together so he wouldn't have to embarrass himself by asking his wife to explain it all to him again. When the photographer had finished her portraits and excused everyone, Liam and Fletcher went strolling off along the pier toward the end, lighting cigarettes as they went; my sisters and mother and I watched them go. "They're making friends," said Emma. "That's nice."

"They're commiserating," I said. " 'What the hell were we thinking? How will we put up with these Thrane girls for the rest of our lives?' "

"They should take Leonard with them," said Emma. "I'm sure he's got plenty of advice on that front."

Amanda burst out, "Lola, you're having a baby? Oh my God, it just hit me!" She swept Lola into a sisterly embrace; I had forgotten about these gusts of sudden affection that occasionally came over my sisters, causing them to throw themselves upon each other's necks in a passionate détente.

I felt in my breast pocket for the envelope. "Amanda," I said. "I have a present for you. Actually, it's for both of you."

"For me too?" said Lola, pleased.

"Come on," I said, herding my rosy-faced, embracing sisters toward a row of empty folding chairs set along the edge of the pier, facing down-river. "It's a surprise."

They settled into chairs on either side of me, quietly excited the way they'd been as little girls whenever I told them I'd written a new play, and they could have the smaller roles if they promised not to fidget during my soliloquies.

"Wait for us!" cried our mother, flocking toward us with Irene on her heels. Both their faces, when I turned to look at them, were agog with an avid, transparent eagerness to be part of whatever we young folk were up to. They took the chairs on either side of Amanda and Lola, giggling and fussing with their chairs until they were as close to my sisters as they could get. My mother rested her chin on Amanda's shoulder, her eyes on the envelope. I didn't look at Irene.

Amanda took the envelope, unsealed the flap, and slid out the card.

"A Hallmark card?" she said, laughter catching in her throat.

"Read inside," I said.

She flipped it open. It took her a moment, but then she looked up at me, amazed. "I don't believe this," she said. "Really?" She burst into tears and clasped my hand.

"What?" said Lola, taking the card from her.

Irene read it over Lola's shoulder, moving her lips exaggeratedly, as if she were a silent-movie actress and the audience had to read her lips to figure out what it said.

"You found him," Lola said calmly as her hand fluttered down to rest lightly on my other hand, her brown eyes clear and dry, her expression quizzical. She had been barely out of diapers when Angus had disappeared. Unlike Amanda and me, she hardly remembered him.

"I think so," I said. "Unless it's some other Angus Thrane about his age who used to be a lawyer in San Francisco. It's possible, I guess."

"But," said Amanda, teary-eyed, "how did you get this?"

I explained about calling the American Bar Association.

"The San Juan Islands," said Emma. "Remember, Irene? The camping trip we all took up there when Jeremy was a baby?"

"Angus didn't seem to like it there much," said Irene. "He complained about the weather."

"Should we call him?" asked Amanda.

"Do you want to?" I asked.

"We could do it tomorrow," said Lola.

"Oh, I'd like to be there," said our mother. "For this historic moment."

"Would you mind very much if I came too?" said Irene with her "charming" laugh, her lips pursing so much on the word "too," I thought for a moment she was going to kiss someone. "It would be great to say hello to Angus after all these years!"

My sisters pressed each of my hands at the same time, informing me that I was expected to handle this to make up for the fact that I'd had so many perks and privileges when we were kids: more authority and power, a later bedtime, a bigger allowance.

"I think we need to call our father alone, just the three of us," I said, looking out at the water so I didn't have to meet my mother's eyes. "We'll tell you everything afterward, Mom, all the gory details."

"Of course," said Emma promptly, through obvious disappointment. "I completely understand."

"That seems unfair," Irene began querulously, but I cut her short.

"Irene," I said. "It's none of your business."

All four women sighed simultaneously in a general, unanimous expression of indulgence toward me and my crabby, intolerant masculine predilections. I'd seen some or all of them react in the same way to Leonard when one of his lectures exceeded its natural limits of length and fever pitch, or Richard Rheingold at the instant when the joke he was telling became too shaggily unwieldy to sustain its weak punch line. It was a sigh of female solidarity, expressing their superiority to men, their half-fond, long-suffering comprehension of our blunt and hapless simplicity.

I stood up and silently walked away. Coming toward me along the pier were my two brothers-in-law; we met at the bench where Leonard still sat alone, and surrounded him all at once. He looked up at us. "Boys," he said precisely.

The three of us looked at one another. "That's us," I said. "A bunch of guys."

"A mess of lads," Liam agreed.

"About time," said Leonard, his eyebrows writhing. All four of us laughed.

"A passel of mates," Fletcher put in heartily, a beat too late.

All around us, people were drifting along in nuzzling twosomes, drinking champagne, coming off the boat or going back onto it. A wet gust of wind came at us from the river, but the rain held off, and a moment later a low beam of sunlight struck the side of the *Skillet* with watery-gold evening light. Looking up at the railing, I saw a small crowd of guests looking down at us; the contrast of shadow and light seemed to show the sadness and terror behind their smiles, like the faces in Felicia's paintings; the illusion was as starkly shocking as if their skulls had suddenly been revealed under their skin. Then the sun was covered by a swiftly moving cloud, and they turned back into happy wedding guests again.

Leonard stood abruptly and said to no one in particular, "All hands on deck," then stumped his way over to the gangway.

"Maybe we should go with him," said Liam anxiously.

He and Fletcher moved toward Leonard, flanked him, and each took one of his arms. He allowed them to lead him up to the *Skillet* and down into the hold.

I headed off the pier, back toward dry land. I lived only eight blocks away; I could easily go home and take a shower and change and spend the rest of the night in comfortable clothes that fit me and didn't make me itch. It felt good to be back in the streets, anonymous again, a free agent. I unlocked my building's front door and climbed up to the apartment; Scott and Matt were gone, and the place felt refreshingly small and quiet. All the excited voices, the wind off the river, the strong emotions of the ceremony, felt miles away. I stood under the hot jet of water with my eyes closed and let it pummel my skin and run off me in rivulets, down the drain.

I reboarded the *Skillet* half an hour later, my hair still damp, wearing clean black twill trousers and my favorite shirt, a long-sleeved red cotton crew neck. I went down into the belly of the boat and waited in line at the bar for a good long spell, bantering with all the other thirsty guests, staring out through the portholes at the darkening sky and river.

Finally, I wrangled another vodka on the rocks from the bartender, who by now was looking even more battered, and whose former ahoy-there-matey cheer had curdled into a parboiled resignation. Drink in hand, I went forward to stand on the catwalk. Below me, on the dance floor, a crowd of people seemed to be jumping and jogging and doing the twist. Amanda's band was playing a raucously good-humored set that consisted primarily of requests yelled out from the dance floor, an agreeable mish-mash spanning five or six decades and genres. The burly blond fellow who'd been conscripted to play guitar in Amanda's place was, I gathered, the accordion player's boyfriend or roommate. I liked the way he played. Instead of Amanda's fancy plucking and strumming, he banged on his guitar as if he just wanted to get the job done as efficiently as possible, which changed the whole tenor of the band so much, it could have been a different set of musicians. He was the locomotive that drove the whole thing; he kept his movements and stage business to a minimum, con-serving all his energies for making the appropriate noises on his guitar and singing in a strong, no-nonsense voice.

My skittering eye alit on the three Rheingolds, standing below, holding their drinks in their right hands at waist level, as if they were a trio of backup singers frozen mid-routine. Since the last time I'd seen her, last fall, Beatrice had chopped off all her long brown hair. She'd got herself a minimullet, short on top, long in the back, that proclaimed her sexual orientation to anyone who chose to see it; I guessed that her par-ents had not, and might never. Irene's eyes were hooded, her mouth hung slightly open, her cheeks looked long and white; her unguarded expres-sion, if that was what it was, contained equal parts loneliness and arro-gance. She looked old and careworn, even though she was flanked by her family while all around her, people were dancing a free-for-all hora to "Hava Nagila," the most cheerful minor-key song in existence. I won-dered then, with sudden real curiosity, what had kept her from attend-ing the ceremony, and realized that I would probably never know.

Liam stepped up to the microphone and gestured to Amanda, who had been hoisted aloft on a chair by a group of her friends and kept up there, despite her writhing and laughing injunctions.

"I'd like to sing a song," Liam's voice boomed into the mike, "for my beautiful new wife on our wedding day."

"This'll be lovely," said Feckin, who had been lurking at my side for a while, looking down with me in amused silence.

"No doubt," I said back.

Liam paused for a squeal of feedback, then cleared his throat and muttered, "A-one two three four," and the band came crashing in right on cue. I half expected him to sing an anthem expressing his joy and relief at finally getting U.S. citizenship, but it turned out to be a simple three-chord rock song with a poppy little beat whose chorus went "Blind date, it's a blind date, is she the one for me, I will have to see, it's a blind date and love is blind." Liam's voice was hoarse and tuneless; I had somehow thought all Irishmen were born with mellifluous, resonant tenors, but maybe they'd revoked his the day he'd left the Emerald Isle. Amanda leapt down from the chair, made her way to the stage, and threw her arms around her husband; he threw his around her, and they danced cheek to cheek while he sang the rest of the song. She seemed to be crying again, judging from the quantity of mascara running down her cheeks.

"What is this?" I asked Feckin.

He smirked at me. "The theme song of a show on TV," he said. "The one she absolutely hates."

"She doesn't seem to hate it today," I said, recalling that she'd also cried at my Yeats poem, which would have made her roll her eyes if she'd been in her right mind. It was interesting that qualities she normally deplored, namely my stuffiness and Liam's oafishness, were making her cry today; maybe the parts of the brain that controlled annoyance and sentimentality were right next to each other.

"You must be pretty depressed," I said to Feckin, "losing your best friend to wedlock."

"I'm not losing anyone," he said mildly. "Why would I?"

"Don't you have to move out of their apartment now?"

"I couldn't do that to them," he said. "I'm like their own feckin child."

"How nice," I said, "a ready-made family."

"Believe me," he said, "I wouldn't do it for everyone."

We stood there for a while, amicably enough, with nothing more to say to each other.

"See you later," said Feckin presently. "I'm off to bum a fag."

A moment later I saw him approach the clot of men just below me. One of them handed over a pack, shaking his head at the others. Feckin took three, stuck one into his mouth and two into his pocket; another of the men held a flame to the cigarette in Feckin's mouth, and a cloud of smoke rose around his head. Then Feckin said something else that made them all laugh, and caused the first man to hand over his entire pack of cigarettes.

Nearby, my mother and Leonard were doing a herky-jerky shoulder-rolling sixties kind of dance to Liam's song, laughing at each other. Suddenly, he seized her in his arms and gave her a kiss on the mouth. She seemed too taken aback to respond at first, and her arms dangled at her sides, but as he persisted, she leaned into him and embraced him back. Liam finished singing his song to Amanda; he swooped her into his arms and carried her off the stage to wild applause. The guitar player said something to the rest of the band and made a brief motion with his head to indicate a new rhythm, and they segued smoothly into an old country song with a three-four beat. My mother and Leonard began to waltz as the guitar player sang the lyrics in his warm, gritty voice. I noticed that he neither fondled the microphone nor made pained, self-important faces; he comported himself with the same unadorned quietude whether he was playing the guitar or taking a break, singing or not. He seemed to feel no need to leap around like an idiot or call attention to himself.

It dawned on me that I was in danger of developing a crush on him, so I tore my eyes away from his strong shoulders and fetching face and made my way aft to the bar and found the end of the line for drinks. At long last, when I'd collected a new drink, I continued upstairs to the deck, where I wandered around for a while, eavesdropping, chatting when I had to, taking the warm, river-smelling air into my lungs as I watched the lights sliding along the surface of the water. The river rocked and lapped against the rusty hull; the boards of the pier creaked, rising and falling with the waves.

After a while I found myself climbing the steps to the wheel room, which was empty except for a pile of instrument cases. I perched in the high, swiveling captain's chair and spun the big wheel a few times, played with the knobs of the defunct controls, then put my feet up on the dashboard or whatever it was called and leaned back and looked through the enormous, greasy windshield. A few minutes later, it began to rain. The river and lights blurred together in a sheer wash that ran down the glass. The roof overhead roared dully. When I heard footsteps coming up to the wheel room, I whisked my feet guiltily off the dashboard as if it were the coffee table in someone's living room. I sat up straighter in the chair and began to swivel it back and forth casually with my hips, whistling to myself, just having a pleasant solitary moment before I rejoined the wedding party.

"Hey," said the guitar player as his well-shaped head appeared in the doorway. "There you are."

"Hello," I said with a gladness I couldn't disguise.

"I wanted to find you," he said, "to say hello."

"I'm Jeremy. Amanda's brother."

He came in, holding his guitar by its neck, and put it into its case. "I know," he said. "We've met a few times over the years."

I looked at him, considering.

"I was there last fall," he said helpfully, trying to jog my memory, "when you fainted at Bombshell. I helped you up. Anyway, my name is Henry Tolliver."

I squinted at him, casting back; his face swam out of the liquid darkness of memory at me, but I couldn't see it clearly enough to know for sure.

"I would remember meeting you," I said, resisting the urge to inform him that he had the same last name as poor drowned Maggie in *The Mill on the Floss*.

"Maybe not," he said, and shrugged, smiling. "I don't take it personally." He came forward to stare through the windshield at New Jersey with me. "Did you know," he said, "that this used to be a lightship, like a mobile lighthouse, that went out in storms to help foundering boats get back into the harbor? Sort of like a sheepdog. That's what the bartender just told me."

"He looks like he went down with the boat and came back up with it," I said.

Henry laughed.

"I liked your performance just now," I added somewhat shyly.

"Thanks, but I'm not really a guitar player, I was faking it as a favor to your sister. And I liked the poem you read during the ceremony. Who wrote it?"

I paused. I found him even more appealing close up than onstage. "Yeats," I said curtly. "I wasn't sure it was appropriate, but it's an old favorite of mine."

"It was entirely appropriate," he said. He fiddled with a control knob. "Anyway, so I'm not a guitarist. My actual instrument is a thing I designed and built that some people think sounds like a cross between a cello and a cat in heat. I think it's really beautiful although that's not a popular opinion. Laura says I should be arrested for playing it."

"The accordion player," I said.

"Right."

"She's your girlfriend?"

"My roommate." He hesitated, as if he were considering his next words carefully. "I don't exactly do, you know, the girlfriend thing. You don't either, I take it."

At this, I felt woolly-tongued and light-headed. "No," I said.

"I thought so," he said.

We didn't look at each other. Our shoulders were almost touching. The wet, smeared banks of New Jersey glowed at us through the windshield.

"What kind of music do you play on that thing?" I asked him.

"It's improvised," he said. "I make it up as I go."

"I know what improvised means," I said. "I know this sounds backward and conservative, but how can you control what you do without being able to revise and polish it later?"

"I try to revise as I go, in the moment," he said. "The process is not all that different from making more quote-unquote conventional kinds of art. You look for the surprising but inevitable in the chaotic and arbitrary. You try not to be self-indulgent or obvious, but to take risks and challenge yourself."

"That sounds sort of pat to me," I said, disappointed. "Are you sure you're not pretentious and full of it?"

"No," he said thoughtfully.

"Oh my God," I said as another thought struck me. "Don't tell me you play free jazz."

"Why?" he asked curiously. "You don't like free jazz?"

"It never goes anywhere," I said. "It's an excuse for people who can't play their instruments to pretend they're virtuosos and noodle around. It's like the emperor's new clothes; you can't say it sucks, because there's no objective criterion whatsoever."

Henry laughed. "How much free jazz have you heard?"

"Not much," I admitted. "But still."

"Well," he said. "As it happens, I'm playing with a few other people tomorrow night. If you agree to come and listen with an open mind, I'll put you on the list."

"Okay," I said. I paused. "Do you actually make a living doing that?"

"You're kidding, right?" he said. "I make a living as a plumber."

"The most lucrative job in the universe."

"It pays the bills," he said easily, "and I hate it with a passion. What do you do?"

"I'm not quite sure," I said. "I spent ten years writing a novel no editor will have anything to do with."

"Why not?"

"I'm not sure," I said. "Maybe it's no good."

"I doubt that," he said promptly.

"The weird thing is, I spent a week writing an idiotic screenplay that's being made into a movie, and now I might move to L.A. to work for a production company. I never had any intention of doing that."

He leaned his elbow against the dashboard and rested his head on his hand. "Then why are you moving to Los Angeles?"

"I'm giving up my idealistic true love," I said dramatically, aware that he might not have the slightest idea what I was talking about, "to marry the scheming slut."

When Henry laughed, the scent of his breath came to me on the gusts of mirth from his lungs. It smelled so healthy and clean a flash fire shot through my groin.

"There's a poem by Wallace Stevens," I said, "called 'Farewell to Florida.' It's one of the saddest and most purely beautiful poems I've ever read. It's narrated by a man on a boat heading north through a wintry sea, leaving a woman behind in Key West, her 'South of pine and coral and coraline sea': a defunct love, a hated place, or so the poem says, but every line ends on a heartbroken sob."

"Recite some," said Henry.

My mind went completely blank all of a sudden. " 'The moon is at the mast-head and the past is dead,' " I said. " 'Her mind will never speak to me again, I am free.' Then later on: '. . . she will not follow in any word/Or look, nor ever again in thought, except/That I loved her once . . . Farewell. Go on, high ship.' " I paused, suddenly embarrassed, but his intent, penetrating expression didn't waver, which gave me courage to continue. " 'The darkness shattered, turbulent with foam,' " I went on. " 'To be free again, to return to the violent mind . . . carry me, misty deck, carry me to the cold, go on, high ship, go on, plunge on.' "

He gave me a searching look. "What does this have to do with your move to Los Angeles?"

I looked away from him, at my hands, the rain on the windshield. "New York is the violent mind," I said. "And L.A. is 'vivid blooms curled over the shadowless hut' and 'trees like bones and the leaves half sand, half sun.' It's a tropical hell. And freeways . . . I don't have a driver's license, Henry. I have to get one. And I have to write screenplays."

"The darkness is your real life, you know," said Henry as if he were cautioning me. "You won't escape that by going somewhere else."

"I'm not escaping," I said. "I'm joining the fray. I'm jumping into the pool. It'll be all right. I'll be fine."

I felt him watching my profile for a moment but couldn't turn my head to meet his eyes.

"You're not moving to Los Angeles," he said.

His voice was so near to my ear, it resonated in my chest cavity. Why was he standing so close to me, speaking right in my ear, questioning my decisions and assumptions? Who did he think he was? Why didn't he go back to the party? I sensed, without quite knowing how to explain it to myself in words, a stubborn, stalwart quality in this Henry Tolliver, a hunkering-down kind of attention I was profoundly unused to having trained on myself, and which disconcerted me. Although I didn't mind it, exactly.

288

I looked at him. He didn't look away. Our gaze continued until it got a little uncomfortable for me, so I slid my eyes to the ship's wheel. I felt a sudden itch to twirl it and pretend the ship was heading out to open sea, anything to ease up on the unexpected intensity of his focus. I felt like telling him to lighten the hell up and stop taking me so seriously.

"How do you know?" I asked childishly.

Henry splayed his hands flat on the surface of the control panel. They were square, strong-fingered, sturdy. I felt a swooping sensation in the pit of my stomach.

"I just know," he said.

"But you just met me."

"No," he said with a sort of laugh. "You just met me."

I sighed deeply, not out of unhappiness, but in order to punctuate this conversation with something other than words, which I had temporarily run out of.

20 | COCKLES AND MUSSELS, ALIVE, ALIVE OH

Well past midnight, when I got home from the wedding party, I cleaned my room. Although Scott and Matt were sleeping and presumably wouldn't want to be awakened by my bustling and clattering around, I collected, rinsed, and stacked in the dishwasher all the dirty plates, cups, glasses, and silverware that had accrued in my room, then ran the dishwasher twice, with extra soap, to get the dried crud off everything. When I'd set the first cycle going, I changed my sheets, swept and mopped my floor, dusted every surface including the windowsills and moldings, then sponged them with a detergent and a rag, and washed the inside panes of both my windows.

During the dishwasher's second cycle, I folded all my clothes, put all my dirty laundry in the hamper I usually ignored, organized my books into tidy rows, and threw away all papers, envelopes, old Kleenex, and the detritus from my desk. When all was clean and quiet, I stood for a while in the middle of my room and surveyed my new landscape. I could see my reflection in the windows. Then, soberly and carefully, as if I were the kind of person who always did so, I washed my face and brushed and flossed my teeth. In clean boxer shorts and T-shirt, I went to bed and slept deeply in my clean sheets, dreaming the easy, untroubled dreams of the just and righteous, until just before my alarm went off the next morning.

As I drank my coffee in my newly bare, tidy room, I discovered that my mind felt unusually alert and orderly, my emotions clear, my body at ease. Why had I chosen to live in squalor all these years, purposefully surrounded myself with decay, disorder, mess, and the unbeautiful leavings of my daily life? All I could figure out by way of explanation was my psyche seemed to have undergone, in Star Trek parlance, a phase variance, and now for some reason I felt like living in a clean room instead. It didn't seem like an enormous thing on the surface, but internally I was acutely aware of a parallel and seemingly contradictory shift, a loosening of the chest, a removal of certain stringent internal dicta whose weight I wasn't aware of until they were lifted and I experienced their sudden negative absence. For some reason I was free of them now. I could remember other times like this one; they reminded me of knotholes in trees, spots of unusual density and concentration around which the rest of time and space flowed normally. What caused them I couldn't say; I simply assumed I'd undergo future ones, periodically, until I died.

"The term 'a sea change,'" Frederick told me through the partition later that morning, apropos of something else entirely, as we ate our deli-delivered breakfasts at our desks, "comes from Ariel's song in *The Tempest*. A dead body is subjected to immersion underwater for so long, its essential nature changes, gradually washes away, erodes, and is transformed. Bones become coral, eyes become pearls. It's 'a sea-change into something rich and strange.' Formerly hyphenated, now two discrete words. You tell Bianca Mantooth that next time she comes around to harangue you."

"I don't think she would care," I said to the partition wall through a mouthful of greasy home fries doused in ketchup, salt, and pepper. "She would just argue that the meaning itself has undergone a sea change. And she'd be right in both sense and usage."

"What she really means to say here," said Frederick, ignoring me entirely, "is that her wardrobe has 'done a one-eighty' since she got her Jack Russell terrier."

"No," I said, ripping open another little packet of ketchup, wondering half-consciously why they didn't make them bigger, or easier to open. "'Doing a one-eighty' implies a turnaround, as in: 'Ever since she went on Prozac, her whole personality has done a one-eighty.' It doesn't apply to a wardrobe, I don't think."

Although I was managing in the course of this conversation to put away my breakfast both quickly and handily, I had heard very few eating noises coming from Frederick's cubicle so far.

"'Do a one-eighty,'" he said with derision. "What an idiotic expression. It sounds like 'pop a wheelie.' Of course, 'do a three-sixty' is much worse. 'Volte face' is much better, but no one uses it any more."

I squirted the contents of one ketchup packet onto my Western omelet sandwich. It was roughly the same amount as one payload of semen; was this coincidental? Yes, and also sort of disgusting. Why did such thoughts occur to me while I was eating?

"I don't know," I said offhandedly. "If I left it in, I bet no one but us would ever care or notice."

" 'Beauty is truth, truth beauty, that is all ye know on earth, and all ye need to know,' " Frederick replied in a hollow singsong. There was a slight burr in his throat that may have been caused by strong emotion, but could also have been a crumb of toast. "Correct usage is as essential to health as nutrition or honesty or moral courage or loving your neighbor." He paused, but I heard no eating noises. "Or loving anyone, for that matter, no matter how far-fetched."

I realized then that Frederick had a bit of a crush on Bianca, which was painfully intensified by his disapproval of everything she was and did; this sub-Socratic dialogue was probably his attempt simultaneously to vanquish his unwanted desire by exposing the unforgivable silliness of its object and to bolster his chances by proving his superiority to her. I also suspected that I was being used as a stand-in for the fair lady herself, and that he was secretly hoping I'd write everything he was saying on her article, attributing these insights to him, thus somehow causing her to fall in love with him, or at least consent to have dinner with him.

"Bianca is beautiful," I pointed out innocently.

"Not so beautiful as all that," he muttered. "A trifle calculated for my tastes."

I stretched my legs out with leisurely pleasure on the low-pile mouse-colored carpet and waggled my toes in their clean socks. There was a bit of something on my chin; I licked it off. Grease, it turned out, with a deliciously salty, potato-y flavor. I licked again, in case I'd missed a molecule.

"In his short story 'Winner Take Nothing,' " Frederick was saying, "Hemingway uses the term 'sea change' as a lamentable metaphor for the transformation of the ugliness of homosexual love into the beauty of a literary work."

"He was such a he-man," I said. "Do you have any extra ketchup packets over there?"

"More brilliantly by far," Frederick said as three packets came sailing over the partition and landed on my desk, "*The Tempest* is also about the transformative power of love, maybe even the kind of love Bianca Mantooth feels for the small designer animal she calls BooBoo. So by that token, she—"

My telephone rang. I hated to be interrupted when I was eating breakfast. I would have let it roll over to voice mail, but I'd had enough of Frederick's lovesick tirade.

"*Downtown* copy," I barked into the receiver.

"Jeremy," came the voice of Howard Fine, my literary agent. "Is that you?"

"Hi, Howard," I said, my appetite suddenly gone. "What fresh hell do you have for me today?"

"No hell is fresh," he said snappily.

"It's too early for another rejection letter, isn't it? The mail hasn't been delivered yet. Unless it arrived on Saturday."

"This isn't about a letter, Jeremy," he said with his usual amiable tolerance of my attempts to leaven the rejection process with banter at his expense, as if he were responsible for this whole mess. "It's about a call I just got a couple of minutes ago."

"A call from whom?" I asked.

"Well, his name won't mean much to you," said Howard. "He's a young assistant editor at Wilder named Bill Dexter. He's the son of a friend of my aunt's. He read your novel over the weekend."

"As a personal favor," I said darkly. "His whole weekend shot to bits. Poor kid."

"Right," Howard said with a chuckle. "He called me at, what, nine-twenty on a Monday morning to tell me he hated it? I don't think so."

"So then . . ." I said, squinching my eyes against the hope that leapt like a weasel against the trap of my rib cage.

Howard sighed, which made the weasel do a rabid flip. He seemed to sigh only when he had good news; he'd sighed when he'd agreed to represent me and since then I hadn't heard him sigh again.

"He's nuts over it, Jeremy," he said aggrievedly. "He said this is the novel he'd want to write if he wrote novels. Apparently, his own father was a crazy schmuck politico just like yours, dumped his wife and kids, went off to Latin America to convert the peasants, get them to overthrow whatever government was oppressing them. Long story short, he thinks this book is the shit. That's the term he used, the shit."

"The *shit*?"

"He wants to buy it, Jeremy."

"He wants to *buy* it?" My mouth stayed open after I finished talking. I was holding the receiver so tightly, my hand was starting to ache. I didn't loosen my grip. "You mean he wants to *publish* it?"

Frederick's head levitated above the partition, his hair fluttering against his scalp, as if his excitement couldn't be contained by his skull and was venting itself through his ears, creating an upward-wafting draft.

"That's what he just told me," said Howard, "two minutes ago."

"What's wrong with him?" I asked, suddenly suspicious.

"What's wrong with him, he asks," said Howard mournfully, and sighed again.

"No," I said, laughing a little. "I mean, why did everyone else hate it so much?"

"They didn't *hate* it," he said patiently, "they just didn't love it enough to buy it. Listen, nothing is set in stone yet. He doesn't know how his higher-ups are going to respond. He's a kid, Jeremy. He's got very little power or clout. He's just starting out; he doesn't even have his own office yet. This would be the first novel he acquires in his publishing career. He can't promise you a lot of money and he's fairly certain you'll have to do rewrites. But I know he'd be a very good editor for you."

At this point, I felt as if the deli delivery guy would have been a good editor for me. "So now what?" I asked.

"Now he's got to work up some figures, get second opinions from some colleagues, go to a couple of meetings, kick it around. But this is real interest here; this is good."

"Great," I said. My mouth was still open. I met Frederick's eyes and shook my head dazedly. His eyebrows shot up, which caused his hair to quiver on his scalp as if it might take wing any minute and fly away. To a poet, the notion of having an agent was otherworldly enough; the possibility of actual publication by anyone but a vanity press must have seemed as astounding as the discovery of fire to early man.

"Here's an idea he put forward, a kind of offer," Howard was saying. "He'd like to sit down with you during his own free time, just to brainstorm with you, give you his rewrite ideas, hear your own ideas for edits and revisions, see whether you two would be on the same page."

"When does he want to meet me?"

"As soon as possible," said Howard. "Tonight, if you're free."

As I thought the words "Henry Tolliver," a lightning bolt zigzagged through my nervous system. "How about tomorrow?" I said as calmly as I could. "Unfortunately, I already have plans for tonight."

"Can I have him call you at work?" Howard asked.

"I'll be here all day."

I stared at the phone for a moment before I hung up, then forced my mouth closed and replaced the receiver carefully and firmly.

"Now, what," Frederick said, coming around to my cubicle, "in God's name was that all about?"

"An assistant editor wants to talk to me about possibly rewriting my novel so he can have a better shot at buying it, if it comes to that," I told him. Stated baldly like that, it didn't sound nearly as thrilling as my adrenaline level seemed to think it was.

"My God," Frederick said, cocking his head slightly to one side. "Do you have any idea what this means?"

"It means I'll be strangled by the tentacles of the conglomerate beast," I said.

He gave a ghostly smile. "It means you did it," he said. "You did it for all of us."

"All of who?"

"Whom," he corrected me gently. "You did your best work, you put it forward, and it has been deemed worthy." He gave a loose howl of a laugh; his limbs flung themselves about in a brief sort of jig. When he lunged for me, I was afraid momentarily that he intended to embrace or even kiss me, but all he did was clap me on the shoulder. "You know how many writers there are in the world, this *city*, who work all their lives on books and plays and poems and stories, who will most likely die without ever seeing a single word they've obsessed over in print?"

"I didn't sell it yet, you know," I said.

"Yes," he said, "but you will. I feel it in my gut. Let me buy you lunch. Somewhere special. Where do you want to go?"

"All this talk about tentacles," I said giddily. "I've got a hankering for the black squid rice at the Cuban-Chinese place."

"Hey, you two," came Daphne's smoker's growl from her own cubicle. "I don't care who's eating what at lunch or who's the big new literary hotshot, you have work to do, so do it now. We gotta deadline, if you'll recall. Jeremy, you leaving early again today?"

"No," I said. "I promise."

"And you can work late Thursday and Friday this week?"

"Till whenever you need me," I said with a sunniness that surprised me.

At one o'clock Frederick duly squired me to Conchita Chan. We snagged ourselves a rickety, chili-and-soy-sauce-splotched table in the back, where we were served heaping plates of salty, greasy, wonderful food.

"A toast," said Frederick, hoisting his glass of ice water. "May you be despised by the most petty and envious of your fellow writers."

"What kind of a toast is that?"

"Trust me, Jeremy," he said with his half-smile, his glass still aloft. "When your peers think you're worth badmouthing, you've really made it."

"No!" I said. "Please don't wish that on me."

"May they disparage, dismiss, and belittle you to the skies," he said, ignoring me. "May they call you overrated and pretentious, may they roll their eyes at the mention of your name, may they take the time and trouble to write scathing one-star Amazon reviews in your honor. You deserve it."

"Thank you," I said, laughing a little as our water glasses met in midair. "I think."

After the meal we felt a bit torrid; we had to take a short stroll around the neighborhood to get some sun and air after inhaling so much steam from the vats of rice and exhaling so much perfervid banter. Shortly after we returned from lunch, one of the editors, the same male mannequin who'd directed Bianca Mantooth to my cubicle, dropped some fresh copy onto my desk, turned on his Pradashod heel, and then, just before he flitted away, murmured snootily, as if it were an afterthought, "Congratulations on your book."

"Thanks, Jason," I said. "But I haven't—" I watched his willowy, linen-jacket-draped swayback recede down the aisle between the cubicles, then shut my mouth, which seemed to be catching a lot of flies today, and got back to work.

My phone rang a moment after Frederick had gone off in the direction of the candy machines. "*Downtown* copy," I said.

"May I speak to Jeremy Thrane?"

"Speaking," I said apprehensively. Frederick wasn't in his cubicle, where he belonged, to eavesdrop on this important conversation and egg me on. I felt vulnerable and unprotected.

"This is Bill Dexter."

"Bill," I said, and swallowed. How did you talk to an editor who might be going to buy your novel some day? I found I had no idea. "Hi."

"I think Howard has already talked to you, so you know who I am, right?"

"Yes," I said.

"Good," he said. "Then I'll get right to it. I loved *Angus in Efes*. I'd like to meet you as soon as possible to talk about some ideas I have for the manuscript. Howard said you suggested tomorrow night, which is fine with me."

"Tomorrow night would be great," I said.

Very efficiently, we established eight o'clock as our meeting time, agreed on a coffee shop in the East Village, and described ourselves as identical-sounding brown-haired white men, after which we said "See you tomorrow" and "I'm looking forward to it" and "Great" and "Goodbye," and then all of a sudden I had hung up the phone and was staring once again at the article I was copyediting. My heart was pounding so hard, it was almost squeaking. Almost automatically, I deleted an apostrophe, added a comma, queried the author's use of the word "antipodean," but as I did these things, the front of my brain was alight with rapturous dread. He'd sounded so young. I was so old compared to him. I was very likely wholly dependent on this postcollegiate boy for whatever fulfillment and success I was going to have in my chosen career. Had I sounded too desperate and needy and cravenly eager? What changes was he going to ask me to make? What if I hated his ideas? What if I couldn't bring myself to do a single thing he asked? What if I turned out to be not as good a writer as he thought I was? What if I failed?

Just after six o'clock I packed up for the day and rode the elevator down to the street with several secretaries in sneakers. We all pushed one by one through the revolving doors into a piercingly clear, effortlessly temperate evening. As I walked home, it hit me that in the course of this one day, three potentially life-changing things (I refused even to think the word "events" anymore) were happening to me. It seemed that this was how such enormous changes usually happened to me, several of them all at once. It reminded me, as it would have any American my age, of the slogan "When it rains, it pours," written in white cursive under that little girl with her big umbrella on the blue Morton's salt box. Of course, literally this meant that the salt wouldn't cake in humid weather, but metaphorically it seemed applicable to my current situation. I found that I was singing inside: I was keeping my copyediting job! I was getting a new roommate named Andy! I got to listen to free jazz tonight!

My unexpected happiness at these mundane, improbable things made me think of a story my mother had told me when I was a kid about a man whose house was too small. He was miserable, he couldn't breathe, he couldn't hear himself dream or think. He went to the village elder for advice. The village elder thought for a moment, then said positively, "Well, you've got to move your cow into the house with you, that'll solve your problem." The man did as he was told, but this naturally made the house seem even smaller, and he found that he was now even more miserable. So back to the village elder he went, distressed and puzzled. "Move your goat into your house with you," said the village elder after the man had complained at length about how cramped he was. The man did as he was told; this part of the story had always astonished me, not having had any comparable venerable elderly figures in my own life in whom I had this degree of blind faith. But when the goat was under-foot, back the man trotted to complain once again to the elder, who told him to move another animal in, and another, until chickens roosted in the rafters, horses' heads stuck out of every window, sheep baaed in the boudoir, and pigs nursed their piglets under the table.

At the end of his wits, the poor guy went back to the old man, whose wisdom he was finally beginning to doubt. "I asked you to help me make my house bigger, and all you've done is make it even smaller! I can hardly move any more! I'm going crazy! I'm ready to go sleep in the barn just to get a little peace!"

The old man said, "All right, now move all the animals out again." The man dutifully moved his entire menagerie back to stable, yard, and barn.

And lo and behold, his house seemed bigger suddenly than he had ever dreamed possible, a palace, a spacious mansion, a wondrous haven of serenity and order, amplitude and comfort. And so he lived happily ever after in his same old house.

I got home ten minutes ahead of my sisters' arrival. They entered the apartment looking sunburned, windblown, and wild-eyed, wearing sleeveless dresses and sandals and looking so much alike, I was shocked.

"We went to the Statue of Liberty," said Lola. "And Ellis Island. We took our tourist husbands on an outing. And all the parents."

"And Feckin," said Amanda.

"And Amanda's whole band," said Lola. "The whole wedding party, practically, except for you, Jeremy. Shame you had to work today, it was grand."

"We left at the crack of dawn," said Amanda. "I haven't been up so early in years."

Laughing merrily at nothing that I could ascertain, they flung them-selves onto Scott's velvet and mahogany fainting couch as if it were a park bench.

"Did the guitar player go too?" I asked casually. "From last night. Henry."

"Laura's Henry? No, he had to work, like you."

"Look at the little bird!" cried Lola.

"Hey, look at this furniture," said Amanda, who for one reason or another had never been here before. "You never told me you lived in such a nice place."

"It's not mine," I said. "All the nice stuff is moving out very soon. So is the bird."

"Juanita?" said Amanda. "Under her own steam, or what?"

"I gave her away yesterday," I said. "You and her both. Listen, are you really ready to do this? I'm sort of dreading it."

"We have to," Amanda said staunchly. "I have to go in less than an hour."

"I think we need to have a drink first," said Lola. "And don't start about the baby."

Amanda and I exchanged a look. "Beer okay?" I asked mildly.

We sat in the breeze coming in through the window screens and drank cold bottles of beer. It had been so many years since the three of us had been alone together, I couldn't even remember when the last time had been.

"Maybe he's got a whole new set of kids," said Amanda warningly.

"He may not be home," I said. "Or he could be the wrong Angus Thrane."

"He might not remember who we are," said Lola.

Juanita gave a soft peep, then flapped her clipped wings through the air across the room toward Lola's head. The tiny claws dug into Lola's scalp, scrabbling for purchase. Lola accepted the bird's arrival with hardly a twitch or a recoil, totally unfazed by whatever came at her, as always.

"Why did you give her away?" Lola asked.

"She found a better owner," I said.

"Who?" asked Amanda indignantly.

"My roommate Scott."

"Why is he better?"

"For one thing, he bought her that cage."

"Wait a minute," said Amanda. "What do you mean, Scott's a better owner just because he bought her a cage? She's been your bird for years. Have you thought about how she'll feel if you give her away?"

"She's a bird, Amanda."

"She's a living being who's completely imprinted on you. You can't just foist her off on someone else because you've had enough of her."

"Who said I've enough of her?" I said. "She wants to go. I can tell."

"How can you tell?"

I looked at Juanita, who was deeply involved with something in Lola's hair. "I can't make her as happy as he can," I said finally. "She has to go with him."

"That sounds like one of those Motown songs where the guy talks all through the middle verse," Amanda shot back. "You can't give her away. I forbid it."

"Amanda," I said, "this is not a Motown song, and Juanita is not my lady. Should we call Angus now?"

The three of us looked at one another in a sudden panicky silence as the air in the room thickened perceptibly. It reminded me of the way it had been when we were kids, sealing ourselves off in an imaginary bubble whenever things got too unpredictable or confusing, all of our internal schisms and hostilities forgotten.

"You call him," I said to Lola. "You're the best at this kind of thing."

"What kind of thing, exactly?"

"Well, dealing with strangers," I said.

"Our father's isn't exactly a stranger," said Lola, "at least not to you. You call. You knew him best."

"You're the oldest," said Amanda as if that settled it. "And you're the one who found him."

They looked at me with obdurate, challenging expressions.

I picked up the phone and dialed Angus's number swiftly, before my brain could get wind of what my fingers were doing and make them stop.

We all held what felt like a three-way staring contest as the phone rang once, then twice, then three times. Then there was the click of an answering machine, and then a recorded youngish-sounding woman's voice saying, "Hello, Angus and Jennifer aren't home, but if you'd like to leave a—" The machine clicked off as someone picked up the phone.

"Hello?" my father said.

"Is this Angus Thrane?"

"Who is this?" he asked brusquely, no doubt imagining that I was a long-distance company telemarketer, or one of those salespeople who offered you all-expenses-paid trips to Florida and Hawaii in exchange for taking a two-hour tour of one of their horrid condominiums in Atlantic City.

"This is Jeremy Thrane," I said. "Your son. I know this is out of the blue, but I found your number, and I thought I would call and say hello."

There was a silence, during which Amanda and Lola leaned forward, side by side on the fainting couch, both of them almost exploding with curiosity. Juanita, as if sensing Lola's agitation through her head, hopped nimbly onto the back of the couch, cocked her head, and dropped a wet green-white turd neatly onto the velvet, which made me very glad I'd already given her to Scott. His bird, his fainting couch. I thought this to keep myself from saying another word until Angus had said something to me; in the silence since I'd said my own name, I felt myself detaching from his response and this conversation and all my feelings through the decades about him: I had found him, here I was on the phone, and now he could take me or leave me. I had done my part.

"Well," he said in a light, resonant baritone that was as familiar to me still as if I'd just spoken to him last week. "Jeremy. Well, I'll be damned. Where the hell are you these days?"

"I'm in New York City," I said, "with Amanda and Lola. We're all right here."

"All the ships at sea," he said.

"That's right," I replied. For some reason, we both laughed.

"You should see where I'm standing," he said. "I'm looking out my front door at the most beautiful sight you've ever seen. You know I'm on San Juan Island, in Washington State? Our house sits on a sort of cliff over the water; right now the sun is breaking through the clouds in the west and there's a rainbow. It's pretty amazing. Jennifer," he called, "Are you seeing this?"

I heard a woman's voice somewhere in the background.

"My wife," Angus said breezily into the receiver as if he were making small talk with someone he'd just met. I felt a dull thud of rage whose source I didn't entirely understand. How was he supposed to sound, hearing my voice out of the blue? What had I expected? I had thought I didn't expect anything at all, but apparently, I'd expected something very different from this easygoing, amused, elusive voice on the other end of the telephone. I'd expected him to act the way I would have acted in his position, but since he'd never done that, why did I expect him to start now? It made no sense.

"Oh," I said. "Jennifer. The voice on the machine."

"That's right," he said. There was a fleeting pause. "So, Jeremy, what's going on with you now? You're all grown up by now, I guess. You're, what, thirty . . ."

"Thirty-five," I said. "I'm thirty-five."

"And your sisters?"

"Amanda got married yesterday," I said. "Lola's visiting with her husband from Australia. They're right here. They want to talk to you too."

"Is that right?" he asked. "What about you? Are you married?"

"I'm gay, actually," I said, almost chuckling at the irony of telling my father this way. Amanda smiled at me; she saw the joke too. "And at the moment I'm single."

"Well," he said again, not seeming to care one way or another whether I was married, gay, or a registered sex offender, which made sense. Having a gay son probably meant no more or less to him than having no son at all, which was what he'd had all these years as far as he knew. "And what do you do there in New York City?"

"I'm a writer," I said. "Actually, I might have sold my novel today. There's an editor who's interested in it."

I heard Amanda's sharp intake of breath at this news.

"Hey," Angus was saying. "Good for you. What's it called?"

Just then, for the first time in this conversation, I recalled that my novel was about my father, and that it wasn't flattering, and he probably wouldn't appreciate it much, assuming he ever read it.

"It's called *Angus in Efes*," I said. "It's based on your life, after you disappeared. I heard you were in Turkey, so I set it in Turkey."

There was another, briefer silence as he absorbed this. "That's great," he said delightedly. "Will you send me a copy?"

"Sure," I said flatly. The old narcissist; didn't he realize it might not be an entirely or even partially flattering portrait? What exactly did he think I felt about his time in Turkey, or wherever the hell he'd been all those years? I pictured him, for some reason, in sandals, navy blue sweatshirt, and loose-fitting blue jeans, an older version of myself; he was sitting casually in a rattan chair, looking out at the view, half of his mind on the rainbow and the other half on this unexpected but not, apparently, totally unwelcome conversation with his son. "But were you really in Turkey after you—after you left?"

"What year did I leave the States?" He cleared his throat. "Wasn't it the early seventies? My memories of that era are a little vague, but I can safely say that I spent some time in Turkey . . . I drove a truck. Didn't spend much time in Ephesus though. So your book qualifies as fiction."

"Do you have any other kids?" I asked; I'd always wondered.

He laughed. "No, I wasn't exactly cut out for the whole daddy routine. I remember one time when one of you came into the room, it must have been Amanda, I think she was about two. She was calling, 'Daddy, Daddy,' and I had to think for a minute: who? Who's that? Jennifer has kids from another marriage. We see them whenever they make their way out west. You three, and all your spouses and kids and whatever entourages you have, are always welcome. We have plenty of room."

A flock of questions and accusations crowded into my throat and dissolved in a futile puddle of saliva. "Oh," I said. "Thanks. Well, speaking of Amanda, do you want to talk to her? She's right here."

"Sure," he said with a warmth I didn't understand: If he really felt that way, why hadn't he tried to find us? "I'd love to. Hey, before you go, Jeremy, what's your phone number and address?"

As I gave him the information, he repeated everything under his breath at the speed of handwriting, so I assumed he was writing it all down.

When Amanda took the receiver, I stood up and went into the bathroom, got a wad of toilet paper, came back out to the living room and wiped Juanita's poop off the fainting couch. It left a wet smudge I was pretty sure would dry without leaving a mark. Then I collected the three empty beer bottles and took them into the kitchen, rinsed them, and put them into the recycling can. I went back out to the living room and sat down in my chair again. Amanda was saying with strained enthusiasm, "How great. What's your coalition called?" There was a protracted silence on our end, during which Amanda listened to whatever Angus was saying, Lola and I watched her listen, and Juanita, who had hopped onto Lola's shoulder, slid her wing feathers one by one through her beak, grooming herself in her energetic, persnickety way.

"And so will you get the legislation passed, or don't you know yet?" Amanda asked a moment later in that same eager-to-please voice. She didn't give a rat's ass about politics, I knew very well, especially faraway grassroots politics that had nothing to do with her. As far as I could tell, Angus hadn't asked her anything about herself or her life yet. He'd probably used up his entire supply of curiosity about his offspring in his conversation with me. I sent her silent waves of encouraging solidarity as I went to the kitchen to fetch her another beer, which she'd need the moment she handed the phone over to Lola. I got myself one too, but not Lola; my indulgence of her fetal-alcohol-syndrome mongering went only so far, and even then it was provisional. If my niece or nephew turned out to be brain damaged, I was going to have to fly to Australia and strangle her.

After she'd handed the receiver to Lola, Amanda took the cold bottle of beer I gave her and put it to her temple before she took a swig.

"Angus," Lola was saying in her Australian accent. "This is Lola here. Yes, hello." A moment later she gave a whooping, almost flirtatious peal of laughter at whatever Angus had said in reply; Juanita gave a shrill cheep, trying to join in. "That's right," she said. "I'm an Aussie now." She listened to his reply with a wide grin on her face, then burst into laughter again. I had forgotten how beautiful Lola was, even more beautiful than Amanda, not in form or features, but because she was entirely unself-conscious and fully herself in every gesture and expression, every word she said. "No," she said; it sounded like "noy." "That's not true; you know, my husband, Fletcher, says the same thing, but America was settled by Puritans, Australia by convicts. Makes all the difference in the world. Hey, now you've got a grandkid on the way. How does it feel to get all three of your kids back and a grandkid in one fell swoop?"

Amanda and I took simultaneous slugs of beer, our eyes meeting over our bottles.

Lola laughed again, put her hand loosely over the receiver, and said to Amanda and me, shaking her head, "He said it seems like a normal thing to get a call from all three of us on a rainy afternoon, out of the blue. Normal!" she said into the receiver. "In whose life is that a normal thing?"

When she hung up a while later, there was a long silence as we all looked at one another like accident victims taking stock of the others' injuries in order to assess our own. Amanda looked shaken and Lola looked victorious, so I imagined, judging by the differences in their expressions and demeanors, that I looked neither. I imagined that I looked pissed off, which was how I felt.

"That was weird," I said flatly.

"I'll say," said Amanda.

"Weird isn't really the word, is it?" Lola rejoined quizzically. "Like Angus said, it did seem sort of normal, and that's the weird thing. We were all so calm. And he did sound familiar. But I haven't got a clue who the guy is, have you?"

"What was he going on and on to you about?" I asked Amanda. "Did he ask you a single question about yourself?"

Amanda twisted her lips in a sort of smile. "When you were in the kitchen, he asked how my wedding was. What did he say when you asked whether he'd had any more kids since us?"

I rolled my eyes. "He said he'd learned his lesson from us, which was that he wasn't cut out for 'the whole daddy thing.' "

Amanda laughed. "That's like saying you're not cut out for surgery after you've cut the guy open and the nurses are handing you instruments and the clock is ticking away."

"Not that it's any surprise," said Lola. "I mean, what other conclusion could we possibly draw from his behavior over the last thirty-odd years? What did he say about your being gay?"

"Nothing," I said. "Not a thing."

"Oh!" Amanda shouted. "You sold your novel? Why didn't you say so right away when we got here?"

"In all the brouhaha and hullabaloo I—"

"That's right!" said Lola. "What was that all about?"

I explained about the deal with Bill Dexter, and they were gratifyingly excited for me, so excited I might have suspected them of humoring me if they'd been anyone else, but because they were my sisters, I allowed myself to bask a little.

A little while later I put Juanita back into her cage, and then my sisters and I left the apartment together and clattered down the stairs single file. We burst one by one through the heavy front door out onto the street, where we stood for a moment, collecting ourselves, then made our disorganized way to the nearest subway station.

"When will I see you again, Jeremy?" Lola asked. "We're here for another two weeks and we're quite available."

"Well," I said, "I have to meet with that editor tomorrow night after work. Maybe I'll come up to Mom's for dinner on Wednesday night."

"Oh, good," she said, kissing my cheek. Then she flung her arms around Amanda. "Have a relaxing, romantic honeymoon in Europe; you'll need it when the reality of marriage sets in."

"Oh, reality set in for Liam and me a long time ago," said Amanda. "It was good to see you, Lola. It was good to meet Fletcher. I'm so glad you came all this way for my wedding."

"Glad we did too," said Lola. "Come to Australia and see our farm."

She waved at both of us, ran down the subway stairs with her hair and dress fluttering behind her, and disappeared.

Amanda took my arm and we headed downtown into the warm evening.

"How's married life?" I asked her.

"Whatever," she said, waving her hand dismissively. "Same old me, same old Liam. I love him, I can't stand the sight of him, he's my soul mate, I want to kick him in the head. But now it's permanent." There were tears on her cheeks. "God, I wish Lola lived nearer."

"Me too," I said.

"Where are you going now, Jeremy?"

"I have a sort of date, I guess," I said shyly. "With Henry."

She looked at me. "Laura's Henry?"

"He's hardly Laura's."

"Anyway, he's had a crush on you for ages," she said. "It's about time. Where are you going?"

"We're meeting at the International Bar for a drink, then he's playing somewhere on Ludlow Street, and then if I like his music I'm going to ask him out for dinner afterward."

"That sounds like fun," she said. "But what if you don't like it?"

"I don't know," I said nervously. "If I don't like it, what am I going to tell him? Have you ever heard it?"

"Yes," she said. "But why do you have to like his music if you like him?"

"Why do you ask?" I asked hollowly, suddenly terrified. "Is he that bad?"

"He's amazing," she said shortly. "But why are you testing him like this? Isn't it kind of a lot of pressure to put on a first date?"

We stopped walking and faced each other. We were on Sixth Avenue near Fourteenth Street; people hustled past us in both directions, but we took no notice of them. I stared uptown for a moment at the elegant spiky spires of the Chrysler and Empire State buildings; the breeze rounding the corner from off the Hudson cooled the sweat on my forehead.

"I can't explain it," I said stubbornly. "But it's essential."

"Okay," she said, smiling, checking her watch. "Oh my God, it's way past time for me to go. Our plane leaves at eleven, and I still have to finish packing and do a million last-minute things."

"Wait," I said, suddenly reluctant to say good-bye to her. "I'm going all the way over to First Avenue. We could walk together."

She hugged me a little impatiently. "I really have to go now, I'm late."

"I'll miss you," I said mournfully.

"Well, thanks, but I might not miss you," she said with a laugh. "Wouldn't it be a bad sign? Missing your brother on your honeymoon?"

"It might be a little strange," I said.

I stood at the top of the subway station and watched her run down the stairs, her hair and dress fluttering the same way Lola's had. She blew me a kiss just before she ducked out of sight.

I headed down Broadway toward Astor Place, pulled forward by a node of concentrated warmth in my solar plexus that was the closest thing I'd ever known to absolute certainty that I was going in the right direction. I looked eagerly and hopefully into all the faces that approached me, an old black woman in a white canvas sunhat, a kid with a Walkman, bearded man in sunglasses, open-faced redheaded girl, but they were all strangers and had nothing to do with me. The people I knew, the ones who mattered to me, who loved me, were all going about their lives, probably not thinking about me at all; meanwhile, I walked quickly and without pausing toward my night with Henry Tolliver, a mystery that would soon open to reveal further mysteries, and beyond those, more unknowns, and so on.

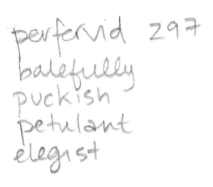